J.J. Connolly's first published work was a short story in the *Brit Pulp!* anthology. His first novel, *Layer Cake*, has received universal critical praise. Connolly lives and writes in London.

What the critics said:

'If the brilliantly written and intriguing *Layer Cake* is anything to go by, his will soon be a name to whet the appetites of readers and critics alike.'

Francis Gilbert, The Times

'Given the current glut of crime'n'caper novels, I approached J.J. Connolly's debut with faint enthusiasm. Happily, *Layer Cake* is a storming piece of work: funny and serious by turns, with an abiding sense of conviction … Set in a teeming north-east London world of seriously criminal business types, the novel has a grasp of street argot unparalleled since Kinky Friedman first sashayed out of his front door and nailed a checker straight out of the bat.'

D.J. Taylor, Guardian

'Once I'd read a few pages I was hooked … Connolly's style is fast and funny and just frightening enough to make you sit up all night finishing the book … Flashed as *The Long Firm* meets *The Sopranos*, it knocks the former into a cocked hat, whatever that is, and could easily emulate the latter's success if made into a television series.

Welcome to the layer cake.'

Mark Timlin, Independent on Sunday

'Funny, hectic, hard-hitting debut novel … Tart, tough and riveted at every juncture by unmistakable authenticity … sheer, unstoppable joy to read from the first page to the last.'

Philip Oakes, Literary Review

'The best crime novel I've ever read.'

Bruce Reynolds

LAYER CAKE

J.J. Connolly

Duckworth

This impression 2006
Published in 2004 by
Gerald Duckworth and Co. Ltd
90-93 Cowcross Street, London EC1M 6BF
Tel: 020 7490 7300
Fax: 020 7490 0080
inquiries@duckworth-publishers.co.uk
www.ducknet.co.uk

First published in 2000

A CIP catalogue record for this book is available
from the British Library

ISBN 0 7156 3335 X

Typeset by Ray Davies
Printed in Great Britain by
BOOKMARQUE Ltd, Croydon, Surrey

Contents

Hello, Hello, Hello

I parked the motor under a streetlight so there's less chance of anyone breaking into it. I locked it up, got my briefcase outta the back and was walking towards my gaff. I'm preoccupied with my work. Suddenly a flashlight's pointed straight in my face. I've squinted, I'm alarmed. The light's gone down my body. It's the law, I've thought. The game's up cos I've got in the case two kilos of top quality, very pukka, recently imported, cocaine. It's about forty kay or twelve years' worth, depending how you look at it, what tariff you wanna use. I've got electronic jewellery scales and Manatol, Italian baby laxative, on board as well. I'm gutted cos I very, very rarely take my work home with me and to get nicked on this rare occasion would slaughter me. Don't do anything stupid, don't do anything at all, take a deep breath and don't even think about running. Relax, work it out, stop holding your breath, cos if they had come for you, you'd be on the deck now, cuffed up and getting the old 'you do not have to say anything, blah blah blah' routine.

'Sorry, Sir, you okay?' He's genuinely apologetic. 'Only we've had reports of a prowler in the area.'

'A prowler, you say, well well. And there's only the two of you? Maybe you should call for some assistance.'

'We're a bit stretched already tonight, Sir.'

'That's too bad. I'll ring the station if I see or hear anything.'

'Thank you, Sir. Good night. Be careful.'

'Oh, I will be.'

They carry on looking for the burglar in among the bushes and I go upstairs to weave that special kinda magic that turns two kilos into three.

April Fool's Day 1997
Welcome to the Layer Cake

'Well, where the fuck is he?'

'I don't know, Morty. I really can't answer that question. Ask me one on sport.'

'Fuck off. What time does your watch say?'

'Probably the same as yours, exactly two minutes past four.'

'And he said he'd be here at four?'

'Yeah.'

'On the dot?'

'Yeah.'

'And he's usually on time?'

'Yeah. He's usually very punctual.'

'So where the fuck is he?'

I'm waiting and I fuckin hate waiting. A guy's meant to be turning up to buy from myself and Mister Mortimer a half-kilo of the finest, purest cocaine this side of the River Thames for twenty thousand pounds cash sterling. If you were an alien looking down on this little scene, one earthling giving another earthling the year's earnings of most people for a bag of white powder that started life growing on a tree, you could be forgiven for thinking it was all a little bit strange. I must admit that some days I still, after all this time, find it a tad surreal. Thank fuck it's illegal, I say.

So now it's Friday afternoon and me and Mort are waiting for a party by the name of Jeremy to turn up and collect the half-kilo that we've put aside for him. It's gonna cost him the twenty thou and we're making out we're gonna be doing him a big favour cos we'll have to find other people to take the rest of the key. We usually try to move only whole kilos. Sometimes it's a problem, but then again, sometimes it's really handy to have half a kilo knocking around. We always make out it's big probs for us to be chopping kilos about. We always make a bitova fuss but we always do it. Business is business. This particular half-key is just pure bunce cos it's the result of us chopping and cutting a little bit more than usual over the last couple of weeks, so Jeremy's twenty can be carved up between us cos we don't owe anything or anybody for it.

I've got my Gucci loafers off, my feet up on the desk in the back office of the letting agency I've got a stake in. The April sun's blasting through the window and I've got a slight breeze blowing through my toes. We've just had a nice bit of lunch in an Italian gaff offa Marylebone High Street where they do some very sexy things with chickens and tomato sauces, the weekend is upon us, and Terry and Clarkie, the kids, as Morty calls our junior partners when they're outta earshot, are out and about running errands. Things are very sweet and I'm as content as my nature will allow. I just wish that Jeremy would hurry the fuck up because I'm starting to get a little bit anxious, I always do when people are running late. I get a wee bit twitchy.

The Golden Rule: Stay as far away from the end-user as humanly possible otherwise it's gimme a freebie, gimme a clue, gimme a move, gimme shelter, gimme a bitta bail chief, gimme a drop of unsecured credit and I say gimme a fuckin break, gimme a day off, gimme fuckin strength. Some days in this line of work you can be left thinking, Is there civilised life anywhere in this whole fuckin universe? In this whole fuckin solar system? Sometimes I doubt it but all this insanity's good for business. We're making so much money playing neat and tidy that we're running outta places to plug the loot. Life is so fuckin good I can taste it in my spit. Demand is high and so is supply but I just wish to fuck that la-dee-da Jeremy would hurry the fuck up.

We always work neat and tidy, we always work as a small team. I try and turn away people who are messy, who are noisy, who'll get us nicked big time, who have to be seen as players, the loud-mouths and braggers. People who are neat and tidy like ourselves we can do business with. All that being flash with racy motors, wearing gaudy diamonds and gold trinkets, the big fuck-off attitude, is just begging to get yourself nicked. No point rubbing the law's noses in your success. What's called for

3

is some peace and quiet, discretion, a low profile so you can crack on uninterrupted and let the Other People go after the noisy, boisterous folk. Some people will say you've got no business being in the game if you ain't double flash with your ill-gotten gains, really upping the old bill with 'em. Why have big dollar if you can't let people know you got big dollar? In this game it often helps if you can agree to disagree with some people, but it ain't always possible.

Don't get me wrong, I ain't saying we live like monks or anything and we ain't exactly on our bellies chipping away at the coalface of life either. On the face of things I run a very successful lettings agency but my legit partner takes care of that on a day-to-day basis. It gives me a bit of income and the pick of some very creamy gaffs to plot up in for six months at a time, but most important it provides a very tidy front to lose myself behind. I've always said I wanna be outta this game by the time I'm thirty. I'm twenty-nine now so this year's gonna be all about getting all my shit together in the one pile. I've seen guys hang around too long in the game until they either get them-selves nicked or they simply lose the plot, start doing far too much of the product, get weak or paranoid or both and end up losing everything, become sad cases. Some guys are just too fuckin greedy.

A lot of operators in this powders game only know this swindle, it's their whole fuckin life. They don't know anything else so if they did manage to get out they'd be fucked for something else to do with their time. Everyone, even dealers, needs a sense of purpose. It's not about the money anymore either cos they got as much as you can spend in a lifetime anyway so it's become a fuckin powder power trip for them. Year after year they plod on, some of them don't even get to see the stuff, just take the prime cut on pay day and how bad's that, but that was never my plan cos you still gotta watch your back twenty-four-seven. In and out before I'm thirty but set up for life, a gentleman of leisure. All my moneys spun and back in the system clean as a whistle. I wanna be nicely set up with legit business interests spread all around, a portfolio, a bit here, a bit over there and that'll do nicely thank you very much. I wanna be un-fuckin-touchable.

Am I getting there? Very much so I'm getting there. We place a lotta stuff with a lotta people. We're very close to the top of our particular pyramid, to guys who actually bring the goods onto British soil, the importers, the real big-time money-men, the vicious international players. We get our supply at a price that's right. When these guys start talking they're talking in millions of pounds, hundreds of kilos. Maybe some of the guys I work with will make the leap up into the big leagues and manage to stay there, but I won't be going along with them. Thirty and I'm out. Have a plan and stick to it.

A kilo of very high-grade snorting cocaine, even with the very top, the very very best stuff, skimmed offa the top to make crack, is gonna cost the guy I sell it to twenty-seven and a half grand at today's market price. We, obviously, get it for a lot less than that from the guy who deals with the international players, an old-school Don, name of Jimmy Price, gawd bless him. We work with his blessing and protection but at a price. Jimmy will allow us bail, or credit, up to half a million pounds because over the time we've worked through him we've built up a very good credit rating, so now we just call on what we need and it ain't a problem. Jimmy wouldn't know whether to snort the coke or rub it on his genitals, it ain't his thing, although some of his generation have been known to go totally wobbly with it. Jimmy has no fuckin interest in the effects of the stuff whatsoever, don't like seeing people getting outta control. He's probably very rarely laid eyes on the goods and he certainly don't put his hands on the product. Sir James oversees, if you like, the sometimes messy business of getting it from A to Z. He gets his handling charge for handling something he doesn't even touch. He's a hands-off senior management executive. Having Mister Price's protection is no guarantee of anything cos there's too many hounds about, but I can tell you that it helps being connected. He trusts us to go to work with a high degree of tact and discretion. He knows we're not sloppy wankers and it's certainly in his interest for us to go to work unhindered.

The funny thing is that I've only met Mister Price twice in my life. Once I shook his hand at some seriously moody boxing dinner and another time we were introduced at the wedding reception of Clarkie's creamy younger sister, very briefly and with a minimum of fuss. Morty works with Gene McGuire, who's what the Sunday papers would call an enforcer for Jimmy Price, but he's more a bodyguard-cum-professional-best-mate. He does Jimmy's bidding and Jimmy trusts him with his life. The money and goods go backwards and forwards through Morty and Gene and everyone gets fat together, very fat, baby-chubby.

Morty looks after getting the supply and I look after the selling-on of the product. Having a geezer like Mort around means that nobody who's got any sense is gonna fuck with us cos he's a fearless and ruthless cunt is Morty and he's got a squad of other ruthless and fearless cunts to call on if need be. There's many myths and legends surrounding him and the gist of them all is that you'd have to be fuckin mad or suicidal or both to mess him about. He don't suffer fools for a minute cos first they're very irritating and second they can get you very seriously nicked in this game. I've never actually seen him perform but with guys like Morty you don't have to have seen it to know it can be done. I've seen him warn some very fuckin heavy guys away from our drop of work and they've stayed warned for a long time after.

Morty looks like a cross between Marvellous Marvin Hagler and Sugar Ray Leonard, taller, but maybe Morty would weigh in at light-heavy these days in spite of spending all those hours in the gym. He's a class act. He likes his ladies, his clothes and a quarter mill a year in his kick. Mister Mortimer is a highly respected geezer and to a lot of firms around London it's the one thing they have in common is a mutual respect for Morty. He's even been asked to sort out disputes, but he don't get involved cos he just don't need the aggravation. He's earned his respect across the board through a drop of charm and a dose of violence, but Morty will tell you it is sometimes necessary. Morty says he will explain but not justify.

About fifteen years ago Morty was running around with a

team of guys who were seriously spun out. The loonies' loonies. Morty had known these guys through borstals and young prisoners' nicks and although he was only a fringe member of the outfit he was, as ever, extremely loyal to them in that very fuckin weird way those guys are to one another, bordering on the insane I would say. They're turning over any business that couldn't go running back to the Other People, sex shops and massage parlours, doing blags long after they went outta fashion, doing loads of drugs and not giving a fuck about keeping a low profile. One night after a party with loads of booze, hookers and chemicals, one of this team, who was always regarded as severely unstable even by this wired crew, has, in a tearful and quite pathetic outburst, told all these geezers he loves them and then put a shooter in his mouth and shot himself dead in front of about ten witnesses. Now this is a dilemma cos this desperate posse can't very well go calling an ambulance because they're wanted all over London and the Home Counties. Even if they did explain the truth, all ten of them telling the exact same story, cozzers, the police, ain't gonna believe a fuckin word of it.

'What, he just decided to put the sawn-off in his mouth and pull the trigger?'

'Yeah, that's how it went down.'

'Oh right, that's all right then.'

Like fuck it was gonna happen like that. They're gonna think that there was some kinda dispute among all these volatile nutcases, who could fall out over a perceived dirty look, and this geezer, Kilburn Jerry, got topped or it was a party game gone wrong. Morty was somehow roped into getting rid of the mangled, headless body but someone fucked up by being just too fuckin untogether and Morty got nicked big-time. He was charged with disposing of a body unlawfully or accessory after the fact and was given eight years, of which he served five and a quarter. The crown actually accepted that the guy had killed himself and the guys who had been originally charged with 'murder due to joint venture' were getting acquitted at the Old Bailey while Morty was being weighed off. All the time Morty kept schtum and did his time. Name, rank and serial number was all they ever got out of him and this earns the respect of his peers, both inside and out, both now and then. I can see why he don't entertain any nut-nuts.

Clarkie is the youngest child in one of those fuckin huge families that you just don't get anymore, not since the arrival of the pill anyway. If this business had an elite officer corps then Clarkie would be a product of it. The Clark family are still a major force in this part of town, in any part of town come to that. The Old Man Clark and the elder brothers have given up robbing banks, mainly cos they can't get out the front door to put a bet on without the Robbery Squad ready-eyeing them there and back. A couple of them got fitted up very tight last time out so they've moved on to less obvious undertakings to provide the corn. Anyways, all that hitting the high street banks with the jolly old sawn-off went out with sideboards and radio-grams, three-piece whistles with twenty-four-inch lionels, although it still goes on, of course, but it's very much a desperate pursuit these days, very much the preserve of crackheads and junkies. It's not the giggle it once was.

Clarkie spent his early childhood years being shunted around the country from nick to nick, from Parkhurst up to Durham, to see the Old Man or one of the older brothers, cos the Prison Service kept them on the move, dispersed around the country, otherwise they might have caused a whole lotta grief if they were to get too comfortable for too long in one place, but I reckon the Clark family still gave the Home Office a hard time. They always made the kangas earn their shillings. The Junior Clark must have taken all this in and decided that a career on the pavement with a shooter was not for him, too risky, too much like hard work if you're captured, so he fired his dough and his lot in with me, Morty and Terry. He decided on a career in commerce if you like. I think Old Man Clark musta hada word with Jimmy Price cos one day me and Morty suddenly had junior partners by virtue of a decree handed down by King James. It was diplomatic to cut them a deal cos otherwise they would have ended up as serious rivals for our bitta business. It stuck in the throat to start with but in the end it made a lotta sense.

When I go it'll be Clarkie who'll be doing what I do now,

brokering the stuff, working with the contacts I've made, keeping track of the money, working out who's owed what, keeping a healthy float stashed, making sure the gear's up to scratch and when we cut it we don't completely tear the arse outta it. So far I've only hinted that I'm on my way out but my mind's made up. I'll let these geezers know when the time is right.

If Clarkie's next in line for my job and I work things out with him then Terry works more closely with Morty on the security side of things. He can be a hothead can Terry but Morty's taken him under his wing and will eventually round the rough edges offa him cos you can't have guys around you who are forever going ballistic. If people keep losing their temper and ironing people out all the time it starts to lose its mystique, it's no surprise anymore, the threat's gone, but Terry's young and he'll learn. Down in the lower levels of this swindle you need your bashers, people respond, but in our neck of the woods you gotta have a drop more savvy, a bit more brainpower to oil the wheels and get the job done. You have to threaten diplomatically. The thing with Morty and Terry is neither of them is all that big, not small either, but you can sense something about them. It's a I-don't-give-a-shit attitude like you'd have to kill the fuckers to stop them coming at you and I guess you would an all. They're like those cartoon characters that keep coming on towards you even after they've been blown up, had boulders dropped from heights on their heads, had dynamite strapped to them and been fired outta cannons and all that shit that by rights shoulda seen them off. It's in the eyes, there's a certain crazy little twinkle, it's in the walk, there's a kinda strut that just lets the other guy know that you're not to be fucked with, it's not an over-the-top plastic-gangsters bowl either. It's in the way these two talk to people, they let other guys know that there's a limit on how far they can have a laugh and a joke and you better keep your wits about you and not cross over that invisible line or you'll wake up in hospital regretting it. As the Roman general said, 'To keep the peace you must plan for war.'

I have to sometimes take a risk and let certain people know a bit more about our business than I would like, cos if guys don't know what you got for sale then how the fuck are they gonna be able to punt for it, and this means using a great deal of discretion. We can't advertise. I can really only entertain people who are somehow connected, who come to us quoted, that's to say someone has vouched for them, says they ain't undercover gathers or agent provocateurs, says they can pay their bills, ain't gonna be skanking anybody, gonna be talking to everyone with a bitta respect and ain't gonna be generally fuck-arsing around, calling stuff on, ordering gear, and then changing their minds at the last minute. We need to know that they mean business and, like the very best working girls, a policy of 'discretion assured' goes without saying. Like any business we're looking for the no-fuss repeat business.

How did I get here? A combination of rapid promotion through the ranks and having greatness thrust upon me. I got into the business by accident. I didn't leave school wanting to be a coke dealer, nobody did in those days, not like today where all these kids want to be in on the swindle. Everybody wants to be a drugsman. I reckon it must look very inviting, like piss-easy money, which it is when all goes well. Ten years ago when I started there wasn't the supply or the demand. A drop of charlie was still for pop stars and a birthday treat, something special, something worthy of comment. Nowadays it ain't even a fuckin luxury anymore to a lot of folk, it's more along the lines of a necessity. I'm sure they don't even notice they're tooting half the time. Sure, you always had your hardcore of cokeheads, like you always had your hardcore of smackheads and a few who couldn't make up their minds which camp they were in, but it wasn't so firmly entrenched in the heartland as it is now, it's everywhere you fuckin look, for fuck sake. There's guys I know who ten years ago were venomously anti-drugs. They would stand at the ramp in naff wine bars delivering speeches along the lines of 'I wouldn't touch that shit, it's fuckin poison and people who deal it are evil, scumbag, lowlife cunts, bloodsuckers.' Now these very same guys do all their shillings on charlie, in cold blood, fuck the consequences, grafting all week just to get charged up or maybe serving up a few grams to pals to pay for it. It's like someone's done a public relations job on dealers as well. They've gone from parasites to the guys everyone wants to know. If you know a good charlie dealer, it's like having the correct connections, like a tricky accountant or a crafty mortgage broker. It puts you in the swindle. All those guys who serve up in gram deals, good gram deals mind, not with all the active ingredient chopped out, live like fuckin princes, get to go to all the best parties on one big freebie, cos everyone wants to be their bestest friend. No party's complete without the bugle. I've watched nineteen-year-old kids from scuzzy council estates tell pop stars and other household names to fuckin get in line and talk to them nice or they ain't getting nuffin, fuck all, not a fuckin sniff bullseye, and the celebrity punters have jumped to attention, apologised to the kid and waited on them to be served.

That's how I started, on the shop floor, serving up to who-ever wanted the toot, a gram at a time, no shit no tick, don't try and find me, I'll find you, I'll be about. I had my round and I got a good reputation very quick so people would always wait until I showed up to be served. It's like selling anything else, washing machines, blow jobs, handmade shoes – if you don't take the piss people'll always come back. Then I was one of the first guys to have a pager. On Friday afternoon and evening the fuckin thing used to light up like a fuckin toaster, every two minutes, beep, beep, fuckin beep, the fuckin thing would be going off. The fuckin thing got red hot. In the end I got so I resented making money. Well, that's not true. What I got to resent was being at the beck and call of all these fuckers who, when I was nineteen and thought I knew it all, came across as real up-their-own-arse types but looking back they were okay, just okay. I hated being talked to like I was some kinda Joey, a fuckin delivery boy. I had stumbled upon the kinda yuppie come trendy come music biz come fashion crowd in the re-emerging Soho and they were all seriously wedged up and dying to get stuck into the product. I would take their readies just as quick as they were willing to part with it and I never got a moment's grief. It was cash on delivery every time. They thought I was cute with a capital Kay, cherub-faced, turning up with the candy and then disappearing back into the night. I started to tell this crowd, who all seemed to know one another anyway, that in future I would only sort them out if the order was anything over quarter of an ounce, seven grams. The idea being that they club together, I do one drop and they do my distribution for me. If they wanted only a couple of grams they were to page another number cos I'd set up a couple of pals with pagers and little franchises of their own. We dealt on reputation and I still do.

So now I was shifting parcels I went to the Spanish guy I was getting my supply from and asked him for a better price cos I'm moving ninety per cent of the powder that moves through him and I think I deserve a bigger whack. He laughs at me and calls me a lippy little bastard, fucks me off with a real flippant take-it-or-leave-it attitude. Now I'm fucked. I've got two choices. I can wrap the operation up, spite myself with my own pride, or go back to the Spanish cunt and eat myself a great big shit sandwich and buy at his price until I can sort out something else, find another supplier, and that's what I'd made up my mind to do. But out of the shadows appeared Mister Mortimer, the legendary pothouse of the parish, who had heard about my supply problems on the jungle telegraph.

I met Morty in a hotel bar in Knightsbridge. Mort likes a meet in a hotel bar, he still does. The lispy barman asked if I was old enough to drink alcohol, I got offended, Morty laughed, and the barkeep apologised saying, 'I've got to ask, chuck, you understand.' Morty told me to go back to the Span-yard whole-saler and the guy would be more sympathetic because he'd had a word and the guy wanted, wanted mind, to negotiate a fairer price. I musta asked Morty about ten times what he wanted outta the deal and every time he says he don't want anything at this moment in time but in the future he may want something from me. I was young and I told Mortimer that if he wanted a fee to put the fix in to tell me now so I can make up my mind if it's worth it or not. I didn't like all this 'One day I may ask you for a favour' bollocks. I didn't want to be beholden to any fucker no matter how much of a house-trained lunatic they were. I didn't put it quite like that at the time. Morty was genuinely amused by my cocky attitude. He thought I had balls, he told me years later.

Mister Mortimer got up, shook my hand and walked out leaving me confused and I didn't lay eyes on him for exactly another five years. I went back to the supplier who was really pleased to see me or at least made out he was. It was like something outta a Mafioso movie cos he's givin it a large dose of the old 'Shit, man, why didn't you tell me you were an acquaintance of Mister Morty. I'm very, very sorry, man, about the misunderstanding, truly sorry I am, brother, all forgiven?' routine. I drove his price down and fuckin down so he was fuckin robbing himself. He was sick and I could see it on his face no matter how hard he tried to disguise it. He wasn't actually losing money but he musta been gutted that Morty decided to get busy cos I had made up my mind that I was gonna go in and pay the going rate. Years later I asked Mort what was it all about. He says he likes to see youngsters get ahead and he never liked the geezer, the Span-yard, always thought he was a slippery, smug cunt, halfa grass. Years later he came crawling to us to punt and I cut him a deal. I still didn't like the guy but business is business. A while after that, three or four years ago in fact, I heard he got slung outta a fourth-floor apartment over in Dalston, landed on a railway track. I guess someone's credit rating went outta the window so the Span-yard followed it out. The law found no drugs on the premises. Such is life.

Soon I've got five or six good pals working for me on a day-to-day basis. I supply them, pager and tackle, and point them in the right direction of where to unload it so we're all making really fuckin good dough and times are truly good. We've got a Junior-Yuppie-Mafia thang going down, living the life, with JPG suits, Suzuki jeeps, Champagne and whistle all the way. I've got other guys starting to come to me for seriously large amounts and I'm running around all day sorting this shit out. The Span-yard got dropped out cos he couldn't keep up and I eventually found what I'd been looking for, some guys out in leafy Highgate who could do the business big time, nicely low-key and nicely sensible. They wouldn't touch the Naughty and neither would we. These guys didn't blink as I called on

13

more and more and more. It was just order, delivery, money, crash, see-you-next-time, I'll be in touch.

I needed the supply sorted cos in '86 the business went into orbit. It was like being around when those guys invented gunpowder. Everything changed overnight. Guys who'd spent their whole lives being paranoid and uptight, going around chivving other uptight guys with Stanley knives and sticking glasses in each other's boats, suddenly wanted to kiss and hug you after a couple of ecstasy. Very straight, square birds were downing Es at a rate of knots and getting chopped, fucked, in khazis. People were begging to pay three ching to party in a field up by the M25. I was doing the catering and could name my price and get it. It was a seller's market. Guys were making fortunes so everybody wanted in.

It soon became amateur hour and guys who worked very sensible, very meticulous for the last couple of years started getting outta their heads. They became shunters. I'd sit them down and try to remind them that what we were engaged in was called crime. All I'd get for my trouble was a loada gobbledegook about freedom and love. They all started going weird on me. You'd go to collect money, and they'd be dancing round the gaff, arms in the air, button music blasting out at maximum volume, every waif and stray of the parish plotted up, poncing and earwigging. You'd try and find a guy you was working with and he'd have disappeared down to Ibiza, said he was going for a couple of days, and was still AWOL two or three weeks later.

One thing that really put me ahead in those days and keeps me ahead now is the simple fact that I don't really like drugs that much. I'm not a fan. I can take 'em or leave 'em. I see them as just another commodity to be bought and sold and the fact that they're illegal makes it more risky and so the rewards are higher for the guys who are bold enough and brave enough and who manage to stay ahead. It obviously helps if you ain't out of the old canister all the fuckin time. Some guys deal cos they're chasing a habit, they deal so they ain't a shunter, they plunder all the profits, they have a loada mackerels hanging round to make them feel good about it, to feel a bit superior, but the

14

reality is that they're simply a better class of mug punter and when the star burns out and the show's over the entourage move on to the next up-and-coming guy. I've tried everything I've ever sold. I've never tried the brown but then I've never punted it either. It's not a moral thing with me, it's just I know for a fact that to get involved in smack in London is just too much pure aggravation and the guys I deal with have got enough going on already. They let the Turks, the Chinks and the Indians take care of all that. I don't try and justify it, I just crack on and do it. Anyone who get webbed up in the brown get seriously dropped out cos it's a known fact that they'll bubble you up when they're clucking.

The papers at this time, '88, '89, are full of scare stories about the evils of drug use and the cozzers are chasing round like madmen trying to put a few bodies away to make the big example of, to pacify their governors in the Home Office, to get the tabloids off their backs cos they're writing it from the point of view that the kids are being corrupted and nobody's doing fuck all about it. The reality as ever is that the kids are fuckin mad for it, can't get enough of it, they don't see a problem. What happened next is still the stuff of rumour and legend. A lot of guys started getting fitted up or the law would use agent provocateurs to set up drug deals and then move in and nick as many people as possible for being involved just to keep the body count up. Contrary to common belief, the Other People only really did this when they needed the result really bad. If they got caught out by some clever Queen's Counsel up the Bailey they could end up in the dock themselves. Scotland Yard had a squad within the Squad to target the whole rave scene, to make arrests, to go undercover, to gather information through grasses, mostly small-time dealers they'd managed to turn informant in exchange for a squeeze if they got nicked any-where in London. These little toe-rags had a licence to go to work with immunity. Everything on this scene was an open secret anyway and there was an awful lot of loose talk, people knowing stuff they shouldn't by rights know. I began to get very seriously worried about getting captured or fitted up. A DJ I know for a fact had fuck all to do with any dealing got a seven-year sentence simply cos he was, very foolishly, sat in a motor when a trade went down. I began to see signs, omens, and decided to leave town for a while. I cashed in my chips and went to look up some pals down in Oz.

I loved it, fuckin loved it. I went over there with a loada pills and let them go a bit at a time. The groovy crowd in Sydney almost took our hand off for them cos they couldn't get them down there at the time. I had a couple of pals in tow as ever and everything was sweet until they started falling out over anything and everything. I got my shit together and headed up to south-east Asia and hung out there for a while. It taught me a very good lesson about doing things with pals, you can trust 'em, sometimes, maybe, but you can't always rely on them. I had some guys doing bits and pieces, running things backwards and forwards between there and the UK so I always had money coming in. I got rumped a couple of times, nothing serious, not cos the dudes were even mischievous or anything, more cos they were so fuckin untogether, outers all the fuckin time. They're doing too much product, it's the fat-bloke-down-the-chip-shop-can't-stop-eating-all-the-chips syndrome. Again it was a lesson learnt, quite cheaply as it turned out, that you should try and avoid doing anything with people who can't control their drugs, who let the drugs control them. They don't mean to fuck up, it just happens.

I went from there over to the States, Califuckinfornia, and had a real good look around. I was having it, associating, with a totally different kinda people, people who were movers and groovers on the arts scene, actors and actresses, film-makers, musicians, sensible ones not the deadbeat, lowlife variety. I was in LA with people who were making moves, the real in-crowd, living near the beach, but I started to miss all those things that are so typically English like cold rain, stodgy food and good old verbal abuse. When I arrived back in jolly old monochrome England things seemed to have calmed down a bit. The ecstasy trade had become highly organised very quickly. The price had tumbled and it was run mostly by teams of bouncers and obvious heavy muscles so I gave all that a big wide. I had moneys to collect from various sources so I wasn't in any kinda

16

hurry to go to work but I made sure I was seen out and about the parish and waited for something to turn up. A lot of the old team I'd palled about with back in '88, '89, were either away doing time, away down in Goa or away with the fairies so I was well open to new suggestions and new accomplices. After a few false starts and offers of hare-brained, get-rich-quick schemes that would only get me put away for stretches, I started moving bits and pieces around town just to keep my hand in really and to top up my dwindling cashish reserve.

Then almost five years to the day after our last meeting Morty rang me. I was sitting, on my jack, in a dusty old saloon bar deep in the backstreets of the old manor. It was midday and I was reading the early edition of the *Evening Standard* and drinking a bottle of Pils. This is something I very, very rarely do. I was about to cut out when the old boy came round from behind the jump to tell me I had a phone call and would I please follow him.

'I think you've made a mistake, pal,' I said. 'Nobody knows I'm here.'

'Oh no. It's for you all right.'

'Who is it?'

'I don't know. I was told to just come and get you.'

He was lying about that but it's no big deal. How the fuck did this old geezer know who I was and who I wasn't, he didn't fuckin ask or anything. I followed him through the door marked private. Everyone likes to walk though a door marked private. The old fellow pointed at the receiver silently and left. It was Morty on the phone. I reckon he wanted me to be a bit freaked out and be asking him how he knew I was there. I didn't cos I knew that's exactly what he wanted. Mortimer loves all that dramatic fuck-about, getting your nut, so I spoke to Mister Mortimer like it was the most natural thing in the whole wide world that he should be ringing me in this out-of-the-way boozer, unarranged, like it was my business office or something. He wanted to meet me in the same hotel bar that we had the meet back in '86, he had a proposition he wanted to run by me, wanted me to come and listen and see what I thought. This afternoon, sure, no problem, no time like the present is there,

17

I'll see you there, Mister Mortimer, three o'clock, wonderful, okay, I'll see you then.

I put the phone down and walked back into the bar and asked the guy for a five-star brandy. I was excited although you wouldn't have guessed it. I was outwardly calm but my heart was pounding cos this was like being asked to join the Freemasons. It was like being welcomed into the big time. Morty wasn't going to introduce me to a car-stereo-thieving syndicate. Mister Mortimer was a major player.

The old boy wouldn't take any money for the Andy Pandy, simply waved away my fiver and got on with his bottling-up, like any friend of Morty was a friend of his as well. It's the little things that let you know you've arrived.

Same bar five years on, same camp guy behind the ramp, same glitzy wallpaper, same high-class hookers hanging out, five years older. Morty's already sitting down facing the door as I arrive. He don't fuck about, straight down to business. He tells me that he can lay his hands on as much exceptional quality cocaine as we can shift, the very, very best gear and from a very safe, very secure source, Mister Price I know now. He's also got people who are up for buying the product offa him but Morty really don't know that much about dealing. He looks on it as a trade or a craft like any other, which it is I suppose. Morty wants into the business cos otherwise he's gonna be left behind in the age of the dinosaurs and he's already a late starter cos he's about four zero so he's leaving it late. What he does have going for him is the connections he's built up over the years, in the boob and out, and a very solid reputation as a merciless cunt with charm. A straight question needs a straight answer, no Jack and Danny, are you willing to come on board as a partner? Equal shares, carved straight down the middle? Yes or no? I need an answer today, right now in fact. He talked about prices and availability like he already knew the job. Why me? I asked and he replied Cos you think like a guy who don't wanna get captured and spend years locked away. I've done too much bird already. You think like a criminal not like a convict. I don't know you but I know of you and people tell me that you're the best man for the job at this moment in time. You ain't no

18

loud-mouth and you go about things with a minimum of fuss but for you to go up a gear in the business you need to start making a few sensible allies. Do you wanna start moving right away from the shopfloor? I need a partner cos some things are always done best with a partner. Do you wanna be a face or do you sincerely wanna be rich? I promise you I don't wanna shag you or anything, son, I just want us to do the business. Okay, I said, but one thing, don't ever call me son again cos I fuckin hate it, I don't even like my old man calling me son. Okay, he said, never again. We shook hands.

We both pulled up ten grand each, put it in the middle. In a matter of weeks we had our money tripled and we were running kit all over London, making meets to sort things out, let certain people know what we were up to, and the rest as they say is history. I was serving the troops up in Highgate now cos we could give them a better price and product than they were getting. It was another two years before Clarkie and Terry arrived and brought with them a whole lot more work. Doors opened to me that would otherwise have been shut or slammed in my face. I talked as an equal to geezers who really just wanted to reach over the table and squeeze my head till my eyes popped out or strangle me and kick my body round the yard for fun, but having Morty at my right shoulder prevented this. I soon learnt that in the Premier League the only thing people understand is power expressed through violence or more accurately the threat of violence. I thought the higher up you went the more civilised things would become, but the reality is that the threat just becomes subtler. Guns hover in the background, you hear stories of disappearances, people simply going missing, going out to collect their dry cleaning and never coming home again. Shit like that starts entering the equation because the stakes are so much higher. Everyone's a lot more paranoid and edgy cos it's such a long way down.

Because Morty wasn't performing on a daily or weekly basis his legend grew through Chinese whispers and I felt we could do anything. We worked together well. We had an understanding. If I didn't think something or someone was kosher we dropped it out. He took the piss for a while about me being so fuckin over-cautious that I suspected everyone and everything, but if something didn't smell right we didn't do it. Soon all the pukka business wanted to come to us cos they heard we only did business with seriously conscientious professionals. If we had started out with a long-term strategy to only deal with sensible guys to lure in other sensible guys then the strategy worked beautifully and I took the kudos. Some sloppy little teams got the zig cos we wouldn't trade with them and then confirmed our suspicions by creating a fuss and slagging us off all over the gaff. In a way it was a compliment.

I was then faced with another kinda problem. I had bundles of cash wrapped round me and there's only so much you can do with cash without people getting suspicious or jealous. I was sent to see an accountant an hour's drive outta London. My card had been marked, I could be completely straight with him. He, Mister Lonsdale, told me that I had better start paying taxes on my drug profits, obviously not declaring that I was a dealer but start opening and investing in as many cash businesses as possible. Start flushing as much cash through these seemingly legit fronts as would look feasible. Go to people you know and trust and tell them you'll put them in the swindle if you can fire some money through the books and get paid a partner's dividend at the end of the year. Start looking to open clothes shops, snack bars, flower stalls, car washes, ice-cream vans, gyms, hot-dog stands, driving schools, recording studios. If any of your pals come to you with a business plan that's half-way sensible, stick your money in, so long as it's a cash-heavy business, don't matter if it don't make money in reality cos on paper it's fuckin thriving. Don't worry if you got lock-ups full of rotting flowers and burgers or you're knee-deep in a river of melting ice cream or the hot-dog stands are spending all day padlocked up in a garage, cos on paper you're selling every single bit of stock you buy at top fuckin dollar. You're fuckin golden bollocks, the Chamber of Commerce young business-man of the year, you've got the fuckin Midas touch. Avoid night-clubs, bars, restaurants and mini-cab firms because they're a total headfuck, his words not mine, and a favourite target of the Inland Revenue and VAT Mafioso. It's the exact opposite of what someone trying to run a cash-heavy business would be doing.

At the end of the tax year I got a tax bill, which I paid by cheque, and Mister Lonsdale sent me a bill to keep the books straight. I gave him a good few grand cashish in an envelope and an ounce of flake-coke at Christmas. The important thing was we'd both got the other guy firmly by the bollocks.

A year or so later Mister El has advised me to start getting into property, introduced me to solicitors and mortgage brokers who could be bent and it starts to become apparent that once you've got your money into the system, skull money goes to straight money. I live in a rented flat, in spite of the fact that I own a few, and work the rents through the lettings agency. I keep readies plugged up in cash and in banks dotted around the place. I've got accounts in Jersey and the Caymans. Having accounts out there's not as flash as it sounds cos anyone can walk into their London offices, plonk their readies on the counter, those cunts'll suck your dick and it don't matter where the paper comes from.

Jeremy shows bang on the dot of half-four with much profuse apologising. We buzz him up. He's dressed like a barrister with black jacket, pinstripe strides and a fawn coat with a crimson velvet collar, totally convincing. He's saying he's terribly, terribly sorry, he's been stuck in traffic due to an accident on Battersea Bridge. We're saying 'no fuckin problem, Jeremy' in spite of the fact that a couple of minutes earlier we were going to abort the mission and scarpa. We lock ourselves in and let him test the gear but he knows it's gonna be good cos it always is. I get some jewellery scales outta a filing cabinet and we check the weight together. Jeremy is pure public school so he don't trust any cunt. He always checks the quality of the powder with his little chemistry set and always weighs the parcel and we always check the money even though we've been doing the business for years. It's good business practice, good manners and keeps standards up. He's happy with his goods and brings out the money from his briefcase and Morty starts running it through a counting machine.

21

For a counting machine to work properly all the notes need to be facing the one direction, all the Queen's heads are the right way up. Some of Jeremy's notes ain't so the counting keeps stopping. I get a little pissed off at this and start to think that maybe he should sort this kinda shit out before he comes fuckin over here, but in reality it's a sure sign that you've been in the game too long, when a guy turns up to give you twenty large and you're getting the hump cos it ain't all facing the right way. Maybe I've grown blasé and take things for granted, maybe I'm just spoilt rotten.

The money tops up to exactly twenty grand. We're happy and so is Jeremy and he cuts out. He'll have the half-key broken down into smaller deals in a couple of hours and it'll all be shifted again by tonight. It's all on order anyway. Morty is rubbing the wedge up against his bollocks. Twenty grand in fifties is about the size of a house brick. Morty chops it into thousand-pound lumps and then puts four elastic bands around the notes, three width-ways and one long-ways. It's a beautiful, compact, taut, sexy little brick. I laugh. Morty finds the actual cash sexy, not what it can buy or the freedom it brings but the existence, the sight, the smell, the feel, of a large amount in the one place, preferably his hand, a fuckin big turn-on, like it's a heart-warming thing in itself, a thing of great aesthetic beauty, a work of art. I can see his point cos to see a fuckin great pile of loot and know some or all of it's yours gives you some kinda thrill, a tingle in the testicles, like spotting a real stunning woman on a real sunny day, it's a mixture of lust and the appreciation of a beautiful thing. Morty laughs and throws the wedge over to me.

'I don't want it, not after it's been where it's been.' I throw it back and he catches it.

'This is money for jam,' he says, slinging it on the desktop and rubbing his hands together. 'And now,' he declares, 'it's time to go off-duty for the weekend.'

'Shall we crave that bitta cash first?'

'Will you indulge, Young Sir?' he says, getting his little bitta personal out and starting to chop himself a line.

I shake my head.

22

'Won't have something for the weekend, Young Sir?'

'No. I'm okay, Mort, but you go ahead, have one for me.'

'Thank you,' he says, a little bit sarcy.

'Moderation in all things, I say.'

'I'm only having a fuckin livener,' Mort says a bit defensively.

'I know you are, Mort, I'm only saying ... '

But Morty ain't listening. He's got his nose down to the tabletop and he's snorting up his line, quite a small one really, hardly worth bothering with some people would say. Morty ain't no cokehead. Although he does have his moments, he don't lose the plot like some guys, he's got respect for the gear, he don't surrender to it like some users.

'Now you've powdered your nose, my bitta cash outta that comes to all the sixes – six thousand, six hundred and sixty-six quid.'

'Right, you and me take a third each and Terry and Clarkie split a third, yeah?' He's counting money onto the desktop.

'That's what we agreed.'

'And how much did you say it was again?'

'Six, six, six, six.'

'Here's six, six-fifty.' He's grinning.

'Morty, you fuckin do this to me every fuckin time.'

'Well, do you have some change?' he says in innocence.

'I'll tell you what. You give me six, seven hundred and I'll owe you the change.'

'Anyone would think that you was starvin the way you go on –'

'This ain't about money, Mort.'

'– living in the bunhouse.' He's tutting now.

'This ain't about the sixteen quid.'

'So why are you makin such a big fuss about a few pennies?' he shrugs, his face a picture of innocence.

'Okay, Mort, I'll tell you what we'll do. You keep the money, cos you so obviously need it, but you gotta wash up the scales and that. Okay?'

And as I turn to point at the scales he's up, out the door and down the stairs, laughing, going down three and four at a time like a big kid, howling like a wolf, leaving me to do the fuckin washing up, again.

Saturday
To Be in Loveland

Saturday morning, quarter to ten, the phone's rang and it's Morty with his business head on. I'm half asleep and half awake.

'You still in bed?' says Mort.

'It's Saturday mornin. I'm havin a lie-in.'

Like a lot of guys who have done a bit of bird he's up every fuckin morning about seven, wide awake, and thinks everyone else should be as well.

'Listen, something's come up, nothin bad, someone wants to meet you.'

'Man or woman?'

'Be serious. It's business.'

I know better than to ask Morty over the phone just who it is.

'Okay. Where?'

'He wants us to have a spot of lunch with him. You up for that?'

'Sure.'

'Meet me at Loveland at about twelve-thirty, okay?'

'I'll see you there.'

Morty had an interest in a string of sex shops called Loveland, one quite large one that operated as a clearing house and store plus four or five satellite ones dotted about near the mainline railway stations. About a year after coming out of the boob having done his five and a bit he was approached by the owners who were having all sorts of problems with hounds turning them over, not unlike the kamikaze firm that Morty had been an associate member of, much to his cost. The owners, who always preferred to keep well in the shadows, thought that Morty could turn from poacher to gamekeeper if they offered him a chunky slice of the profits. The word would get about that

24

Mister Mortimer was on the firm and they would get less aggravation. I don't think it had occurred to him to go robbing sex shops or asking them for protection but when the offer came he accepted with a wink and a handshake, like he had been waiting to be asked all along. So now Morty was like one of those crafty ex-MPs or brigadier generals who sit on the board of directors of major corporations, sign their name to the annual accounts, turn a blind eye to any skulduggery and claim their hefty remuneration. He, like them, only had to show up two days a month to collect his readies, and whereas their names looked good on the letterheads Morty's moniker brought with it a certain respectability in dubious circles. When there was a big football game in town or a full moon Morty stuck a couple of bashers in the lolly pops but apart from that they never gave him a moment's worry.

I've got there about twelve-thirty and the kid in the shop's sent me through to the back office. Morty's sat in a kinda armchair arrangement that's been made outta boxes of sticky books and sex aids. It looks almost like a throne. He's drinking a cup of coffee outta a polystyrene cup, looking at the pictures in the morning paper and smoking a snout. He barely looks up when I come in. Nobby, who's got a piece of the gaff and runs it for the other partners, is sitting at the desk punching numbers into a calculator and writing down figures in a ledger, cursing under his breath every now and again.

Up on the ceiling there's a blow-up doll that they've had filled with helium so it's just floating around under its own steam, grazing the walls and bouncing off the corners of the room in slow motion. Its bug eyes are wide open staring off into the faraway distance. Its mouth is stretched open as if she's just received a terrible shock or she's waiting for a delivery of some sort. The doll's arms are outstretched and legs are wide open but bent at the knee. Its vivid yellow nylon hair has been pulled roughly into two ponytails and has grubby red gingham ribbons tied around the ends. The kid comes in from the shop to ask Nobby if a delivery of Danish rubber-wear mags has come in yet cos he's got a punter who's been back three or four times waiting for something specialised, some odd kink or other,

25

nuns in PVC or something, but Nobby shrugs, no joy as yet. The tiny draught coming in from the street sends the doll bouncing across the ceiling but Morty and Nobby don't so much ignore it as simply don't notice it anymore. Morty lights another fag and folds the paper back on itself and carries on reading. I fuckin know he's dying for me to ask about the doll.

'Some punter brought it back,' says Nobby, noticing me looking upwards, 'said it was worn out in under two weeks and he wanted a replacement or his money back. We fucked him off of course but he's gone down one of those law centres to see if they know what's reasonable wear-and-tear on an inflatable doll. The geezer's a total fuckin nut-nut.'

'I'd kinda worked that out on my own.'

'He's got legal aid to take the whole fuckin caper to small claims court, and that –' says Nobby pointing up at the dolly '– is Delectable Donna and nobody can work out if she's an exhibit or a witness. His brief was taking the whole fuckin thing very serious – you know, rights of the little man and that, he may be a sleazy perv but he's still got human rights – but then the geezer tells her that he's used the bitta kit approximately eighty-nine times, approximately, mind, so he may or may not have been counting. In under two fuckin weeks he's got eighty-nine offences to be taken into consideration, work it out, that's over six times a fuckin day and his brief has got the fuckin thing on her desk in a fuckin Tesco's bag so his fuckin human rights have gone out the fuckin window. She tells the Billy Bunter to take it home and–' he mimics a bird '– "totally cleanse it, use some extra strong bleach on its, you know, working parts, soak it overnight and then scrub it and then scrub it again" so that's what the sticky cunt does. Now our man, our brief, says that in doing so he's perished the plastic so we can't send it to the lab, to forensic, like they do in the movies so he's fucked our chances of getting a fair result.'

'By interfering with Donna?'

'Exactly. His brief, who's totally fuckin spooked by now with the geezer, agrees with us. She tells him to settle with us or fuck off, cos we were offering him a new doll to avoid the thing getting in the local papers and that, cos if they get anything juicy they get on to the nationals. It could end up in that fuckin rag,' says Nobby pointing at Morty's paper.

'It's right up their fuckin street.'

'I fuckin know they'd have fuckin fighting funds and everything. We support your right to be a fuckin sex case. We gave him a new doll, those things only cost us about a tenner from Holland, we told him to be gentle with her, take your time, treat her like the lady she is. We even gave him a few old books that have been knocking around donkeys, not of donkeys you understand but shit that's been on the fuckin premises too fuckin long and ain't movin.'

'And Donna comes home.'

'She becomes our property again and she's become a bit of a mascot.'

'I think it's disgusting having that thing up there, it's fuckin unhygienic,' says Morty getting up and giving Nobby his paper back. 'You've been around these fuckin perverts too fuckin long.'

'That thing's been industrially cleaned, it's cleaner than when it left the factory.'

'It'd fuckin wanna be, Nobby.' He gives me a little wink.

'So, Morty, before you go, what am I gonna do?' says Nobby.

'I fuckin told you, Nobby. Anything you didn't order, can't sell or is not up to scratch, send it fuckin back.' He turns to me to explain. 'The people over in Holland who supply this outfit keep sending Nobby here stuff that's no val to us. Either it's dodgy quality or it's just too fuckin much. It's basically all their old shit and every time Nobby tells them to stop they just keep sending more.'

'Have a look at this,' says Nobby, getting a magazine out from under the desk. He opens it and unfolds the centre page so now it's a poster-size picture of a bird reclining. 'When you scratch the scratch and sniff, it don't sniff,' he says, scratching at it and going to hold it under my nose.

'Fuck off with that!!!'

'And they got a very funny idea of what's obscene and what ain't, like if the donkey in a video's wearing a condom that's

27

all right cos it's safe sex, ain't it,' says Nobby. 'And if you watch one of those films to the end, which is a fuckin hair-raising experience in itself, definitely not a first-date movie, they got a little caption saying that no animal's welfare has been harmed during the making of this production. They got things a bit mixed up.'

'Slightly,' I say.

'Like it's okay if some poor bint's getting chopped by a beast just so long as Muffin the Mule's got straw to sleep on and a few barley sugars,' says Morty.

'See, those people have got no fuckin idea,' says Nobby. 'Your British are very straight really in what they want. What's hardcore over here ain't worth a wank, literally, to them on the Continent, it's softcore, show it on the telly, no problem. That's why we're getting all this shit getting sent over.'

'Is it paid for?' I ask.

'No way.' Nobby shakes his head. 'And they don't seem to mind, but it's cluttering up the fuckin place and stuff we can sell, got punters for, ain't coming through. See you're up against the internet now so if the gear ain't up to it then you're fucked.'

'Listen, keep all the paperwork straight and send the rest back, pay for what you take. Bookkeeping is your forte, young Nobby,' says Morty.

'Yeah, I suppose so, Morty. It's just–'

'Listen, Nobby, you fuckin asked my fuckin advice so you got it,' says Morty, suddenly annoyed now, giving Nobby the pointy finger down his nose. 'Anyway, I'm outta here. Me and my colleague here have got an appointment. And Nobby–' he speaks slow like he's talking to a child '– Send That Fuckin Gear Back, Okay?'

We're out on the street and walking towards where our cars are parked.

'He's okay, that Nobby, but he can get on your fuckin nerves at times, lets people talk to him like he's a fuckin teabag, he's a benefit-of-the-doubt merchant. Been around these fuckin sex cases and nonces too long.'

'You get people asking you for kiddie porn back there?'

'Yeah, all that stuff's on the internet now but we still get asked.'

'And?'

'I tell the geezers in the shop to tell 'em that we do have it but it's far too dodgy keepin it on the premises and to come back later, when we shut, when nobody's about, you know, kid 'em on, get 'em to come back later.'

'And then what?'

'We beat them up.'

'Bad?'

'I don't know any other way.'

'Not you and Nobby?'

'No, for fuck's sake. He couldn't swing a golf club, let alone a punch. No, you can always find volunteers to beat up a nonce.'

Strangers, Role Models and Heroes

'You've got no plans for this afternoon, have you?' says Morty as we walk to his car.

'No. Where are we off to, Mort?'

'We'll take my car and I'll drop you back later.'

'What's the appointment about?'

'Have you eaten yet?'

'I've had breakfast.'

'Are you hungry?'

'I'm getting there.'

'Cos it's a bittova drive to where we're going, so you'll be hungry when you get there.'

'So, Mort, where the fuck are we going?'

'To have a spot of lunch, a late one.'

'Yeah, I'd gathered that, but where? With who?'

'It's meant to be the bollocks, this gaff we're going to. Someone's asked to see us, well, see you really.'

'Is it business?'

'Oh yeah, it's business all right, it's always business with this guy.'

I think I'll just wait till he tells me. A minute goes by.

'I got a call this morning from Mister Price,' says Mort. 'That's who we're going to see. Why, I don't know, so don't ask.'

'Why'd he wanna see us?'

'I said don't ask, so you ask.'

'Didn't he say anything?'

'No, I said that, didn't I. He just asked or rather told us to meet him and Gene in this gaff called Pepi's Barn out Epping way, so it's a bit of a drive.'

'I guess so.'

'He says to meet him at two o'clock. Jimmy's driver's given me some instructions and a fuckin grid-reference cos the place is so fuckin exclusive it's hidden away from the riff-raff, it's tres exclusive, unlisted, a well-kept secret, says James.'

'I bet it's not a café he's got us driving halfway across London to eat in. I bet Jimmy likes his grub.'

'You'll be able to ask him yourself in a little while.'

I'm thinking that I'm gonna let Jimmy ask the questions here today, cos people don't get to where he is without being a cute old fucker and a ruthless one as well. Round our way the likes of Jimmy Price were looked up to like great statesmen or magnates, self-made men who had come up the hard way from nowhere to command respect. That's the romantic view, like the made-for-TV movie. The reality is that these gents could be horrible, nasty cunts when necessary and it was necessary a lot of the time.

He's to be admired, is James. He is as cute as fuck. He's got interests all over the place, straight and not so straight. He was one of the first to realise that taking libbos, believing too many Jimmy Cagney movies, taking the piss outta the old bill, was a mug's game cos they just get the zig and come at you with more legal firepower. Far better, thought Jim, to keep a very low profile and crack on, retain all the best lawyers and barristers just in case it all goes crocked and avoid any kinda attention. This might seem like stating the fuckin obvious nowadays but this geezer's from a different era where it was par for the course to show out that you was at it. Depending on who you listen to, Jimmy's one of the few guys in London who could straighten the very top old bill, the top players up in Scotland Yard, with a few bob or one of the only guys in London that the old bill would actively fit up. They would put their pensions and solid reputations on the line to place Jimmy Boy in the boob for a score of years. Some guys wanna tell you that he's a fuckin genius, some folk wanna tell you he's a visionary, others that he's to be avoided or watched.

Of course there's the sub-species at the bottom of the pile who are simply envious of the man, the lagging boats down the boozer, the Born Losers Arms, who start running off at the mouth once they've had a bucket saying the geezer's a wanker and next morning they wake up shitting themselves hoping, praying, that nobody's heard them and they'll spend the day hiding under the blankets, sobbing and shaking with that particular brand of paranoia that the booze brings. It's pure old-fashion jealousy. They've got a fat old cunt of a misses that they would dearly love to strangle and bury off the motorway somewhere, they're getting grief from the local gathers who know they're wrong 'uns and drive 'em mad, they've been in and out the shovel since approved school, still doing the same old shit and getting nowhere, they're eating dogshit that passes for food, they got ill health, no fuckin future and they turn round and look at Jimmy. Is it any fuckin wonder that these sad cases can't handle it? He's off the manor, nice fuckin tan cos he's just got back from a little working holiday over on the Costa del Crime and when he comes down here he's like the Pope waving and walking on rose petals and they, the fuckwits, are either grafting against all odds, bubbling one another up or bleeding starving. Terrible thing, envy, it can eat you away like fuckin cancer if you let it. They can resent the man cos he's never done his big lump in the jail. He's done all the kid stuff of course, the borstals and DCs and that, but he's never had his collar felt as an adult which is pretty fuckin remarkable seeing all the knavery and skulduggery he's into, but he's shot through with pure animal cunning. Fair fuckin play.

Jimmy was what the Yanks would call an underboss to old Dewey and he was a fuckin legend, no two ways. He was a fuckin gentleman, a fuckin naughty one, but a gent none the less. Sure, he could be a lunatic but he commanded respect from all the underlings and even people who ordinarily would have only contempt for geezers in his line of work. My old man, who was a straight-goer all his fuckin life, driving his trains to fuck-knows-where, had great respect for old Dewey. The man was a Don. If Dewey had've been born into a different class he would've ended up running the fuckin railways or a big city bank, but it turned out how it did and he ended up running large parts of London with his allies.

When Dewey died of heart failure Jimmy smelt what was in the wind. Drugs changed everything. He spotted the new, younger, hungrier, seriously talented, ruthless families and clans coming up and moved sideways before he was bulldozed over like so many old relics. He realised his limitations and downsized, as big corporations do, his operation. What Jimmy did was carve himself out a principality among the bigger nation-states and kingdoms. It wasn't about turf or territory, you couldn't draw a red ring around it on a map, it was about Jimmy and his teams being given the respect to march on, doing their business unhindered. James' operation became lithe and flexible, less graft, more profit. It moved away from the factory floor.

I've got a feeling of fear mixed with excitement cos I know that if Jimmy's sending for me it's got to be important, but also I'm on my way to meet a fuckin legend of my youth. Old Dewey, Jimmy Price, the Tylers, Crazy Larry Flynn, the Archer Boys, the O'Mara family, seven brothers and five sisters, the girls as fuckin mad as the boys, and not forgetting our Clarkie's clan, they were like the royal families of Europe when we were growing up. Their fallings-out and feuds, their treaties and pacts, arranged marriages and messy divorces, their myths and legends, bar-brawls and escapades, their betrayals and treachery, were like a drop of poor man's Shakespeare to us kids who played three card brag in pissy stairwells and hung around smokin snout on cold street corners. We got hear-say and rumour, Chinese whispers and fuckin gross exaggeration and there was kudos to be earned if one of the greats' shadows fell upon us. We would have collected their pictures on bubblegum cards if we could.

'What do you think of Jimmy Price, Mort?'
'We've had this conversation before.'
'And you've never given me a straight answer before.'
'He's very good at his job.'
'Meaning?'
'He's very good at what he does.'
'Very diplomatic, Mister Mortimer.'
'I try.'
'I mean, do you like the geezer.'
'I don't think guys like Jimmy are there to be loved.'
'I know that.'

33

'So why ask?'

'A moment of temporary insanity, Morty, I don't know what came over me.'

He draws a deep breath and does that thing he does with his eyes, rolls them skyward. 'To answer your question, no, I don't like Jim, but I tell you what, I fuckin respect the geezer.'

'Don't take this the wrong way, Mort, but are you scared of him?'

'I won't take it the wrong way, and no, I ain't scared of him or anyone else. What's the worst they can do, they can only fuckin kill ya.'

Only.

'But you respect the guy?'

'Yeah, for holding things together after the old boy croaked. It was all up for grabs. He was a hard act to follow was Dewey.'

'So they tell me.'

'But Jimmy sorted it. Don't get me wrong, I ain't saying I'd like to go on me holidays with him or anything cos between me and you, cos we're the only ones here, he's a leery, bullying cunt is James at times, and to answer your question, no I don't like him all that much.'

'He's snide?'

'How can you call him snide in this game? Everyone's snide in this game. He loves a fuckin mind game, loves to let people know where the fuckin power lies, who's fuckin boss. If somebody's got a weakness, Jimmy can smell it out like those sniffer dogs the customs have got.'

'And then he's on it.'

'Fuckin dead right he's on it. This is a geezer who's bent old bill. Cute's a better word than snide. But if he don't like ya he'll put it right on ya.'

'So you know where you are with him.'

Morty laughed. 'Did I say that? You ain't been listening, brov. No, you never know where you are with a slippery cunt like Jimmy.'

'Thanks for warning me.'

'You'll be okay, cos you're a talent and talent's in short supply. Jimmy don't sit down to eat with any muggy-cunts, you know. What's the very worst that can happen? He can have you killed.' Morty laughs at his little joke.

'How very reassuring you are at times, Mister Mortimer.'

'Killed very slowly.' Morty really liked his little joke. 'As the song says, don't you worry about a thing, Mama. You can take yourself too fuckin seriously, you know.'

'I'm paid to worry, remember.'

We're in Hackney High Street.

'Is this the way to Epping, Mort?'

'It's the only way I know so it's got to be the right way.'

It's Saturday afternoon so the whole gaff is fuckin smashed out with shoppers.

'You see that building? The carpet warehouse? The big one over there?' Morty's pointing up and across the street at a grimy pile, a cross between a prison and a church, the whole front splattered with gaudy posters in lime greens and oranges, promising sale prices, never to be repeated offers and wholesale prices direct to the public.

'Yeah. What about it?'

'It was once the parish workhouse.'

'It looks like it.'

'And after that it was like a hostel for people who got fucked up in the war, the First World War not the last one, people who got fucked up in the head, not maimed or wounded but, you know, shot away inside the head. My great-grandad had a dose of that.'

'What, he fought in the war?'

'Yeah, fuckin right he did. He signed up in the West Indies, lied about his age. Dead keen, he was, but I don't suppose they give a fuck.'

'How old was he?'

'Fifteen and a half he was but he did look older.'

'He'd fuckin wanna.'

'He ended up at this gaff called Ypres – Wipers, the troops called it – getting the complete shit pummelled outta them by the German guns, but they ain't like what we call a gun, a shooter, these guns were on fuckin railway trains, with about twenty geezers loading the fuckin thing with one-ton shells.

Heavy artillery, heavy gravy. The top kiddies, the officers, won't go up to the front cos they don't want to get their fuckin uniforms muddy.'

'That wouldn't do at all.'

'Anyway, a fuckin huge shell has landed on this dug-out that the great-grandad's in. A direct hit. The little outfit he was with are buried and he's buried alive. It turns out later that he's in there for twenty-four hours before they dug him out and he's wide awake for the first part in among all his pals who have been blown to fuckin bits, one guy's arm's over there and his legs are over here, there's body parts all over the fuckin trench and he's covered in bits of their blood and brains and fuck-knows-what.'

'And he's in amongst all that shit.'

'Well, he had no fuckin choice, did he,' says Mort.

'And conscious for the first part?'

'Yeah. He's woken up about two weeks later in the Brighton Pavilion. Have you ever seen the Brighton Pavilion?'

'I can't remember if I have.'

'You'd know it if you'd seen it cos it's like the fuckin Taj Mahal in fuckin downtown Brighton. It's all spindly towers and nutty arches. It's a total fuckin crack-up on the outside and inside it's all mad gold and felt-flock wallpaper like a curry house but to him it's like a palace cos he's from the sticks on one of the little islands. Then he thinks, hang on, maybe I'm dead already and this is fuckin heaven, and he's panicking but it turns out that the gaff is being used for a hospital for an Indian outfit. In the confusion and mayhem they've got him booked as an Indian and shipped him over to Brighton.'

'What was the matter with him?'

'He's got a couple of broken legs and a fuckin huge bandage round the canister but they said nothing was broken, but from then on in he became a right fuckin headbanger, a complete fuckin head-the-ball, he's gone completely the other way from all that King and country bullshit, it's turned him inside out, it has, he's never the same again but you wouldn't be, would ya.'

'I don't suppose you would, not after you've been covered with your spar's blood and brains and that.'

'He's caused fuckin havoc everywhere he's gone for the next sixty years. He used to wake up screaming, thinking he's been buried alive again, fuckin shit ya right up to hear it, cos it was a fuckin insane scream and he'd be gulping for breath like he was suffocating all over again, poor old cunt.'

'They'd call that Post-Traumatic Stress Disorder these days. They'd give him fuckin therapy from arsehole to breakfast time, he could sue 'em for a fuckin lump sum or a bittova war pension.'

'Too true. And they'd sort him out a medal as well, but this was back in the days when people thought they were being really fuckin polite calling a black geezer a coon or a nig-nog.'

I'm laughing.

'I know, you can fuckin laugh,' says Mort, 'but it's true, fuckin mad ain't it, but what I'm saying is that all these good people thought that black people lacked a bit of the old moral fibre. See, the whole fuckin gaff was streaming with soldiers who had been fucked up by the war, call it shell-shock or post-traumatic stress whatever, and it was put down to either cowardice or character weakness or both and the old boy was just another crazy and a Johnny Darky into the bargain.'

'In the grief stakes I reckon he musta got double bubble.'

'Sure. So he ended up in that gaff back there. He used to bring me over this side to show me all the places he'd lived in, done a bunk outta, boozers he's had the tear-up in, he'd bring me over to see the sights.'

A lot of the people on the pavement look shell-shocked from plain old ordinary everyday living. They've got a look of deep fatigue from years of attrition. Their faces are weary, young and old alike. It's the look of poverty and scraping by week after week, year in year out, stretching out the Monte Cairo till next pay day, living on subs and Christmas clubs and it's at times like this I'm glad I'm in the business I'm in. Most people are simply fucked, fried and lied to.

'You know what he used to say to me? I was just a kid but he used to say it over and over again and I just used to fuckin nod my head and think what the fuck's he on about the old cunt but years later it all makes the most perfect sense.'

37

We're sitting at the traffic lights. Mort's looking out the window, out into the shop windows, no doubt thinking about the trips over to the Eastside with his crazy old trooper of a great-grandad. He's got this faraway look in his eyes. I suppose this is a bit of a trip down memory lane for him.

'Well?' I says.

'Well what?' says Morty, coming to.

'What did he used to say?'

'Oh right, fuck me, I was gone then. He used to say that your intelligence, your imagination and your integrity are yours and yours alone and no cunt can make you give them up unless you want to. You can give them away, you can sell them to the highest bidder, you can let people think that they've got you where they want you, but you know you got a different deal going on in your head, and all the time you're letting them believe what they fuckin wanna believe, but you, and you alone, know different. He used to go on about the "three eyes, remember the three eyes," and I thought as a chavvie that he was on about some fuckin big old three-eyed monster, I was well spooked. See, a lot of people just saw him as a crazy old black geezer, screaming and shouting in the street, getting nicked for fighting or getting a good hiding for wrecking some old spieler cos he's flipped out or for just fuckin growling at people he shouldn't have done, but he was a fuckin deep thinker in spite of all that shit.'

'I like that, though, about your intelligence, your imagination and your integrity, it's good gear.'

'It's good simple home cookin, ain't it. When I got sent down that time for that Kilburn Jerry business, that was the moment, the exact fuckin moment –' he clicked his fingers '– that I knew what he was on about. See, eight years ain't a long time and it ain't a fuckin short time either. It used to go round and around in my nut. It kinda kept me sane and drove me fuckin mad at the same time if you know what I mean.'

'Kinda.'

'See, in the boob ninety per cent of the cons are complete fuckin gobshites, as they say up in County Kilburn, mug 'em-selves off the whole time, fuckin idiots who ain't got a clue. My uncle, Winston, and my grandad used to talk about knowing your own history. They were both always readin every fuckin history book that they could get hold of, Winston still does. See, it's important that I know about their struggle, although I didn't get on with the old man when I was younger, but if I know all the shit that's gone down over the years, with him, the grandad and the great-grandad, to get me here in this motor, sat talkin to you, then I ain't gonna be givin up so fuckin easily. You understand?'

'Kinda.'

'If you know your history, the struggle, your lineage, you know who you fuckin are.'

'That makes sense.'

'You know who had it, had it in lorryloads, ferocious they had it and it was very fuckin impressive, those IRA geezers down on the Island. The Parkhurst Brigade of the Provisional IRA. If you can forget about what they've done to get in there, forget that they're always banging on that they're POWs, we're all fuckin POWs I used to tell them, but if you took the time and you actually sat down and talked to them they had that knowledge in shitloads.'

'I can imagine, as it goes, cos they believe they're soldiers.'

'And they are. They didn't blow anyone up for fun or cos it was a good earner or anything like that, they did it cos they believe they're at war. See, if you associate too much with those guys it goes down on your record and it affects your parole. The authorities see it as another way of punishing them, keeping them isolated and some of the muggy-cunt, lowlife, petty criminal, half-a-sex-case rubbish play the game cos they wanna earn a little squeeze from the kangas. They give the Provo geezers a hard time, but they don't see that they're being used as mugs and anyway those Irish boys can look after themselves, they can give as good as they fuckin get, they stick together.'

'I can fuckin imagine that somehow. They come across as headcases.'

'In a very cool, calculated way they are, but like you say, they're soldiers. But, and this is the point I'm making, if they ain't got their head in a book on Irish history going back about

39

ten thousand years, about that fuckin fat –' he holds his thumb and forefinger about four inches apart '– then they were discussing it and some of them were writing poetry about it, but they knew where they were comin from. You see what I mean. A sense of where you come from gives you a sense of where you're going. Understand?'

'I see what you mean.'

'I read all that Irish history and every other fuckin history book I could get hold of as well because, first up, I liked the stories cos fact is always stranger than fiction, it's the fuckin truth, and so while all my pals were off doing nightclasses trying to suss out how people's minds work so they could be more effective crims, you know, psychology, sociology, theology and every fuckin other sort of fuckology, I'd be away in my cell readin my history books. To be honest, most nights I was glad when bang-up come so I could be on my jack with a puff and me books.'

We hit a bitta dual carriageway heading north. Morty's in full flow.

'See, people reckon that studying history teaches us not to make the same mistakes over again, but we do again and again as if we as a species like to fuck up, prefer it maybe.'

He weighs it up in his head. He pulls his quizzical face but continues.

'Maybe, maybe not. See, huge empires or countries live in fear of the other guy upping them before they can do it to the other guy, so it keeps on kickin off over and over again. So while my pals are learnin about "this is how the old canister works, bish, bash, bosh," and I guess that there is a lot of truth in that old voodoo, I worked out that you can never really know what anyone's thinkin cos as soon as you write the formbook on them they'll go and do something that totally fucks up your theory about their motives, whys and wherefores. I could give you examples, Hitler or Alexander the Great, whoever, you never know what they're going to do next.'

'Too fuckin true.'

I'm wondering if this is some kinda word of warning for my meet with Jimmy Price or it's just Morty shooting the breeze.

'You do love your history, don't you, Mort.'

'I fuckin do, which is funny cos I fuckin hated it when I was in school. I could go on that quiz show on the telly, you know, specialist subjects and that. But remember that about your intelligence, your imagination and your integrity cos that's been handed down and now I'm handing it down to you.'

'Cheers, Mort.'

We pull off the carriageway and into some small lanes with heavy woods on either side. Mort's following the directions he's got written down on the back of a fag packet. After about ten minutes' driving we stop at a crossroads.

'Very good directions. There should be a sign here somewhere.'

I spot it. 'Over there.'

A tiny wooden sign saying 'Pepi's Barn' pointed down another smaller lane between two of the branches of the crossroads. There's no way you would have spotted it without knowing it was there already. Looking at my watch, it's exactly one-thirty. We drive down the lane for a couple of hundred yards, through an avenue of trees that meet at the top and block out the light. It really is quite beautiful and a touch eerie at the same time, like something outta a kids' fairytale. When we emerge at the other end it's a mighty fuckin contrast. We turn a sharp corner at the end of a tree-lined avenue and suddenly we're on a gravel forecourt in front of a massive country house as far away from a barn as it's possible to get. It's on two floors, about three hundred years old. In the front there's a beautifully manicured lawn with Roman statues dotted about, David and the armless one, Venus de Milo, and clipped privet hedges about three feet high. They probably called this a villa when it was built, it's moody classical with large columns on either side of the double doors. A guy in bottle-green and gold livery opens the door of the Audi. Morty gives him the keys and he drives the motor off to park it out of sight.

'Remember, he'll be checking you out, maybe pushing a bit, keep calm, don't bite, remember the three eyes,' says Morty as we stroll into the gaff.

A Spot of Luncheon with
Mister Price

Pepi's Barn inside is something else. It looks brand spanking new and really old at the very same time. The floors are laid in white marble. On the walls are mosaics of what look like Roman gods and goddesses doing battle with the forces of nature in an almighty big frieze. The oak supporting beams have been exposed back to the original wood. The reception area is on an upper level. Down three steps is the main floor of the restaurant and down another three steps a conservatory has been added on. Beyond that again is a garden that has been laid out around a water fountain. Huge plants, almost two floors tall, are in each corner of the room. The vibe is of pure luxury and, sure enough, on the lawn peacocks and white doves roam aimlessly about. I realise that the original villa had been built on a slight hill cos you are higher at the front door than on the main floor. There's a fountain inside as well, up against the far wall. It's a slow, gently cascading number to add to the ambience of calm. In the bottom sit fish, valuable koi carp, motionless in the clear, crisp water, not for frying in batter.

Half an hour ago we were sitting in the motor in two-egg-and-chips-guv Hackney and now we are waiting to be seated in a gaff that simply oozes affluence. Thirty tables, every one of them full, and you had to be a boy scout to find the place. All the waiters look like male models with chiselled cheekbones. They're all wearing long aprons down to their ankles and they move across the marble decks noiselessly. Lorryloads of flowers are everywhere, arranged by experts, you can tell, sitting in crystal vases that I know cost two or three hundred quid a pop. Ceiling fans spin gently at half speed. Nothing gets too frantic here.

We leave our jackets and phones with the cloakroom girl. I see everybody's wearing that off-duty look that the rich kids, the genuinely caked, seem to get without even trying. It's all Ralph, cords, Timberland deck-shoes, Burberry and Mulberry. The men and the women are dressed the same except some of the gals have Gucci, Hermès or Chanel silk squares around the neck. The atmosphere's very relaxed and laid-back. Morty tells the Major Dee that we are with the Price party and he leads the way through the main room and out to a little side conservatory with one big table for about six or seven on its own in the middle. The spring sun's shining through the glass and I can see cherry blossom on the trees outside.

Jimmy Price is sitting with his back to the far wall, looking out so he can see all the comings and goings around him. He's relaxed, off-duty, with a large vodka and tonic in his hand and a leather cigar box on the table in front of him and a fat live one in his hand, a Cuban Montecristo for sure. He's wearing an argyle cashmere golf sweater that's cost about three or four hundred quid. His ginger-grey hair's swept across his nut trying to cover up his baldness but some of the sun from behind him still glistens on his shiny head. He looks older than I remember him from our previous two meetings. Jimmy's had a shave about an hour ago and his face is still glowing red-raw. He's got red cheeks and broken veins around his nose. He's wearing too much of that expensive aftershave that smells too sickly sweet and it mixes with the cigar smoke to tell me that he's got the money of the folks next door, he's got it in spades, shitloads, but not necessarily with the easy class and style of those people. He never will.

Next to James sits Gene McGuire, his Chief of Staff, who I know quite well already. Gene's wearing a nondescript blue pinstripe suit that makes him stand out among all the weekender casual. He never looks properly relaxed in a suit does Gene but he wears them like some guys wear overalls. The top button of his shirt's undone and the tie pulled to one side. He's black Irish with mad bushy eyebrows. He's got two packs of Rothman's in front of him and he's pulling relentlessly on the one in his other hand, rolling a battered gold Dunhill lighter over and over in his hand with a slow, steady rhythm. In front of him on the table he's got a large chunky tumbler of whiskey, half full. It's like giving cherries to an elephant giving whiskey to Gene. He's got that crazy little twinkle in the eyes and, like Mort, he can be great company but also a total psychopath when he's on active service. He ain't tall but he's fuckin solid and he's got the biggest hands I've ever seen on a human being in my life, like he could literally tear ya apart.

'They put us out here cos of the smoke, you know, what with the kids and that.' Jimmy gets up to greet us. We shake hands, his chubby and slightly clammy. Gene shoots me a sly little wink and carries on rolling the Dunhill without missing a beat. We sit and make small-talk – nice drive? good directions? nice gaff, ain't it.

'You wanna see it on a Saturday night,' says Jimmy. 'None of this dressing like farmers, it's top 'king notch. People pull out all the stops, no dinner suits or anything but not short of it. In summer they have an outfit, a band, like, violins and that playin classical music on the grass. It's fuckin beautiful I can tell ya.'

'It sounds very nice,' I say.

'You know who I saw in here last week? Go on, guess,' he says to me and Morty.

'I don't know,' says Morty.

'Well, have a fuckin guess.'

We shrug our shoulders.

'That's no fuckin good. I'll tell ya, shall I. Rod Stewart. Rod fuckin Stewart, that's who. I could have reached over and touched him.'

Jimmy grabbed me tight by the arm.

'That fuckin close I was.'

'Who was he with?' asks Morty, half impressed.

'Loada tossa footballers.'

'Did you get his autograph?'

'Don't take the 'kin piss Mortimer, you'd be showin yourself right up. It's not the done thing in this gaff.'

'No, no. It's a serious question,' says Morty. 'If I saw Stevie Wonder or Barry White in a place I'd wanna get their autograph, go over and say hello.'

'Not in fuckin here you wouldn't, not with me you wouldn't.

My misses was well chuffed, seeing him like that. I went out and bought her all his records the very next day, the fuckin lot.'

Gene gets the waiter over. He's grinning quietly to himself. The waiter empties the ashtray every time Gene kills a Rothman's.

'Same again.'

'Large Chivas Regal, Sir?'

Gene nods.

'Yeah,' says Jimmy, 'and let's have some menus. The food here, it's cooked with love, ain't it, son?'

The waiter says nothing but he looks embarrassed.

'No, seriously chaps, the grub here's like nothing you've ever tasted in your life. They get all the top chefs. Ain't that right, son?'

'Yes, Sir,' says the waiter and goes to fetch menus.

'I ain't all that hungry,' says Gene. 'I think I'll just have a steak and a couple of rolls.'

'For fuck's sake, Gene, that's all you ever eat, fuckin steak, try something different for a change. Look,' he says as the waiter comes back with the menu, 'they got duck, rabbit, veal, but like beautiful veal, chicken done in herbs and spices, like secret recipes that'll make your fuckin bollocks tingle, look, fish, good for the old ticker, fish. Here we go, salmon, Dover sole, trout.'

'I'm gonna just have a steak.'

'Look, liver done in devil's sauce.'

'Just a steak –'

'Lamb.'

'– if that's all right with you, James.'

'Fuckin hell. What's the fuckin point of coming to one of the best fuckin eating places in the country, if not the world, if all you're gonna fuckin have is a 'kin steak.'

'That's what I want, Jim.'

'You may as well go down a fuckin kebab house.'

'Jim, listen, I didn't want to come here. I'd sooner meet the boys down the boozer, any one you like. It was your idea to come here.'

Gene spelt out his objections in his smooth Donegal accent.

45

'Okay, okay, don't fuckin go on, fuck sake, Gene.'

Jimmy says it like Gene is a ranting, foaming-at-the-mouth lunatic, like 'what's his fuckin problem'.

The waiter takes the order. Me and Mort order the same thing, the duck pâté and the poached salmon with new potatoes, watercress and baby lettuce salad, while Jimmy makes a great show of ordering, showing off his snob's limited knowledge of food and wine, like a bittova wanker really. Gene tells the waiter he wants a steak.

'No problem, Sir.'

'How big is the steak?'

'Eight ounces, Sir.'

'Bring two.'

'Yes, Sir. How do you want them cooked?'

'Fried fast on the outside so it's raw on the inside and stick two fried eggs on each.'

'How would you like the eggs done, Sir?'

'Over easy please, son.'

The waiter just writes it all down. Jimmy is shaking his head.

'Fuck's sake,' he says, sighing and looking over at me and Morty. 'No style, no style at all.'

On the contrary, I'm thinking, Gene's showed great style. He's told them what he wants and how he wants it cooked. In a five-star place like this one that's how it works.

More small-talk as the starters come and go. Jimmy's telling stories, all the old stories, the good-old-bad-old days. 'The CID was blokes you could have a drink with, could have a 'kin laugh with. They was fellas you'd been to school with only they'd made a different career move. It coulda been them in your place and vice-versa. It was all a bit of a fuckin game back then compared with now, it was a fuck-about, cops and robbers.'

Gene tears through his steak and eggs and a small basket of rolls. He seems to be getting more hungry as he goes through them. The food, Jimmy ain't fuckin lying, is ecstatic. We finish up and compliment Jim on his good, no excellent taste in choosing this restaurant, which I suppose was the idea. Life tastes good.

Jimmy calls the waiter over and orders coffee, brandies and

bring Mister McGuire another two of them, he says, pointing at Gene's Chivas. A small team descend on the table and clear everything away and even brush the tablecloth so everything is neat and tidy again. We're sitting in stuffed satisfaction. The guy brings a tray back heaving with drinks, unloads them, and goes to stand against the far wall to await any further instructions, but Jimmy calls him back over.

'Can we have a little privacy, son. We'll give you a shout if we need you.'

The kid disappears. On cue, Gene sits up straight and looks attentive for the first time. Morty's looking to Jimmy to start talking. He's become the boss. The expression on his face changes from I-can-clown-with-the-best-of-them to a slight frown, his eyes develop a micro-focus and his eyebrows become heavy in an instant. He transforms from chubby, puppy dog into poisonous cobra. I feel I've been caught thinking out loud that he's a cunt, like he can look into my nut and read my mind like it is the runners and riders page. I suddenly feel very stupid for thinking that a geezer like that could get to where he was in the scheme of things by being a fuckin tosser, having top-ranking dudes, the Spitfire pilots of the criminal world, on their toes and putting up with all his bollocks-talk.

I suddenly feel very small fry, there's a voice in my head saying, 'You're the cunt, pal.' I've realised that Mister James plays his mind games to the sixth and seventh degree, like some ruthless chess Grand Master thinking ten moves ahead or an ancient Chinese general leading the enemy, laughing in their stupidity and arrogance, into the fatal ambush. Jimmy flexes his arms, clicks his fingers. I wonder how many you and the Old Fella put away in your time, how many disappeared off the face of the earth never to be seen again? He's toying with the pinkie ring. Is he toying with me? I can hear him thinking, You think I'm a cunt, do you? a clown? a fuckwit?? Well, do you son? I'm speculating, How many got fed to the pigs? How many got dropped into lime pits? How many skeletons got put through the concrete crusher, put in cement in oil drums and dropped into the sea? Mister Price's eyes have become locked onto mine now, they're looking at a point exactly two inches behind the

47

bridge of my nose, he's clicked in and locked on like one of those state-of-the-art missile systems that once they've got ya they ain't fuckin letting you go until you're dead. Jimmy's placed a cigar in his mouth, let Gene light it with the Dunhill, tilted his head back and blown the smoke upwards into the air. A small puddle's formed in the small of my back.

'What do you want, son?'

'Sorry?'

'In life, what are you after? A shot at the title? A seat by the band?'

He opens his hands like one of those pictures of Jesus Christ. I say nothing.

'What do you want from life? Fuck's sake, talk to me, son.' His voice has changed. It's on target, dry and flat.

'I don't know, Mister Price. It's a very expansive question,' I says with an assurance that surprises me.

'And that's a very good answer. You know, years ago some people would have thought you were a homosexual if you used a word like "expansive" but times change. You're not a homosexual, are you?'

'No, I'm not. Definitely not.'

'Not behind with the rent?'

'No way.'

'I didn't think you were. No harm in it I suppose. Let me put it another way. How far do you want to go? What sacrifices are you prepared to make?'

Price, Gene and Morty sit in a semi-circle looking at me, waiting for my answer, but I don't really know what the fuck he is on about. Morty is on their side now.

'Give me an example,' I say.

'That's good, that's very good.' He laughs but the laugh is different, it's loaded with all the old cunt's cunning and sinister intent. 'Never, ever commit yourself, say as little as possible. That's a little tip for ya, son,' he continues. 'I'll tell you why I ask. I ask questions and I get answers, people tell me things. I like to know about people.'

He pauses to gulp his brandy.

'I collect information up here,' pointing at both his temples

48

with his index fingers. 'Information is power, it was said two thousand years ago, and it's still as true today. In fact it's what I trade in, and other things of course, but substance or wealth or property or whatever, they're only there to keep the score. You understand?'

I'm nodding but I ain't got a clue.

'I talk to Gene and I talk to Morty and I talk to other people and they tell me about you. They tell me that you're a good, clean, tidy worker, that you ain't even got a CRO file, you make money for everyone in your chosen enterprise, you keep your own counsel which is important because there's far too many loud-mouths out there who just love to let anyone and everyone know their business. I'm told you just go about your business with what I like to call stealth. Fuckin lovely word that. Stealth. You ain't out spunkin your dough down the clubs trying to impress some old sploshers, pissed and on the powder, having the big nose-up.'

He pauses for breath, a gulp of Cognac and a pull on his cigar before continuing.

'There's too many fuckin jokers out there who could get us put away for stretches if you told 'em anything worth knowin cos they can't keep their fuckin big mouths shut. Do you think of the future? Have you got a plan, son?'

Shit. Now he's put me on the spot. I really wasn't expecting this. He's asked me a straight question and he's gonna want a straight answer.

'How old are you, son?' he asks.

'Twenty-nine.'

'You make a lotta money, don't you?'

'Yeah.'

'And you've got it invested? You've been sensible with it?'

'Yeah, I suppose I have.'

'I admire that. It shows that you're thinkin of the future and we all have to think of the future. You put me in mind of guys I've known over the years who've made a tidy little stack and walked away. They were gonna do the business until they were, say, for the sake of argument, thirty and then vamoose, gone. I knew blokes who were blaggers, in and out of banks with sawn-offs, they worked until they could set themselves up as straight legit businessmen then they walked away. Some of them could drop it out and others just couldn't resist the buzz. They kept coming back for another portion. I knew some guys just weren't allowed to simply fuck off and leave.'

'Why?'

'Too good at makin money for other people.'

He leaves it hanging in the air, brushes some ash off the linen tablecloth and shrugs his shoulders.

'Myself,' he struggles to re-light his cigar, 'I wouldn't do that to anyone, hold them against their will, not to my worst enemy.'

I'm fuckin glad to hear it. Jimmy knows my plan. I can't see how but he does. Maybe he's seen or heard something in my behaviour that's convinced him but sometimes with guys like him it's pure animal instinct.

'Oh yes, we must think of the future otherwise it tumbles over us and before we know it we're extinct, like dinosaurs. I was talkin to you about the good old days, it's bollocks, it's a music-hall turn. I could see you thought so too.'

I move to speak but he raises his hand to stop me.

'No no, son, it's not a problem. The world, London, it's changing by the week, by the fuckin day, and people like me, people like you, Gene and Mister Mortimer here, if we don't change with it we gonna get left behind, we'll be fuckin relics like the old bruisers havin tear-ups on the cobbles that we used to laugh at when I was your age. You understand?'

'Definitely.'

'We need the young, flexible guys like yourself to stand any kinda chance of staying ahead. What I'm saying is we need geezers like you. Listen to this, an acquaintance brings a Russian to my house to discuss a little something, yeah?'

We nod.

'The Russian geezer don't speak no English so it's all that thumbs-up-and-smile business but the guy who's doing the interpretations, who's Russian as well, is calling the guy "The Cannibal". This Russian guy's a spooky cunt, you only got to

50

take one look, there's a naughty vibe offa him. If you upset him, gonna die, no two ways.'

Jimmy wipes the palms of his hands together dismissively. Gene and Morty nod.

'I'm beginning to think they call him the Cannibal cos he's a merciless cunt, a real animal, but it transpires that they call him the Cannibal cos he eats human flesh. I said, "WHAT!!" The guy explains that in those Soviet prisons it happens all the time, no grub, they're literally starvin, so if someone dies they fuckin eat them.'

'I bet they don't wait around for people to die either,' says Gene.

'I hadn't thought of that,' says Jimmy. 'Anyways, this cunt has developed a taste for it and even after he's released he occasionally tucks into a feed of human being. Think about that mentality and he's sitting in my fuckin house grinning.'

He shrugs.

'Did you ask him how this guy cooked them?' asks Morty, as ever the food and drink connoisseur.

'Cooked?' says James.

'Yeah, did he fry 'em or roast 'em or what?'

'For fuck sake, that's sick, Morty. What you fuckin after? A recipe book? Can you fuckin believe that, Gene? Course I didn't ask this barbarian how they were cooked. I fucked them outta the fuckin door. Listen, this is the point I'm making here, we've got to start realising that if we don't get our shit together we're gonna be in trouble.'

We all nod solemnly.

'To a lot of people the streets of London are still paved with gold. They don't give a monkey's who they gotta fuck over to get to the prize. Life is very cheap to these geezers. Some of these people have come from fuckin war zones. These Slavs they'll cut your fuckin throat for a few quid, no problem, yeah? These are hungry boys, they ain't content with Bee Gees records and tins of Coca-Cola anymore. Everything is up for grabs or so these fuckers think. Do you know the meaning of the word solidarity?' he asks me.

'It means sticking together, don't it?'

51

'Ex-act-lee. Think about it, the meanings in the word, think about "solid", the word, to remain solid, that's solidarity. For guys like us that's what that word means, to stick together against our common enemy.'

I nod my head. I'm being led by the dick somewhere by Uncle James. I'm about to be asked to pay for being on the team. He goes on.

'There's a price to be paid for that and the price is loyalty. From here on in people are either for or against us. Loyalty, that's our greatest strength, you understand, son?'

'I sure do, Mister Price.'

'Please son, Jimmy, call me Jimmy.'

'Okay, Jimmy.'

'That's better, ain't it. Now there's something I want you to do for me. I've got a hunch that you're the best man for the mission. Now you look like the kinda bloke who knows the lay of the land, yeah? Morty says you've been all over the world, the States, Oz, down the Far East, but you also know your way round London better than most. Am I right?'

'I know my way about but I'm no cab driver.'

'Oh yes, very good, but what I meant is that you are more capable of moving in different levels of society than most of the folk of our acquaintance, am I right? You can move in different social scenes, Nob Hill to Hungry Hill, highlife to lowlife, without attracting too much attention. You would have the savvy, the nous, the plain old fuckin intelligence to fit in. Now, am I right for fuck's sake?'

'Yeah, I suppose so, but compared to who, Jimmy?'

'Work with me on this one, son, work with me. Fuckin 'ell.'

He's brought out a brown manila A4 envelope onto the tabletop. I know he ain't got no holiday brochures in it.

'I want you to do this mission for me, strictly as a volunteer, mind, as an almighty personal favour. Now, if you don't want to do it I can always get somebody else, just say, I won't be offended.'

'Go ahead, Mister Price, I mean Jimmy, I'm game.'

'Maybe it's best I start at the beginning.'

Big Jim's Big Pal's Big Problem

'I have an old friend from years ago. We did all the normal stupid kids stuff, you know, housebreakin, warehouses, terrorising the local market traders, nicking anything, a right pair of gunnifs we were. We got nicked together and ended up in approved school. Those fuckin gaffs in them days weren't like they are today, a fuckin squeeze. They wanted to break you down and leave you broken. I went back a few times, there and Portland Borstal, before I wised up and got the point, maybe not the point they wanted me to get. The thing is be smart, play safe and don't be gettin yourself pinched. Be cute, be quiet, don't be flash half the time and a jailbird the other half. Some cunts never work that out. Anyways, my pal is gifted. He's makin moves that are decades ahead of their time. He's in what's laughingly called the straight world but he's forever tellin me that the so-called straight game is a million times more crooked than any criminal enterprise.'

'I can well believe it.'

'He says the crims, outta the two sets of people, have a lot more honesty, there's certainly more loyalty and integrity. When was the last time you heard that little word, ay? He says the criminal fraternity can be trusted more but I don't trust the criminal fraternity very far myself, total toe-rags most of them.'

'I'd say there's some truth in his argument.'

'Let's not go losing our heads either, the world is full of shite-hawks and envious ne'er-do-wells. My pal's given me a few tips over the years, helped me bury some of me ill-gottens. He's one of the few people I would ask for advice if I'm in schtook and he's always done the same cos he knows that I ain't gonna shaft an old mucker. You know –' Jimmy's carved up the table with a chop of the hand '– he went his way and I went mine but neither of us forgot the place we come from and who we could depend on.

'Now, my pal has become a minor celebrity on the business

53

pages. He's held up as a snotty-nosed kid from a dustbin who's done the business, come up with a lot of hard graft, sixteen-hour days, seven days a week, and now he's taken his foot off the pedal to enjoy the fruits of his labour, off to Ascot, off to the polo game. He may have worked hard but in the early days he got up to a lot of skulduggery to oil his passage. The newspapers have got him booked as a shining example of how you can leave all that knavery and mischief behind you if you knuckle down. Of course it's come out that he's did a bit of bird as a wee lad, made an error, took his punishment like a man, learned his lesson in the approved school, an example of how the system can work. The story goes that he shook the governor's hand on the way out and told him "You won't be seeing me again, Sir." That's complete bollocks, a fiction, it never happened.'

Gene and Morty are grinning at the thought.

'Now he's got a problem and he thinks I can help. I can't tell you who this bloke is and I don't need to explain myself, but needless to say that this guy is well worth knowing. He won't be ungrateful. Okay?'

'Okay.'

'He's been married twice. First time out he's got himself hitched up to this bitta posh who's half a duchess, connected, Hooray Mafia. She's gone to all the right schools, knows all the right faces, got the double-barrelled surname, the real deal. Needless to say the duchess and her family are fuckin potless. Apparently a lot of the so-called aristocrats in this country are boracic. What shillings her old boy left when he fell off the twig went on death duties. My mate don't give a fuck cos by this time he's got money coming in quicker than she can spend it. He's seriously caked. His business has gone through the roof. He's mega-rich, jumpin on and off aeroplanes, doing deals with foreign governments. She just stays in England spendin it. She's ironin out huge wads of loot every day. Soon, however, he starts to realise that for all the poise and beauty she's nutty as a fuckin fruitcake. It's not just the spending, he can handle that, it's drugs. He don't hold with drugs, not for his wife. She's off wandering round the local villages naked in the middle of the night and the local plod are having to bring her home.'

'Sleepwalking?'

'No, just out for a bittova stroll in the nude. This is happening on a regular basis, this and a million other crazy things. Him and the blue-blood have a daughter who he adores, Charlotte, or as he will have it, Charlie. Him and the missy have gone their separate ways but he's still coughing up so they want for nothing. I reckon she had the kid as a means of entrapment cos they're devious fuckers these aristocratic cunts. Her lot can trace their family back to William the Conqueror, 1066 and all that. They refer to our Queen and our beloved royal family as "The Germans" and only then with a face like somebody's holdin a turd on a stick under their nose. They think they're fuckin better than them!!?'

'I can well believe it, Jimmy,' I say.

'My pal puts this insanity down to inter-breeding. I says, "I know mate, it's like Dalmatians, crazy fuckin dogs, never mind fuckin pit-bulls, a Dalmatian will turn on you like that."'

He snaps his fingers. Gene and Morty nod gently in agreement. 'They drown them if they ain't got enough spots,' says Gene.

'Who? The royal family?' says Jimmy dryly.

'No, Dalmatians,' says Gene.

'I'm kiddin, Gene,' says Jimmy, looking skyward. He goes on.

'Anyways, little Charlie has the very best of everything, schools, ponies, trips abroad, pretty clothes, but he's genuinely devoted to the child while the mother is gettin madder and madder. She puts the chavvie into boarding school and moves back to town, she's surroundin herself with all these fuckin pounces and mackerels. All the time she's out the game on booze and pills from some quack down Harley Street then she's started dabblin with the real naughty gear, you know.'

He winks at me.

'The gaff he's bought for her is fuckin open house to riff-raff and lowlife.'

'But didn't he try and get custody, show she was an unfit mother?' I ask.

'Good question, son. My pal's fighting tooth and nail to get custody for the child but every time they go to court she turns up sober, like everything's tickety-boo, and it's him who's the mad one, tellin tall stories. Cunning fuckin bitch. I reckon there was a bit of the old-boy network at play as well.'

Jimmy looks around conspiratorially. We instinctively lean towards him a bit.

'I said I'd help out. I suggested kidnapping the bitch, bugging the gaff, a drop of the old blackmail. I said I'd have her favourite little gigolo shot in the groin, maybe carve up one of these parasites who got her bitta tackle. Razor slashin's across the arse were very popular around that time. I had blokes around me in those days, nice boys, good to their mothers, desperate to please, but total fuckin pothouses. He just wouldn't have it. He says it'll get out of hand. I said maybe it needs to get out of hand. Say the word and she'll wake up one morning dead from an overdose, but no, he's always had a streak of the squeak in him, fuck knows where he gets it.'

Jimmy's slowly building up a bitta steam. It sounds like he resented his old pal not allowing him the opportunity to wreak havoc. It sounds like he really wants to flex his muscles to impress his old school chum.

'That chinless fuckin trout was blatantly takin the fuckin piss outta him, fuckin bla-tant-lee.'

Jimmy chops the table three times to enforce his point. She musta looked upon James Price Esquire like he was a nouveau-riche reptile who belonged under a rock. He took it personal.

'Anyways, fuck her, the bitch, she ain't of no importance. She's probably in some fuckin gutter somewhere.'

Translation: He hopes she's in some fuckin gutter somewhere. He dismisses her with a flick of the hand.

The waiters are hovering outta earshot, but they look a bit edgy cos the gaff is emptying and Mister Price is slapping the table and using profanities. He's got a thin line of spittle coming outta his gob and he's getting mashed on the hundred-quid-a-go brandies.

'Well, after years of banging his head against the wall my pal wised up and cottoned on to the fact that you can't beat those establishment fuckers at their game cos it's their crooked game. He's carried on divvyin up the sovs and he's recruited a little team of ex-soldiers, special forces, not your average bolt-through-the-neck squaddie types, to keep a beady eye out, like guardian angels, just to make sure that Charlie's okay. The mother's changed the family name back to the original la-dee-da double-barrelled affair cos it gets you in places where they wouldn't normally entertain ya.'

'Maybe she's right. Like you say, they do have a network thing going on. Bit like us really, Jimmy.'

'You was right about this geezer,' he says to Gene and Morty, pointing at me. 'He's a live-wire.'

He has a gulp on the brandy, a big pull on the cigar.

'It's her motives that are nasty. She wants the best for the girl but she also wants to fuck my mate's nut up. Spite, there's a lot of malicious spite in this bird.'

'I'm beginning to get the picture,' I say.

'Good. Now, Charlie's plotted up in one of those jolly-hockey-sticks girls' schools down on the south coast but it soon begins to transpire that she's a chip off the old block on her mother's side. She's developed a taste for wacky baccy and bad company. She's thirteen and going over the back wall of a night, into town until five in the morning. The old man's little obs team has tipped 'em the wink. She's been varfted outta school after school until they've run outta schools to send her. If she was down the local madhouse comprehensive she'd fit right in but all those birds in those posh schools are right into their studies. Charlie just can't be arsed, it's not that she's thick or anything, it's like she's schizoid, you know, like split per-sonalities. One half the sweetest kid you could ever meet, big old brown eyes, gentle, real loveable, but the other half of her was like a fuckin possessed demon, a banshee. I've seen both sides of her on different occasions.'

'Maybe she needed specialist help.'

Jimmy slaps the tabletop. 'That's exactly what I said. She's been put through her paces by the very top trick-cyclists, child psycho-whatsits, and she behaves like a very well-behaved young lady who nobody can believe is anything other than a perfect angel. She makes promise after promise to everyone but next thing the old bill are ringing up to say that she's been nicked for wreckin some restaurant or shoplifting or assaulting cozzers. She's developed a taste for public nakedness like her mother. There's no need for her to steal, it's senseless. The old fellow's at his wits' end. Everything else in his life is hunky dory, well, better than that, it's like he's got the fuckin Midas touch. Everything he touches turns to gold. He's married this young sort who's unbelievable. This bird, I'm telling yer, straight up, you'd lick shit off a stick for this bird. She's beautiful but she's got the smarts as well, cos this geezer ain't the type to be burnt twice.'

I'm sure I spot a tiny hint of a smile across Jimmy's lips.

'At this point in the tale the mother has disappeared, posted missin in action. Spooky it was. The house was empty but lookin like it had been vacated in a hurry, nothin's been packed. The kid's away at school, there's a joint in the ashtray, an old Jimi Hendrix record playin over and over again, blastin out, there's a drink poured out on the table, there's grub in the kitchen, the old bill found a loada dope in the fridge, there's enough brown and charlie for a fuckin Rollin' Stones tour but there's no sign of any struggle so she wasn't being turned over by bogeymen. There's cash slung around, in vases, drawers, in pockets, so it wasn't a case of aggravated burglary gone wrong. She had people comin round that night, appointments made the next day, but she ain't cancelled none of them. It's like she's been beamed off the planet. Old bill couldn't find a fuckin trace of her but those seventies throwbacks are renowned for goin walkabout and she did have previous for that kinda turn-out. Anyway, she ain't been seen since. Good fuckin riddance, I say.'

I'm looking hard into Jimmy's face for any clue that he knows more. Outta the corner of my eye I can see Gene's left eyebrow go up about a quarter of an inch like he wasn't convinced either. Maybe Jimmy put the old stuck-up blue blood on the back burner until he granted his old pal a freebie. All that bollocks about her being in the gutter could have been a decoy.

'My pal came to me and asked me if I knew anything but...'

He shrugged his shoulders and put his hands up. 'What could I tell him?'

Subject closed and we'll never know.

'Charlie's left school and she ain't got a clue what to do but it ain't like she's got to trot down the employment exchange. She don't really need to get money cos the old man's got her on a trust-fund arrangement, she's got an almighty allowance. He's sent her out to Switzerland to some top finishin school and everything's fine until he gets the inevitable phonecall to say she's gone crazy so he's off over to Zurich to collect her or bail her out.'

'What triggers off these outbursts?'

'I don't know, daylight, darkness, full moons, fuck knows.'

'How did she react to her mum's disappearance?'

'It didn't seem to register. Some clown's suggested that it may be an idea if she was earnin her own money, don't cut her off or anything just get her makin her own moves. Good for the self-esteem.'

'Could work.'

'Everyone's always tellin her how pretty she is, you know, the English-rose type, so the old man's arranged to have her smudges done by one of the guys who charge a couple or three grand a day. They've had the pictures done and then his new wife has told him to keep outta the way cos otherwise it don't mean shit if she is successful. He wants her to make it on her own merits.'

Now Jimmy goes into the envelope and brings out two pictures. He pushes them over to me so they sit side by side on the linen tablecloth. The first one's a glossy, professional one of Charlie, head and naked shoulders and the very beginnings of her tits, soft focus round the edges. The photographer had obviously gone for the just-goosed or the just-about-to-be-goosed look cos her hair was designer messy, bottle blond and windswept, highlighted and lowlighted. There was a light behind her head and Charlie's face was like a mask stuck in a look of surprise, with her eyes startled, her lips deep red and smothered with lip-gloss. It all gave her the look of a vulnerable sex-kitten-cum-sex-toy, but something in the picture told me that Charlie's heart wasn't in the modelling game.

The second picture is a colour photocopy of another photo that had been cut in half. Charlie was cuddled up against a big guy who had been cut out, her father no doubt. His arm, in a navy blue blazer, was hung across her shoulders and she looked up snugly, shyly and lovingly to where her pop's face would be. She was cute, pretty, but she wasn't model material. Her hair was just plain young-girl untidy and it looked better for it. She was wearing what looked like one of her father's old jumpers, a cricketing type affair, that she looked completely lost in, and jog pants that were huge. Her arms were folded tightly across her, hands pulled up into the sleeves of the jumper so she looked happily protected and fragile at the same time. I prefer her in the second shot, she looks more like a human being, even fancy her a little bit, but there's something a touch spooky about her.

'Don't you think she's beautiful, son? A beautiful bewildered little girl?'

'Yeah, she's very pretty.'

'She's like a precious bird that's been kept in a gilded cage. Girls are helpless and unworldly at twenty-one.'

Jimmy obviously doesn't know some of the twenty-one-year-olds I know.

'It does sound like she's been a bit overprotected.'

'Maybe. She's gone up for this bit of work, a really fuckin big campaign for make-up or underwear. It would have been exactly what she needed at that point in time, it would have given her the foot in the door, but Charlie went on the missin list, turned up a couple of weeks later. I don't think she knew where she'd been half the time. She's havin it with some right fuckin losers, wasters, scumbags, dopers, the same story as her mother, don't know who's good for her and who's a user. She's got a lovely little mews house, a motor, money, but she's still fuckin up and she's hangin around with people who are givin her drugs to get her hooked so she'll start to buy them.'

That's a bit too simple, Jimmy Boy. In my experience girls like Charlie, and I'm starting to get a pretty good mental picture of sweet but not so innocent Charlie, Daddy's little girl, will take your arm off at the shoulder to get the prize.

'Soon it's gone crooked and the law's startin to poke about. My pal had a few heads banged together, a couple of geezers have been told to keep away from her. They've got the message. He's sent her out to the States but she's got in trouble over there as well so it's back here and the same old bollocks, but now she's into the powders heavy and as you know, with that gear you can indulge yourself into the boneyard.'

I smell the faint whiff of hypocrisy. His angle seems to be that she's a victim in all this but she's a more than willing participant.

'The old man didn't wanna cut her off and leave her penniless cos then she really would be at the mercy of every scumbag on the planet. Somebody says she needs tough love. It's an American idea, you walk away and leave 'em to it, you just stop helpin them to fuck up. They put them all together in a rehab, fuckin Yanks again, you get a load of sleazy cunts, alkies, junkies and coke fiends and put them all together under one roof and they're supposed to help each other kick the habit.'

Jimmy shakes his head very gently.

'You'd think only in America but it turns out they've got them over here as well. He's listenin to one of his new wife's hoity-toity mates who's tellin him "It's all the fucking rage nowadays."'

'What's her poison?'

'Oh right, well, uppers, downers, laughers, screamers, you name it and she's up for it. Whatever it is it's got to be top quality. She likes coke to go up –' he points up at the ceiling '– and brown to come down,' he points back at the tabletop.

'I can't see why they just can't stop,' I say. 'It's about discipline.'

'Exactly. Some people just ain't got none, no backbone.'

'Self-discipline,' I'm saying, wagging a finger and nodding, knowing full well I'd be a great deal poorer if more people had it. I think I've found my range with Jimmy as well, know how to jolly him along.

'You're right. Anyways, Charlie's shipped out to this place

61

Chipton Grange, Chip-on-the-shoulder Grange my mate calls it. It's a big old country house down in the West Country in acres of grounds, up at seven, in bed at ten, country air, loads of good old-fashioned grub to put some flesh back on her bones. Fuckin lovely!! It's a tough regime but apparently it works.'

'Like your old approved school.'

'Oh yeah, very good, you're a card, son. Well anyway, first she hates it then she likes it but she's got webbed up with some geezer in there and that ain't allowed. They ain't in there to be courtin so one of them has to go.'

'Makes sense.'

'Aha, makes sense to you but love is blind, my friend. Rather than be parted they've fucked off together, into the night, into the lovers' moon, cab to the station and were last seen gettin on a train to London, arm in arm.'

'So she's disappeared just like her mum?'

'Well, she's missin, but that's what I'm comin to.'

I'm getting warm about Jimmy's favour. 'When did she do the bunk outta the treatment gaff, this Chipton Grange?'

'About three weeks ago.'

'And this guy, who is he?'

'Trevor Atkins, otherwise know as Kinky. Why he's called Kinky don't ask cos I don't fuckin know but that's his AKA. Trevor John Atkins to Mister Plod and Kinky to his confederates.'

'Should I know this guy?'

'I very much doubt it. He wouldn't be on your beat. I think you'd only ever meet if you ran him over. I had someone get his CRO file pulled and he's just a fuckin hound, loads of previous for petty thievin and jumpin bail, in and out of the boob and the detox, a recidivist waster. I'm not one to get all holy about these things but it's a fuckin waste of time lockin them up and it's a waste of time lettin them out, pure boob fodder.'

'They make a strange couple, the lady and the bitta rough.'

'To you and me, yes, but no surprise to the good folk who run these gaffs. In the misty, murky world of the drug scene and these facilities you get lords with whores, titled ladies with housebreakers, real posh birds with –'

'– guys like Kinky.'

'Exactly.'

'And how the fuck do these guys get to be in there? How do they afford the fees?'

'They run a kinda assisted places scheme. You know, like all those public schools. It's part of the philosophy behind the set-up. They entertain people from all levels of society.'

'What's this Trevor's, this Kinky's particular tipple?'

'The dear boy has a weakness for crack cocaine.'

'I thought he might. And what part of London's he from?'

'Originally from over East Ham way but from the arrest sheets and the addresses he's given he's from all over the place, Tottenham, Kilburn, Willesden, Down South, Stockwell, Brixton, all over the place.'

'He's a black geezer, right?'

'Yeah, he's a black geezer, what of it? Listen, I don't give a toss if he's black, white, yellow or green. I don't give a fuck if he's from outta space. I'm not interested in him, he can fuck off and die. I want you –'

Here it comes.

'– to find Charlie. It's that fuckin simple.'

It ain't fuckin simple at all. It's a whole fuckin heap of aggravation, a wild goosechase into the Hades of jobbing junkies and twitchy crackheads, into a whole world I've always done my very best to avoid like the plague for fear of catching one.

'What makes you think I can find her?'

'You're bright, you're of the new breed.'

'But what about the old man's SAS johnnies? Surely they would be better equipped to find her?'

'Those army types are far better goin native in Belfast or Kuwait than London. People sniff 'em out in London. And anyway, I want you to find her for me. Okay? Any questions? No? Good.'

So there you have it, that's the deal pure and simple. For whatever reasons Jimmy's got in his head, he wants me to find

Charlie so he can bathe in the kudos with his pal. He's got a hunch about my retirement plans and he could easily nause the whole thing up. If I'm smart I play the fuckin game and wait for the love bubble to burst between Charlie and Kinky and make sure I'm around to pick up the credit. It shouldn't take them too long to implode in on themselves.

'It's one of those things that can take a day or it can take forever, Jim.'

'Find her.'

'I'll do my best to find her.'

'Do your best and find her.'

'I'll see what I can turn up.'

'Fuck's sake, just fuckin find her, okay? Gene's got more stuff for you that you might find useful. I just wanna know where they are. We'll decide what action to take.'

'I know it's none of my business but –'

It was someone else talking, it wasn't me, but the words were coming outta my mouth. Shut the fuck up will ya.

'– he ain't gonna disappear is he?'

Gene looks out the window and Morty looks straight down into the tablecloth. Jimmy takes a fresh cigar from the leather case in front of him. He patiently lights it, getting a good glow going.

'You're right, son, that ain't none of your business. Like the old song says, "Don't piss on your chips if they're a pinch too hot." One day you're gonna be a million miles away from here and this'll all seem like it happened on a different planet.'

His eyes lock into mine but he points out the window.

'I've got as much concern about this Kinky as one of those bugs on those roses. Let me spell it out for you, I-Don't-Give-A-Fuck.'

'I'm sorry. I was bang out of order. I'm really sorry.'

'I know you were, son, and now you've apologised so it's okay, all right?'

He reaches over quick as a rattlesnake. I jump back a bit cos I'm surprised at how fast the old bastard can move. He grabs my cheek between his thumb and first finger and shakes it.

'Look at his little face, so serious, so told-off, look Gene, look Morty, look how serious he looks.'

We all laugh with our crazy Uncle Jimmy.

'You report to Gene.'

I nod.

'Details, details, things to do, things to get done but don't bother me with details, just tell me when they're done. You know who said that, son?'

'I dunno. Winston Churchill? Durin World War Two?'

'No, I did, James Lionel Price, just now.' And with that he laughs himself bright red, fit to burst.

'There'll be a nice bonus in it for ya when you turn her up,' he winks.

Jimmy's clicking his fingers for the bill. He just signs it like he's got an account with the place, pulls himself outta his seat and pats his stomach contentedly.

'We'll keep in touch, it was nice to meet ya. No, seriously, it's nice to meet people with some savvy, and some manners too.'

'Thanks, Mister Price, it was nice to meet you properly at last.'

We've all got up, left the table and started walking back up towards the entrance. Jimmy stops and silently points back at the table. I've left the photos of Charlie and the envelope, on the tabletop. I go and retrieve them.

The receptionist gives us back our jackets and our phones. As I'm walking into the khazi I realise that Jimmy's tailed me in.

'Need a good drain-off before I get in the motor. Look at all them fuckin flowers,' he says. 'It's like a flower shop in here, or a fuckin funeral.' He laughs. We both take a piss and wash our hands and as we're about to go back out the door Jimmy puts his foot against it. He looks around but he already knows that we're the only ones in there.

'Listen, son, you do this thing for me and you can walk away and nobody, but nobody, is gonna give any grief, okay?'

He's giving me the pointy finger. I nod. There's someone trying to open the door Jimmy's holding shut.

'You'll be out, if that's what you want, history, yeah?'

They're banging a bit and pushing a touch harder. I can hear them cursing on the other side of the door.

'I'll make sure no cunt says anything. You have my word.'

The person on the other side of the door now knocks like they're room service knocking on a hotel-room door. He pats me on the shoulder and winks. Jimmy takes his foot away and swings the door open wide in one swift movement. The Major Dee is standing there.

'Is everything all right, Mister Price?' he says with a bit of alarm, looking past us into the khazi.

'No problem, Angelo. This door's a little tight at the top here. It must be all this rain we've been havin.'

He winks on Angelo's blind side. It hasn't rained in weeks.

'Next time I'm in for dinner I'll bring my tool kit and we'll have a bit off. It only needs a smidgen,' he says, running his fingers down the side of the door and eyeing it up.

'Yes, Mister Price. And thank you, Mister Price.'

We walk out the khazi.

'They fuckin love me here, son,' says Jimmy.

I see that Gene and Mort are waiting outside on the gravel. Jimmy's a bit pissed so the sun and the fresh air give him a kick up the arse. He's slightly unsteady on his feet. His driver pulls up in his Jag and holds the door open for him.

'We'll talk,' he says to Gene, holding a hand to his ear. As he climbs in he gives me a little wink.

'He likes you,' says Gene as the motor speeds up the drive. 'You're like the son he never had.' He's laughing. 'We'll have to call you "Son of Jimmy" from now on, won't we, Mister Mortimer?'

'Call you Jimmy? Only if you insist, Mister Price, sorry, Jimmy,' says Morty.

'You two can fuck right off.'

'He'll be arrangin for you to be meetin his daughters, a bittov an arranged marriage,' says Gene.

'They nice?'

'They're more superlager than supermodel but you'll be

okay. They're a bit rough around the edges. Mister Mortimer told me you like fat girls. Two at a time. Is that right?'

'Sorry mate, it just slipped out,' says Morty. 'Anyway, fat birds have tight pussies, mate.'

'I've got some bits and pieces for you,' Gene says, turning to go. 'I'll ring you first thing in the mornin. Adios, amigos.'

Back to the Hacienda

Driving back into town, busy thinking. We drive in silence for a while. There are a lot of guys who after spending an afternoon with Jimmy Price, after being courted by him, after being bought dinner or lunch in a gaff that he obviously used to impress people he wanted to impress, would be delighted, over the moon, like some old-school footballers who had scored the winning goal in the last few minutes of the Cup Final, the rest of their lives would be an anticlimax, downhill all the way. Their lives would have peaked and no amount of booze, birds or Chas up the hooter would ever match that moment of pure exhilaration. So they were on a loser all the way down. They would retell the story, blow by blow, be forever telling the other toe-rags down the boozer about how they and Jimbo were 'Like Fuckin That', fingers crossed. They'd boast about how their good pal James took them out for a spot of lunch, to ask a favour. Ask away, Jimmy Boy, very civilised it was too, don't you know.

It's like that old pop once wrote about it being the best of times and the worst of times at the very same time. On one hand Jimmy has endorsed my walking away from the business so if anyone has a problem with that I can simply tell them to take it up with Mister Price. Walking out and staying intact can be a problem. I only have to find this genetic time-bomb misfit with the crackhead boyfriend but I consider it real progress. I realise that the whole thing smells a little bit fish, like I've been watching a film at the pictures and at a very crucial point in the plot I've popped out for a hot dog. When I've come back I'm missing something, so the story don't hang together like it should. Why should ruthless Mister Price cut anyone a deal? Why should I be any different? Could I have turned him down even if I wanted to? Would he have just leaned over the table, poked his finger in my chest and simply told me to do the finding or else? That would mean moving abruptly away from

68

everything, most importantly my paper-pot, my assets, that're hovering up around the million-pound mark. Remember at all times: He's one slippery cunt, likes to spin a yarn. Give him credit, he can tell a tale, but strictly speaking he's telling me stuff I don't really need to know. If we were working on a need-to-know basis, he could have sat me down in the café by the market, ordered me a ham sandwich and a cuppa milky tea and told me to crack on and find the bird. Should I feel privileged, blackmailed or both? The answer is probably the last one, bitter-sweet, sweet and sour.

Looking out over the top of the motorway coming back into central London, the sun's going down across row upon row of uniform roofs. I start tripping out. I'm imagining mile upon mile, street upon street of houses, like they go on for ever and ever, all the way to the sea, all the way to Scotland in one direction and to Cornwall in the other, like the whole of mainland Britain is just row after row after row of two-up, two-down, terraced houses and all the fields and farms and forests are buried somewhere underneath. In one of those houses, in one of those rooms, Charlie and Kinky are plotted up, either safe and sound, loved up, pet names for private parts, lazy sex in the late afternoon with an orange sun pouring through a tiny chink in the curtains, or in a mutual hostage situation, lick some rock, boot some brown, boost two brew. Kiss and cuddle, sleaze or kamikaze, what's your mission?

Morty's waiting for me to talk. I'm quite content looking across the skyline and watching the sun go down. It brings up a smidgen of melancholy in me cos I've always fought like fuckery, put my liberty on the line daily, to avoid ending up in one of those houses down there, sitting down with child-like naiveté to tick off the lottery numbers, eating the defrosted, microwaved chicken Kiev, soggy oven chips that never look like they do on the box, living in hope and not the real world, maybe next week, maybe next year, maybe next lifetime, maybe never, maybe fuckin maybe. I say avoid ending up in, but what I mean is avoid ending up back in one of those little gaffs, eating sausage, egg and chips for me Saturday tea, the old man checking the pools coupon he kept behind the clock he

69

inherited from his old man and the best he ever got was the free credit for the next week. He never got close. He could never go to work and tell his pals, the other straight-goers, that he'd almost hit the jackpot but Halifax Town or Alloa City had let him down badly, cos the most he ever got was about ten points and you needed double that to even win a four-figure sum. It kept his hopes up I suppose. I'm like that geezer, the apprentice gunslinger, in that movie the *Magnificent Seven*. He hates the townsfolk, he's got contempt for them, he calls them gutless because he's from a little spit of a town just like it and it scares the shit outta him that one day he may end up back in a place just like it if he ain't too careful. And where does he fuckin end up? Back in Ba-loo-ga-ville.

'Can I change this tape, Mort?'

You gotta be in the right frame of mind for Marvin Gaye.

'Turn it off altogether,' he says.

I turn it off.

'You find her and you're in,' he continues. 'He likes you, seriously, no fuckin about, I ain't takin the piss like back there. He needs sensible people around him.'

'But he put it like an ultimatum.'

'As is his right, brother. Look at it this way, we've come a long way with him lookin out for us, five years, not a bitta grief. He's callin in a debt. It's the business you're in.'

'I better give it a try.'

'Like the old song says, "One day we'll look back on this and chuckle." Son –' Morty does a very passable impression of Jimmy Price complete with pretend cigar – 'Soooon, don't take yourself so 'kin seriously, son.'

He reaches over to grab my cheek just like Jimmy.

'Fuck off, Morty.'

'Don't become too fond of tellin me to fuck off. Get those photocopied,' he says, pointing at the photos.

'Good thinkin. It's a shame we don't have a smudge of Kinky.'

'I know exacly what he looks like–'

'How?'

'Like a million other pipin niggers.'

70

'Now if I said that you'd be all—'

'Shut the fuck up, will ya. In case you ain't noticed I'm black. I can say that shit, white person say it, they get boxed, okay? Black person can talk all that nigger shit.'

'What this needs is subbin out. We need to sub-contract it out.'

'But to who?'

'Findin Kinky is most definitely the key, Mort.'

'You know who I thought of, your pal Billy Bogus,' says Mort.

'That's it. Why didn't I think of him?'

'Cos you ain't as clever as me.'

'That ain't his real name, you know. He don't like being called it either.'

'What, he wasn't christened William Bogus?' says Morty sarcastically. 'Well I never.' He's got a look of mock astonishment on his face.

'I'll try and find him. I'll ring round. He ain't always in the country. It'll be a touch if he's up for it.'

The drive across town only seems to emphasise what a job it is. London is really dozens of little towns grafted onto one another. Morty drops me off at the motor and I head for home. I spot a place doing colour photocopies that's just about to close. I dodge inside and have the guy run off five copies of both pictures. I get home, I make calls to a couple of people who are mutual acquaintances of me and Billy and, yes he was in town, and yes they'd pass on a message for him to get in touch straight away. They also suggest I try a couple of clubs in the West End that he could be hanging out in. I get a bitta sticky tape, double it over and stick Charlie's smudge on the bathroom mirror, like in the movies, have a quick shower, some Thai food sent over, eat, get dressed and go out for a bittova drive and a think. I do some of my best thinking while I'm driving.

71

It's Saturday Night

I don't feel like getting involved in any hi-jinx tonight. There might be halfa chance I'll bump into Billy. I slip into the places in the West End where I'm told he might be on a freebie, cos I know the people who run the gaff. In this end of town it's all young babes with tit-jobs, messers, chancers and hustlers, double-lemon rag-trade guys, lemon meaning flash, wannabe models, wannabe wannabes, mega-rich girls who look like hookers, show-biz folk, hookers who look like Daddy's girls, a wagonload of charlie in one-gram wraps that's been slapped about and a binbag fulla pills. The drinks are a tenner a pop and the place is heaving. It looks like a big jolly-up, a bit wild and decadent. These people do their drugs, they have a dance, they have a booze, hopefully they fuck one another and if anyone dies, which they never do, it's gonna be self-inflicted rather than the result of any fisticuffs or mindless violence.

I rarely feel in the mood for a nose-up, it's just a bittova sex-aid really. If the mood takes me, I like to get it on, get the lines chopped out. The whole scene can end up going places it may not usually go. I keep a couple of grams of very, very pure totally uncut stuff that's pure yellow, almost crystal, tucked away behind the bathroom medicine cabinet. It's real pukka gear that me, Morty, Terry and Clarkie keep for ourselves and our lust ones, but I can take it or leave it.

I'm sitting in the back bar of a place just offa Berkeley Square talking small-talk with the barman. I'm away from the dance floor and Saturday night crowd. Suddenly there's a guy walking straight towards me calling my name and he's on me before I know it, which is a drag cos if I'd seen him coming I would have swerved him. He's seen me first and he's on me. The guy's from an out-of-town outfit who we work with every now and then. I'm usually very good with names but I can't for the life of me remember this geezer's name. He's not dangerous, not like some of his team, he's more of a camp follower, a delivery boy. He's slapping me on the fuckin back, pumping my hand and calling me 'mate' over and over, which is something I hate.

He's connected to a gang of jokers who would turn up every now and then and almost demand to do business. From over the border, over the state line, over the M25 so we called them 'The Yahoos' or 'The Banditos'. They would arrange a meet through Jimmy or Gene so you couldn't just tell them to fuck off or they'd come riding into town like the outlaw baddies in the westerns and start shooting the gaff up. They're still very stuck in that attitude of what's the point in having loot if you can't let every fucker know you got it, even the law. They had all these wild fantasies about being the direct descendants of the old double-flash geezers of the sixties and seventies, you know The Twins and all those pavement-job gents. They'd read all the books, seen all the movies, heard all the myths and legends. The three things that weren't comical about these firms was the totally senseless violence they inflicted, mostly on each other, to try and impose some kinda loose pecking order, the telephone-number figures that they dealt in and the amount of bird they could get you with their sloppy work and shit attitude. These comics could get you sent down for decades, serious time, tens, twelves, fifteens, twenties. They couldn't understand the idea of peace and quiet and it wasn't my place to educate them their jobs. Morty had it right when he said they were in the disorganised crime business.

Everything was cash to these guys. We would even take a cheque from one clean account to another from teams we did regular business with, guys we trusted, guys with the peace and quiet principle. I know guys who pay for their stock from abroad by sending diamonds over by courier service. They stick the glass in a padded envelope and have it collected from wherever they happen to be eating lunch that day. Morty once took a four-bedroom house in Southall in exchange for two-and-a-half kilos, but price of oats was higher then. Clean money already in the system was worth more to us than bundles of cash in carrier bags although we would never turn it away. We had front outfits that were very often very successful in their own right, showing that we were, first and foremost, good business-men. These guys don't bother with all that, too difficult for 'em. They're living in big drums, two new motors parked up outside, flashing the cash and even signing on the Kid Creole every fortnight. Balls, they called it. Rank stupidity and greed I'd call it. It's like asking to get yourself chored, making yourself conspicuous, putting yourself on offer.

So they would show up and we would be gracious and polite but try and keep them at arm's length. We would entertain them up to a point, we'd explain our position that we were either over-stocked or under-stocked depending if they were buying or selling at that time. We'd actually try and avoid a trade but we'd have to keep greedy Jimmy P. sweet into the bargain so it took a lot of tact. We'd only do stuff with them if it was really foolish not to and even then we wouldn't encourage them to hang about. Our whole team would be going on at them end-lessly about security, talking out the side of our mouths, looking over our shoulders, acting twitchy the whole time, making out we were being targeted by the Other People's Criminal Intelligence outfit, SO11, some of the Yard's top boys.

One time we had a little team of sensible guys we serve, from Finsbury Park, make out they were old bill ready-eyeing us, got us under observation. We gave them a special-offer price on a key on condition they take it serious and they played the part to perfection. They needed to be obvious so we had them plotted up opposite this meet with the outta-towners in a flower van, like in a movie, with a big fat telephoto lens hanging out the window, clicking away like mad. You can't be too subtle sometimes, it coulda been an ice-cream van with the chimes on. They had the cameras pointed at the Yahoos, who were giving the pretend cozzers two fingers, grabbing their dicks and shouting, 'Suck this, you cunts,' up the street towards the van. We even had the smudges developed. It started off as a bit of a crack, half as a joke between us and this Finsbury Park firm, to show them what we had to put up with, but it really showed us how they behaved around the Other People, even if they were make-believe Other People. Only very stupid people believe the police are stupid. Half that lot, Crim-Intel, have got degrees in Political Science, whatever that is, so a loada mugs childishly abusing them is only gonna make them even more determined to send us, Uncle Tom Cobberly and all, down the Island for double figures. Morty took the photos off to show Jimmy and Gene, who thought they were hilarious, a real crack up. The message came back that we were to continue to keep these jokers sweet cos in the words of James Price, 'Outfits like ours, like countries in time of war, need our lunatics. They may come in handy at some point.' Fair enough, but we were left with the job of humouring the lunatics cos Jimmy wouldn't be seen dead with them. To me they were just big, rude, bullying, useless cunts.

I'm running through names in my nut trying to get his. He's wearing a naff designer-label-logo top that's some jumped-up cunt's name on a two quid sweatshop top. He's a big old lump so the sleeves are too short in the arms and body's above the top of his strides. He looks like a big kid whose mum has stuck his clothes in a boiled wash and then left them in the tumbledryer to shrink-to-fuck. In tow this guy's got a girl who's delicious. The real what-the-fuck's-she-doing-with-him scenario. She's blond with a scattering of freckles around the bridge of her nose, only a smidgen of make-up, a beautiful face that's inno- cent and horny both at the same time, and a little crop-top that shows off her flat stomach, her deep, healthy tan and pierced belly button. Her tits are standing up all by themselves, nipples pointing at the ceiling. She has a really fit, taut, athletic bod.

'How you doin, good to see you –' I'm smiling, lying, patting him on the shoulder '– How's tricks?'

'Good, mate, good. This is Tammy,' he says.

'Hiya, Tammy.'

Nice smile, nice eyes, deep blue. Is it my ego or my dick or is she showing out just a bit? She's fluttering the eyelashes just a bit too often, throwing her shoulders back just a tiny little bit so her tits go even more skyward.

'Hi,' says Tammy. She's looking at me with big eyes.

'Who you with, mate?' asks Gormless.

'I'm just out for a look around on my own. I was gonna

shmyes in a little while. I'm only in the mood to look tonight, anyway. I've had a long day.'

'You want some shampoo, mate?' He's got a bottle of Champagne by the neck in his hand. The pair of them have got glasses well topped-up.

'No. I'm all right. I'm not drinkin tonight.'

'Well, you can have one glass, just to be sociable.'

He's well coked up and so is Tammy, who's sniffing away like mad. I still can't think of his name but I've got him narrowed down. This guy is a pal of an operator from across the border, a capo called JD. His name is Tom, Dick, Harry, Bert, Eric, one of those real old names that go back before the war, real old-school.

'What are you doing up this end, brov?' I ask.

'Fancied a change. Tammy wanted to check it out.'

'You two been seeing each other long?' I says to Tammy.

'Nah, we've only been out, what, three or four times? Ay, Sid?'

Sidney. That's the name. What she's saying is it ain't serious. Tammy, I'd get the gear outta the medicine cupboard for you.

'Four times.'

'Sorry, Sid?' I say.

'We've been out four times.'

So Sid obviously was counting. He saw it as a bonus to run into a face he knew, even if I didn't leap up and engage in an orgy of backslapping, cos you could sense that they had been traipsing around the gaff, charlied and boozed up to the gills. I reckon that Tammy was using him as a driver-cum-coke-supply, she wasn't all that into him romantically or sexually. To steam into Tammy would be more than tricky cos it's all about protocol with these guys, it isn't the done thing, they take it all very personal. So now I'm talking bollocks-talk about nice club, nice people, nice DJs, but what I'm really thinking is how good it would be to have that little top straight off over Tammy's head, have her kick off those flimsy little sandals, unzip those silky, satin jeans and have her wriggle outta them and then peel off her, no doubt sexy, little knickers and have her standing naked in front of me. I reckon she could be undressed in about four seconds top whack. I wonder if she's thinking the same thing too. Meanwhile, Sid's going waffling on in my ear'ole about some old bollocks but really the canister's gonski. I realise I've got a hard-on tugging away in my strides just sitting here thinking about this little soft porn scene. I don't want the little head telling the big head what to do. I make a double effort to listen to Sid, be polite, not give Tammy any blatant encouragement. What I'd dearly love to do is nick her for a session of freestyle, points awarded for wit and imagination, lust, coke, animal passion.

She's looking at me and she's a real love-a-player type. She knows I could bury her up to her pretty little neck in powder. There's telepathy or a chemistry going on here that Sid, poor cunt, is totally oblivious to. She can tell instinctively by Sid's slightly crawling attitude that I'm most definitely a connected dude and that, to her, is a turn-on. She's dancing on the spot, starting to let go, getting horny on the music, the coke and her prick-teasing, moving her hips in a figure of eight, but like slow, her eyes half-shut, her head thrown back. I'm thinking what it would be like to have her in my bed right now, to put her on top of me so she's dancing and fuckin me senseless at the same time, moving to the bass thump, pleasuring herself with my dick, tweaking her clit, biting and scratching. What it would be like to stick a pillow under her arse and ride her slow and long, to spin her over and bite her firm little bottle. What it would be like to be down on her, running my nose along her wet lips, in among her slippery, slidy pussy with her groaning with pleasure, begging in anticipation, 'Now, now, now!!!!', the very tip of my tongue making dollar signs on her clit, $$$$$$$$$.

'Do you wanna line, mate?' Sid's shouting and nudging me at the same time, waking me up.

'A what?'

'A line, do you want one?'

'Oh no, sorry Sid, no, I'm all right. You have one,' I say.

'Tammy, do you wanna line? a bittova livener?'

She nods and he hands her a wrap. She turns away, swaying,

and as she turns she gives me a sly, naughty look, a kinda be-right-back look, but Sid just don't spot it, thank fuck.

We're sitting on a couple of barstools, side by side like we're best mates. The bar's starting to empty out. Outta politeness more than anything I ask him about a few faces I know from out this way and he starts to tell me this story about a pal of his, I think he may even mean JD's cousin who I've met once or twice. He always tries to stay in the shadows this guy, fancies himself as a Mister Big, Charlie Large-potatoes.

'This is a funny story, mate, this'll make ya laugh.'

'Go on, mate, I'm all ears.'

This is the story he tells me. A pal of his, an old friend, they went to school together, did a lotta shit together, grew up together, tore up the old neighbourhood together. (Now where have I heard this before?) The guy's name is Darren, but he likes to be known as 'Duke' or 'The Duke'. Duke's doing really well, he's into shifting powders, pills, steroids, ringing motors that end up abroad, moving bootleg copies of movies before they've come out, distributing home-made porn, financing booze cruises, buying and selling guns, a real live-wire.

He's bought himself a big house, the whole number, swimming pool, whirlpools, three-car garage with three motors to go in it, all stuck in a few acres of land. For Christmas one year, for half a joke, this guy's bought his live-in girlfriend a little can of CS gas with a twenty-four-carat-gold cover that you slip on and off, like those covers you put on those cheap throwaway lighters that you get from the Continent. He's had it knocked up special by a goldsmith, to order, so it looks like a bitta very expensive jewellery on her key-ring, dead flash, like, with the keys to the Merc sports, the house keys, the Gucci and Chanel key-rings so it don't look too suspect. He thinks his little joke is hilarious.

Her name is Sarah but she likes to be called Sacha, but behind her back people call her Slasher. The two of them have got a very serious cocaine problem. From wake-up bugle in the morning, all through the day, they're snorting line after line of charlie so in the end they're both dead paranoid, neurotic, and she's dead thin, which she don't mind. Duke is also injecting steroids, drinking liquidised rump steak and lamb's livers, maniacally working out in the gym. They've got, very foolishly, toot all over the gaff, in sugar-bowls on the coffee table, on mirrors in the bathroom, by the bed, but he's got his private stash that he keeps hidden from her and she's got her stash that she keeps hidden from him, in case the supply should dry up, thinking about if times become lean, which is the sure sign, a dead give-away in fact, of the dedicated coke addict. She reckons he's got a bit of a problem and he reckons she's got the makings of one but in their delusion they think that all this decadence and living extra-large is a sure sign that they've arrived. In reality, for all the big drum and scattering of creamy motors, they're barely holding their shit together, they're winging it in grand style, but getting by each day by the skin of their teeth.

They ain't got no kids cos she don't wanna fuck up her dolly-bird figure. She's got an arse like two peas in a hanky after all the coke. What they've got instead is two thick-as-pig-shit Dobermanns. What he's trying to do is teach the dogs back-commands, meaning that if someone says 'Kill!' the dog don't do nothing, maybe lick their face, but if someone says 'Sit!' the pair of cunts will tear any stranger's throat out but he don't know how successful he's been at this cos he ain't got nobody to try it out on. It's a method he's invented himself so he don't know if it works or not. Not very Kennel Club.

In his highly frazzled state he's always telling the bird that he don't give a fuck about cozzers.

'Fuckin cozzers, I piss on them,' Duke's telling Slasher. He's more worried about being turned over, skanked, by someone who's madder, badder and a drop more naughty than him, which would be tough cos he's very mad, bad and totally para two-four-seven. All this ranting and raving is going in under her radar so she's getting more and more edgy and twitchy. His paranoia's feeding off hers and hers offa his so the atmosphere is really quite electric. It's crackling. The needle's in the red.

It gets worse. He's got shooters all over the gaff as well, just in case a team of bogeymen rush the gaff, try and skank him for whatever loot and chemicals he's got stashed around the place.

They're real state of the art as well, laser sights, six hundred rounds a minute delivery, same bit of kit as the Yard's Diplomatic Protection Unit have got. At first he's got them stashed away very snug but soon he's getting them out to show his cronies and not putting them back in the hiding places he's had specially built by his cousin who's a dry-wall liner. Soon there's Glock and whats-his-name down the back of the leather sofa, under the pillows, a Uzi 9mm pistol knocking about under the kitchen sink. The paranoia level is climbing steadily up into the danger zone. The old bill round there are, compared to the Met, a bit of a joke, carrot crunchers, and they ain't been near these two. Their firm is feared by all the local hounds so the threat has been largely conjured up in their imaginations and fed by their deluded fantasies and enflamed egos, but to these two crackling cokeheads it's all very real.

One morning a geezer's turned up from the local council while Duke is out and about. The guy's there cos they've had this fuckin great fence erected so people, like the cozzers, can't be looking into the plot, but, one, it's about two feet into the common land that backs into the rear of the property, and two, in his 'I don't give a fuck, I'm Al Capone, I rule the planet, OK' delusion, Duke's not bothered to apply for a drop of the old planning permission. Maybe he thought that nobody would notice this hundred-yard-long, twelve-foot-high fence with discreetly placed razor wire along the top going around three sides of the plot.

The council bloke is dressed from head to toe in plastic and polyester, carrying a plastic briefcase stamped with a crown. He looks exactly like a bloke from the town hall turning up to explain about the problems with the fence but to her, who's totally wired, been primed with the Duke's paranoid bollocks, he looks like a master of disguise, too fuckin geeky to be true, a bit too much like a council joe, so she ain't taking any chances. Between the time he's rang the intercom on the outside gate and she's buzzed him in thinking it's all very feasible about the fence, and him arriving on the doorstep, she's lost it, panicked big time. As soon as she's opened the door she's let him have it full blast, bosh, a double dose of the mace right in the poor doughnut's eyes. He's started screaming the place down, let go a personal alarm gadget that those council guys get issued with these days cos there's a few nutters about. It's like a mini-siren, high-pitched and ear-splitting, so she's got more panicked and given him another helping. Bosh. The dogs have come running out to see what all the noise is about. They start barking at the pair of them cos she's saying 'sit' meaning 'kill' and he's shouting 'sit' meaning 'sit' so the two child-substitutes are just plain baffled, plain old confused.

Slasher's thinking that the rest of the team of robbers mustn't be far behind so she runs off to find one of the bits of hardware that's cluttering up the place. She comes back with a fully loaded Uzi. Mister council man is up now, trying to escape, but he can't see fuck all. He's falling over, colliding with posts and motors that are parked in the driveway. She, purely by accident, lets go a three-second burst on the machine pistol and it completely saws one of the dogs in two and takes out the windows on a Mitsubishi jeep. She drops the shooter, it's hot metal, and starts screaming hysterically at the top of her voice. The guy's weeping, pleading, 'Please don't shoot me, please don't shoot,' getting up and falling down, stumbling around the front of the house. She's jumped into the Merc sports and is driving away down the drive to just get the fuck away from this nightmare. Slasher don't care where she's going cos she's gone into a dose of shock. She clips the geezer on the shoulder just as he's getting up, blinded, and now he thinks that she's trying to run him over, the poor bastard, to finish him off, but she smashes through the gates and takes off. One dog's sniffing around the other's dead body, yelping, the frontdoor's wide open, there's an Israeli army sub-machine gun lying on the deck with a shot-up jeep with it's anti-joyrider alarm going full blast, a half-blind council official stumbling backwards and forwards, hooting, screaming after a double dose of mega-powerful German-police-issue CS gas and the lady of the house is driving about ninety miles an hour down curvy country lanes trying to get some bugle up her hooter, like that's really gonna help.

Sid's telling me this tale of gross insanity like it's the best yet, a real hoot, what a scream, birds, ay? what are they like? I'm thinking that it only goes to show why I don't like working with these outfits. They've got totally different priorities. They're loons.

'So what happened then, Sid?'

'Well, she got her old man on the mobile. He was well pissed off at first cos it meant walkin away from everythin that he'd worked for and he was pissed off that she'd shot Mike Tyson.'

'The boxer?'

'No. The dog –'

Of course.

'He gave her a few slaps but he forgave her. Maybe if he'd been home that day it wouldn't have happened.'

It could've been worse. Hostages, sieges, shoot-outs, body counts and a very large chunk at the beginning of *The Nine O'Clock News* come to mind.

'And what happened to the house?'

'Well, over that part of the world you can see straight across the fields with binoculars so Duke sent a couple of boys up to see what was goin on, and the filth were around the drum pullin it apart. They were like flies round dogshit.'

'Did anyone get a pull?'

'Oh, fuck yeah! It was on the news up our way. They didn't say exactly what happened. But they showed the house, all that tape, the old bill with guns goin in and out, team-handed they was.'

'Right, but did anyone get a pull?'

'Oh yeah, all the chaps got a visit cos Duke had our phone numbers in his book or on bits of paper round the gaff.'

'It was more likely they come from his phone bill. They go and get the records straight away, see who he's been talkin to. What did you tell 'em, the law?'

'Oh. I said I'd gone to school with him, known him years. Every now and then I bumped into him in a boozer, had a drink with him. What would you have told them?'

'The same. It's not good to over-elaborate, keep it simple. The old bill were happy with that?'

'They seemed so.'

82

'Did what's-his-name, Duke, have the numbers of anyone up our way in his book? Think. It could be important.'

'He could have done.'

'But you don't know.'

'No I don't. Fuckin hell, I wish I'd never told you now.'

You fuckin useless cunt, you clueless wanker, it's all a fuckin funny story to you, ain't it, it's all a game to you and the dumb collection of cunts you move with.

'Oh, don't be like that, mate. I'm only askin,' I says, patting him on the shoulder.

Right on cue Tammy comes back. She's been queuing to get a cubicle. Me and Sid are sitting side by side with our backs to the bar. She leans into his face and gives him a kiss on the lips, she rubs their noses together like they're a couple of Eskimos and hands him back the wrap.

'Thanks, Siddy baby,' she says.

At the very same time she pushes something into my hand. I know by instinct that it's not for Siddy baby to see. I can feel it's a bit of torn glossy paper. I close my fist around it. My heart starts beating a bit faster and my dick wakes up again. The kiss was a decoy.

'Ain't she a darling,' says Sid.

'Ain't she, mate,' I say.

She's draped all over him, nibbling his ear. What she's doing with a plank like Sidney fuck only knows. Is this for my benefit I wonder. He's grinning like a idiot. The card's burning into the palm of my hand. I'm dying to look. Whatever it is I can't make any move on Tammy tonight. I've just gotta learn a bit of patience. I gotta sit tight for about another five minutes till I can cut out with grace.

I'm thinking that maybe Sid'll go for a nose-up but he sticks the wrap in his back pocket. Tammy's dancing with her arms around Sid's neck but she's looking straight at me. She knows what I'm thinking and she's getting off on it. There's danger of it getting a little bit weird like it can on coke. If I get another hard-on I could be stuck here for another ten or twenty minutes or all night trying to get rid of it. One, two, three and I'm up, and in one movement I've got the bitta card into my pocket ready for the off, the handshakes and goodbyes.

'People, I'm gonna cut out.'

'So soon, mate?'

'I only come out for a breath of fresh air. I'll catch you later, Sid. Very nice to meet you, Tammy.'

'See you again soon,' says Tammy, nicely loaded.

'Yeah, see you later, mate, you take care,' says Sid.

'Yeah, you look after yourself, Sid.'

You look after Tammy for me I'm thinking as I'm giving his hand a good shake, and then I'm away. A few quick goodbyes to people hanging out, then down the stairs, into the street and the cool spring night air. I get the bittov card outta my pocket. It's a corner of the flyer for a club. In girlie handwriting, she's half written, half scratched, 'You are one sexy motherfucker. Ring me soon.' An outta-town number and a PS: 'Don't tell Sid.' First prize for stating the obvious, Tammy. She's kissed it so it's got a big pair of lipstick lips on it. This is a touch, it was well worth going out tonight after all. I must keep this bitta card safe. It's worth its weight in gold. You, Tammy, are one sexy motherfucker yourself and we two sexy motherfuckers must get together real soon. Whatever scene she's got going on with Siddy baby she's taken a big risk giving me this under his nose, maybe that's the thrill. I'll have to get her down here for a session real soon. For the time being I better just switch off the blue movie in my nut or I'll end up driving myself mad or the motor into a lamppost. It ain't easy. I drive home trying to shift an image of Tammy, sexy little Tammy, dancing round my bed, naked, except for a pair of pointy-toed, hi-heel black-leather ankle boots.

Sunday
In the Rose Garden

Eight in the morning, the phone's gone, it's Gene.

'Do you know the rose garden in Regent's Park?'

'No, but I can find it.'

'Okay, I'll see you there about eleven. Sit and read the paper, I'll find you.'

The rose garden's in the middle of the park. I've plotted up on a bench where I can see the comings and goings and waited with the papers. There's hundreds of different types of roses, each with different names, but they all look pretty much the same to me, not being a flower lover. I walked through the China garden and they've got herons standing on one leg, little bridges and lakes, very quaint, amazing really.

I'm reading the colour supplements, thinking this is all very civilised, very tranquil, maybe I should do this more often on a spring morning, when outta the corner of my eye I see this figure in a tracksuit and woollen cap. At first it's just the silhouette coming up the slight slope but as it gets nearer I can make out that whoever it is has got a rucksack on his back and is wearing hobnailed boots. The steel in the bottom of the boots is making a rhythmic crunching sound on the gravel path. He's still a way off but I'm thinking that it's gotta be one of the loony-tune soldiers from one of the barracks around that part of town, practising for one of their cross-country gallops. The pack is tightly strapped onto the guy and it's obviously very heavy from the way it's behaving. Just as I'm thinking that the geezer's got to be a total headcase to make so much work for himself the runner gets close enough for me to make out that it's our Geno. The crunch becomes louder and he approaches with a big grin, which is unusual for him cos he's notoriously poker-faced. Sweat's dripping out from under his hat, down his face and off his chin in big drops. The grey old-school tracksuit is drenched like he's run through a pond to get here, there's steam coming offa him. The rucksack is from the same era, an old rambler's affair with buckles and leather laces. He pulls up huffing and puffing, bringing up huge lumps of recycled snot, spitting them over into the roses where they connect with a splat. In one movement he's got the rucksack off and places it on the floor in front of my bench. It's heavy even for Gene. It lands with a brittle chink.

'Good morning, Young Sir,' he says.

'Good morning, Mister McGuire. What's in the bag?'

'Oh, bits and pieces, odds and sods for you.'

He goes in the bag and brings out a plastic bottle of water and has a long swig, gurgles and spits, pours a little over his head and neck and offers me the bottle. I shake my head. It's got bits of spit and phlegm floating about in it.

'Haven't you found the lady yet? You won't find her lazin around in the park on a Sunday morning either, reading the fekkin paper.'

'For fuck sake, Gene, I was only fuckin –'

'I'm jokin, honest, it was only a little joke.'

'I know. Anyway, that bottle didn't make it that heavy.'

'Oh, there's a few old house-bricks in there as well, just to make it a contest.'

I peek into the bag and there's eight house-bricks in the bag, bits chipped off the sides, splinters and red brick dust in the bottom of the bag. He goes into one of the pockets and brings out the Rothman's and the Dunhill, lights up.

'How often do you do this running business, Gene?'

'Two or three times a week, just to stay nimble. Three or four miles, that's not far really, I know blokes who run whole marathons with full kitbags on their backs.'

'You must know some very funny people.'

'Don't we all, son.'

Gene goes into the bag again and comes out with some papers.

'Family, friends and all that shit, mostly young Kinky but some more on the princess.'

'I'll look but I ain't sure what I'm meant to be looking for. This is all fuckin damp, Gene.'

'You can dry it out later.'

'Love is blind, ay Gene.'

'Too true, but do you really believe she's as pure as Jimmy's makin her out to be? Well, do you, son?' Gene laughs gently.

'No way. She's a right box of tricks is Princess Charlotte. She's probably got the poor cunt jumpin through hoops as we speak, dumb bastard.'

'Won't know what's hit him,' Gene says, pulling on his snout.

'I've got an idea who I'm gonna try and get to help me out,' I say.

'Who?'

'A guy called Billy Bogus. You know him?'

'It rings a bell.'

'I wanna get this sorted as soon as possible.'

'Give it time, son. We cast our bread upon the water.'

'Very biblical, Gene.'

'Old Testament.'

'I suppose it is Sunday after all.'

'Read that about Kinky,' says Gene pointing at the papers. 'It makes for grim reading, he's a depressing no-hoper, could end up feelin sorry for him.'

'Well, he's got his break now ain't he. He's lucky in love with the princess, could marry into the good life, nicely set up.'

'Then he really would disappear,' says Gene with a slightly raised eyebrow.

'I fucked up saying that about Kinky disappearing, didn't I?'

'Yeah, you did. But he likes you and he was in a particularly good mood yesterday. He probably had the ride before he came out so he let it go. You had me worried though, son.'

'I don't know where it come from.'

'You put him right on the spot. If he didn't like you he woulda made you suffer, gone right into one, you know, made you sweat. It's all about –' Gene's searching for the correct word '– protocol, etiquette, if you like.'

'I understand. I don't know who was talkin.'

'When you get round guys like Jimmy, don't get me wrong, I really do like the old bollocks for all his faults, you learn to say as little as you can get away with.'

'I realise that now.'

'He thinks you've got balls and brains. See, if you'd crawled up his rectum and went to sleep he'd think you was a wanker and he'd treat you like one. He'd have you washin his car and mowin the lawn, just for the laugh, for a giggle. I've seen it before with guys who reckon they're tasty. He's just took the piss cos guys set themselves up but he's given you a job to do, placed his trust in you, cos you confirmed what me and Morty have been tellin him, you're a talent.'

'Thanks.'

He flicks his fag-butt with his finger and thumb away into the roses. We both sit in silence. We nod to the good folks out walking their dogs. Looking through a gap in the privet hedges, we're watching a guy throwing a big lump of wood and have his Labrador catch it on the first or second bounce. Gene lights another snout and pulls hard.

'They're clever dogs, Labradors,' I say.

'They can't do crosswords,' says Gene.

A small grin appears on his face. 'Your best mates have been in touch.'

'I'm not with ya.'

'The, what do you lot call 'em, the Yahoos?'

'Oh fuck,' I say. Gene laughs.

'I knew you'd be pleased.'

'They're a pain in the arse.'

'They make money.'

'They make trouble.'

'They're okay.'

'They're dangerous.'

'I've had more dangerous kebabs.'

'They're messy.'

'So be very careful,' he says with a pointy finger.

'Funnily enough I ran into one of their team in a club last night. He was tellin me about some right nutty escapades.'

'How wonderful for you,' says Gene, dry as fuck.

'Sidney. And he was with this bird, fuck me, Geno, she was fit.'

Gene looks totally disinterested. Maybe I'll tell Mort instead. He'll appreciate it.

'Fit. My dick was standin to attention in the gaff. Has that ever happened to you? You coulda hung a wet fur coat up on it. She was sendin over blimps, you know, she had the hots for me big time.'

Gene's got that look that says 'I really didn't need to know that'. The sort of look those Catholic schoolboys get when you get too graphic.

'Gene, you know what she did, she –'

'Listen,' he interrupts, 'don't, okay? Don't under any circumstances be shaftin any of those boys' birds. Okay? Do you understand?'

'For fuck sake, what do you take me –'

'Yes or fuckin no, son? Do you understand?'

'I wasn't going to do anything, Gene,' I lie.

'Okay. This is serious business we're doin here. Don't let your bollocks do your thinkin for you. Okay?'

'He's only a fringe member of their outf –'

'Will you be fuckin told. I don't fuckin care.'

'Okay,' I says, my face all hurt and innocent. I'll have to be sneaky.

'What are they after? Do they wanna buy or sell?' I says to change the subject.

'They've got a fuckin big load of tablets from over the sea, but like a wagonload, and they reckon they're the very best quality. Jimmy won't let us turn it down. He don't want them fucked about like sometimes happens.'

'We call it protectin ourselves.'

'I know that and I know why you do it but this time things have got to be done without the shenanigans, blokes in fuckin ice-cream vans.'

'It was a flower van.'

'Whatever,' says Geno.

'Will this be regular work?'

'No, I asked them that last night –'

'Last night?'

'Yeah, last night me and yer man met them last night. I got home, he rang, I had to head back out that way again. I didn't like it but there you go. It's a one-off.'

'Thank fuck for that.'

'You really don't like them, do you?' He knew the answer already.

'Fuckin right I don't like them. It's all a game to them. They don't seem to mind goin away for stretches.'

'They can't do things quietly,' he agrees. 'And you're a bit of a soldier. Was Jimmy right about you wanting to be out soon? Be honest with me, son.'

'Well, between you and me I think I've got an agreement that if I find Charlie for him I'm free to walk away.'

'When?'

'In a few months' time.'

'Well, you two must of been talkin in riddles cos I never spotted that. When was that? Yesterday?'

I ain't gonna say anything about the business in the khazi.

'That's how I saw it.'

'You got your retirement planned?'

'I just thought it best to get out first. And if it was left up to me I'd give these headbangers a wide, politely mind, at this stage of the game.'

'But it could be a good bitta business. Maybe what you got is a big old dose of what's called gate fever in reverse.'

'Gate fever?'

'When guys are comin to the end of a bitta bird they start panicking, gettin anxious, cos they can see the end. You're sweatin about gettin captured.'

'This is my opinion and I'm entitled to it, I just happen to believe this outfit is more grief than they're worth. No joke, I'm serious.'

'You'll think differently when you have your wedge out.'

'I'm surprised to hear you, of all people, talk like that, Gene. How much can you spend in Long Lartin or Gartree? I'd rather be potless and on the out than have a loada dough waitin after I've done a twelve or fifteen.'

90

'Will I tell him you're not interested? Nobody's forcin you to do anything, you can walk away now.'

'If I thought I could … I'll do it but I want it put on record that I don't fancy it.'

'Duly noted.'

Gene's now got a brittle tone in his voice. He lets it sink in before continuing.

'I'll get them to contact me and arrange a meet early this week. You sort out the details with them but I'll be about when you meet them so don't worry, okay?'

'How's this gonna work out moneywise?'

'Basically you're gonna buy the parcel from this crowd and sell them. Jimmy reckons you might have people tucked away up north, and the profit gets carved straight down the middle.'

'What, fifty-fifty?'

'That's right, son.'

'That's bollocks, and you know it, Gene. Half the whack for setting up a meet?'

'There's a fuck of a lot of money to be earned here. Maybe I should be talkin about this with Mister Mortimer.'

Bit snide that, Mister McGuire.

'How many bits are we talkin about here?' I say.

'I don't know for sure but it's somewhere in the region of two million.'

'Fuckin 'ell, that's a fuckin lot of tablets.'

'And that's a lotta shillings. And when they tell you that it's the first time you've heard it, okay?'

'Sixty-forty sounds better.'

'I'll see what he's sayin but I think you're being greedy son.'

'This only came up last night?'

'Yeah. We had a meet last night, all cloak and dagger, just the way they like it.'

'Why do they always come to us?'

'You're victims of your own efficiency.'

'I don't feel flattered.'

'They were sayin what a lovely geezer you were last night, what a good worker.'

'I'll thank them personally when I see them.'

'Sarcasm doesn't suit you.'

'I could very easily live without these people. I tell you what, Gene, this bitta work sounds like we can nick a good few readies, but if I thought that this was gonna be a regular bitta business, I'd walk away right now. I'd walk outta this park and I'd just keep walkin –'

Geno's laughing.

'– I couldn't afford to be webbed up with these jokers full time, my health wouldn't stand for it, I'd be twitchy as fuck. They see things that ain't there and they don't see things that are.'

'They want it done in a hurry,' he says.

'Oh, I bet they do. Where do they think we are, Disneyland? Who's got that kinda money sat around?'

'When?'

'I'd like to see them as soon as. I don't really know what's happening pills-wise at the moment. I'll have a better idea by Wednesday or Thursday. I'll have an idea of what we can realistically do.'

Gene nods. 'I've changed my number at home again,' he says. 'Have you got a pen? I'll give it to you.'

I give him my pen and he writes it on the top of the Rothman's packet, tears it off and gives it to me.

'You know the sketch, ring very early or very late. You can try me in between but they're the best times. You're gonna be a busy boy.'

'I don't mind bein busy. Maybe you're right about gate fever, maybe I'll bring my retirement forward. This could be my last coup before I sing "My Way".'

'You're a sly little fucker, you never let on.'

'My mum used to call me that, sly. I'd rather be workin while I'm young, make me dough and get out.'

'We'll talk soon. I'm coolin down. I better get goin.'

He throws the rucksack onto his back, adjusts it.

'Adios, Young Sir. Oh, one last thing, there's a –'

'Listen, Geno, I really don't want to hear it. Please leave me alone, I've got enough to be getting on with. Please don't think me rude but I'm not sure I can handle it.'

92

This is the most I've ever seen Gene smile.

'All I was gonna say was there's a rose over there that's named after Sir Bobby Moore.'

'Who?'

'I don't believe this. You know, he won the World Cup with England, don't ya know that? 1966 and all that? Fuck's sake, you must know Bobby Moore.'

He's shaking his head. So am I.

'A bit before my time, Geno.'

I'm lying. My old man never shut up about him, what a gentleman he was. I was almost named after him.

'Only Jimmy would be mortified if you'd been here and I hadn't shown it to ya. It's over there somewhere. Anyway, adios, Señor.'

Off he goes down the path, crunch, crunch, crunch into the distance. He's right, there's a lot to do. We really are attacking on all fronts. I can really start to smell the end but for the time being I'm as content as my nature will allow to sit here in the cool spring air. I read the papers for a while, business section. In here are the comings and goings of the real-deal multi-national top outfits, with the Bosses that the likes of Jimmy Price call Sir. They're up to swindles that make me and Morty, Gene and Jimmy, the top guys who Jimmy gets the oats from, Terry, Clarkie, the lot of us, they make us look like clucking junkies hoisting down Oxford Street or a team of crackhead muggers, desperado on a Sunday evening. They do aggravated burglaries, tie-ups, on whole countries, crashing in, beating up the occupants and ransacking all the natural resources. One day the government and the public will say all this illegal drug dealing has got to stop cos it's all getting totally outta hand. They'll ask some sober-minded citizens from the clubs of Pall Mall and the City of London to come in and sort out the whole game properly. They'll even give them start-up loans, non-repayable of course, tax-breaks and grants, and the whole scam will be made to look like these heroes are doing us all a favour, putting themselves out, by coming to the rescue of the nation when things are getting perilous. Their media will turn the whole issue into the tired old law and order debate. Any renegade souls still dabbling in the chemicals trade, taking sovs outta the coffers of the monopoly, will be hit hard, profits seized, banged up, big-time, long-time. I suppose you'll get some die-hards and cry-babies who wanna keep going on about the good old days, how it was money for jam, 'Oh what fun we had!!' before this new regime came along and spoilt everything. You can hear the rumblings now, and when the establishment Mafioso realise how much gilt, paper, cashish, wonga, wedge, corn, cutter, loot, spondos, dollar, readies, shillings, folding, dough, money is on offer, slipping through their soft, dry, manicured hands, billions not millions, the likes of me will be taken out and shot if necessary. If we don't get the message.

I think they want it to get bad, but like really bad. I think they want it to go up in the air, but like really up in the air. I think they want it to get to the verge of civil war, no-go areas in London and some northern cities, paramilitary dealing teams, evil baddies. Not around where they live of course. They'll want the British Army on the streets cos Mister Plod can't cope, not with a wooden truncheon, with an enemy equipped with the latest hardware. The chief constables will plead with the government to just legalise everything cos they can't fight this thing for ever. Just give it over to somebody who can handle it, organise it, collect taxes on it, to pay for treatment, maybe even find a cure and make a handsome profit for their trouble. The government will be told the terms and conditions of the carve-up by their paymasters, the money men, and being joes who take it up the arse from the City cartels anyway they'll go along with the swindle in the hope of getting a few meagre crumbs brushed their way off the high table. I don't believe those guys in Parliament run anything anyway, they just do the bidding of those masonic, on-the-level, funny-handshake geezers, brandied-up on the cherry-red leather sofas in the gentlemen's clubs of St James's, the real string-pullers and puppet masters.

Do they give a fuck about most of the people living in this country anyway? I don't think they give a shit if they send themselves stupid. You could even say it helps keep people quiet and in line. The syndicates that end up with the drug monopoly will be courted as champions. They'll make grand stirring Shakespearean speeches about how they've come to save Royal Britannia, this precious jewel, in its most self-destructive hour, when it's under attack from within, by the weakness of its own wicked children, by the rabble who have grown soft and spoilt by hand-outs and ill-discipline, by the low morality of felons and delinquents. After the public relations coup of all time the slippery fuckers will walk away with a licence to print money. Recreational Drugs UK plc will give the people what they want, when they want it, stupor today, good times today, fuck tomorrow and fuck the consequences. If it becomes chaotic, like no doubt it will, the rich and privileged will soon be going back to live in castles and city forts anyway. They'll be laughing all the way back to the banks they own with everyone's praise and blessing, the pay-off to a nice bit of work, a job well done. Perfect, really. If you take a step back and look at it logically you have to admit it's a brilliantly thought out and executed piece of manipulation. You have to admire the cunts. I won't be hanging around for any repercussions or reunions. I'll be long-gonski.

Monday
Tommy, AKA Cody, AKA Billy,
AKA Hugo

The guy I wanted to help me with the Charlie business was Tommy Garret, AKA Cody, AKA Billy Bogus. His real name was Thomas Roger Garret but one Friday night when we were kids *White Heat* was on the telly and after that Tommy was always Cody. The name just stuck, it suited him, and he preferred it. Only his mum called him Tommy now. He didn't like the nickname Billy Bogus but it was kinda convenient for him that a lotta mugs didn't know his real moniker either. He wasn't on the bogus lawyer, bogus Foreign Legionnaire, bogus gynaecologist tip either. This guy was a different class. Cody's game was deception and he'd worked his way up from kiting, lying down Jekyll paper with a cheque card, through credit cards, and into something a whole lot more sophisticated.

Cody has a gift for mimicry, can look and sound like anyone after being around them for only a few minutes, but at the same time he's no party-piece. When he comes to dress the part his attention to detail is masterful, tiny details matter, old school ties, pinkie rings, correct magazine under the arm, wear the right cologne. The secret, he told me once, is not to strong it. Go gentle, play it simple and don't become a caricature. Don't ever try and convince anyone who you are or who you ain't, it's not your problem. Your job is to convince yourself.

Cody's a very good actor. The major banks and credit companies are his stage. He earns very good money, always works very tidy, has very good contacts, who he looks after well, keeps a low profile. Cody would avoid the festivities, hanging out and talking shop. I like him because he can talk about life, not just work and skulduggery, who's up to what with who and all that bollocks. Work for Cody, like myself, is a means to an end, and the end is La Dolce Vita, the good life.

Cody has put some very tidy business our way and I've always weighed him on for it. I've lent him wads of cash or given him cheques to play with so he can send it through different accounts in different countries to give the impression of heavy financial traffic, big amounts moving back and forth to convince whoever needs convincing that commerce is vibrant, above board and legit. When the time is right, after much patient approach-play, he hits 'em up for the massive loan, crash, thank you very much, see you later. Cody goes abroad for long holidays, sometimes working, sometimes not, and had arrived back in London from Hong Kong only a few days before. He'd got my message and rang me late last night. I told him nothing over the phone.

Cody wanted to meet in the restaurant of one of the more superior department stores along Piccadilly after the lunch-hour rush had died down. He wanted to be in the area to visit his barber while he was up that way and he likes to steam into the kinda birds you get up around these places, the Quality Street Gang, rich gals out shopping or up in town for the day to hook up with old school chums, well-bred girls with plummy accents and a healthy outdoor attitude to sex, young ladies who were up for a robust ride over the gallops.

The place had obviously just been severely revamped, so it's all chrome, purple and orange up the walls. He's already plotted up in a booth along the back wall, three steps up, slightly off-centre, the very best vantage point to observe the comings and going of the clientele, and the very best place for them to get a good look at Cody. He's looking good. He's picked up a nice tan on his travels. Tommy Garret, from round the flats, is dressed like an off-duty polo player, all battered faded Levi's, tweed jacket with leather patches on the elbows, a peach-coloured silk hanky in the top pocket, tan riding boots and a proper polo shirt, the ones they wear when they actually play the game for real, collar up, a large number four on the front, the same number as Charlie Windsor wears, don't you know. The barnet is all messy, all curly and flyaway. He's got the little pinkie ring and the huge fuck-off Rolex. Cody's got a small pile of newspapers, the pink money ones, but he's lazily thumbing through

97

the *Herald Tribune* with a nice air of indifferent arrogance and wealth, spaced-out but worldly. The whole outing is sending the shopaholic, trust-funded girlies wild. As I walk in I can feel the vibe. The whole air of not giving a shit was sending them haywire. They love a bounder. No need to change the bait, Cody.

Cody gets up and greets me with a firm, dry handshake and much back-patting and playful shoulder-punching.

'Good to see you, old boy, good to see you.'

The accent is straight out of some old black-and-white movie, all those actors your nan likes, pure Eton and the Brigade of Guards. He shoots me a tiny wink. I can see all the little ear'oles tweaking to hear better. We sit back down, Cody gets the waitress over and orders two seafood salads. We sit closer to talk.

'How's your bitta business?' he asks.

'Good. Almost too busy. Where there's people there's toot.'

'You could translate that into Latin for the company motto,' says Cody.

'It'd make a nice little slogan if we could advertise.'

'The need for chemical stimulation comes from a deep core of emptiness, ingratitude and a lack of sense of purpose.'

'No disrespect, Cody, but it's a bit too early in the day to be gettin into all that.'

He laughs. 'You said you may have something for me.'

'Are you up for a bitta work?'

'I could be, it depends what it is. At the moment I've got funds going round in circles down in the Far East, nice fronts, a very tidy piece of work. It'll be very good when I get to collect.'

'Then this could be a bitta you, Cody.'

I explain the problem with Charlie and Kinky while we eat. He seems to think that it'll be easy.

'Why?'

'Desperadoes. If you make yourself busy with a bitta wedge, someone to watch your back, these fuckin drugsters will tell you anything. Soon as you get a sniff you follow it relentlessly.'

'Jimmy Price will pay a bonus when she's back in the bosom

98

of her family and I'll give you that bonus and I'll give you two grand cashish over the top.'

'How much is the bonus?'

'He didn't say.'

'That's no fuckin good.'

'I didn't wanna push it. To be honest I just want her found. I'd pay to get it done.'

'So he's asked you to do this for him, and you just wanna slip through and get someone else on board to do it.'

'I would do it myself but I've got shitloads goin on already.'

'But if this is payment by results I've got no idea what I'm workin for. Jimmy Price, the slippery bastard, could buy ya a shandy and a cheese roll and call it a bonus, thinkin he's a Don. You gotta be serious about readies, sort out all the shit before you start work, otherwise people start fallin out.'

'Cody, I'll tell you what I'm gonna do. I'll put up seven grand of my own for you to find the bird and, if you find her, I'll bin the bonus from Jimmy Price.'

'So if he drops you ten kay, let's just say, then you're three grand ahead mate.'

'That's right. So it's make-your-mind-up time, Cody, but you can't have it both ways. Let me tell you something as well. If Jimmy gives me a bunce, he'll just let me have a key tax-free. Then I've gotta get my loot away from Morty cos he'll think he's entitled to a good lunch outta it, so this little outing could end up costin me money. This could be the easiest few grand you ever earned. It could even be a laugh.'

'Behave. Don't graft a grafter.'

'Have you got readies, Mister Garret?'

'I've always got readies. I'll tell you what, I'll take the seven-grand option. Three and a half a body.'

'How the fuck do you work that out?'

'Three and a half for Kinky, three and a half for the tricky princess.'

'I don't give a fuck about him. I only want—'

'You gotta give me a squeeze, mate. Look, I'm not even sure I wanna go huntin around lookin for anyone. I'm back here on

99

holiday, catch the end of the football season, bitta shoppin and birdin it up, you can get tired of all those Oriental –'

'Okay, Cody, three and a half a body, the bottle gets ya seven. It'll be a bitta pocket money for ya.'

'The most cunning clown to walk the face of the earth,' says Cody.

'Who is?' I'm puzzled.

'Jimmy fuckin Price.'

Our noses are about six inches apart and we're talkin in whispers. Cody looks serious all of sudden.

'I'll do this bitta business, I'll try my hardest, for you, but I don't wanna have to be talking to Price. I'll do it as a favour to you.'

'Thanks. I appreciate it.'

'Well, you've helped me out with tank money in the past.'

'I've got some photos, info and that.'

As I pass the envelope across the table I feel a sense of relief.

'Be careful of Price, mate. I wouldn't wanna see you get in any trouble,' says Cody.

'I kinda worked that out on my own.'

'Be very careful. Is Geno still with Price?'

'He's like his right-hand man. He really likes the geezer. He's very loyal.'

'And loyalty's a very admirable quality in people but it can be a stupid thing as well as a good thing. It can blind you to facts.'

'Very true,' I says.

'I've known Gene since I was a kid. I used to run to the bookies for him from the Old White Bear. If he won he'd collect the winnings himself but he'd always bung ya a fiver. You could buy a pair of shoes for a ching back then.'

'And still have change for a slap-up meal and the pictures up West.'

'Don't take the piss. Gene's loyalty goes way back, to the regime of Ol' Dewey. He picked up Geno when he was on his arse, always laggin drunk. His missus had taken the kids back to Ireland, back to Donegal, left Geno in a right state.'

'How many kids has he got?'

100

'Three. Daughters.'

'I can't imagine Gene as a family man.'

'Well, neither could his missus so she jogged on back home.'

'He never talks about havin kids.'

'Gene don't talk about anythin much, does he, he's the fuckin closed book. Anyway, it's not the way with those tea caddies. They send a few bob home if they've got it, spend their lives pissin it up and greetin in their beer.'

'They're either fightin or cryin and they do love a melancholy air on the jukebox.'

'That's how Old Dewey and Pricey got Geno on the book. He's battered the shit outta these six mad Galway geezers, the whole western tear-up scenario, chairs going over people's heads, geezers going through windows, and he's done the fuckin lot of them. He's wound up cos the missus has gone home, he's totally on his arse, ain't workin, ain't havin a wash, a shave, nothin, he's right confused cos he's always been a good provider, out real early in the mornin, ganger-man on the railway, but that ain't enough for her, can't talk about it to nobody around him cos, well, you don't, do you, a fight's started and he's created havoc, absolute chaos, wouldn't stop even after they'd surrendered, waved the white flag, fought the cozzers to a stand-still and everything. They had to get the SPG, as it was back then, and even they had the full-scale battle with him to get him in the van, a couple of them went to the blood factory. As an audition it was quite spectacular.'

'I can imagine it. I bet he's a total bread and butter in the John-Wayne-style straightener.'

'So they've spotted his potential as a fearless, completely loyal, no questions asked, no talkin back bodyguard-cum-how's-your-father.' He gives me a little wink. 'He was Dewey's Foreign Legion and now he's Jimmy Price's Foreign Legion.'

'I don't follow, Cody.'

'Well, some French king, back in the day, couldn't or wouldn't trust his own armies, thought they would turn him over if they could, so he got his sidekicks to recruit a whole

101

army of foreign mercenaries who don't give a fuck about the internal bish, bash, bosh of France just as long as they get their readies.'

'You're sayin that Gene's a mercenary?'

'Not exactly. What I'm sayin is that he don't get into the politics. Where there's people there's politics. Gene is loyal to Jimmy P. cos Jimmy P. showed him a shitload of compassion.'

'No doubt in a very calculated and cunnin way.'

'You've been payin attention. And he needed a guy like him what with Crazy Larry on the fuckin rampage. But what Geno, who's a lovely man, don't get me wrong, I've got great time for him, don't understand is that any debt he owes Jim has been paid over and over again.'

'But he still hangs in there with him.'

'Sure, cos Jimmy still feeds him something. He make him feel wanted, like he's good at his job. It's funny what motivates people. Even big old lumps like Gene are like kids themselves, if you look behind the façades. Maybe he's lookin for, deep down, approval from grown-ups, something he didn't have as a kid.'

'Hold fire, Cody. You've gone a bit too fuckin Californian for me all of a sudden. Have you been at those airport psychology books again?'

He laughs. 'I have more than a layman's interest in knowin what makes people tick.'

'I think Geno's a lot smarter than we give him credit for. He plays up to Jimmy as much as Jimmy plays up to him. They keep each other sweet.'

'It's a deal, like any relationship.'

'Fuckin hell, thank you Professor Cody fuckin Garret for your expert insight.'

'I'd make a very good head-shrinker, a fuckin natural.'

'I think you're right.'

'I fuckin know I am.'

'Listen, one thing, Cody, if I'm not around and you catch up with Charlie and Kinky you get in touch with Gene or Morty, okay?'

'If I catch up with Charlie and Kinky and you're not around I'll wait until you are, okay?'

'Okay.'

'I ain't gonna get into any heroics. I'll tell ya where you can collect the Richard, and that'll be my end of the deal. I'll do me best for ya, scout's honour.'

'Scout's honour and seven large.'

He laughs. 'Now I've got to get a haircut round the corner. You could use a trim. This gaff'll interest ya.'

'Why?'

'It's a crack-up. It's a right old-fashioned barber's. It's got royal warrants all over the windows, it's the real McCoy. Have a haircut, go on, I'll treat you. You get the meal and I'll pay in the barber's.'

'I've got things I should be doin.'

'Oh, fuck all that. You could learn somethin in a gaff like this.'

'Like what?'

'You'll see.'

We arrive at a shop with an old wooden front. The windows, plastered with crowns and crests in goldleaf, are crammed full of shaving and grooming paraphernalia, leather and pewter flasks, silver-framed pictures of pheasants and pike, all things wholesome and countrified. Cody's talking the same as me but as the door opens, a bell rings, we're in the shop, he's straight back into his swell's voice.

'Hello, Sir,' says the woman behind the jump.

'Hugo, please, Hugo,' says Cody.

'Yes, Sir.'

'I need a haircut but I'm afraid I don't have an appointment, been away, down China way, Honkers.'

'Are you known, Sir?'

'But of course, Jenkins usually does the old thatch.'

'I'll see if Mister Jenkins is available, Sir.'

'Okay, very good.'

Off she goes to find Jenkins. The inside of the shop is like the outside, all old dark wood and display cases from ceiling to floor with cut-throat razors, shaving brushes, leather strops for sharpening the cut-throats, mirrors, hairbrushes and all the pukka kit for a gentleman's grooming. The whole wall behind the ramp's piled high with bottles and boxes, tubes and jars of colognes, aftershaves, creams, hair tonics. The whole place smelt of the aristocracy, of richness, luxury and indulgence.

The woman returns. 'Mister Jenkins will be with you shortly, Sir. He's just finishing with a client now.'

Then a guy who I guess is Jenkins comes out from the back. He's seeing the punter off the premises, wishing him a safe journey back down to the Shires, bowing and tugging at his forelock, asking the old geezer if there's anything else he requires. It would serve him right if the old boy wanted his arse rimming. At the door the guy pushes a pound coin into his damp palm and Jenkins pulls the forelock harder and bows lower.

'Thank you, Sir, thank you.'

Get a fuckin grip, pal. It's only a quid.

'Ahh, young Lord Hugo,' says Jenkins, spinning round to greet Cody. 'How are you, Sir? You look well.'

'And so do you, Jenkins. Need the old thatch tidying up. Any chance?'

'Of course, Sir. We can always fit you in, Lord Hugo,' says Jenkins.

'Oh, and this is my very good chum from the pampas, Pepe Gon-za-lez, doesn't speak a bloody word of English. Tell a lie. He does understand one word. Don't say –'

Cody mouths the word 'dago' behind his hand so Jenkins and all the people behind the counter can see. They laugh, slightly embarrassed.

'Pepe's a bloody polo mercenary, from Chile, doing the tour. Bloody good player, though. Needs a bit of a trim, any chance? I said you need a bit of a trim, Pepe,' he says, raising his voice to me. I'm giving it a large dose of gracious, oui, key, yes, good, thank yous in my best Chilean accent and nodding my head.

'Oh, I'm sure it can be arranged, Sir, Lord Hugo. We're not very busy at the moment. Please come through.'

He leads us into the rear of the shop and it opens up into the barber's with about eight leather chairs in two rows on either side. Four of the chairs are occupied. A couple of the old guys are tilted back having a wet shave with lethal-looking cut-throat razors while girls give them manicures and generally pamper them. On the walls are testimonials, photos and letters of thanks from guys who are historical figures, Churchill and JFK. The place is like a museum of famous statesmen and here's me and Cody being shown to our seats. Fuck only knows who's sat here before us. For a wonderful split second I've got a gushing feeling of what a great place London Town is. You can cash your giro cheque in Tottenham or Brixton, Kilburn or Aldgate in the morning, jump on the Oxo cube, come here and spend the afternoon ironing it out, getting pampered and rubbing shoulders with peers of the realm and old money and still have time to be back at the dole shop before closing time to report Monte Cairo missing. I get a rush of civic pride as the barber sets about my hair, knowing that we can, and do, rise above our station in life.

'A littlesome, no, trim, yes,' I'm saying in a pidgin-English. 'Lord Hugo say trim isa dix millimetres, no littlesome.' I'm placing my thumb and forefinger about half an inch apart to show him how much I want off. He asks me if I talk English.

'No, Señor, Spanish, I'ma speak –'

'You're right there, chum.'

'I'ma specking Spanish? Yes? Chile?'

'It is round the Khyber Pass. Now listen, you, shut the fuck up, okay you oily bastard, you comprehendi? Shut the fuck up or I'll shave you like a chicken.'

'Trim, yes, dix millimetres, good.'

'For fuck sake shut up, you don't have to understand anything, you wop cunt.'

Further up I can hear Hugo ranting about giving Hong Kong back to the slopeheads, how on give-it-back day we should tell the Communist bastards 'to go fuck themselves' and if they don't like it we should tell the buggers to 'fuck off, stick to cooking beanshoots'. I can hear a couple of the old pops agreeing. One goes as far as to say that if there were more young people like Hugo around 'we wouldn't be in the damned mess we're in now'. Jenkins is agreeing all the way but he would have agreed to let young Lord Hugo come round his house and chop the wife and teenage daughters at one sitting.

'Trim, I trim, we trim, you trim,' I'm saying.

'Stop fuckin talking, you bastard,' he's hissing.

I'm picking up bits of cut hair and holding them up to the light, measuring it, estimating its length.

'Trim isa dix millimetres, no?'

'Fuck millimetres, you can't even see 'em.'

I can see what Cody gets outta infiltrating the upper echelons of the status quo. Cody's in the chair with his feet up, boots off, having the works, shampoo, haircut, wet shave, hot towels, manicure and buff up. He's pontificating on an array of subjects, including law and order, where he thinks a hard line approach to the problem is the only way, especially fraudsters and drug dealers, let's try a return to boot camps, transportation and penal servitude. The old boys mumble in agreement. The geezer finishes cutting my hair and he hasn't done bad at all. He finishes up, mumbling to himself.

With the job done, me and Cody are back in the shop having a load-up. I'm taking advantage of the fact that Cody's paying to get about a hundred quid's worth of tackle, aftershaves and shampoos, on Cody's bill. If he's bothered he ain't showing it. He pulls out a fat snakeskin wallet and pays the bill, about two-fifty, in crispy cash-point-fresh twenty-pound notes. We leave with great fuss. Cody puts a tenner into Jenkins' sweaty palm and I give my man about twenty-seven pence in shrapnel and my biggest dago smile.

'Anyway, Lord Hugo, nice to see you and stay in touch.'

What's the Big Deal?

I've put Tammy's number into my phone three times under
different names, kept the original bitta card in a safe place, just
in case I lose my phone or it decides to erase all the numbers.
I've even taken the precaution of writing it in pencil on the wall
behind the sofa cos in the past I've lost birds' numbers and it's
driven me mad and I desperately don't wanna lose this one. I'm
about to press the little green button to connect me to her
number, to arrange a little baked-bean, my old gent's getting
twitchy at the very thought, when as if by magic the phone
starts to ring. Gene's mobile number appears on the screen.

'Hello, Gene. You all right?'

'Fine. Where are you?'

'Location is corner of Dover Street and Piccadilly, over.'

'Don't fuck about. Where's that?'

'You don't know where Piccadilly is, Gene?'

'Only in Monopoly. If I knew I wouldn't ask.'

'It's in the West End.'

'If I ever ask you that question again, son, just say "West
End", okay?'

'Okay, Gene.'

'We gotta collect ya. Your mates wanna chat tonight. I ain't
comin there to collect ya, it'll take for ever. Get a cab up to
Highbury and Islington tube station.'

'It's quicker to get a tube from here.'

'Then get a fuckin tube. Fuckin hell.'

He can be very fuckin moody, Gene, Pink Panther one
minute, Snappy Crocodile the next. It comes with hanging out
with Jimmy Price too much. I can hear him lighting up.

'Where will I meet you, Gene?'

'There's a bar outside the station.'

'What's it called?'

'Don't matter what's it's called. You get off the fuckin train,

107

up the stairs, out the station and there it is. You could fuckin fall into it.'

'When?'

'I'll see you there in twenty minutes, half-five.'

'I bet it's really dirty and 'orrible.'

'Will I meet you in a fuckin launderette somewhere then?'

'They always are, boozers outside railway stations.'

'You can be really fuckin anal sometimes, son.'

'What's that mean? Queer or something? I bet I've fucked more –'

But he's gone. I click the phone shut. That's what it's like in this game, someone gives you a hard time, you just give it to someone else. If in twenty minutes I asked Gene what he meant, people would holler I was bearing a grudge, he wouldn't remember or he'd tell me to fuck off. I had big plans for tonight as well.

Thirty minutes later I'm in the bar. As Gene said it's right on top of the station. It's lively, clean, but there's no sign of Gene. Fifteen minutes go by before Morty comes walking in and tells me that Gene and Metal Mickey are going round and round the roundabout. We walk outside and seconds later Gene's BMW pulls up with Mickey driving. We head up the Holloway Road through the early evening traffic. Gene turns back in his seat and explains that he's arranged a meet with the Yahoos in a lock-up they've got up in Edmonton, just to see what they've got, what sorta money they're lookin for, to get the full SP. They're anxious to get things moving. I've got my little bag of gentleman's toiletries, costing a hundred quid, sitting on my lap. Gene looks at them and raises one eyebrow. It's not the right time to be pulling him about that anal remark.

Nobody's saying much, there's not a lot to say. Geno's playing a tape of Johnny Cash, *Live at San Quentin*. Metal Mickey can't drive for shit, thinks he's driving a tank. I ain't gonna be the one to tell him cos he don't say shit, don't say a word, but he puts out a vibe of pure sadistic intent, unquestioning obedience and loyalty. He reminds me of something outta one of those sci-fi movies about dodgy androids whose wonky wiring has led to a malfunction in the communication circuits.

I'm sat behind him looking at the back of his head, the kinda head that iron bars would bounce off, leaving the poor guy holding the bar with sore hands from the vibrations. His neck is the same size as his head but he's got the most tiny piggy ears, like a child's. Mickey's ex-army and most ex-army types I've met are wankers. They all leave the forces thinking that they're going to set up the elite little security outfits, looking out for pop stars and other assorted VIPs, and half of them end up as shop-cops, long hours, moody uniform, patrolling the booze aisle down the supermarket. Some of them end up doing bits of freelance work and they've got the audacity to look down their noses at ya, like they're better than this.

If you get captured by Mickey on a bad night, when he's had about ten pints with chasers, he's lagging, all Queen and Country, up the Union Jack, he's a right pest. He loves to tell stories about how happy he was back in the Old Regiment over in Ireland, the best days of his life, Paddy bashing, fuckin Fenians and cuntin Prods as well, cos they're all just shit-shovelling Micks, ain't they, all the same. He'll regale us with his tales of smashing up old biddies' houses for a bit of a crack on a Saturday night. Nuisance or not it's good to have him riding shotgun tonight.

We drive into a small industrial estate just off the North Circular Road in Edmonton. Mickey slows the motor so he can read the numbers stencilled on the roller shutters of each unit. When he finds the one he wants he stops the motor and gives Geno a tiny nod of the head. We get out. The two boys are looking off in all directions, down the street, along the rooftops and over into the big bitta wasteland the other side of the wire fence, but everything looks peaceful. Mickey thinks he's back on the Falls Road. Gene and Mickey, satisfied, lean back into the motor and have the rubber mats up from under the front seats, rummage about, and when they come out of the motor again they've both got bulges under their jackets, the kind that are meant to be noticed. Mick's got a nice content look on his face, anyone wants treatment can have it. He shoots me a wink. I feel better having these head-the-balls watching cos I wouldn't fancy my chances on my lonesome with the Banditos.

109

Gene kicks the bottom of the shutter three times, a door in it opens and we step inside. It's quite dark at first. My eyes take a while to adjust. The whole space, it's bigger on the inside than it looks on the outside, is stacked with boxes from floor to ceiling, except in the middle where there's a scattering of chairs and a huge table. It's like an office set-up has been plonked down from nowhere, a few phones, fax machines and a lorry-load of paperwork, neatly stacked and filed, well organised. It could be that someone's up to a little bittov the old pile-it-up-and-clear-it-out fraud.

I'm relieved to see that of the three guys from their team here, I know two, Big Frankie and JD, and they're about the two most sensible. The other one, the one who opened the door to us, is only the gofer. It's a relief that they haven't sent any of the more belligerent cunts to organise the trade cos we'd all be here all night while they acted the fool, did their Jekyll original-gangster impression for our benefit. JD especially, who seems to be in charge, you can talk realistically to. He's no mug, no walk-over, but he ain't gonna let a little thing like pride or stubbornness get in the way of making a nice bitta wedge.

As much as I don't like working with these reprobates we could all have a right tickle here. If everything goes down as I'm planning it we could have a right touch. I personally wanna come outta this thing with about, at the very worst, a hundred large to squirrel away overseas with the rest of my pension. That figure could be anything up to double or go to the quarter million, in which case I'd be chuckling, hoping Cody does the biz, and booking a nice long holiday somewhere. If this outfit have got two million pills then every penny we can nick comes to twenty thousand pounds in the final count-up. I can't calculate anything until I've got a buyer either and there's only a couple of teams, or cartels if you like, in the country who I would trust to even mention this parcel to.

'Gary, get the chaps a beer,' says Big Frankie.

Gary the gofer opens the brand-new fridge that's been set up in the corner. It's like an off-licence fridge with different brands of beer on each shelf. In the door there's cans of Cola and a mouldy bottle of milk.

110

'Do you wanna a beer?' says JD.

'Do you have any water?'

'Only in the tap in the khazi.' He laughs, tres amused by his own little joke. 'No, hang on mate, I'm only joking. Do we have any water, Gary?'

'No. We've got a Coke. Will that do?'

'Yeah, that's fine, Gary,' I reply.

Gary sorts everyone out. I sit down on one side of the desk and JD sits on the other. He lights a Benson, breathes deeply and exhales long, gives the back of his neck a little massage, rolls his head from side to side and takes a long hit on a can of Stella. He's on edge, anxious to get the best possible result.

'Okay, JD. What you got?'

'Two million ecstasy tablets with a high level of MDMA.'

Very Nice. He's pleased with himself.

'And what do you want from us?'

'We don't want anything from you. We want to know if you want them off us.'

'Well, maybe, maybe not. As I understood it, you want us to shift them, sharpish, correct?'

He nods.

'One thing,' I say. 'This is just me being nosey, but why did you get hold of so many if you couldn't shift them?'

'That's none of your business. Don't get busy, okay?'

He gives me a couple of seconds of harsh eye-to-eye contact to make his point. He's sitting back in his chair getting twitchy, huffing and puffing. I imagine Morty doing that thing he does with his eyes, a roll to heaven. I lean into the table, elbows on it, put on my soothing voice.

'One minute, now hold up JD, mate. Please, and it's important we both understand this, JD, I ain't gonna take anything you say to me while we're sat down here personal. Please don't take anything I say as a dig.'

'I'm sweet.'

'This is business, Jay.' Hands up, palms out, leaning back, pacifying gesture. 'Is there more where these came from?'

'There could be, yeah, very possibly,' he says, grinning to himself now.

'Now, why don't you hold fire with them and just let them go, say hundred thou a week?'

'No way. We wanna take our money out right now.'

'But that means knockin them out in one big hit.'

'That's the way we wanna play it.'

'That means flooding the market, dropping the price. Two million Es is about how many pills get launched over a week-end in Britain, that market is covered. If a firm like yours let go another two mill it would send the whole thing crooked.'

'You guys wouldn't want to buy them and let them go a hundred thou at a time, would yer?'

'That means tying up cash. We could maybe place them with some people we know but that would mean drivin the price way down. They'd want them for pennies.'

'I thought people pegged the market?'

'That's a myth, JD. I wish it was true.'

JD signals Gary that he wants another beer. He crushes his empty can, slings it into the corner. I really wanna turn this into a buyer's market without scaring them off altogether. I really wanna do this deal.

'That watch, it's nice, a Rolex?' I say.

'Course it's a fuckin Rolex.'

JD's watch is one of those real gaudy, opulent numbers, all diamonds on the face and a great chunky gold and steel strap. It's snide. Even those Arab camel-drivers up the Edgware Road would have said it was over the top.

'What did it cost?'

'Well, somebody sorted me out. It's worth about twelve grand but it cost me four and a quarter.'

He's looking at me quizzically.

'Well, I'd argue with that.'

'You'd argue with anything, pal. What you mean, anyway?'

'You say it's worth twelve grand but I'd say it's only worth what someone's prepared to pay you for it. You see what I mean?'

'No. You've got me baffled.' He looks it.

'What I'm sayin is the value of anything, bags of pills, gold bullion, powders, human life, even, motors, houses and Rolex

112

watches are only worth what I can get someone to pay me for them. It's no good me pegging the price high if the market says low.'

'Are you saying my fuckin watch ain't worth shit?'

'No, no, I'm just trying to explain the market value of anything is determined by the rarity, the scarcity of the article, the vendor's willingness to part with his cash. In other words, market forces.'

'You're not tryin to tell me that I've been had over?'

'No way, JD. You got the bargain.'

'Yeah?'

'I'm only tryin to explain that the price I put on your truckload of pills is governed by loadsa considerations. Think about it, you got legality, rarity, quality, quantity, availability, seasonal adjustments, currency fluctuations, adverse publicity, police activity–'

'Listen.' JD leans into the table, locks his eyes into mine, gives a little twitch of the head and points at his Rolex. 'Do you like this watch?'

'Yeah, it's lovely.'

'That's okay then.' He leans back and spits.

JD's brooding, arms folded across his chest like a big sulky baby. His outfit have sent him up to work out a deal with the smug Swell Mob and they've talked to him like he's a fuckin teabag, a wanker, told him he's gotta take any deal that they sling 'im. JD's disappointed cos his job was to organise the pay day but it's looking like they're going to be getting less than they thought, still a very tidy sum.

'Listen, JD, we all want the best deal but it ain't gonna just drop into our lap. I promise you this. I'll try and get a deal that makes everybody happy.'

'You do that, pal, you do that,' he says.

'You gotta trust us but if we have to cobble together great lumps of cash money to buy the goods, it means findin great lumps of readies –' I'm fuckin about with a calculator the whole time just for fun, punching in numbers and making out I'm doing calculations in my nut '– and that means pullin it outta of

113

other things for a while, it's very disruptive. It would help the price if we could have bail on the goods.'

'No way.'

'Hear me out. I'm only askin you to listen to somethin. If you could get your team to agree to givin us credit it makes the whole business a lot more attractive.'

'We want cash. C.O.D.'

'What I'm sayin is for the sake of a few days it could mean as much as twenty-five per cent more in the final tally. That's a lotta loot.'

'We want cash or nothin, okay?'

'You realise for the sake of a few days you could be muggin yourself of half a million pounds.'

He laughs. 'This geezer's deaf. You tell 'im something but he don't hear ya, just goes on and on. You lot make a pile of money for makin a few phonecalls. You can earn it, you pull up ya cash up front, then you can do what ya like.'

'Jay, I'll bring you a price and then we can talk again, be patient, give me until Thursday or Friday.'

He leans over, grabs my hand, squeezing it hard. 'I won't say it's been a pleasure doin business cos you're fuckin hard work.'

'I'll take some samples and be on my way. I've got to get busy.'

JD gives Gary a little nod. He disappears round the back of the wall of boxes and comes back with a brown medicine bottle and hands it to me. It's labelled multi-vitamins and minerals, high potency, one hundred tablets. I open it and shake out a couple of the pills. They look real fuckin serious, the size of the top joint of a little finger. I haven't seen Es like this in years.

'Let's hope we can do some business,' I say.

We get out at last. It looks increasingly like we can have a nice big pay day. It's a drag they haven't agreed to bail cos cobblin together big amounts is a problem for us. Going to Jimmy for cash is always a non-starter. It could be done but it meant letting other firms in on your moves. I put the jar snugly in my inside pocket. It feels like the tip of a seriously lucrative iceberg. I wanna do some serious calculations but Mort's anxious to know what I think we could move the parcel on for. I

114

have to tell him to be patient and get Mickey to drop me outside Seven Sisters tube station.

'I think you upset them back there tonight,' says Mort as I get out.

'Fuck 'em,' I reply.

I jump on a train and it takes me about ten minutes into the Cross, straight upstairs, cabs waiting and nobody in the queue. I jump in the first cab and tell the cabbie to take me down to Hoxton Market. This is where Sir Alex, chief chemical taster, resides. This is a boy who knows his drugs. I hope he's in. I'm sure he'll be glad to see me, he usually is. I always check things with Alex cos he's straight with me. If it's shit merchandise he'll tell me so and if it's pukka he'll tell me that as well.

The lights are on and there's somebody home. I'm right, he's glad to see me. Alex gives me a big fucking bear hug and a big old slap on the back. He drags me up the stairs like I'm his long lost brother. I ain't seen him for about six weeks but you'd think it's six years. He wants to drag me into the front room to introduce me to his entourage but I ain't really got time.

'How are you?' says Sir Alex.

'Busy, really fuckin busy.'

'But you're okay?'

'Yeah, I guess so. Tricks are good but I ain't got time to enjoy things. Anyway, what are you lot up to tonight?'

'One of the guys is playin later and we're gonna go down and hang out.'

'Good, cos I got some stuff that needs checkin out on a scale of one to ten. You know the score.'

'I sure do.'

'The geezers who gave me this reckon it's a bit fuckin special, really powerful, old-school, like the stuff from eighty-seven, eighty-eight.'

'They all say that.'

'But check it out, okay Alex?'

'Sure.'

'I need to know about midday tomorrow, Alex.'

'If you wanna hang about an hour you can know now.'

'Ain't got time.'

Twenty minutes later I'm indoors. Morty's left a cryptic message – he's had a word, we're going on a trip, pack a bag, meaning we're going up north, saying he'll be round at one in the afternoon, meaning nine in the morning. I put the brown sample bottle in the bathroom in among all the other medicines and aftershaves. There don't seem to be much point plugging them. I eat, have a roasting hot shower, pour myself a brandy and crush half a Valium into it to really switch off cos I know if I don't I won't get a fuckin wink of sleep all night. After a couple of gulps of the rich spirit it hits me it's been a long day so I turn it in at five-past eleven, which is some kinda record for me. I really believe in beauty sleep.

Tuesday
Oop North

Morty just grunts 'Okay' as I get in. He don't look up from his paper. Mister Clark's got a brand-new, rented, top-of-the-range Rover using a moody licence and the credit card. In an emergency we simply walk away from it. It's good that Clarkie's driving cos he can work a motor like it's part of him, the ride is tranquil, not like Morty's crazy, hurry-up-and-go driving, racing between traffic lights at sixty miles an hour like we had old bill up our tails. Clarkie goes on those advanced driving courses with ex-old-bill instructors, the kind those driver-cum-body-guards go on. You learn how to avoid getting your charge kidnapped, pursuit evasion. He picks up a lot of insight into how the Other People work. Clarkie's driving round in big circles trying to work out if we're being ready-eyed. A regional crime squad team will use anything up to six motors, in relays. Local gathers will only have the impounded shit-heap motors they've got knocking about in the yard. Morty's obviously told Clarkie that he wants some peace and quiet, so Clarkie's taken a powder.

Clarkie times traffic lights, holding back or speeding up, so that we get over exactly on the amber light, then turning sharp to the left or the right, nothing illegal, but anyone following would have to do the same and show out. As we sail over, Clarkie's checking the rear-view mirror to see if anyone's jumping red lights. He drives round the same roundabouts three and four times with his eyes glued to the rear-view. We cut into Regent's Park and round the inner circle. It's bright, fresh and there's cherry blossom on the trees, the world is coming alive all over again. We stop for petrol in Hendon. Clarkie's checking the tyre pressure, the oil, the water, but most of all he's checking the other cars parked up on the quiet street. He goes inside, pays, and comes back with bottles of water and packets of snout and we head for the dearly beloved Motorway One.

I fuckin hate leaving London. I love it for different reasons to the cor-blind-me-gov, we-woz-at-our-best-in-the-blitz, ain't-it-a-bloody-shame-they've-done-away-wiv-rationin gang. I love it cos it is so brand-new, vibrant and nicely anonymous. People are too busy to be curtain-twitchers. Looking out the back window of the Rover, looking at the signs on the other carriageway, watching the miles to London increasing, I always get a feeling of sadness. Clarkie keeps the motor at a constant hundred all the way. I'm just looking out the window and dreaming, plotting, going over the business with the Yahoos last night. Certain things don't really add up, like what they're doing with all those pills, when they've got no idea what they're worth. If they had come to us a couple of months ago and said they were going to manufacture a huge batch and would we be up for helping shift them, that would make sense. It's like in any business, you always have your distribution in place before you go calling on your stock. I always know where the oats is going before I call it on. I wouldn't ask Gene to send round seventy kilos and then try and riddle out what to do with it.

Suddenly Morty puts on a drum and bass tape, cranks it up and starts to tell me and Mister Clark that our youth is wasted on us. Clarkie tells him that a man of forty-five should be at home listening to a nice bitta Nat King Cole and smoking a lickle draw instead of tooting powders, listening to jungle and chasing young Richards.

Around Birmingham, Clarkie's telling us a story about these four Turkish guys who've chipped in to fuck this brass, score for half an hour, up on Green Lanes. She's doing the biz in a flat upstairs from one of those social clubs they shift the brown outta. They all pile upstairs and it turns out it's one of the guys' sister.

'So did he still fuck her?'

'Well, would you?' says Clarkie.

'I don't know what his sister looks like. Did he? I bet his mates all fucked her,' says Morty.

118

'That'd freak ya right out,' says Clarkie.

'He's probably already fucked her,' says Morty. Another hour, off the motorway, into the outskirts of Manch, beautiful leafy suburbs at first then through the lively Asian part of town. I can smell the spices from the car. There's signposts on the roundabouts and buses saying 'To the city centre', always a bad omen that for the Cockney abroad. I look at my watch. It's twelve-fifteen. Alex is late in ringing. Soon we're off the main drag, down into terraced, two-up, two-down houses. He slows the motor cos the streets are tiny and the dwellings packed close together. It starts to get grim. Every third house is bolted up with steel shutters on the windows like the former occupants have simply snapped and shipped out in the middle of the night. Satellite television dishes are secured at the very tops of chimney stacks on the ends of long extension poles, and DIY, install-it-yourself alarm systems seem to have been a popular Christmas present. A couple of houses on the corner have been burnt out. Parked up, side by side outside these gaffs are rust-buckets, held together with spit and gum, and some real lemon, double-flash gangsta rides. Morty's surveying the scene from the front seat, taking it in, noting the slightest detail, like a five-star general driving through a defeated land.

He spots a papershop and tells Clarkie to pull over cos he wants some chewing gum but really he just wants a mooch about. Morty calls me into the loppy-pop to show me all the choccie bars and sweeties, under glass like jewels on Old Bond Street. The Asian shopkeepers look scared. Their eyes follow us everywhere, double-edgy, thinking we're gonna rob them. Maybe we do look sinister in our raincoats and shades. Morty senses this and talks to them very slow, trying to be gentle and reassuring, saying please and thank you, but it only sounds more spooky and threatening.

We go outside. In the short time we were in the shop, a gaggle of kids have gathered round the motor checking it out. These kids are fearless on their own turf. Black kids, white kids who look Irish with red Barnets, mixed-race kids with dreads, white-on-white kids who look apple-white, going on luminous. Kids of ten and twelve, smoking salmon and spitting non-stop, with faces like hardened old geezers. Clarkie's leaning against the motor watching them drag their grubby mitts down the brand-spanking-new paintwork leaving sticky marks, deliberately trying to provoke him, but Mister Clark don't bite. The sad thing is that in a few short years these kids will be real live grown-ups and some may escape, like our man Ronnie, but most will end up fucked-up one way or another, spitting at the world, the girls with more chavvies than they can handle or love and the geezers doing hard time, inside or outside the shovel. One kid, a good-looking mixed-raced kid, is screwing me, with hate and envy in his eyes, like I ain't never been where he is now. I feel like saying, 'You look at me like I put you there and now you look at me like I give a shit.'

One kid asks Clarkie for a fag.

'You shouldn't be smokin son.'

'Fook off. You fookin Cockneys?'

'Might be,' says Clarkie.

'Fookin watch yaselfs round 'ere,' says his pal in his nasal voice, miming a handgun and shooting Clarkie with it. Morty laughs hysterically. I laugh at Morty laughing.

'Charmin, the hostile natives, Mister Clark.'

'You know something, Mister Mortimer, I think we've been ambushed by Apaches. I think they're gangsters,' moodying he's scared.

Morty gets a twenty outta his pocket and shows it to the kids. He rolls it into a ball and throws it into the middle of them and immediately they start fighting amongst themselves, except for a couple on the outside who know they don't stand a chance. One kid emerges victorious and he dances away from the rest of the crowd. In the meantime Morty has pulled another note and slung it, but this time it catches on the slight breeze and flies off down the street with the kids in hot pursuit.

Morty thinks this is splendid entertainment but points at us to get back in the Rover, to saddle-up while all the commotion's going on. As we pull away I spot the handsome kid standing on the pavement outside the papershop, uninvolved in the mêlée. As we go round the corner he makes a pistol shape with his hand, takes aim and shoots. I pretend to duck but his face remains stony hard.

Ronnie could never bear to drag himself away from this area cos he knows everything and everybody there is to know. We've done business with Ronnie and guys he works with on and off for the last five years. If something good comes our way, we give them a shout and vice versa. Morty had arranged on the phone last night to come up and see the chaps. The jellied eels, pie-and-mash fraternity totally underestimate the intelligence and cunning of the northern boys. They make the mistake of believing that they have no class but if you do the biz with the right guys they just want the same as your very good self: lotta dollar, peace and quiet. If you judge all northerners by the hordes of football supporters tumbling outta King's Cross and Euston on match days, hooting and pissing everywhere, you will only draw a negative conclusion.

These guys, Trevor, Ronnie, Shanks and Victor, are bigtime, big hitters, bigger than our little team. They control a large chuck of the wholesale business in north-west England, which is very impressive. A lotta people think they're buying straight off the boat, but in fact it comes through these guys. Dudes who hate them with a vengeance, cos of envy or fear, who wouldn't give 'em the steam of their piss, buy pills and powders from them through third parties. These are the kinda guys who could buy the two million pills, hold them up, sit on them, and not have to worry about cash flow.

As we pull up, Ronnie's out with his coat on, ready to go. He jumps in the back and it's handshakes all round. He's relaxed and in no hurry, scrubbed and groomed, a class act. Ronnie's telling me that he's got three houses knocked into one and they each weigh him in at about twelve gee each, so for thirty-six kay you got yourself a palace. In a war-zone, I'm thinking. The hounds round here ain't dressed right if they ain't carrying metal, and are reckless with the firepower, shooting each other up, kidnapping one other. They treat shooters as a fashion accessory. Ronnie's got the creamy wife, three chavvies, an Italian designer anorak addiction, keeps a low profile and a box at Maine Road. I myself would be very much of the 'born in the north, laughed in the north, cried in the north, love the north but now I gotta great big chunk of readies I'm fuckin straight outta the north to go live in London' school.

We're driving back outta Manchester, following the signs for Liverpool. I always thought they had grown together at some point, into one huge city, but Ronnie thinks that this is blasphemy. There is still a drop of grass between the two and the character of the Manks and the Mickey Mousers is vastly different. The Manks are droll, dry, think every cunt's soft, whereas the Mickeys are the gobby, have-the-crack-at-all-costs, jokers in the pack. Scousers are very similar to true Londoners, flash, up-front and knowing. They both have a natural talent to inspire irritation in plums and logs world-wide.

Mister Clark has done his homework and don't need any directions. After about twenty minutes we pull off the motorway, up the slip, round a mini-roundabout and down a dual carriageway for about three hundred yards before Clarkie rolls the Rover into the car park of a nondescript roadside hotel, the kind businessmen use schlepping round the country. It's a very convenient rendezvous for any kind of business meet, legal or otherwise, being plonked down right between the two cities. We've decided to stay overnight and have booked a suite of rooms. This sounds grander than it actually is. What it is in reality is like renting a three-bedroom flat with a large front room so you can entertain business clients, Brazilian hookers or whoever you want to meet. All the walls are concrete with vinyl wallpaper, all the wood and brass is plastic and everything's got a floral design on it. If you bump into any of the staff in the corridor they grin at you and say, 'Good afternoon, Sir' like they're taking the piss.

Just as we're booking in, Clarkie putting it on the moody card, my phone rings. It's Sir Alex ringing from a call box in Brick Lane. First he's profusely sorry that he's ringing late, it's one twenty-five. I walk back outside to get better reception.

'Hiya,' says Alex.

'How ya doin?'

'Good, mate, good.'

'Those whatsits?'

122

'Good, very good.'

'Really?'

'Yeah, really good.'

'Scale of one to ten?'

'Ten.'

'Really?' Alex takes a bit of impressing.

'You know what you said the other geezer said and I said …'

They were like the old days.

'Oh yeah,' I say.

'Well, he was right.'

'Is that right?'

'Yeah. Dead right,' says Alex laughing.

'That's all right then.' I can hear pips going. 'Thanks for that.'

'No, thank you, ma –'

He's gone. Well, that's good news. If Alex says they're good they must be excellent. Any kiddie shunter's gonna think that they're the best ever. Everything's coming together just beautiful. I can see the end of my career, my final curtain, another quarter of a million quid in the pot, a big, wet goodbye kiss.

Trevor and Shanks from Liverpool, as well as Ronnie's pal Victor, who lives Cheshire way and has made his own way over, are all sitting in the bar already. We ask the lads to give us five minutes and then follow us over. These guys are very heavy and shrewd, very sound, very professional. Between them they've formed an alliance that by rights shouldn't really work, rivalries should turn it ugly. It's mostly down to the force of personality of Trevor that it does work. Trevor is the top kiddie and, strange in a business where everybody is onto the slightest sniff of weakness or kindness, he manages to be a real gentleman. Trevor has gotta be about six-and-a-half foot tall with a really intelligent-looking face for such a big geezer.

The chaps arrive and Shanks brings out his little gadget for detecting listening devices and goes all through the rooms with it. Ronnie and Victor smile thinly, like it's a bit of a private joke between them, Shanks and his toys. He also unplugs the tele-

123

phone cos they can be used to earwig conversations by clever-dick cozzers.

'You never know,' says Shanks, sitting down in an easy chair.

'Is it warm up this way, Trevor?' I ask.

'It's all action, everyone wants a slice.'

'People get envious,' says Ronnie. 'Think they're owed a living, start shooting up the place and then the law do get busy.'

'The filth want it quiet as much as anyone, stands to reason,' says Shanks.

'But some cunts are never satisfied,' says Trevor.

'Same problem wherever you go, greedy cunts,' I say.

'Well, you'd know all about that, wouldn't ya,' says Shanks.

'What's that, bro?' I say, offended.

'Well, not you personally, but that outfit who do your runnins.'

'Who are we talkin about?' says Morty, looking as confused as me.

'That fuckin team from down your end, like you don't know,' says Shanks, getting a bit twitchy.

'But who, Shanks? Fuckin talk to me.' My voice getting higher. Shanks leans forward.

'You mean you don't know?'

'Shanks, until you tell me, how the fuck do I know if I know or not?' I say in a strop. I can smell something nasty on the wind.

'Listen, pal, you ain't talkin to one of yer fuckin Cockney bitches now, okay?' says Shanks, screwing me.

'Shanks, I ain't got a Danny La Rue what it is you're on about. You know something we don't?'

'Right, okay.' He takes a deep breath. 'Your outfit, the Cowboys, the Yahoos, the fuckin Here-we-gos, what the fuck do you call 'em?'

'They ain't our outfit but I know who yer mean.'

'You do, okay? I can't believe you don't know.'

'Fuckin 'ell. How the fuck am I meant to know what you won't tell me?'

'Watch yourself now,' says Shanks with a pointy finger.

124

'Fuckin cool it, brother, you gotta chill,' says Victor to me, talking for the first time. 'Shanks here is tryin to help you if you let him.'

'Shanks,' says Trevor, 'stop fuckin about and explain.'

I'm double-uneasy. I can feel in my gut something slipping away.

'Right,' says Shanks, taking his time. 'We had someone come into us for some acid, but like a real lot, but none of this lot could be bothered so I sorted it out myself, an earner for myself. I nip over to Amsterdam and while I'm over the Dam the gaff is alight with chat about that team from down your end turnin over an ecstasy factory.'

This is very bad news, especially as it's common knowledge up here.

'Like how? I'm sorry, Shanks, but it's important.'

Shanks looks towards Trevor, who gives him a tiny nod.

'They get over there and get busy. They let the right people know that they're in the market for a lotta gear, they put the word out but nobody'll entertain them. They don't trust 'em, too fuckin loud. Eventually they find this German outfit, more like a little army really, who are into the whole Nazi thing, like neo-Nazis.'

'Skinheads?'

'No. They ain't a loada poufs with big boots and braces. They're all suited-up, into the ideology thing but they're into all sorts of shit to raise funds. I know for a fact that the top kiddie, Otto, got the big old townhouse on one of the pukka canals worth about one mill sterling. He's out and about town in the black Porsche with a different bird every night, blonds, naturally, so not all the money gets in the fightin fund.'

'Ain't it a weird thing for neo-Nazis to be into, dealin and makin tablets?'

'Well, not if you think about it. If you wanted to justify it you could say that you're supplyin decadent youth their own poison, letting it corrode their souls, weeding out the weak. To be honest I don't think the top boys give a fuck. Look at the Provos, the IRA, they've got the political firm, the armed wing and the lot who just see it as a money spinner. We sorted this guy out one time, he was UDA or IRA or some fuckin tribe from over there. Trying to talk to him about anything that wasn't gee-gees, didn't wanna know.'

'He was on a bandwagon.'

'Now you got it. See, this right-wing lot in the Dam have got a few shady things going on and if it comes on top they'll be screamin that they're political prisoners and all that shite. A little bird told me that this lot have got websites soliciting contributions for the final armed struggle and they're gettin sent loot from all over the place, but mostly from the States cos they're all gun-crazy loonies over there, ain't they.'

'That's a good idea, to skank money, very sweet and simple,' I say.

'Maybe we should start one,' Morty says to Victor, who's also black.

'The top boys don't want no fuckin race war, no way, they're havin too good a time, it's the last thing they want. The Northern European White Alliance,' declares Shanks, 'they've spotted a gap in the market. Anyway, this firm from down your manor order up a loada stuff. They tell these guys that they only want the pukka gear and they don't mind payin for it. The Germans – I say Germans but this firm's from all over, Scandinavia, Holland, Belgium but mostly Germans – they want a deposit and some people you talk to say they got one and others say they didn't. See, nobody's got the full SP. Next thing, the two outfits are out and about, on the piss, all over Amsterdam which is unusual cos mostly they're dead unfriendly, really ignorant, very loud, very rude.'

'They're pigs,' says Trevor. 'Let's have it right.'

'See, you've got the very top kiddies, who are right smooth, see it as a swindle, then you got the foot soldiers who are real divs and probably believe all that master race bollocks, that's the lot your hoolie mates was out and about with.'

'They ain't our mates,' I say wearily, 'but they would have a lot in common.'

I can see it all now, the pitchers of beer, the schnapps, the whores, the pidgin-English from both sides, the arms around

126

the shoulders, the big plans for the future, the you're-my-best-mate bollock-talk. Inside I'm liquefying.

'Come the day of the trade,' continues Shanks, 'they're all best mates, but when the stock's all counted and the Germans want their money the English team go at it with semi-automatic assault pistols. No one was meant to be tooled-up, turns out that both sides were. The rumours, the Dam is always full of rumours, say the Germans were gonna turn over the other lot but they were quicker.'

'Can't trust anyone, can ya?' says Morty.

'It gets worse,' says Shanks. 'There's a bitta argy-bargy and one of the Germans, who is in fact Belgian, gets shot twice through the guts. He dies later cos they wouldn't risk takin him to hospital with a gunshot wound.'

'So he bleeds to death,' I say.

'Yep. And this team of white power loonies hold your lot responsible,' says Shanks, who's on some kinda scally wind-up.

'Now hold on,' says Morty, getting up, all didgy. 'Them cunts are nothin to do with us. Will you guys be told.'

'Hold fire, Mort,' says Victor calmly. 'You say they ain't but everyone in Amsterdam thinks they are. This German posse think they are.'

'But why us?' I shrug.

'Cos your monikers were banded about for a drop of credit-ability.' He goes on, 'It ain't us you gotta convince. You guys have got a bittova problem.'

That's a bit of an understatement, Victor. We've got a serious misunderstanding with a deceived nightmare outfit who, Nazis being Nazis, ain't famous for their ability to consider reasoned argument and, more importantly, we're sat in a room with some very capable geezers who may be thinking that we're here to mug them off a lorryload of bushwhacked pills. That would stink of slackness and disrespect. Not knowing the real origin makes us look like amateurs, mug punters. Shanks definitely thinks we're at it.

'When did all this go off?' I ask.

Shanks is looking at me like he's still unconvinced.

'Ten days ago, maybe twelve. Here's a clue for yer. A guy I do a few moves with over there knows this German outfit. He drinks with 'em to keep 'em sweet, yeah. He says the top mover from over this side was a guy called Duke. Do you know any Duke? Ever heard of any Duke?'

Morty and Clarkie shake their heads. We look at one another to see if any of the others knows a Duke. Sidney's little slapstick tale don't seem so fuckin funny now. I can see it all laid out before me. Duke, toot, missus, toot, council man, mace, dogs, shooters, flit, gonski, pals reunion in the Dam, plot, scam, raid, pension, start-up money, dead Belgian, oops, irate Germans, looking for readies, meet with us, pills for sale, dead cheap, big eyes, mugs, us.

'To be honest, chaps,' says Trevor, 'I thought you were a bit cocky when you walk in. You really didn't know about this turn-out, did yer?'

'I think we've been set up,' I say, indignant.

'By who?'

'By the geezers who hijacked the pills. We was asked if we could punt the gear in one hit.'

'With who?' says Trevor.

'Well, work it out. Why're we here?'

'But you didn't know they were skanked?' he says.

'Not till now. I swear on my mother's life.'

'How many bits are we talkin about here?'

'Two million.'

He takes a sharp intake of breath. 'That's a lotta pills. You know we're talkin pennies.'

'This ain't worth fallin out over, ain't worth gettin indigestion over.'

'Very true. Different story if they were legit,' says Trevor.

'But someone's gonna make a lotta dough outta these cunts,' says Morty to Victor.

'Someone's gonna get very seriously fucked-up as well,' replies Victor.

'See, you guys might be better off gettin word to the Germans that this ain't your coup,' says Trevor.

He's up, walking backward and forward, patrolling the room. He goes on.

'This madness ain't any good to anybody. They're gonna want one of yous as payback. That's how it works, one for one and it could be yous –' he points at us in turn '– or yous or yous.'

'But it's got nothin to do with us,' says Clarkie, ignoring the mounting evidence.

'Like fuck it ain't. You three are up here lookin to sell the fuckers to us,' says Trevor, towering over Clarkie.

'But we never tea-leafed the cunts.'

'Okay, so you didn't, okay, let's say we accept that. How's it look?'

'Bad.'

'Thank you.'

Trevor sits back down.

'Hang on,' I'm saying, 'have you ever heard of us goin on the rob, skankin? I ain't talkin about toe-rags from the sticks.'

'Well, put like that it's not a problem,' says Shanks, 'but are the North European White Misfit Alliance gonna ask us for a reference?'

'Shanks, we didn't send anyone over there, okay? These cunts are tryin to mug us into doin the biz.'

'And you're fuckin doin it, pal.'

I turn my chair to face Shanks.

'This guy you know in Amsterdam. What's he like?'

'He does trips for us.'

'Trips where?'

'No. Acid trips. He makes them. He's a chemist of sorts.'

'Is he okay?'

'Not really. He's a bitter, fucked-up old hippie, went over there in seventy-six and never left.'

'But would he do as an intermediary, could he handle it?'

'For money he would. You want me to talk to him?'

'Not yet, hold fire. I need to talk to some people in London first.'

'Listen, if you need geezers who can do the business, you know –' he makes a gun shape '– we can sort that as well.'

'That's handy to know,' I wink. You never know with people like Shanks if he's just letting you know he's got some right naughty hounds on the firm, so don't fuck him about.

'See,' says Shanks, 'it might be that the only way they believe you weren't in coup would be if you deliver this Duke geezer. There was a dispute between two firms over there and one lot had to serve up this geezer's head in an icebox, you know, what you take on a picnic, to show good faith.'

'Some picnic.'

'They might just want some compensation.'

'Why from us?'

'They think they've got a genuine grievance against ya and a good few guilder might do the trick.'

'I ain't givin 'em fuck all,' says Morty, shaking his head, eyes alight.

'Shanks is sayin how it could go down,' says Trevor. 'If you do need specialists we'll work out codes before you go back.'

'Thanks. We appreciate it. So you don't want anythin to do with the pills,' I say, getting up.

'Let's not be hasty,' says Ronnie. 'If they were at a keen price we might.'

'These are like pills were ten years ago,' I say, sitting down.

'Everybody says that. We'd wanna keep it quiet for obvious reasons.' He puts his finger up to his lips. 'We'll have to have a chat among ourselves.'

'Fair enough. I think we need to do the same,' I say. 'I'll leave you some samples.'

'If we ain't interested,' says Ron, 'I'll just ring ya and say, no code, you'll know.'

If I was sitting where they're sitting I'd be thinking on the lines of half a million quid the lot, take it or leave it, twenty-five pence per an article. They're the big hitters.

'You really didn't know?' says Shanks, getting up, shaking his head.

'Clarkie –' says Morty.

'What?'

'Tell this lot about that fuckin Turkish geezer.'

Quiet Night In

I wake up suddenly from my dream, feeling right weirded-out. I dreamed that I was watching this huge battle, a set-piece affair, armies from different periods of history marched into one another in ordered fashion and began fighting in vicious hand-to-hand combat. A Spitfire appeared above and strafed a Roman legion, while redcoats from Waterloo battled it out with Waffen-SS troops. All this is taking place on a large oval field like a cricket pitch, with pendants and flags on poles around the outside. I'm sitting at a raised table on a grassy knoll picnicking with Jimmy Price. The fighting has the atmosphere of a sporting event but the death-cries of the combatants seem very real. Jimmy's head is twice the size it is in real life. He's pushing food into his face in pure gluttony, laughing at the slaughter, choking and spluttering, pointing and slapping his thigh. The table is laden with grub of the finest kind, game birds and dressed fish, like a medieval royal feast. Servants in livery from Pepi's Barn bring more and more all the time. Suddenly large droplets of rain start to land on the tablecloth and soon a summer shower has started. Jimmy glances skyward with a look of distaste on his massive face, as if to say 'What's this? Rain? I didn't order rain. How fuckin dare you.' But then he abruptly snaps outta it, slaps me hard enough on the back to leave a bruise and laughs himself red raw, then the hotel reception buzzes through with my alarm call and wakes me. I get left with the feeling that I can't make my mind up if it qualifies as a nightmare or not.

Morty and Clarkie are gonna have a night out in Manchester with Victor and Ronnie. I can tell by the look in Mister Mortimer's eyes that he's up for a mad one so I decide against it, and just when they're all giving me serious grief, Trevor invites me to come over to meet his wife and kids, eat dinner, cos his missus cooks amazing Thai food, and chill right out. A couple of spliffs, a bottle of good wine, nothing excessive. I leave them

131

in the hotel bar and sneak off to have a kip about half-four and it's now on the dot of six. I order some coffee from the reception and turn on the telly in the room. What was that fuckin dream all about? I reckon after you wake from dreams it's sometimes hard to lose the feelings and weirded-out, spooky shit I don't need. I can't seem to get any sense outta this telly either. I can't get it to change channel, maybe you gotta pay to change the channel, which is a fuckin liberty. I sling the remote control across the room, hitting a wall, and instantly regret it cos it shatters into bits. Now I'm stuck with the local news and weather, something I don't really give a toss about but I ain't getting outta bed until I've had my coffee. Then I'm gonna jump in the shower and that's gonna wake me right up. I'll probably get charged for a whole new set by these conniving bastards.

The main story on the local news is a grisly murder, and if it's on the telly I don't mind a grisly murder. It seems a boat-broker, whatever the fuck that is, has been found murdered in his home-cum-office on a boat in a harbour about ten miles up the coast from Liverpool. There's a cozzer being interviewed but he's being very tight-lipped but what he is saying is that in all his time on the force, twenty-three years, he's never witnessed a more brutal, horrifying and callous act and I believe him. He looks jittery and a deathly white, like there's something wrong with the colour on the telly, like it's suddenly gone black and white. There's TV crews sticking microphones under his nose and asking loadsa questions and every time he says he can't answer that particular question they just jump back in and try a different tack. He's trying not to get too graphic but it turns out that the guy was tortured before he was killed and one look at the old bill convinces me that they really did go to town on the guy.

My coffee arrives. 'Was this a robbery gone wrong?' asks one of the reporters. 'No,' says the cozzer, and goes on to explain that sums of cash and other valuables were not taken from the scene and the perpetrator or perpetrators were at the scene for some time and the place was ransacked. Maybe the work of a professional contract killer, another reporter suggests. The cozzer thinks it's too early to tell and they, the old bill, are keeping an open mind and asking the public for every assistance. Contract killers, I'm thinking, don't hang around, it's the old one-two in the canister and offski, maybe they got a killing-for-kicks nutter on the loose up here. All this don't really help my spooked-out mood but I find watching it very compelling with a nice cup of coffee and a complimentary Amaretto biscuit. They interview one of the neighbours. The old dear says he was a very nice man, Mister Van Hire or something like that, always said good morning if I met him while out walking the dogs, he kept himself to himself, and went about his business. It always is, love, the quiet ones, the inconspicuous ones, who get ironed out brutally in their own homes. Funny how, if the dog wags its tail at ya, you couldn't be a bad person. Waking up at six in the evening in this fuckin bunker is enough to send ya twitchy without lucid dreams about Jimmy Price in a military theme park, this afternoon's disappointment over the Jack and Jills and a carve-up being shown live on the local TV news.

I take a leisurely shower, letting it run as ice-cold as I can stand just before I get out. That livens me right up. I get dressed, sky-blue polo neck, jeans and black suede Gucci loafers. This afternoon's meeting was a fiasco, a real show-up, but I'm glad I ain't the one who's gonna have to go back and tell Geno or Jimmy about the Yahoos' little raiding party. Tonight I don't even wanna think about it and right now ain't an opportune time to be discussing tactics with Morty or Clarkie. I'm sure I saw them popping a sample each earlier on. We'll have the journey back tomorrow morning to discuss it at length.

Trevor's said he's gonna send a car round for me at exactly seven-fifteen and to be waiting outside. As I walk past the bar I can see Morty holding court with Clarkie, Shanks, Victor and Ronnie. They all look well on the way to getting mighty lashed, getting noisy and making merry, so I sneak past without popping in to say hello. As I walk out the driver simply opens the back door of the motor and I get in. The engine's running so we're off straight away and soon we're going down country lanes at about fifty miles an hour but the driver inspires confidence with his control. Looking out the window, across fields lit by the nearly full moon, it looks like a picture-postcard landscape, with valleys and small villages. Soon this gives way to woodland and it gets denser as we go on. I make a point of never engaging taxi drivers in conversation cos you never know what you're gonna get, but this geezer ain't said a dickey-bird all the way and we've been driving for fifteen minutes.

He begins to slow down on a curvy wooded lane, pulls up suddenly. I realise that it's the start of a driveway going up a slight hill. You would never see it, especially at night, if you didn't know exactly, and I mean ex-act-lee, what you were looking for. The driver pushes a button in a panel that seems to be buried, covered with ivy. It beeps for a few seconds and then stops and the mute driver continues up the drive slowly. Fifty yards further on there's a set of heavy steel gates wide open and the very second after we drive through they start to close again automatically. Lights come on, as if by magic, as we drive further up the drive, bathing the forest in a harsh white light and throwing up eerie shapes and shadows. There must be invisible infra-red laser beams flying about or sensors buried in the road. Another hundred yards up the drive we pull up in front of a house that looks Swedish. It's made entirely of wood, is tucked away into the side of a small hillside but blends into its surroundings like it's camouflaged. Two motors are parked in the garage, a Saab soft-top and a Land Rover Discovery. Above the doors and garage are CCTV cameras, so Trevor's got the whole place ready-eyed up. This place being so isolated, I bet anyone living round here would have serious security, but Trevor's are there to give him a bitta warning against more than communal garden burglars. His would, hopefully, give him extra protection against the busies, as they still call 'em, bogeymen, skankers or kidnappers.

The driver pulls the motor up noiselessly in front of the house, gets out, walks round, opens the back door. I get out, he gets back in and drives off. All the time he ain't said a word, not a peep. I'm impressed in a funny kinda way. I find the bell and push it and it chimes away inside. Trevor opens the door, grinning, with a huge Great Dane on the end of his arm, pulling it back on a massive steel choker. The hound is friendly enough, not like those evil small dogs that have an inferiority complex and have to make up for it by being extra nasty. It's the kinda dog you can give kids pony-rides on. He's panting and jumping about in excitement, he's about five foot tall and must weigh in at about twelve or thirteen stone. He looks like Goofy, so now we got Mickey Mouse and Goofy.

'This is Albert, daft as a brush,' says Trevor.

If dogs are like their masters then Trevor and Albert were made for each other. If anything Trevor's size makes Albert look smaller than he is, but not much.

He brings me in and the house is beautiful, with wooden floors and beams everywhere, not old wood, but fresh blond pine. Everywhere shows taste and thought. There's a pungent smell of coconut and lime, lemongrass and other Thai spices wafting around. Trevor shows me into the kitchen. 'This is Mandy,' he says.

She's quite small and petite. Again, stood next to Trevor she looks smaller still cos she only comes up to his chest. Mandy's blond and pretty, got a good vibe about her. Two kids, about eighteen months and three years, are up at the breakfast bar eating cod-shapes and baked beans. The younger one's in a highchair and Mandy's helping her with her food. This is what I need tonight, a homely glimpse of family life and home cooking.

'The kids are eating now and we'll eat later. They're up late tonight.'

'This house, did you have it built?'

'No I didn't, but if I did have one built,' says Trevor, 'this would be it. No, it was built for a Swedish firm who come over in the eighties, built a factory nearer town. These houses were for the top executives, there's another dozen or so dotted up and down the road.'

'They're very hard to find.'

'That's Swedes for ya. Their angle is to be at one with nature, not to be hard to find.'

'What happened, the factory went bust?'

'Lotta people reckon it was another government scam, tryin

135

to get jobs brought into the area, but it didn't work. The Swedes cleared out and left the houses for sale.'

'So it worked out well for you.'

'That's one way of lookin at it.'

He shows me round and you can tell he's a proud man, happy to be a good provider for his kids and he's seriously loved-up with Mandy, his childhood sweetheart. She puts the kids to bed while Trevor lays the dining table by the window.

'In summer we have these doors open and we eat out on this deck. These doors all fold back so it's like there's no walls at all. This house is really beautiful in the summer.'

'It's very nice now.'

'Not bad for an ex-con, mini-cab driver.' He gives me a sly little wink. I know bits and pieces about Trevor.

'Is that how you got started then, Trevor?'

'I got out from a lumpa bird and a mate sorted me out a car buckshee and a job so I went to work drivin.'

It ain't the done thing to ask what the bird was for, ain't ethical, Geno would say, but I already know the gist.

'You know I was inside with Morty, not great pals or anything but our paths crossed at some point, some nick or other. I didn't know him well but then he gave everyone a wide. He was kinda aloof if ya like. Well, as aloof as you can be in nick.' He laughed like aloof was not the kinda word he used every day.

'He told me he didn't like the company that much,' I say. 'Thought most of them were riff-raff, grasses, geezers who went guilty cos they thought the law might cut them a deal, losers, mugs, junkies. He's a bit of a snob, is Mister Mortimer.'

We're laughing.

'I tell ya what,' I go on, 'if you get him on his high horse, get him goin, he can sound like some old Tory geezer. His voice changes and everything. He starts to really pro-noun-ce his words. Recidivist lowlife smugbags, stealing old ladies' purses, where's the morality, where's the get-up-and-go that made this country what it is today. Let these fuckers rob someone who can afford to be robbed. Do away with Social Security, let the work-shy fuckers starve.'

136

'He's not really like that, is he?'

'No, is he fuck. He just likes to spin people's nuts, a black geezer talkin like that, gets 'em at it, see if they'll bite cos he likes an argument, does Mort. I'll tell ya what, he preferred being with Cat A cons than petty crims. It's a pride thing I guess.'

'He used to walk along the landin with a face like there was a really bad smell and he used to have a uniform –'

'A what?'

'The prison-issue uniform. He had it pristine, pressed to perfection, the shoes polished like a soldier. He'd walk around the gaff like looking down his nose at everyone.'

'In his uniform?'

'Not every day, but on Sundays and that. If he had a visit he'd really go to town but every day he'd put on a clean shirt, and underwear I guess, some blokes don't change that stuff for weeks.'

'So he'd look a dandy in the shovel.'

'He had a tie sent in.'

'Sent in?'

'Cos they don't give you a tie.'

'I don't know.'

'Well they don't, but Morty's got one from somewhere and if he's out and about on the wing, suited and booted, and he sees a screw with his top button undone he'd be ordering them to do it up and you know a lot of the time they'd do it. It'd be summer, a hundred and twenty degrees, fuckin boilin, and he's got a woollen uniform and a tie on.'

'Did anyone else wear a uniform?'

'You'd have a riot if you tried. Really straight-faced he'd say to them, "Do that button up you scruffy bastard," so they weigh him off as a nutter, not your fraggle rock, ravin loony kind but the give-him-a-squeeze, keep-him-sweet kind. It'd be like "Come, Morty, we don't want no trouble," cos you only have to look at him to know he can perform, it's in the eyes.'

'I wouldn't dispute it,' I says.

'I did my time quiet, couple of scrapes but nothing serious. You know what I was away for, don't ya.'

137

I do but I have to let him tell me, protocol. 'You wanna tell me?'

'I was working on the door of this club and this fight's kicked off cos we wouldn't let some drunks in. This geezer's tryin to bite me ear off so I thought I'd run him into a wall but we've both gone through a shop window. He's cut to pieces, big bits of glass in him, blood everywhere. I ain't got a scratch. This guy dies cos he's cut main arteries in his leg and his arm. He actually got out the window and ran away but collapsed round the back of some shops and died. He lost the blood faster cos his heart was pumped up from the fight. Busies followed the blood-trail to find him.'

'Might have lived if he hadn't run.'

'Possibly. The law's charged me with murder cos they're saying that I slung him through the window. His pals are prepared to say I did. The law don't believe it but it's a dead easy conviction for murder, looks good on their records.'

'It's good at promotion time.'

'I'm in the frame so these cunts get a better pension. But common sense prevailed. A couple of boys spoke to his mates, told 'em givin evidence was not on. The charge gets dropped to manslaughter. I shoulda sacked me brief cos he let a loada stuff go he shoulda jumped on, medical reports and that, useless he was.'

'You got what?'

'Five, cos I had previous, did about three, looking at life at one point. When I got out I wouldn't spit my gum out on the street. Then I realised that if you don't take a short cut you ain't gonna get nowhere.'

'Very true, Trevor.'

'See, at that time in Liverpool there was a kinda mini-cab war going on, offices getting burnt out, people getting sent out with a big bag of change and told to ring up and send cars round to moody addresses all day long, drivers getting beatings, informing the dole if guys were scratching and working.'

'Very snide.'

'Petty, I would have said. I was offered a partnership by this pal of mine whose heart wasn't really in it. He figured that thirty per cent of something was better that one hundred per of fuck all. I went to see the geezers who ran the other firms and we carved the city up. I pointed out that all this bad blood wasn't good for business, get us all nicked. Think about it, if you can talk to one other, you can peg prices, stop undercutting and if anyone comes along, opens up, you can sort it.'

'Sounds good.'

'In the end we took over the other firms, started doing the very top end of the market, executive cars, limos, no one had seen one up here back then.'

'So how did ya get to the dark side?'

'Well, we was always runnin parcels around for various people we knew so one thing led to another and it grew and grew. You know yourself once you're a player ... ' He shrugged.

Everybody wants to know ya. Things can snowball in weeks, not months, so you gotta be wide awake to keep up. I'd heard it was heavier, bloodier than that. The mini-cab wars grew into the contraband wars. Once Trevor had built up the momentum and allies to take on the other cabbies, he marched straight on into the drug trade. Those two are first cousins anyway. People got seriously ironed out and a few got posted Missing In Action. If certain people in certain businesses know you've killed another human being, call it manslaughter or murder, making one or serving 'um up, offing or topping, it ain't gonna do your reputation any harm.

I can hear Mandy coming down the stairs. Trevor puts one finger up against his lips and gives me a sly little wink. She starts to bring the food from the oven and put it on the table and at the same time wok-frying some noodles. If she put this together at short notice she's a kinda culinary genius cos there's a king prawn curry with coconut and lime leaves, jasmine rice, a whole fish baked with ginger and spring onion, satay chicken and beef, and a Thai salad with peanut sauce. Trevor opens a bottle of wine and puts water on the table. It looks like a feast.

'Do you eat like this every night?'

'Yeah, unless we're going out to eat. Why not?' says

Mandy. 'He,' she nods at Trevor, 'would eat the whole lot on his own. You gotta eat so why not eat well?'

We sit and eat.

'You in the same business as Trevor?' she asks.

'Yeah,' I say, not knowing if that means dealing drugs or cabs. Some guys tell their wives everything, some guys nothing. I'm sure Morty wouldn't tell his Richard his name if he thought he could get away with it. We talk about London. Mandy says she's been to London, she liked it but she wouldn't wanna live there, too impersonal, but ain't all big cities like that, ain't Liverpool. London's the Original King of Impersonal and the reason I fuckin love it. I can lose myself without trying too hard. The area I live in is very plush, with big townhouses that have been carved up into three or four luxury flats, but nobody knows their neighbours. They may nod at me in passing but then they jog on and mind their own business. There's no cosy chats or exchanging gossip over the garden fence down our way. If I ended up brown bread, like the geezer on the local news back at the bunkhouse, all my neighbours would be out on the street, talking to the TV and papers, paying me the ultimate compliment: 'He kept himself to himself.'

The food is delicious, as good as anything I've eaten in Thailand. Trevor carries on eating until there's not a scrap of grub, not a grain of rice or a strand of noodle, left on any of the plates. He sits back and lights a fag with a very satisfied look on his face. He's quiet, savouring the tastes, pulling on his snout, blowing smoke-rings inside smoke-rings to amuse himself. Then suddenly he's up and opening the back doors.

'Here, I wanna show you something.'

He flicks some switches on the wall by the door and a path gets lit up going way off into the massive wooded back garden.

'Come on, bring your drink. You come as well, Mandy.'

'I better stay here in case one of the little 'uns wakes up.'

'Okay, we won't be long, babes.'

We walk out into the cool night air onto the decking, then down five or six steps onto a lawn. It's a bit chilly, a bit misty, but Trevor don't seem to notice, he's only wearing a gym vest. He beckons me across the slightly rising lawn, with tall, skinny

140

trees on either side, and into the wood proper. There's a gravel path, lit with lanterns that have been strung along the low branches of the trees every few yards. They sway gently on the breeze. We walk into the wood for about a hundred yards. The shadows make faces in the dark and the clouds are rushing overhead. I can hear owls in the distance and small creatures moving in the bushes. Suddenly we emerge into a clearing by a small river and in the middle there's a mini version of the main house. It's lit up with spot-lights that have been half buried in the surrounding turf. As I walk round the outside I can see that it's half on the river bank and the other half is perched over the water supported by hefty wooden stilts.

'The summer house,' says Trevor, beaming.

He leads me onto the overhanging balcony. It's got benches and we sit down.

'Very impressive, Trevor. Did the Swedes build this as well?' I ask.

'Oh yeah. They know how to live, the Swedes. There's a sauna in there with a plunge pool, and I guess you sit out here in the nude with the family and all your neighbours, very adult, the Swedish.'

He laughs.

'So, do you have your pals round for the all-over suntan?' I ask.

'Do I fuck. Most of the people I know, I wouldn't let them through the front door. You should feel privileged.'

'Thank you.'

He points across to the other bank, about twenty feet away.

'The river's very shallow at the moment, very dry, but if it's been raining heavy or the snow's melting it's white water, really fuckin powerful, gets ya going.'

It hasn't rained in weeks. The flow is down to a trickle. On the other bank I can see the high-water line where rocks and small branches have been thrown up by the force of a torrent. Where the river curves away outta sight, the power has eroded the bank away leaving an overhang waiting to drop.

'I come down here most nights and smoke a spliff,' he says, lighting one that appeared from nowhere. 'Whatever the weather, I smoke a spliff, relax, look at the river, look at the stars. It kinda sorts me out, you understand?'

'Sounds good.'

'If it's freezing cold and the river's rushing, I fuckin love it. You ever done bird, brov?'

'No. I've been lucky.'

'I heard you've been careful. You know, the one good thing that came outta that last bitta bird was I can really fuckin appreciate all this.' He sweeps his hand across. It's dark out on the balcony and I can only see Trevor's features when he pulls on the spliff, the glow lighting up his face.

'It may sound like old hippy bollocks but if you've never had your liberty taken away, can't do things you take for granted, you can never really understand freedom.'

'But some geezers go back time and time again.'

'Cos they don't know any different, or they're looking for the last big prize, but waking up in there and seeing the same old faces, day in, day out, it depresses the shit outta me to even think about it.'

He seems to have got well stoned really quick. The puff smells seriously pungent, mega-strong, but he ain't exactly gonna be smoking chicken-shit and henna.

'And that's what you think about down here?' I say.

'And other things, plans for the future.' He takes a long draw on the spliff, holds it down. We're silent for a few seconds, listening to the river trickle by.

'Do you know what "Cosa Nostra" means?' he says.

'It's the Mafia, ain't it?'

'Sure. But the term "Cosa Nostra". Do you know what it actually means?'

'No.' I shake my head.

'It means "This thing of ours", yeah? You get it?'

I ain't sure what I'm meant to say here. I obviously ain't had enough spliff. Trevor can see I look mystified.

'See, what I'm gettin at is the idea of being in something, this thing of ours, with people, geezers you respect, sticking together, working for something you all believe in, trusting one another to be straight with each other. It can only pay benefits.'

142

'But the reality of all that is it's fucked.'

'Now, maybe, but at the start it was a noble idea. I've read all those books about the Mafia and ... '

Trevor's talking but I ain't listening. A little alarm bell's ringing in my head. It's always a bad sign if guys have read too many books about the Mafia. To read all that shit you'd begin to think it was quite noble and heroic. Guys who have got too far into that tip have ended up causing themselves and people working with them a whole lotta grief. They wanna start pulling strokes in broad daylight. They seem to forget it's called crime. When those old-school Mafioso guys were up to their tricks, the fuckin world was a different place. They were as strong as a government, they selected presidents of the United States, ran whole cities, ran the police, ran judges, ran sports, ran the unions, and after that what's left to run?

' ... You know what I mean, brother?' says Trevor, grabbing my arm.

'Sure, sure. You're right, brother.'

I'm clueless.

'I knew you'd understand. Talk to some people about this sorta shit and you lose 'em straight away cos they're just lowlifes. What I'm talking about is trusted guys, sensible guys coming together to do their work, to give the public what they want. Nobody forces this on anyone.' He holds the spliff up. 'We just supply a demand that's there and it works a whole lot better if you can trust a few people.'

'Who have the same aim.'

'Now you got it.'

'But this is a messy business. These are different times from when those geezers did what they did. I've read some of those books and some of those guys had a lotta class but a lot of them was just fuckwits, lordin it up, livin large until–'

'Listen, what I'm saying is don't ever lie to me or my boys, okay? We'll have a Cosa Nostra.'

'An understanding?'

'Yep,' he says.

I hope he ain't on about those fuckin pills. I better change the subject.

143

'But Trevor, people get greedy, people get ironed right out, people don't know when enough's enough. We have chosen a dangerous way to make our living. These are dangerous times for everyone, even straight-goers are gettin mashed up in their own homes.'

'There's a lot of loonies about, it's true.'

'I saw on telly before I came over here, some poor fucker, mindin his business, he gets totally ironed out, in his own gaff.'

'What happened? I didn't see it,' says Trevor, relighting his spliff.

'Quiet guy, lived on a boat, someone held him captive, tortured him and then offed him.'

'On a boat, in a boatyard?' There was a bit of concern.

'Yeah, about ten miles up the coast. The cozzer was right ups –'

'Did they give the guy's name. He wasn't Dutch, was he?' He was hoping he wasn't.

'He was, as it goes.'

'Fuck sake.' He flicks the glowing butt of the spliff into the river. It dies instantly. 'Tell me exactly what they said on the telly.' He's on his feet, pacing. I tell him as much as I can remember. 'Now, think, was the guy's name Van Tuck?' he asks.

'That's it, Van Tuck,' I say, clicking my fingers.

'I gotta get back to the house and make some calls.'

Trevor's off immediately, leaving me sitting on the bench confused, but he appears single-minded and serious so I act the same. Where the path meanders in a gentle loop Trevor runs straight across, sticks breaking under his weight. Soon he's ahead of me, then out of sight completely. As I come through the door and into the kitchen, he's punching numbers into the wall-phone, cursing and swearing at Mandy to bring his mobile phone over. She brings it immediately and he starts running through the memory and pushing numbers on the speed dial. Suddenly he smashes the phone off the wall so it's dangling by its cord, swaying backwards and forwards.

'Where the fuck's Shanks? ... Where the fuck's everyone?' He's got the two phones up against his ears, waiting for someone, anyone, to answer. The last time I saw Shanks he was in the hotel bar with the lads getting well hammered and that was about three hours ago. I'm baffled, standing in the doorway.

'Give us a minute,' says Trevor to me. Then he turns to his wife. 'Mandy, where's that address book I keep tucked away?'

Mandy goes down on her knees and removes one of the drawers in the fitted kitchen and taped to the back is a standard black pocket address book. She brings it over right away and Trevor starts flicking through it, still with one phone jammed to his head with his shoulder and the mobile in his hand. When he finds the number he wants, he disregards the phone under his chin, lets it fall to the floor and starts punching the number into the mobile. Someone answers.

'Good, you're there. Listen, I'm coming over right now ... Fuck that. Listen, I'll be there in about twenty minutes, okay? I'll see you then.'

He flicks the phone shut.

'Listen, babes, something's gone off. I'll be back as soon as possible. Keep ringing Shanks, tell him to ring me.'

Where's that leave me? I'm thinking.

'And you,' says Trevor with a pointy finger, 'you're fuckin comin with me.'

Van Tuck's Rude Awakening

'Van Tuck is, or was, a mover. He moved stuff around for people, transportation was his thing. He would trade boats, some thieved, but mostly legit for the sake of appearances.'

Trevor's throwing the Discovery around the dark country roads. Small branches whip across the windscreen. I instinctively jump back. He don't appear stoned, either.

'So he was a smuggler,' I say.

'You're sharp. He put things together, people in touch. Van Tuck was a fixer, very handy he was, too.'

'You did work with him?'

'All the time. He was a fuckin genius, poor cunt, he could do anything. We'd get him to deliver our stuff from over the water. I've got a nasty feeling we had something on its way right about now.'

'Something big?'

'Anything else just ain't worth the hassle, kid, course it was big. You ain't talkin to a fuckin day-tripper, pal. Shanks was doing the business on this bitta work.'

'It ain't that acid Shanks was on about earlier?'

'If it was those trips I'd laugh it off but I could be going down for a good few quid here if my parcel's in transit. I won't know till I talk to Shanks.'

'He made the arrangements with the Dutchman?' I ask.

'Yeah. We buy over in Holland mostly, it gets delivered to Van Tuck then back to us in the UK but it's our property once it's with Van Tuck. You keeping up? Now, I can't go back to the people I buy from, tell them Van Tuck's history, I never got my gear so I ain't payin ya.'

'They heavy?' I know the answer.

'Course they're heavy,' says Trevor, shaking his head. 'But we've done a deal, we owe them, don't we. Ain't their fault people get murdered.'

'Ain't no one's, really.'

'Don't know about that. Someone's to blame. I bet this has something to do with your pal's trip to the Dam.'

'How much we talkin here, Trevor?'

'Our whack coulda bought your poxy pills a few times.'

We're talking millions and tonnes here.

'We ain't goin to the boatyard, are we?' I say, thinking Trevor might be on a kamikaze mission.

'Don't be stupid. It's gonna be crawling with filth.'

'Did Van Tuck have the paperwork for your consignment?'

'It wouldn't lead back to us. It gets landed in Van Tuck's name. He was a cautious cunt, looked a div, did everything in codes, kept it all up here.' Trevor points to his temple. 'Thousands of codes and numbers.'

The roads are getting wider, straighter and better-lit.

'Do the law know about this geezer?' I ask.

'That's what I'm gonna try and find out now. Can't wait for Shanks to turn up.'

'You got a cozzer on the firm?'

'I wish. We've got this reporter on the local paper who's really sweet with all the CID, their big drinking buddy.'

'So they tell him and he tells you.'

'Or he gets his balls sawn off and I've told him that. For the time being he gets anything he wants, readies, coke, birds, holidays, but mostly he wants readies. See, the filth, race apart ain't they, and he's in the thick of it picking up titbits. Every now and again they tell him, or he earwigs, something juicy.'

'It's worth the readies?'

'Well, we've got a lot knocking about, ain't we? Don't worry about this guy, we've got him well stitched up.'

Trevor's chain-smoking, throwing the Discovery round corners without looking. We hit a bitta dual carriageway leading into Liverpool. Trevor puts the pedal to the floor. I'm pushed back by the force of the acceleration. Five minutes later we're on the outskirts, two minutes after that Trevor's slowing down and we're into streets that look exactly like the sedate, leafy suburbs of London, rows of moody Tudor and Edwardian houses, Liverpool's Nob Hill.

Trevor pulls the motor up, parks with two wheels on the

pavement, gets out, don't bother to lock it, flicks his fag into someone's front garden and walks up one of the paths, gesturing for me to follow and fuckin hurry up 'n' all. The house has been chopped up into three flats. Trevor puts his finger on the middle bell and holds it there. After ten seconds the ringing starts breaking up so he takes it off for a split second then replaces it. He's banging the knocker with his other hand. A light comes on behind the glass and a silhouette fumbles with locks and catches.

'For fuck's sake, hurry up you fuckin dozy cunt,' says Trevor encouragingly, kicking the bottom of the door.

The door opens and there's a sheepish-looking guy in a robe looking up and down the street to see if any curtain-twitchers have got us under observation, he gestures us up the stairs, puts us in the front room and says he'll be back in a second. The room's comfortable in a catalogue kinda way, like those mock-ups they have in furniture stores complete with nice lampshade, nice rug and curtains. You can see where some of Trevor's readies went cos in one corner the guy's got the state-of-the-art, top-of-the-range, Bang and Ollie hi-fi, wide-screen TV and video. I make it about twelve grand's worth, almost what a reporter on a local paper would make in a year. Our host comes back into the room and pulls the curtains shut. He's tense, fretting about, trying to tidy up the remains of an Indian takeaway, but in his nervousness he keeps dropping the tin containers. The brown paper bag it came in is splitting at the bottom cos it's soaked in cooking oil. I notice that the meal was for two. He eventually gets it together and takes it out to the kitchen.

'Trevor,' I say, 'that meal's for two. Someone's here.'

'Duncan,' says Trevor in a whisper as the guy walks back in the room, 'is there someone else in the flat?'

'Well,' he says, grinning like a naughty schoolboy, 'I've got one of the floozies from work in the other room. We were el copulas, you know, when you rang.'

'This girl, does she have a name, Duncan?' asks Trevor, quite gentle all of a sudden.

'Yes, of course she does,' Duncan replies, looking puzzled.

'What is it?'

'It's Joanne.'

'Go and tell Joanne to get dressed, give her some cab fare and tell her to fuck off. I need to talk to you.'

Duncan doesn't like being told what to do in his own house but off he goes anyway. We can hear slightly raised voices, Duncan trying to pacify Joanne. Trevor gets himself a bottle of brandy from a drinks cabinet, uncorks it and starts swigging it, sits down back-to-front on a dining chair, looking a gunslinger. Duncan's apologising and a woman's telling him to 'go fuck yourself, ya fuckin prick'. The front door slams. I can hear him coming back up the stairs two at a time. He swings back into the room breathless. He's got a bit more composure, getting his balls back. He thrusts out a hand in my direction.

'Good evening. I'm Duncan and you're … ?'

'It doesn't matter.' Nobody likes a sneak.

'Oh, you're a Londoner, are you?'

'Like I say, it doesn't matter.'

He's about thirty, his barnet's swept over in a wedge, cad-dish, his hands stuck in the pockets of a Bahrain Hilton dressing gown. He looks like the public-school prefect who confiscates the younger kids' snout, only to smoke them himself. Duncan ain't got the scally accent that Trevor and Shanks have got.

'Listen, Duncan, don't worry about him. What'd you know about that geezer who got killed in the boatyard?'

'It ain't in the area I cover. Do you have an interest?'

'Course I've got a fuckin interest. I wouldn't fuckin be here otherwise, would I, ya divvy cunt.'

'Can I take a glass of that?' says Duncan, pointing at the brandy.

'Get a glass and get my mate a beer. And hurry up.'

Duncan goes out to the kitchen again. Something inside me likes the fact that Trevor's giving this arrogant cunt a hard time. Duncan comes back in. He gives me a Stella and Trevor pours him a very large drink.

'Now, Duncan, sit down there,' says Trevor, pointing at the cosy armchair. 'In the past I've asked you to do me favours and

149

I've always given you a bitta wedge for your trouble. Have I been fair with you?'

'Yes,' says Duncan, nodding his head.

'Now, this might not be in your area but I want you to stick your neck out for me, okay? I want you to ring one of your detective mates and ask them what's the score with this Van Tuck business, was he killed cos of his connections. See what you can find out.'

'There's no way I could do that.'

'What are you saying? You don't have the numbers?'

'I do but ... ' You can tell he wishes he'd lied.

'But what?'

'It ain't appropriate. I've never done it before.'

'There's a first time for everything.'

'I'm not sure how they'd react.'

'Well, we're gonna find out, ain't we?'

'But what if he cottons on to what I'm doing?'

'You've got someone in mind, ain't ya?' says Trevor. Duncan looks sick cos he's bubbled himself up twice in seconds.

'There's a detective sergeant, thinks the sun shines out my arse, one of life's Labradors, lonely bastard.'

'Okay, but will he know anything?'

'I don't know.'

'Until you ask.'

Duncan takes a slug of the brandy.

'Trevor, I really don't want to do this.'

'Listen, bum-fluff, you've taken my cash and what you've come back with has been canteen gossip.'

'And a lot of good information, you said so yourself.'

'Granted, lad. I've always looked upon you as an investment for the future and now it's the future. I always knew your day would come and today's the day.'

'Couldn't it be tomorrow? It'll look less blatant.'

'I don't give a fuck,' says Trevor.

'But –'

'But nothing, you little cunt. Every-fuckin-thing in this place is paid for with my money. Don't think I don't know about your safe deposit box, yer sly little fuck.'

Duncan looks startled, like his big secret, the source of much smugness, hasn't been a secret at all.

'Now, Duncan, pay attention, you're gonna ring this detective sergeant, box clever, sweeten him up, say maybe you can meet up for a shandy, but while you're here, what do you know about this mischief up the coast.'

Duncan is thinking how it could be done. 'It isn't for publishing, just morbid curiosity,' he says, bucking up.

'That's it, Duncan. See, my confidence wasn't misplaced,' says Trevor, 'and Dunck, if he ain't got the low-down get him to ring someone who has.'

'That could be very, very tricky, Trevor,' says Duncan, slightly deflated.

'But not impossible.'

'It could be done. Let me think.'

He gestures for a refill. I can see blood and arrogance returning. He's busy thinking about how to carry this off, about superiority and dominating others. Suddenly he looks at his watch, picks up the remote control and turns on the local news that's just started. It shows, lead story, the murder of Van Tuck. We watch, sniffing for clues. The story changes and Duncan turns it off. He goes next door and returns with a Filofax. He has a man-sized slug on the brandy, rubs his hands together and punches the numbers into the phone. I hear it ring three times.

'Alan, it's Duncan, you old bugger. How's tricks?'

Alan and Duncan start exchanging small-talk. You'd really believe that they were the best pals in the whole wide world, through thick and thin. Duncan's telling Alan that he should have got promotion over some other geezer. 'He's a good solid copper but how can I put this politely? I don't think I can. He's a wanker.' They both laugh, now they got a naughty secret together, slagging off Alan's superior. I can hear this Alan laughing from where I'm sitting. It must be murder to be in the same room as him. Trevor's gesturing for Duncan to get to the point, cursing under his breath, but Duncan simply nods his head and carries on. He tells Alan a couple of jokes – 'A Spook and a Paddy go into a boozer,' blah, blah, blah ... 'This Welsh chap goes into a brothel … ' I can hear roaring at the punchlines. 'Remember that one, Al … that's a good 'un.'

This Duncan is a real grafter. Cody Garret would be proud. I'm almost sorry for this Alan, plotted up in some scuzzy bedsit, half pissed, all the other cozzers gone home to the wife and coffin lids. It wasn't happening down at the divorced and singles so he's slopped off with a carry-out but, hang about, things are lookin up, his jolly good friend Duncan's rung up. The saddest thing is that if he knows he's being grafted he don't care.

Duncan gets Alan onto a couple of old war stories of the all-the-gang-together variety. What about the time the strippers got the extra score apiece for doing the lesbo routine at Chas's stagnight, the brawl they had with the bouncers at that night club before the lads pulled out their warrant cards. We must have a drink together soon. Friday night? I'll ring, Al.

Trevor's shaking his head. It sounds like Duncan's bringing the conversation to an end. He's even moving his head towards the phone rest on the coffee table. Trevor's on his feet moving towards Duncan. He's waving a massive fist about six inches from Duncan's nose and pulling an evil face.

'Maybe it would be easier if we arranged when and where now, better than me trying to catch you tomorrow. You're a busy man. How about we say six-thirty in the Freemasons? Okay, I'll see you then and bring plenty of money.'

I could hear a laugh from the other end. Trevor's gonna throw Duncan outta the window cos the conversation's over, the business done.

'That was a bad one up the coast today, wasn't it?'

Trevor looks like he's going to kiss Duncan. He gestures for Duncan to hold the phone so he can hear the gist of what's being said.

'They said on the telly it was a very sadistic piece of work. We ain't got a serial killer on the loose, have we Al? Very good for circulation.' He laughs.

Again a pause.

'You've whetted my appetite, you old bastard. I know it's against the rules, but that's never worried you. You know I'd

152

never print anything that would drop you in the proverbial brown stuff, but I like to have the inside story. I've got a sicko's interest in this. I'm just a sick bastard, don't quote me.'

Alan laughs at that. Trevor puts a fag in Duncan's mouth and lights it for him. Duncan covers the mouthpiece.

'He's saying he'll ring a bloke he was on a sergeant's course with, who's on the investigation, tell me Friday when we meet.'

'Ask him to ring the guy now. You're on a roll, Dunck. Try and find out if they think Van Tuck was iffy.'

Duncan puts up a hand to silence him.

'Alan, is there any way you could ring him now? If you were at school together and you're old chums, maybe he'd welcome a call, a chance to catch up. You know what interests me, Alan? Why did they pick on this guy? Was he kosher? Could you ring your comrade as a favour to me? On my honour, my solemn oath, I won't breathe a word to anyone. Could you ring him and ring me back?'

Duncan listens intently and then laughs.

'The first round's always on me anyway, you old tosser. Ring me back. I'm going nowhere, Al.'

He puts the phone down, takes a hefty hit on the Andy Pandy and a long drag on the snout.

'I think we're pushing it, Trevor,' he says. 'I think his nose was a bit put out of joint.'

'Fuck him and his nose. Listen, your best pal ain't gonna say shit cos he'd look a cunt in front of the other busies. You fancy a cup of coffee, Duncan?'

'Yeah. That'll be nice.'

'What about you?' he says, turning to me.

'I wouldn't mind,' I say.

'Away you go then, Dunck, three cups of coffee but you better hurry up before your bum-chum Alan rings back.'

Duncan reluctantly gets up and goes to the kitchen. Trevor calls me over conspiratorially. His eyes are darting like he's gone a bit psycho, a bit worrying.

'I need to know if the gear's been shifted yet, how Shanks worked it with Van Tuck, cos sometimes he sends the bill of lading over to Shanks so he can collect.'

'The bill of landing?'

'No. It's the bill of lading, L-A-D-I-N-G. You've never shifted any cargo, have ya? A container arrives in Liverpool dock and it gets opened and the cargo gets broken down into consignments. The bill of lading is like a receipt for your bitta that cargo. You produce the bill of lading and show that you're the person named on it or it's been endorsed on the back, like a cheque, and away you go.'

'It sounds really easy.'

'It is most of the time. Now, if that bitta paper was on Van Tuck's desk when he got killed, it's now in an evidence bag with the CID and tomorrow morning they'll be down the docks either pulling apart my crates, finding some very choice Greek marble and my loada puff, or they'll be plotted up waiting for it to arrive, in which case it's a write-off, it's seized.'

I realise we're whispering.

'Are you saying that the bill of lading could be with Shanks?' I ask.

'Possibly. What I'm really hoping is that it's not even been delivered and we can get word over there to hold fire until we can work something out. And all this, I think, is to do with that lot rumping the German outfit.'

'Trevor, it could be that some hounds from up here have topped Van Tuck and are planning to collect your load.'

'He was our ace in the hole. Only me and Shanks knew about him.'

'To your knowledge, Trevor.'

The phone rings just as Duncan returns with a tray of coffee and a plate of assorted biscuits. He places the tray down on the coffee table and waits.

'Well, answer the fuckin thing!' roars Trevor. 'Stop fuckin about and answer it.'

Duncan picks it up on the sixth ring. 'Alan,' he says like it's a surprise, 'any joy?' Duncan's eyebrows go up, pulling faces like it's some very disturbing stuff, like he's eaten something sour. 'Really ... that's strong ... they did what? ... That's fuckin sick, that is ... there's a maniac on the loose ... no, of course I won't. You're bloody loving this, ain't ya ... And Van Tuck, anything known?'

A pause while he listens.

'Right, I see. Well, poor bastard. The fat lady's sung for him ... No way, Alan. I wouldn't dream of publishing anything ... I almost wish I hadn't asked now ... We couldn't print that anyway, people would throw up.'

I can hear a huge guffawing from across the room. Alan sounds quite tickled, loves the gory detail.

'But seriously, don't you think that's sick ... that's the word ... Okay, I'll love you and leave you, see you in the Masons, Friday, on parade eighteen-thirty hours ... If you hear anything let me know.'

He puts the phone down.

'Are these blokes after you or something, because if they are, you've got a problem,' says Duncan.

'Tell us exactly what your friend told you,' says Trevor.

'He's not my friend, by the way, but anyway. He tries to ring the fella he knows but this bloke's out. He's a bit pissed, he's got balls, so he rings one of the guys on the investigation and he welcomes the chance to download because it's heavy. The victim, the Dutch bloke, was held for about two days before he died. They know that because the decay on the wounds showed some were forty-eight hours old and others were fresh. Also, two smartly dressed men were seen entering the boatyard early Sunday afternoon. They've worked out, you really have to trust pathologists because they're seldom wrong, that he was tortured for the whole two days. He was given a rare beating. He had a fractured skull, ribs and forearm. They've then wired him up to the electricity mains by his goolies, his swinging bits, burns of the electrical variety on the old testes.'

'Poor Van Tuck,' sighs Trevor.

'Oh, there's lots more, they didn't stop there. They were only getting started. They put his eye out, pop, something sharp or something blunt in the eye.'

'Sounds like they wanted information,' says Trevor to me.

'I may continue,' says Duncan. 'They started cutting his

fingers off, one by one, a couple off each hand. The wounds on the little fingers were older than the others.'

'Charming,' says Trevor. 'If it was a hit, someone woulda walked on that boat, bang-bang with a silencer and away.'

'It's brutal but not very professional,' I agree.

'Exactly. They risk getting caught in flattette.'

'What? Talk English, Duncan!'

'On the job. But if I can finish before you two offer a critique. He had water in his lungs, so they reckon they half drowned him in the bath and then they cut off his two big toes in the bath and dragged him around a bit so there's blood everywhere on the boat and the police are spooked by it because they reckon that these two were cooking meals and having naps. And the final coup de grâce, the grand finale, they left him wired up to the mains so he was slowly cooked alive and they carried on lobbing bits off him.'

'Like?'

'Ears, nose –'

'Bollocks?' asks Trevor.

'You know, Trevor, I didn't think to ask.'

'How was he found?' I ask.

'By the cleaning lady, little Irish woman,' says Duncan. 'She'll have a job getting that place ship-shape.'

'What was the cause of death?' I says.

'Loss of blood and heart attack.'

'What do the busies think Van Tuck was about?' asks Trevor.

'They never had a sniff of anything on him, no files, no Interpol circulars, nothing here or in Holland.'

'Do the law think it could be just a nutter?'

'Possibly, but they'll go through ever bit of paper, every phone bill.'

'Where's the fuckin khazi in this place?' says Trevor, getting up and walking out the door.

'The door directly in front of you, Trevor.'

Duncan sounds quite pissed on the brandy.

Trevor's phone rings. I pick it up from the coffee table and the display says 'Shanks' and a land-line number. I answer it.

'Trevor?' says Shanks, his accent exaggerated two-fold.

'Shanks, it's me. Trevor's in the khazi having a piss.'

'I just came home and there's about twenty messages on the machine, from Mandy 'n' all. You okay?'

'I think Trevor better ex –'

'Did I hear my fuckin phone go?' says Trevor, rushing back in still doing up his flies. 'Give it here.'

He snatches it outta my hand.

'Shanks, listen, someone's been topped, yeah. Now think, where was that bitta how's-your-father? Listen. Was it with the Dutchman or was it still in the shop?'

Trevor asked the question like it's the final question for the big star prize on a TV quiz, slow and deliberate, pronouncing every syllable. Trevor listens intently cos he has a couple of million sovs, maybe a year's work and possibly a lot of attention from the cozzers riding on the answer. He's nodding continually throughout his conversation with Shanks. I can hear Shanks' voice faintly but it seems to have gone up an octave so it's high and shrill.

'Saturday, you say, and he had it then, the paperwork, on hand. The goods were where? Well, Shanks, maybe, just maybe, there's a fuckin chance.'

Duncan's phone rings and he picks it up. Trevor's still marching up and down while Shanks rabbits on like mad. He covers the mouthpiece and gives me a wink.

'Shanks reckons we've got nothing to worry about, we sit tight and don't panic, he's got people in the docks.'

I've got half an eye on Duncan. He's jotting down notes in a reporter's notebook. He starts to deflate, like someone's letting the air outta him.

'Trevor,' says Duncan, putting the phone down.

'In a minute, Duncan, fuckin hell, can't you see I'm busy, are you fuckin mad?' says Trevor, shaking his head.

'I have to go out, something's come up, like right now, Trevor,' says Duncan.

'Well, fuck off then. We'll let ourselves out,' says Trevor, who's cheering right up.

157

'That was one of my contacts with a story,' says Duncan, looking down at the carpet.

'So ya off to win the fuckin Pulitzer Prize, are ya? Shut the fuck up, will ya. No, not you Shanks. I've got that fuckin nuisance paperboy with me.'

'He works in the docks,' says Duncan.

Trevor only hears the word docks. 'One second, Shanks. Don't go away. You –' he points at Duncan '– speak.'

Duncan still can't look up. His voice wavers as he speaks, the fear has returned.

'This chap who works for a shipping agent says the police, acting on information received, just seized approximately three tonnes of hashish resin, very high quality, in a consignment of Greek marble. The whole place is alive with police and customs. He says they arrived earlier with bills of lading and started to pull the place apart. After two and a half hours they came up trumps.'

'Shanks,' says Trevor into his mobile, 'we just gone down a snake. I'll see ya tomorrow, laters.'

He clicks the phone shut very calmly and tucks it into the back pocket of his jeans. He picks up the coffee table at each end. I watch as the tray of untouched coffee and biscuits slides off onto the floor in slow motion. He holds the table above his head for a split second and then fires it, like he did it every day and practised for hours, into the wide-screen television in the corner, letting go a howl of deep rage. The glass on the telly disintegrates instantly and shoots splinters and shards of glass back into the room. Next he picks up the stack system and propels it against the wall. Trevor's throwing everything in the room that'll break against the wall or overturning it. He pulls the dining chairs apart and moves on. He's screaming 'fuuuuuuuuuuuuuuuuuck' over and over again. I'm stood in a corner trying to look as inconspicuous as possible and Duncan, bless him, is doing the same while Trevor completely destroys the room. Every last breakable object, lamps, plants, the carriage clock, vases, video, is smashed. Now he's trying to throw an armchair through the front bay window but it won't have it. The upstairs neighbour is banging on the ceiling but luckily for

158

everyone Trevor is oblivious to it. After about thirty seconds of intense destruction Trevor is suddenly calm but breathing hard like he could suddenly see the pointlessness of it. He looks around. He's surprised by the debris around him, baffled.

'Come on. We're going,' he says to me. Duncan's shaking in the corner and looks literally about to shit himself. 'Sorry 'bout that, lad,' Trevor says to him in passing. 'I'll pay for any damage.'

Wednesday
Dan Saff Again

Morty finds last night's turn-out hilarious and my reaction to it even funnier still. Trevor dropped me at a petrol station in the fuckin middle of fuckin nowhere and the fuckwits behind the jump thought I was asking for a fuckin spaceship to take me home rather than a fuckin taxi. When I did manage to communicate this to them, through a travelling salesman who acted as an interpreter, it took about an hour to fuckin arrive and the geezer driving got lost and wouldn't admit it so after about twenty minutes we drove past the same fuckin petrol station again and I swear I saw him waving at his 'You're from London, ain't ya' mates. Then the geezer wants to charge me twenty-five quid for a sightseeing tour so there's a bittova row and a bitta barter and he eventually settles for fifteen quid after the hotel night-staff was gonna call the old bill and neither of us wanted that.

At about four in the morning I got woken up cos I felt a hand on my dick. Coming to, I'm greeted by the sight of some junkie hooker kneeling by the side of my bed smoking a snout and about to give me a blow-job with Mister Mortimer and Clarkie egging her on, telling her that I've just got outta the boob and I'll really appreciate it, ain't had it polished for a five stretch, darling. It's fuckin sad and repulsive cos she's half gouging, stinks of Tennant's, snout and junkie constipation smell, but when I fuck her off she's straight on Morty saying she wants her cash anyway. Morty and Clarkie are out of it, crying with laughter, doubled up.

'I want me fookin money, you two. You said you'd pay me here, ya cunts.'

She's now got her arse about a foot from my face, screaming, and her off-white leggings are far too small so they're stretched to fuck. I can see right through them. I'm trying to

160

make out what the fuck the pattern on her knickers is. I sometimes think of the strangest thing at the strangest time. Morty
gives her a score.

'I want some fookin cab fare. You said you'd fetch me
back.'

Teddy bears, that's what they are, fuckin teddy bears on her
knickers. That's a sad state of affairs, I'm thinking, she's
sucking cocks for a living and she's got teddy bears on her
drawers. I wanna go back to sleep. Morty gives her another
forty quid and she starts to relax a bit. They turn the light out at
least. I fall back to sleep listening to Morty howling with
laughter. Maybe she'll get my cab driver on the way back, they
were made for one another.

This morning we got to the dining room at one minute to
nine and breakfast finishes at nine on the dot. The staff didn't
look pleased to see us. Apparently the night manager had to
knock about the noise at five o'clock after complaints from the
other guests. Morty gets himself the full-on breakfast from the
serve-yourself counter and is tucking in. I've got some fruit and
a pot of coffee and Clarkie's got four tall glasses of orange juice
lined up in a row in front of him. He's also got a glazed look
that suggests that he wouldn't pass any random drugs test.

'I thought you'd appreciate a little souvenir of Manchester
last night seeing as you did the corporate entertainment bit with
Trevor,' says Morty, a bit too cheery after only three hours'
sleep.

'He's a fuckin pothouse, that Trevor.'

'Do you hear that, Mister Clark, our colleague here is
shocked and surprised to find that one of the most feared and
respected drug dealers in the north of England has a vicious
temper.'

Clarkie grins.

'He seems such a nice geezer,' I say, 'but he changes when
he's stoned, had a spliff and –'

'He becomes some kinda hippie Mafioso, a right pest with
all that stuff. The wind and rain and honour, brotherhood and
all sorts of shit. When I was in the boob with him –'

'You remember him from the boob?'

161

'Course I fuckin remember him from the boob. We did time together. How d'ya think we found Trevor? In the yellow pages?'

'Well, he says you wouldn't have remembered him.'

'I don't know why he's said that cos you'd remember Trevor all right. These fuckin eggs are dead.'

'If they weren't they'd be chickens.'

'I mean they've been on the fuckin hotplate too long. This gaff reminds me of Sunday mornin in the shovel. And that lot remind me of screws,' he says, nodding at the waitresses in their black uniforms.

'Well don't eat the eggs then. So why would you remember Trevor? He says he did his lie-down quiet and –'

'Trevor?! The Trevor who was here yesterday?'

'Yes, Morty. He says he went in to do a five and ended up doin a three so he musta –'

'No. He went in to do a three and ended up doin a five, other way round mate. Someone's got their arithmetic wrong and I can't believe one of the biggest dealers in the country can't do simple maths.'

'So why would he tell me that?'

'Fuck knows. Maybe Trevor has problems with his memory. Listen, Trevor's party piece was throwin screws over the landing from the threes.'

'What, killin 'em?!'

'No, silly bollocks. He'd still be there if that was the fuckin case. No, they have a net, like what you get under the trapeze at the circus, and they'd land in that, screws and grasses.'

'And they thought it was a giggle as well, did they?'

'No way. He'd get a serious beating from the mufti, the heavy mob, but he's a bit mad is Trevor.'

The sensation of walking out of Duncan's last night over all that broken glass in the shag-pile carpet is still very vivid.

'He had you booked as the Chris Eubank of the prison system,' I says.

'What?'

'He said you had a tie and a uniform.'

'That was only to raise a laugh for the chaps. See what I

162

mean, Trevor takes everything too fuckin serious. This Van Duck geezer, nothin to do with us, or the firm from down our way, or any fuckin Continentals. See, these fuckin scousers –' says Morty, pointing at the gaggle of waitresses with his knife '– when they ain't singing "You'll never walk alone" or "He ain't heavy, he's my brother", they're nickin the gold fillings outta each other's heads. They got a right nasty side to their character. Some cunt's tortured the geezer to death for his PIN number when all the time they coulda gone down the docks with this bill of whatever and won the scally lottery, three tonna puff. I don't know why you even mention it.'

'He went down for three tonne a block last night cos someone done a number on his travel agent so I think he's a bit entitled to be –'

'And another thing. We ain't givin no fuckin readies to any Germans. If we can find a home for those pills we pay the Apaches or whatever you call 'em their whack, Jimmy his, and we jog on.'

'Is that cos they're fuckin Nazis?'

'Listen, I don't give a monkey's who they are or what they fuckin believe. They ain't getting a fuckin penny. Subject closed.'

'And you still wanna find a buyer?'

'Yes. Maybe this outfit'll wanna make up their losses.'

'Shanks rang, actually, to say maybe wait a few days until Trevor's in a better humour. Sounds like they're all in mournin for their three tonne of black.'

'Thanks for lettin me know.'

'We've never punted skanked gear before, Mort, it's aggravation.'

'It's big bucks. Let's not get carried away here. You ain't trying to get elected, are ya?'

'No!'

'Good.'

I think a healthy gung-ho attitude, a large drop of the old bravado, has its place in the jollying-along process but I think Mister Mortimer is starting to move into what Americans and West Londoners call denial, a blanking of unsavoury facts. Did

163

the captain of the *Titanic* tell the passengers and crew 'Icebergs, I piss on 'em'? I think not.

A waitress comes over to shift the plates and Clarkie goes to stroke her arm but she moves away frightened. She looks at us like we're cannibals. Clarkie ain't touched the juice, it's still lined up in highball glasses in a perfect row. The waitress retreats back to the safety of the other girls. They're having a little conference of their own, waiting for us to finish. We're getting disapproving looks.

'How many of those pills did he have?' I ask, nodding at Clarkie.

'Two. And you know what he says they're like?' says Morty, looking at Mister Clark like he's behind glass at the zoo.

'Don't tell me. They're just like the old days?'

'He says he's been doin pills since he was twelve and these are the best he's ever had.'

'I ain't in the mood for one of Clarkie's "I was shiftin ounces of charlie at primary school" stories this morning, Mort.'

'He says if he usually does only two, it don't touch the sides but look ...'

Clarkie's staring up, open-mouthed, at the white-washed, plasterboard, suspended ceiling, with neon striplights and sprinkler system, gazing like it was created by one Michelangelo.

'Let's get the fuck outta here. I'm having fuckin lunch in Soho, civilisation, if you wanna tag along,' I declare, 'and I think I better drive.'

Tuna Can Be Life or Death

This is more like it, this is what I joined up for. Me and Morty's getting seated in this gaff in Soho that's highly recommended. It's the latest trendy spot for all the latest trendy people. It's hard to get in, even on a Wednesday lunchtime, but Morty ringing every five minutes all the way down the motorway, driving 'em mad, has got us a reservation. They wanted to tuck us away in the corner downstairs but he's either bribed someone or caused a fuss so now we're sitting upstairs on the good tables, facing out into the restaurant so we can observe the comings and goings, nut the creamy women and do a bit of our favourite sport, people-watching. We like to get in the watering holes where the most exotic birds come to feed, simply sit back and soak it up.

This place is the nuts, with strange flowers in polished steel vases, orchids floating in crystal bowls on the tables and huge, nutty, a bit psychotic if you ask me, abstract paintings on the walls. Whole slabs of concrete walls are painted in primary colours, orangey red, Irish green, turquoise and a regal purple and whole walls are left bare so they look like an underground car-park. Daylight pours in through the skylight. It's indulgent and luxurious but in a different way from Pepi's Barn. Jimmy wouldn't like it. He'd say there's far too many pretentious wankers in the place. The clientele are mostly media, film, telly and advertising folk. Hopefully that's what me and Mister Mortimer look like, a pair of film-producer dudes hatching a plot to make a movie, and not a porn one either. This is all very civilised, what I need, a nice spot of lunch. A lot of our product ends up going up the hooters of these good people but it's still a bit early in the day for most of them. In fact, most of them stick to the bottled water at four-fifty a go. Maybe it would be different if this was Friday afternoon rather than Wednesday. The good folk of medialand would be letting off, getting nicely loosened up for weekend frolics and a right royal nose-up.

Today it's just the hubbub of talking business and gossip, doing deals, running shit up flagpoles, mixed with the gentle chinking of glasses, people coming and going with hugs and air kisses. I've seen these sedate people at full throttle and it's one mad fucking party, nicely debauched.

Clarkie got dropped off at Kilburn station, got a cab over to see some Richard and we commandeered the Rover. I can't seem to raise Geno on the phone anywhere, home or mobile, but that ain't really unusual. We need to talk to him and let him know about the business with the pills, circumstances of origin, but if he can't be found we might as well relax, take our boots off and have some decent grub. Maybe Morty's denial's rubbing off on me, maybe I feel better being back on familiar turf, I felt like kissing the pavement outside Kilburn High Road tube, but the business about the Germans, the Yahoos, Van Tuck, don't seem like the naughty problem it was when I got out of bed this morning.

We order tomato and orange soup with toasted fennel, tuna Niçoise, steaks well-done cee-voo-play, an olive bread for the soup and a ciabatta garlic bread to come with the main and a bottle each of sparkling and still water. We're simple folk us.

'I was in this gaff Saturday night with this bird,' says Morty. 'I've ordered the tuna Niçoise and when it's arrived it's come with tinned tuna flakes.'

'That's a bit cheap.'

'Not when they're charging about a tenner a go.'

'No, I mean it's cheap of them.'

'Dead right. A tuna Niçoise should have iceberg lettuce, new potatoes, green beans, anchovy, right? Boiled eggs, dressing and a fuckin grilled tuna steak, not fuckin tinned shit. Or better still, a griddled tuna steak.'

'Fuckin dead right. You backed it, yeah?'

'Fuckin right I backed it. I got the head man over and he was dead embarrassed, no fuss, no threats, the bird's well impressed.'

'Did they sort you out?'

'Yeah. I could've stronged it and got the whole turn-out for nothin but I didn't. I just told 'em they got me mixed up with some other geezer, some muppet who pays a cockle for a tuna salad.'

'It's not the money it's the fact that they're takin the piss.'

'Not outta me, they ain't. No fuckin way.'

'So what did you eat?'

'Oh, they found me a tuna steak from somewhere, maybe they sent out for it. Fuck knows.'

'Any val?'

'Very good, it was, after the wait.'

Our soup arrives.

'I knew this geezer once, in the shovel, got killed over a can of tuna.'

Here we go.

'How come?' I say.

'All those guys who pump iron save their wages and buy stuff, you know, tins of tuna and that from the canteen. They open the tuna, eat it outta the can and straight away work out and that way you pump up cos it's pure protein, tuna. That's how it's done. You can bang away for ever on them weights but if you ain't got the right fuel on board it's a fuckin waste of time.'

'Is that right?'

'Oh yeah. So this can of tuna's gone missin from this guy Vinny Taylor's cell and Vinny's got it into his nut that this other guy, Frankie Brown, has chored it outta the cell so he's got himself all wound up, marched into Frank's cell and plunged him in the throat, straight in the fuckin jugular, no fuckin about, crash! Blood's sprayed out everywhere.'

'What, you was in the cell?'

'Yeah, we was havin a little smoke. This soup's cold.'

'It's meant to be.'

'Yeah, three or four of us were just sittin about when in marched Vinny, straight over to Frankie in three big steps, one, two, three and crash –' Morty does a cutting motion with his soup spoon '– all over in about a second, two seconds tops. He's done him twice, either side. He held his head back and he knows exactly, ex-zact-lee, what he was doin so there was fuck all anyone could do about anything.'

167

'So you scarpered?'

'Right, cos Vinny stood over him so we couldn't do shit. The claret's gone up the fuckin walls, over us, it's gone fuckin everywhere.'

'Where did the blade come from?'

'Everyone had a chiv, it was that kinda neighbourhood.'

'All over a fuckin can of tuna. What's a can of tuna cost? Sixty pence? Eighty?'

'Fuck knows. Anyways, it wasn't just about the tuna –'

I'd kinda worked that out on my own.

'It's about all sorts of shit, you know, respect, status. And all that body-building crap.'

'Who's got the best definition and that.'

'Yeah, it's all a bit queer, really. Anyway, it had all been simmering for some time. They're slowly windin each other up, nothin you can put your finger on, but you know ...'

'So what's happened?'

'Oh, the big lockdown, outside old bill brought in, Vinny's been ghosted down to the Moor.'

'The what?'

'Dartmoor. This went off in the Scrubs, D-wing, right, and as far as anyone knows he got moved that night down to the block and then on to the Moor, poor fucker, and he'll have trouble gettin' out of there.'

'They question you?'

'Next day, couldn't tell 'em nothin, but Vinny put his hands up straight away anyway, mainly cos he was caught red-handed stood over Frankie and he wouldn't let the screws in to help him, so there you go. Such is life.'

'Such is life,' I shrug.

'Strange guy, Vinny, but people wouldn't take liberties with him.'

'So he gets lifed off?'

'Well, he was doin life anyway for serving some geezer over a bird so what can they do except give him another life sentence and tell him he can't apply for parole until about the year two thousand and fifty when he's about ninety fuckin five anyway. Double-lifer.'

168

Morty shrugged and tore at some olive bread.

'It was too late for an anger-management course,' I say.

'Too late for Frankie Brown,' says Mort.

'Too late for Vinny Taylor. Did they ever find out who nicked the can of tuna?'

'No, thank fuck.'

It took a couple of seconds.

'What, you nicked the tuna, Morty?'

Morty stays silent, finishes his soup, pushes the bowl away.

'Well, strictly between me and you, yeah –' He lowers his voice and looks about just in case any of the good folk should be earwigging '– it was me. I was hungry.'

'Did you ever, like, let on it was you, tell anyone, like?'

Morty raises an eyebrow slightly then looks up at the ceiling like he can't believe what he's hearing. He talks slow like he's speaking to a stupid child.

'Well, it was, how can I put this? Er, it wasn't like a group-therapy situation, yeah? You understand, brov?'

'Yes, Mort.'

Our main course arrives.

'Well, well, well. Now that looks like a proper tuna Niçoise.'

My phone rings. I don't know the number. It's a land-line number, maybe it's Geno. I push the receive button.

'Where are you?' asks Cody.

'We're in Soho, me and Mort, havin something to eat.'

'You got a pen?'

'Yeah.'

'Write down this address.'

I grab a paper napkin and write it down. 'What's this, Cody?'

'Block of flats, other side of the Euston Road from King's Cross mainline. Come over as soon as, okay? Low profile, hands in pockets, yeah? You drivin?'

'Yeah.'

Cody sounds all business.

'Park right off the plot but ASAP.'

'Is this good news?'

'How long you two gonna be?'

'Half an hour. One or both?'

'The ice cream.'

Freezer. Kinky. 'You should sound pleased, that's three 'n' 'alf.'

'Might need a steward's. Listen, thirty minutes then I'm gone.'

He's off the phone already. Sounded a bit bottley, not like Cody at all.

'That was Cody. He reckons he's found the boyfriend, Kinky.'

'That's a touch, then, ain't it. No bird?'

'No. He says we gotta go over there like right now. We better stick that tuna steak in some of that bread, grab a bottle of water and a cab and go and see what he's got.'

'What, leave the motor in the NCP? Where is he?'

'King's Cross. Might be easier.'

'Fuckin lovely. You can pay for this, seein as I'm givin you a hand.'

I pay and we walk out with a very expensive tuna sandwich and a bottle of water each. The taxi won't take us anywhere until we've finished eating so we could've relaxed and finished in the restaurant.

We get the taxi to drop us in front of the station like we was going on a trip. We go through the subway so now we're on the side of the Euston Road that we want. Addicts and boozers are sitting on or draped over the crash barriers looking for a clue. It's busy round the front of the station with travellers, office workers and a few tourists even. Mort pulls one of the drunkies over and asks him where this street is. The guy, who's a Jock or a Paddy, spots the name of the block of flats written on the napkin, points it out, incoherently mumbling and swaying at the same time. He's trying to focus on me and Mort but it just looks like he's pulling faces, grooning. We laugh. Far from being offended the geezer laughs too. Morty gives him a handful of change and the lagging boat wants to shake Morty's hand but Mort ain't keen.

The block is like a fortress, with a wire fence all around and

170

a private security guard sat behind a concierge desk reading the paper. There's a panel outside and I push in the number of the flat and push the 'Call' button. Straight away the door buzzes and in we walk. The guy doesn't look up as we walk past into the lift. It smells of piss, no surprise there. The flat we want is on the fifth floor. As we emerge outta the lift there's a geezer I know, out on the landing. Tiptoes was rumoured to be able to walk without touching the floor. In reality he walks very light-footed, on the very tips of his toes, hence the moniker. He works in the same game as Cody, he's good, but he ain't in the same league as Billy Bogus. He has his finger over his lips, shooshing us, his eyes are sweeping the locale to see if anyone's watching us. Me and Mort, who are quite boisterous after the grooner, suddenly have to get schtum.

Tiptoes motions us in silently. He's all gloved-up. He gives us a wink, nods over his shoulder and then shuts the door without making a sound. The gaff stinks, it's fuckin putrid and stale, like something's died. There's an accumulation of tram-pled mail on the mat, bills and final demands, a scattering of envelopes that brought Giros, empty and slung back in the pile. There's a commotion going on inside. Tiptoes leads us through into a front room where Cody's got three geezers sat on a dilapidated three-piece suite in front of him. He turns to us.

'Just one minute, Inspector, I think we may be getting somewhere at last,' he says to us as we enter.

'Crack is the devil and you suck his cock, Mister Policeman, you beg, steal and sell your soul to worship at his altar. Kinky is with the Angel Gabriel, safe from harm, gone to join the fight with the good angels against Lucifer's forces, the forces of evil that you represent on this earth.'

The guy's whacked out, frazzled, glaring eyes. He's white and got the beginning clumps of dreads. Something in his voice says he's middle class, home counties and educated, but he's fallen a long way from grace.

'Listen, Graham, maybe you could be quiet for a bit and let the others speak.'

'You can try and silence the word of the Nazarene.'

'Where did the money come from? Listen, I ain't here to

nick anyone. I just need to get to the bottom of this, trust me.'
Cody's talking to a kid who looks about fifteen, street kid,
maybe a rent, dirty, snotty-nosed. Maybe the shunters like it
like that. The kid says nothing, but he carries on absent-mindedly pulling the stuffing outta the arm of the sofa, rolling it up
into balls and letting it drop to the floor. The religious freak
with the hint of crack psychosis rumbles on and fuckin on. I
start to tune him out, blank him, while Cody's telling him to
shut the fuck up.

I turn my back on the trio and whisper to Tiptoes.

'Is Kinky here?'

Tiptoes nods very slightly.

'One of them?'

He shakes his head but says nothing. I hope he ain't escaped
on us. I was getting my fuckin hopes up, could be on the home
stretch. The floor in this room is scattered with empty purple
and gold cans. In the corner there's an old, discarded box of
takeaway chicken that's starting to chuck-up, smell, and it's
made worse cos the curtains are drawn and the windows ain't
been opened for ages. The gaff's been totally trashed. I walk
through the room doing my best impersonation of a police
officer, moving things with the end of my pen. I notice that the
television's missing from its spot on the table that all the chairs
in the room point at. There's a total lack of dust in an oblong
where the TV once was in pride of place. There's an aerial wire,
going nowhere, giving the game away. This place was never
gonna be in any interior design magazines but now it's had the
arse torn outta it.

There's burnt spoons, bloody works, cans, bent and punc-
tured to smoke rocks, pipes made from water bottles, burnt
Jimmy Boyle, lemons, squeezed, hairy and grey and half-eaten
Kit-Kats where the brothers only wanted the foil wrap to have
a little boot, empty wraps. All the ingredients, in fact, of a
toe-rags' picnic. The last of the trio that Cody's trying to get
sense outta is roasting, sweating and ill, a dozen-a-dime junkie,
hustler, hoister, burglar, mugger. The kinda kid Jimmy would
call jail fodder.

'All the devil's disciples name is Satan, I am of the damned,

172

this is our sacrifice, this is our sacrament. We must return to the anti-Christ before it's too late.'

The geezer Graham is off again with more energy than before. It'll take more than two aspirins to sort his head out. I catch Cody's eye and motion him to come out into the kitchen.

'Sergeant,' he says to Tiptoes, following me and Mort out, 'keep an eye on these three.'

'Cody,' I ask as soon as he arrives, 'where the fuck is Kinky? You ain't let him fuckin —'

'Didn't fuckin Tiptoes tell ya?'

'No, Cody. Where the fuck's this fuckin Kinky?'

'Follow me.'

He walks us down the hall and opens one of the doors. He turns the light on with his gloved hand and politely moves aside to allow me and Morty to go in first. A smell hits me first. If it was bad coming through the front door this almost knocks me over. 'Kinky,' says Mister Garret, nodding into the bedroom. I walk in.

Kinky's dead. One look's all it takes. His eyes are open in tiny slits about a quarter of an inch wide. He looks peaceful, frozen in time, like a waxwork or a carving of Jesus on the cross, arms out wide, head tilted slightly to one side. The colour has left his black face leaving it ashen. His lips already look blue. He's on a tatty mattress, with a grubby duvet half covering him, and on the floor by his side are a candle, a spoon, a bottle of water, a Bic lighter, an empty wrap and a tiny, but seemingly very effective, works with minute traces of blood on the inside. The shit and piss have dropped outta him onto the mattress.

'Don't touch anything. Keep you hands in your pockets, removes temptation,' says Cody, whispering.

'Poor cunt,' says Morty, shaking his head.

'Sad way for anyone to end up, but listen, this bottle next door reckon someone give him two grand in readies to drop the bird out,' says Cody.

'So he's spunked the lot on brown,' says Mort, who's got a purple silk hanky held against his nose.

'And rocks as well, 'n' givin the boys next door a good time.

After the clinic he woulda been clean and to suddenly jump back in where ya left off ... '

Cody lets Kinky's dead body speak for itself. He turns to me. 'Would Jimmy give him two key in readies on the old man's behalf?'

'Fuck knows, Cody. Maybe we should be gettin outta here.'

Kinky had bought himself some new clothes, a couple of sweats and a pair of jogging pants. One of the sweats still has the shop labels on. A pair of box-fresh white Reeboks has been placed tidily together at the bottom of the mattress, all ready for the next day's rough and tumble. Kinky's tied the laces with bows at the top so he can admire them as he falls asleep. The box is in the corner, neat, like he wanted to keep it.

'They, them lot next door, had about eight hundred quid when we flopped on 'em.'

'Let 'em keep it,' says Morty. 'It ain't ours.'

'How'd you find him?' I ask, nodding at Kinky.

'Easy, really,' says Cody, 'and a bitta luck. Asked about, put soma your cash 'bout and here we are. He was a bit high-profile when he got back from the country with two grand. That's a lotta money on the street round here.'

Guys like Kinky don't open savings accounts or put themselves on a little weekly pension, they iron it out as quick as possible, cos deep down they think they've got no fuckin right having readies. To them it's a means to an end, and the end is oblivion. Kinky's experiencing the ultimate oblivion right now.

'Whose gaff is this, Cody?' I ask.

'The tenant is up the Cally, in the Ville, doing six months for being a nuisance to society, nothin heavy, and Graham, the nut-nut, is meant to be lookin after it for him.'

'He's doin a lovely job, ain't he,' says Mort, nodding at Kinky. 'Bodies in the bedroom, everything sold, the whole gaff lookin like a fuckin khazi.'

'Let's leave Kinky in peace,' says Cody, showing a side to his character I never realised he had. Me and Cody are walking out the door but Morty's mumbling something, almost to himself, very unlike Mort.

'What's 'at, Mort?' asks Cody, standing in the doorway.

'I was just saying, some guys make it, some guys don't,' says Morty, crossing himself as he leaves.

'Tell them what you just told me,' Tiptoes says to the rent when we reappear. The atmosphere is a lot more subdued. I think Tiptoes might have threatened the righteous one with a bitta ABH or something stronger cos he's a bit jittery and twitchy but mostly silent. Every time he goes to speak, Tiptoes, who can actually have a row, that's why he's on this mission, silences him with a pointy finger and a stern look.

'You're not police, are ya, really?' says the kid in an accent that's pure over-the-pipe Saff London.

'What makes you think that, son? Speak your mind, don't be frightened,' says Cody.

'Cos you don't get old bill, CID, looking like him,' he says, pointing at Mister Mortimer, who grins.

'You'd be surprised, son, what old bill look like,' says Cody knowingly. 'I promise you I could point you out old bill that don't look like old bill, not in a million years.'

'And old bill can't afford shoes like them. You can turn it in now, Graham,' he says, pointing at my black suede Gucci loafers. He's very sharp, this kid.

'They could save up,' says Cody.

'You've all got too much money,' says the kid.

'Would it matter if we weren't the police?'

'I couldn't give a fuck. Can we keep that money?'

'If you behave I'll think about it. Let me tell you something, okay? If any of these three here got upset, you'd fuckin wish they were old bill. Can you see that?'

The kid, who it must be said has got a lotta fuckin balls, surveys us and nods.

'Now, junior, tell me what you told my mate and you, Graham, keep fuckin quiet. Okay?'

'Kinky reckons he got the money to leave the Richard alone but he really liked her.'

'But by who? Did he say?' I ask.

'I dunno, mate, but she said give it back cos it can only do harm but he says that he's gonna keep the money and keep seeing her. She was staying here.'

175

'She was here?!' says me and Cody at the same time. Cody turns and gives me a 'Leave this to me' look.

'Up until three days ago. She wouldn't use no gear or nothin and she didn't want Kinky using it either, she said she could get them both off it but when the money turned up he had a little boot.'

'A chase?'

'Yeah,' he shrugs, 'but she went fuckin mad so he didn't know what to do cos he wants to have a bitta tackle but he don't wanna lose the bird either.'

'Try and think, who give him the money?'

'He wouldn't say.'

'Or he didn't know.'

'I'm not with ya,' says the kid.

'It come through a third party.'

'You've lost me now.'

'It don't matter. How did he react?'

'He was largin it. You'd do the same, but she wouldn't have it with him if he was using, see, so he was fucked, weren't he.'

'Where did she go?'

'Brighton.'

'How do you know?'

'I heard them arguing.'

'And she fucked off? When?'

'Tuesday morning. He got this dough Sunday night. She hung about tryin to sort him but he weren't havin it so she chipped.'

'To Brighton?'

'Yeah. She's givin it "Do ya think it's that easy, do ya, taking the money and messin these people about, do ya?"'

'Who did she mean.'

'I dunno. Gissa snout, mate,' he says to Mort.

Morty gives the kid a snout and lights it for him, which is very rare.

'Giss one for Ron.'

Morty throws snout over to the other two on the sofa.

'I meant for later on, mate,' says the kid.

'Play your cards right and one won't have to worry about salmon for a while, son,' says Cody.

'Okay, Dad,' he says, laughing, trying to jolly-up his pals, who are still rigid with fear. 'I tell ya this,' he says, leaning forward and taking a massive lug on his snout, 'I went in there to try and ponce a bitta gear off Kinky but he was fast asleep, snorin and that, so I tea-leafed a bit. You ever done gear?'

He looks at us one at a time and we all shake our heads.

'I didn't think you had, somehow, but when you gotta 'ave a bitta gear, you gotta 'ave a bitta gear, you know what I mean?'

No. I thought we'd established that.

'So I chored a bit and had a sly one. Little while later, early this mornin, I hear someone creepin 'bout. I think it's Kinky sussed me out, yeah? But it ain't. It's some geezer loiding the front door so I'm thinkin it's cozzers ...'

'Then what?' asks Cody. All six of us are waiting to hear what happened.

'Then I goofed out. I thought if it's a spin, I've had a nice bitta gear, fuck 'em, I'm sweet.'

'Are you sure this really happened?'

'Listen, mate, if you want me to swear it happened, then it happened, and if you want me to go the other way, I sweet with that 'n' all. You tell me.'

'You ever hear of the truth, son?' says Cody.

'Fuckin 'ell. Don't get the fuckin hump, mate, I'm tryin to help you out here, mate.'

'You ever hear of tellin the truth?'

'Listen, mate, I didn't come crashin in 'ere earlier sayin I was old bill.'

'He's got ya there, brov,' says Morty, who's formed an affinity with the kid.

'Is that all you know, son?' says Cody.

'That's it, mate,' says the kid.

'Either of you two got anything you wanna add?'

They shake their heads.

'You got somewhere to go?'

They nod their heads.

'Let's go then. Anything you wanna get before we go?'

The kid jumps up, disappears, but before I know it he's back with the Reeboks, the sweats and the jog pants, stuffing them back into the carrier bag they came in.

'This is what we're gonna do. You listening?' says Cody. 'We're gonna stroll outta here, in the lift, heads down, don't be lookin at those CCTVs, okay? We're gonna walk round the corner, twice to the right. You can tell your left and right, can't ya? Good. Follow me. My pal here –' nodding at Tiptoes '– is gonna be tailin us out and when I think it's sweet, I'm gonna give you these readies back, okay? Any questions? No? Good.'

Tiptoes is already out, quietly checking the landing. Suddenly he jumps back inside and shuts the door. I can hear the lift door opening and people getting out. Tiptoes has his finger over his lips. I can hear myself breathing and a large family of Bangladeshis chattering as they move past the door. The language sounds like a sing-song, like Italian. We're all silent but I can hear the people outside laughing and joking. Then it stops and a door shuts along the landing.

Tiptoes creeps out and holds the lift. At his nod we all pile in and go to the ground floor. Graham points out a back door and we all move through that instead of going past the security guard. When we're out on the street again, Cody takes point and leads us up and over the Gray's Inn Road. He's paranoid about ready-eyes, is Cody, and the whole area is smashed alive with them. Suddenly he darts down a small turning then very quickly pulls the three desperadoes into the disused fire exit of a cheap hotel for the carve-up.

Cody's given them a carpet, three hundred, each and a very quick, very loud, very stern warning about talking too much. Me and Morty are standing on the pavement nonchalantly and we can hear it.

'I'll find ya like I found him and I'll fuckin kill ya, okay? I fuckin said "okay?"!'

The kid emerges from the doorway.

'See ya, pal,' he says, nicking Morty's live snout outta his hand and sticking his readies down his pants.

'Don't be fuckin spendin all that on the brown, see what happened to your pal,' says Morty, shaking his head.

'Kinky didn't go over,' shouts the kid, running backwards, on his way to an important appointment with a ten-pound bag. 'Someone did him in.'

Chance'd Be a Fine Thing

Cody and Tiptoes come outta the doorway, both looking up and down the street but it's deserted.

'Listen,' says Cody with an edge in his voice, 'I think we need a little chat. There's a café two hundred yards up the Cally, George's, give us ten minutes. You two go that way and we'll go this, okay?'

With that they march off at high speed, leaving me and Mort wandering down this quiet back street that still has cobbles on the road.

'That geezer, I knew him,' says Morty.

'Who, Tiptoes? You would, he's a face.'

'No, Kinky.'

I stopped walking.

'Really? How?'

'He's a distant relation, tenth cousin removed or something.'

'Shit, really? I'm sorry, Mort.'

'It's all right. I ain't seen him or his family since he was about five, twenty years ago.'

He lights another fag.

'It took me a while back there to work it out. Trevor Atkins. Cute kid, as I remember, but he was distant.'

'All the same, it's a cuntish way to end up … What can I say?'

'There's nothin to say, is there. It ain't a big deal. I didn't wanna say anythin back there with those two.'

'Don't say anythin now, either. They don't need to know.'

We walk the long way round, enjoying the fresh air again. We walk into the café and order coffees.

'Not eatin, lads?' says the soapy geezer behind the ramp. 'Why not 'ave a bitta cake, lads.'

The cake looks like it's been here as long as he has, the fuckin cellophane's dusty. Morty don't like the gaff. It's a bit too greasy for him. The tables haven't been wiped down properly. They've been wiped with a greasy rag so the Formica's slippery and bit more shiny than it should be. He's got his look on, the look he puts on when it's all a bit distasteful and grubby. He sits down but keeps his raincoat buttoned up, his driving gloves on and his elbows off the table.

Cody motions me outside straight away.

'I know what yer gonna say, Cody.'

'This is a bit fuckin much, mate, fuckin stiffs. I thought this was gonna be a giggle. Did you hear what that kid was saying back there? Someone offed his mate.'

'The kid's spark out, shot away, tell ya anythin. Listen, I've had a think. I'll give ya the three and 'alf I owe ya but if you just find the bird down in Brighton, I weigh you on ten grand.'

'Are we talkin thirteen and a 'alf gee?'

'No. That's bein greedy, Cody. I'm talkin ten.'

'I was gonna give Tiptoes something outta my whack, a coupla grand, even, see how things went, but now he could be webbed up in a murder –'

'The geezer OD'd, happens all the time 'round 'ere, you said it yourself. Listen, you get a train to Brighton from the Thameslink over there you could be ten grand richer tomorrow.'

'You pay Tiptoes his whack, two grand?'

'Done,' I agree.

When I thought they had Kinky and the princess I realised how much I wanted out of this thing. I consider it twelve large well spent. Cody opens the door of the café slightly and calls over to Tiptoes to come outside.

'Fancy a trip to Brighton? Two gee?' says Cody.

Tiptoes nods slightly and away they march back down the Caledonian Road towards the station. I turn round and spot Morty. He's got a faraway look on his boat. As I go to walk back into the café I bump into someone trying to get through the door at exactly the same time as me.

'Watch where ya fuckin goin, ya little cunt,' the geezer gives it, twitching his head and sticking his chest out like he really wants to know. The geezer's got a few naughty Mars Bars. One runs from the bottom of his right eye to the middle of his chin, so he's obviously come second a few times. He's a big fat cunt so I could nut the geezer right on the hooter, leg it and he'd die of a fuckin heart attack before he caught me, but instead I swallow, act the prince, and let the geezer squeeze through first. He's dressed like a total lamp anyway, chucking up a smell of neglect and stale brew. He's having trouble walking so he's got enough problems going on for today and so have I.

'Morty!' the fat geezer shouts as he sees Mister Mortimer. 'Fuckin 'ell, long time no see, ya fuckin cunt, where ya been hidin?'

Morty was looking about as tranquil as I'd ever seen him until this oaf starts hooting. He looks like he's been snapped out of a daydream and landed with a bump. I'll know in the very first second that Morty looks at this geezer whether he's pleased to see him or not. He might not be saying anything but I'll know from instinct. Morty looks up and it's a definite negative, like the geezer's in the exhausting-nuisance category. The fat geezer plonks himself down opposite Morty and when I sit down at the same table he looks at me with a snarl, like I'm the interloper.

'Hello, Freddie,' says Morty in the voice he saves for funerals.

With that, this Freddie-geezer's off into the big Auld Lang Syne number like they were best mates but they lost touch. He's shouting at the geezer behind the ramp, calling on the massive fry-up, and he looks like he eats it three times a day. Morty's a big boy now and if he don't wanna talk to this Freddie character he'll get up and move. I tell Morty I'm going outside to use the phone and this Freddie says, 'Go on, fuck off, then,' and laughs like it's really hilarious.

I try Geno yet again but no joy. I don't wanna go back in just yet so I mooch about in a couple of shops for about five minutes and then stroll back. Morty hasn't moved a hair or touched his coffee but Freddie's in full flow and tucking in at the same time. It's fuckin revolting to watch Freddie eat at close quarters. He's shovelling fried eggs and beans, putting rashers of bacon into his mouth and then pulling off the rind with his chubby fingers. He's eating so fast, it's urgent business, he's getting breathless.

182

He's chatting his rubbish the whole time. Under different circumstances this could almost be funny but the mood ain't right today. He's pronged a sausage in the middle and he's taking bites outta each end. I can't believe this geezer. He's wiping up egg-yolk and grease with bread and marge. I don't like being around mongrels like him any longer than I have to. I'll need a tetanus injection if I do. The cunt revolts me and he's talking non-stop, everyone's a grass, a slag, a muggy-cunt or a wrong'un, or thinks they're Charlie Potatoes cos they've got a few bob.

Freddie clears his plate and pushes it away. He's sitting back in his chair and starting to relax. In fact he's getting a bit too cocky, a bit too confident. I can see his brain clicking over. He wipes his mouth with the back of his hand and reaches over and takes one of Morty's Bensons but he leaves a nasty greasy thumb-stain on the gold packet. Morty clocks it. Only his eyes move. Freddie lights the snout, takes a drag and blows it out like it was a big fuckin chunky cigar and he's celebrating a pools win. He rolls the fag between his greasy thumb and forefinger, with a silly grin on his boat, but then he's up and leaning on the table with his elbows, sucking bits of debris out from between his teeth.

'Morty, how ya fixed for a coupla quid for old times' sake? I can't get to work cos the gathers got my card marked,' he says.

Morty don't say a dickey-bird but like a robot goes into his trouser pocket, pulls out a wedge and pulls a couple of twenties off and drops them on the tabletop.

'Ya couldn't make it a nice round sixty sovs, could ya, Mort?'

Mister Mortimer goes back in his kick and brings out another score note and drops it on the table. This is very fuckin strange cos Morty won't usually entertain mackerels. He'll give people readies but not if they ask.

'This on you, Morty?' pointing at his plate. 'For old times' sake, ay?'

This Freddie's tearing the arse outta things. Morty just shrugs like he's mute. Freddie gives Morty a tiny wink with a sideways flick of the head. He's got a smug little smirk on his face. No disrespect to ya Freddie mate, I'm thinking, but you're a complete cunt.

'All right, Mort,' he says and gives him another sly wink. There is an unspoken 'All right, Mort, you muggy-cunt'. Some people think kindness is weakness. For a split second Freddie is blatantly taking the piss outta Morty to his face and Mort's just gazing over his shoulder into space, like he's had a draw, with a thin smile on his face.

Then it all goes horribly wrong. Freddie, probably the story of his life, sees it too late. His eyes suddenly fill with terror, his arms come up to try to protect himself but Morty is up and in a flash snatches the hair on the back of his head, wrenches it back one time and brings it crashing down onto the tabletop and plates at a million miles an hour. Fred's nose explodes with a damp thud and I hear the crushing of bone. Morty pulls it back and does it again. Blood sprays over my raincoat. I jump back as the table gets thrown across the floor. Fred's just paralysed with shock. He don't even make a token feeble attempt to get away, he just falls against the wall. Morty's got him by the throat and he's hitting him around the head with everything that ain't nailed down. The sauce bottles have got smashed into his face. The heavy glass ashtray's bounced off his jaw, face and skull, once, twice, ten times. Freddie's trying to cover his head with his hands but Morty's totally lost it and the shit's raining down on Fred's head. Morty's moved in close on him, halted for a split second to steady his feet, and then kneed him once, twice, hard in the guts, right in the middle of the ribcage, pushing all the wind outta him. Freddie's gone crimson. His head's thrown back in the air. As he comes back down he's vomiting, doubled over. Morty's held him up by the back of the collar and given him two rapid, one two, knees in the face and let him fall backwards to the deck. His face is smashed to fuckin pieces, a bloody mess. He's dazed and starts pleading with Morty, 'No! no! no!' he's begging, but Morty's just pulling him to bits. He's standing over him screaming, 'You cunt, you wanna laugh, do ya? Wanna laugh at me, do ya? I'll kill ya, ya cunt.'

Now he's kicking him in the side of the head with the heel

184

of his shoe, screaming 'Cunt' as he connects each time. It's almost become rhythmic, 'You cunt, cunt, cunt, cunt'. Morty's trying to break Freddie's neck and Freddie's head is flying off at different angles. His face is pain and disbelief, his eyes rolling back in his head. As Morty's stomping him, Freddie for some strange reason keeps trying to get up, like a drunk struggling to get upright. He doesn't wanna fight, he just wants to get up. Stay down, for fuck's sake, you stupid cunt.

'You wanna laugh, do ya? Let's all 'ave a fuckin good laugh, shall we, you fat cunt,' screams Morty as he takes a swift four-step run-up and kicks Freddie's head like a football. Fred crashes backwards and ends up spread-eagled except for one leg that's tucked under him, on the slippery floor. His head's off at a nasty angle to his shoulders, his nose pouring blood. He's shaking and jerking around, trembling, like he's throwing a fit. Morty kicks him twice more in the head.

'Now fuckin laugh, Fredrick.'

It's all taken about three or four seconds, top whack, and Morty's standing over him slightly huffing and puffing. Freddie looks like he's been dropped from a tenth-storey window. He's lying awkwardly in the sauces and his own blood that's smeared on the café floor.

'You wanna cuppa tea, Freddie? Let's all have a nice cuppa tea and a good laugh, ay, Fred? What do you think? Where ya been, ya fuckin cunt? I ain't seen ya 'round.'

Morty's walked behind the counter. The owner's just put his head in his hands, eyes down. He's picked up the big steel teapot from off the hotplate and come back to where Fred's lying.

'Yeah, a nice cuppa tea, Fred. Don't worry, this one's on me, for old times' sake, put your money away, Freddie.'

He starts to pour the scalding hot tea over Fred's already bloody head. Freddie lets loose a terrifying scream. It's complete agony, torture. He pulls himself into the foetal position, sobbing. I'm shittin myself at this sudden explosion. This is too much.

'He's had enough, fuck's sake, leave him,' I shout at Morty.

Morty stops pouring, turns, looks me right in the eyes, like cold. 'You can fuck off 'n' all, okay? Don't ever try and tell me when enough is enough, okay, son?'

I ain't saying nothing. I ain't risking a hiding on Fred's account. Morty dumps the pot and remaining tea all over Freddie's face in one hit and he screams even louder than the first time. The teapot hits Fred's cheek with a clank, then goes spinning across the floor. He's left with a steaming teabag by his ear.

An old geezer's table has disappeared from in front of him but he's still got the knife and fork held upright in his hands. The waitress has her hand held up against her throat like she's trying to comfort herself, stroking herself gently, her eyes transfixed on Freddie's body as he pulls himself even tighter into a ball and wraps his hands around his head. Morty looks about the near-empty café, just daring anyone to say anything or make a move. Nobody does. They'd wanna be mad cos he's glaring, shaking with energy, spitting, walking backwards in a wide sweep towards the door. The tables and chairs have been scattered so he's picking up the ones in his way and slinging them to the side. In all this shit, I'm standing trying to wipe Freddie's blood off my coat but I only drag it across the cloth making it look worse. There's a trio of builders sitting at a table looking straight down rather than at me and Morty. One of them musta sneaked a crafty look at him. Suddenly Morty's walking back towards them.

'What you cunts fuckin looking at? Ya fuckin mugs,' he says low and cold. I spin round and the guys are back staring down, rigid, scared to breathe. The geezer behind the counter knows the score cos he's very gently, very slowly, moving lower and lower until he disappears altogether. Another time, another place, it would be comical.

Morty walks back and opens the door but he's still sweeping the café with his eyes, like a searchlight. I'm frozen, rooted to the spot. He points at me silently with his gloved hand, then jerks his thumb over his shoulder out the door. He's still looking in every direction at once. The only sounds are the sizzling of the frying food, the hissing of hot water, the sobbing of the waitress and the groans and snotty crying of Freddie. As

186

I step over him to get to the door he starts to gurgle like a baby on his blood. He's got blood coming outta his ear as well, always a bad sign, poor cunt. I carefully pick my way through the upturned tables and chairs cos the floor is slippery with tea, teabags, red sauce, brown sauce and blood. I walk out the door and back onto the Cally Road.

We walk fast, trying to be inconspicuous, heads slightly down. Morty's pulling his mac tight around him over and over again. We move rapid, looking directly ahead. The traffic's moving and people are busy so we blend in. Morty abruptly shoots up a side street. I follow. He's muttering to himself.

'Cunt. Always got something to say, you wanna laugh at me you cunt, do ya? Always chat, chat chatting.'

Freddie ain't even here. He ain't met him in years. Morty's gone psycho, twitching, eyes darting all over, turning round to walk backwards for three or four steps at a time to check to see if we're being followed. He's more crazy now than he was back in the café. He was spookily controlled back there, it was like surgery, it was genuinely callous. Now he's into some kinda delayed-action tip, spitting on the floor, cursing Freddie. Now the adrenaline's really pumping into every cell. I'm seriously scared I may catch some of it, he'll go right into rogue-mode and trip out over some old or imagined slight now the para-noia's rushing full blast, now the juices are flowing. I'm alight, shaking with it, myself.

Morty seems to know the area well, cos we're zigzagging through little streets and housing estates, walking fast and sometimes breaking out into a trot for a dozen steps at a time. Morty's always a few steps ahead, darting round corners, tell-ing me to fuckin keep up for fuck's sake. Suddenly he stops on a bridge by the entrance to a canal.

'Listen, go through that archway there –' He points at an archway leading into a council estate '– and keep going in the same direction, okay? You'll come out on Upper Street even-tually. Buy a paper, get a cab right away, head outta town, don't go straight home, read the paper in the cab, cover your face, yeah?'

Morty doesn't want us getting a pull together. I can hear the

187

first of the wailing sirens. He doesn't want some have-a-go-hero cab driver telling the law that they picked up two people who fit our descriptions.

'Sure, sure, sure, Mort.'

I turn to go. I get three steps but he calls me back. I feel like ignoring it.

'Listen, I'm sorry about Fred but he fuckin begged for it.'

He sounds sane but the eyes are on fire, raging.

'I know, Mort.'

I can hear a helicopter overhead. That ain't unusual for King's Cross but maybe it's looking for us.

'I'll catch you later. Remember what I said, lose yourself.'

I head off my way and he disappears down some steps onto the canal towpath.

'Fuckin cunt, Freddie,' I can hear him saying as he goes.

Aftermath

I came out onto Upper Street ten minutes later. I bought the *Evening Standard* with the exact right change, hailed a cab straight away and mumbled for him to take me up to Seven Sisters station. I did like Morty told me and held the paper in front of my face all the way so the driver didn't even try to engage me in conversation. I couldn't have read it anyway. I thought about Freddie, how one minute he's like one of those big stupid dogs, licking its own bollocks, and ten seconds later he's fucked, simply snapped in two, his life's never gonna be the same again. From Seven Sisters I got on the Victoria Line all the way down to Green Park. I got out the tube and went and bought a new jacket in Bond Street. I had the old raincoat folded over my arm so only the lining's showing.

I wanna wear the new jacket and put my mac in the bag so I slip down a little side turning. As I'm checking to see if there's anything I need in the pockets, I come across the napkin with the address Cody gave me only a couple of hours before. I glance in a shop window and there's a beautiful leather coat with a fur collar but a two-grand price tag. On Monday morning Kinky coulda walked in there and bought that but now he's gonna be looking at modelling a two-quid grey plastic zip-up body bag. If he's lucky. If someone, and it falls to me, makes the call.

Nobody notices me as I walk back down to Piccadilly and wait my turn for the phone-box. I tear the napkin so I've got the part I wrote the address on and use the rest to handle the receiver and not leave prints. I ring 999 and a voice answers immediately.

'Which service do you require?'

'Ambulance.'

'At what address, Sir?'

I give her the address. I'm looking at the entrance to the Ritz at the same time. There's a woman's miniature poodle snapping

189

at the doorman but everyone's laughing, amused by the little whippersnapper's antics.

'There's a body there, a dead one, but I think the door is open.'

'And you are, Sir?'

'I don't know.'

'You don't know your name?'

'No, I don't. Not at the moment.'

'I'm going to need a name.'

'Trevor Atkins,' I say.

'That's you, Sir?'

'That's your name. You said you needed a name.'

I put the phone down, walk up Piccadilly and put the napkin in a litter bin, conscience clear. I stroll in Green Park for a while, have a coffee by the ornate lake and then finally get a cab all the way home.

The canister's seriously spun. When I sit down I wanna be up pacing around and then I just walk from room to room, talking into the mirror in the bathroom like some fuckin nut-case. It was some devastating, short sharp shock treatment I witnessed back there. I go back into the bedroom to try and lie down for a while but I spot the torn Rothman's packet on the bedside table and ring Gene's number. It rings about seven or eight times and I'm about to put the phone down when he answers. 'Yeah?'

'Hello, Gene, how you doing?'

'Okay, son. You?' His Irish accent seems exaggerated over the phone.

'Well, I'm not really sure as it goes, Gene.'

'Come over. Jump in a cab and come over. I need to talk to you anyway. You got a pen? A bitta paper?'

I take down his address. He says leave the car and jump in a cab, ring me again when I'm downstairs.

He lives in this Edwardian block somewhere down in Maida Vale. I get the cab to drop me on the corner and I walk up to Gene's entrance. I ring. He buzzes me in. The lift's a fuckin relic where you have to pull back the folding door yourself. The bits and pieces of shiny brass have been polished till they're

190

round at the edges but the halls seem dusty. Gene lets me in the flat, sticks me in the sparse front room and goes back to the bathroom cos he's halfways through having a shave and he's covered in foam.

There's a hefty leather-bound copy of *Blackstone's Criminal Practice* open at page 685, about halfway through. Gene walks in wiping his face with a towel and sees me looking at his book. 'You know, a bloke I know in a bookshop once told me the most stolen books are academic ones.'

'Really,' I say. 'It kinda figures. Students spunk the grant on beers and chored the necessary.'

'Right. And you know what the most stolen academic books are?'

'I'm gonna say law cos I think that's a massive clue,' I say, ─ing at Geno's light reading.

─nd you'd be right, young sir,' he says, bowing his head ─ously.

─ actually think that's an urban myth,' I say.

─Never let the truth get in the way of a good story,' he says ─ a wink. 'You hungry?'

─ realise that I've not eaten in hours, not since the tuna ─dwich standing on the pavement in Soho, but I ain't all that hungry, I've got a twist in my stomach, but I reckon I better eat cos otherwise I'm gonna get more light-headed, more and more tripped out.

'Why? What yer suggestin?'

'I can have a Chinky sent up, real good gear, delivered.'

'Sounds like a good idea.'

Gene wanders out and comes back with an open can of lager and hands it to me. Then he shuffles through an impressive collection of takeaway menus and rings the number. He orders a 'D' for four and a few other bits and pieces. 'There's never enough in a set dinner for two,' he shrugs.

He doesn't give the guy his name. They seem to know it already. He asks them to collect forty Rothman's on the way up as well. 'Follow the usual form,' he tells the Chinaman on the other end of the phone. Geno puts the phone down, goes into a cabinet and comes out with two chunky tumblers and a bottle of Irish whiskey. He puts the glasses on the coffee table in front of us and pours two very large drinks.

'About half an hour,' he says, nodding at the phone. 'Now, I know you normally don't drink the hard stuff but you look a tad perplexed, not your customary inscrutable self. This here is Irish whiskey. Like the bagpipes, the Irish invented it but the Scots stole the idea and got rich on the back of it. Only the Irish do both with more feelin. Here,' he says, raising a glass to me, 'it'll take the rough edges off.'

'I've had quite a day already,' I say.

'I know. I heard about Kinky and Freddie.'

'You spoke to Morty?'

'Very fuckin briefly but I'll talk to him again, maybe later tonight.'

How come these fucking guys know everything that goes down almost as soon as it happens? What, they got their own fuckin radio station?

'What about Freddie? Does anyone know anything about him?'

'He's in intensive care. He's got a brain haemorrhage, like what boxers get, a couple in fact, touch and go, though. They took him in a helicopter to the London Hospital in Whitechapel.'

'He looked real bad, really fuckin weighed. I thought he might be, you know, dead.'

'Well, it does happen,' says Gene.

'It did fuckin happen, Gene.'

'If he was gonna die, son, he would've died before he got to hospital. I don't know if Freddie was unlucky or what but from what I can gather yer man Fred was always that far –' he places his thumb and forefinger an inch apart '– from a fuckin rare hidin.'

He pulls hard on his snout and very gently shakes his head before going on.

'Mister Mortimer's the wrong man to be givin backchat. You've only got to look at him to know he can have a row. Every single day Morty's not at war with society is a let-off for civilisation. If you had a hundred like Morty you'd have civil war. I'm not saying Freddie what's-his-face Hurst deserved a thrashin but you've got to give the likes of Mort total respect or give them a very fuckin wide berth.'

So I'm learning.

'Who the fuck is this Freddie geezer anyway?'

'Freddie Hurst. Now, when Morty tells you this, and he will, it's the first time you've heard it, okay?'

'Okay.'

'Has Morty ever told you the story about how he got captured for the disposing of the body business?'

'Fuckin endlessly.'

He laughs. 'The main mover on that little firm was Freddie Hurst, big chiv from here to here,' says Gene, running his finger from his eye to his chin.

'Same geezer,' I nod.

'I know, it's sorted already, no worries. Anyway, Freddie was the number one capo, the one the others looked to for a clue. When Morty got caught with the body they coulda got Mort outta it cos they were all going away for concurrent sentences anyway, they were all looking at twelves and fourteens.'

'But how would that've helped Mister Mortimer?'

'The Director of Public Prosecutions, as it was back then, had accepted that there was no murder and that Kilburn Jerry, who I knew, by the way, cos he was one of Crazy Larry's little bum-chums, had shot himself whilst under duress. It woulda only took a few of that fuckin crowd to go in the witness box and swear they threatened to shoot Morty if he didn't help dump the body.'

'But Morty offered no defence.'

'That's the way he tells it nowadays but everyone at the time was waiting for them cunts to do the right thing. Morty couldn't ask them straight out, of course, but it made no fuckin odds to them, one way or another, another concurrent sentence for threatening to kill, to go with all the others. Basically Morty didn't have to do that nursery rhyme but Freddie couldn't be bothered.'

'And that's the first time he's seen him in twenty years?'

'Oh, he's seen him plenty times since but not when Morty's in a bad mood. See, fellas like Mortimer, one day some idiot's having a laugh with him, slapping his back, and it's okay, so they come back the next day, same line of questioning, and crash, he puts 'em in hospital.'

'Crazy Larry was the other way?' I'm a bit shocked.

'Bent as a nine-bob note. Rampant homosexual,' announces Gene, rolling the 'r' with glee.

'I didn't know that.'

'Think about it, son, ain't you lucky you didn't? The first most young lads knew about it was when Larry was doing an attempted burglary on 'em.'

'Shouldn't that be buggery?'

'Same difference. He woulda been after your little ring-piece if he was still around,' he winks.

'No fuckin chance. Whatever happened to Larry, Gene?'

'Fuck only knows,' he says, shaking his head.

That's a fuckin turn-up, Crazy Larry being of the other persuasion, a feared and respected armed robber. I bet he was of the 'It's better to give than receive' school as well, always had one of the waifs and strays in tow. It don't bear thinking 'bout. Larry was shot four times walking into the entrance hall of his apartment block by a masked gunman. The kid who ran and rang an ambulance, who was meant to be a passer-by but after what Gene's just told me may have been chummier with Larry than that, came back from the phone-box to find Larry gonski. Police found shell casings, rounds embedded in the wooden panel-work, a blood trail leading to the pavement, but no sign of sixteen-stone, six-foot-two, Crazy Larry Flynn.

'Hang on, Gene, you said it was sorted already?'

'As good as sorted. I sent someone over to see Mort and then come back and tell me all about it and then I sent the same guy off to talk to this fella who was gonna have a little chat with Danny O'Mara and he sent word back saying if you wanna kill Freddie Hurst he ain't got a problem with that, says he can't believe nobody's done it before and when Freddie wakes up in hospital Freddie's family's gonna mark his card and let him know there's a good few bob waitin so he can go to Disneyland

194

in Florida and piss Mickey and Minnie right off and Danny said he'd ask someone to drop by and have a little word with the café proprietor, ask him if he wants to stay in business and that.'

'Morty'll have to weigh him on?'

'Of course he will. Listen, Freddie ain't gonna be winning any popularity contests or curing cancer but he's still got to have a few bob compo from somewhere and if he ain't getting it one way, he'll go the other.'

'And he'll have to have a conviction to have the claim-up with the criminal compensation.'

'Exactly. Some of these fuckers think they've come up on the football pools, getting a hiding. Morty can afford it, anyway. Ten or even fifteen large ain't gonna mortally wound Morty.'

'Didn't Danny wanna know why me and Mort were up the Cally in the first place?'

'I think Danny's got better things to worry about than where you two eat your din-dins. Having said that, if we didn't send word over and let them know the score then he might have been within his rights to get the hump but as it is he's –' Gene does a very bad Cockney accent '– sweet as a nut, governor.'

'Now,' says Gene, 'I wanna go over this with you in detail, okay? And like you said to JD the other night, don't take anything personal.'

Gene starts to debrief me slowly and with great attention to detail. He's asking me about how it went off back at the café over and over again, like the cozzers would do, over and over, questions, questions. Okay, you come out of this squat-affair with Billy Bogus and Tiptoes. A million questions about Billy and Tiptoes. You had a pow-wow with them and off they went and in walked Freddie. I told Gene I thought that, at the moment of impact, if you like, Fred went into some kinda power trip, like he simply couldn't help himself taking the piss outta Morty. Bad mistake, says Gene. The wink, the nod of the head, the 'All right, Mort'. Very bad mistakes all of them, agrees Geno. He wants to know how it went down from there on in, blow by blow, heel-kick by fuckin heel-kick, but not in the way some blood-thirsty little hound would or even one handyman

195

examining the handiwork of another, but in a very cold, very factual, very calculated way, like he was hearing evidence or preparing a defence. Now listen, did you feel that Freddie provoked Morty into his action? Yes, I guess he did but I could've swallowed it. But you're not Mister Mortimer, are you? Over and over again, start at the beginning, the very beginning, more and fuckin more details. Who were these guys, eating in the gaff? Did Morty take his gloves off at any time? Think. Did he? Are you sure he didn't? That's good. Who paid for the teas and coffees? I think they're still outstanding, we owe for 'em. Freddie was givin it large, slagging everyone. Slagging the O'Maras? Slagging everyone, Gene, tapping up Mort for a few bob, this one's on you, Mort? Those words came back to fuckin haunt him. You, let me double-check this, you ain't got no form, no CRO, is that correct? Good. Did Freddie eat? He was fuckin eatin, all right, the fat bastard. He probably ate in his sleep. I think he'll be on liquids for a while, nil by mouth, anyways. Morty was spitting on him, now I remember, could be a problem, but I very much doubt it, there was probably a fuckin lot of DNA flying about already. Okay, let's kick this can around the yard one more time. Fuck sake, Gene. Blow by blow, from the top. I'm worn fuckin out with it. It's very fuckin important, son, blow by blow, in slow motion. The jacket you get rid of sharpish, you shoulda fucked it into one of those big old bins round the back of one of those hotels up the West End, ripped the sleeves off first so it weren't any good to anyone. It cost me five hundred quid, and as soon as the words come outta my gob I realise how fuckin stupid that sounds. This could be murder, it's that word again, and we ain't outta the woods yet. I'll give you five hundred quid, six hundred, even, right now, out me own pocket if you like, but jettison that fuckin jacket. Sorry, Gene. And no fuckin miracle dry-cleaning jobs or fuckin conspicuous bonfires, either, okay? Okay. I'm sorry. That's okay, son.

Murder, this could be murder. Fuck. Shit. I don't need this, this isn't what it's all about for me. I don't belong here. I trade drugs, no moral bullshit, no justification, it's what I do. I'm way down the list in the criminal stakes but now I've wandered way off beam. It'll be no good me getting all high-handed if the law kick my door off, telling them to spend their time catching some nasty pieces of work, killers and murderers, cos that's what they'll be looking to arrest. Three people sitting in a café, two walk out leaving one dead and that, my friend, is what's called, in ye olde English law, joint venture and the only way out of this little predicament, this oh-so-inconvenient dilemma, is to trot into the witness box, swear the oath and do the business for Regina, lolly your buddy Morty, go Queen's evidence, get him lifed-off. Murder, attempted murder, GBH, malicious wounding, not me, governor, not my style. Anything else you can think of, son? says Gene. No? Start thinkin of an alibi. We sit in silence.

'Nothin you can think of?'

'No, Gene.'

'Okay, tell me all about Kinky and then you can tell me about the Dutch geezer and the Germans. Morty seemed to think you think they're a problem.'

I wish I'd stayed at home and unplugged the phone. For the next twenty minutes I get the servere going-over and I'm sure Gene's interrogation technique was learnt from the Provos cos it's very fuckin thorough.

'Listen, when Morty tells you this, it's the first time you've heard it, right?'

'Okay.'

'That geezer Kinky was Morty's distant cousin.'

'Really. That's a turn-up.'

Gene seems to be filing all my answers away, musing over them, unhurried, then suddenly upping the tempo to start grilling me, lots of questions very fast, bang, bang, bang. He asks all the pertinent questions, stopping me and telling, not asking, me to think harder, then asking me to say the first thing that comes into my head. Fuckin 'ell, Mister McGuire, give me a fuckin break for fuck's sake.

Suddenly the phone goes off right in my fuckin ear. Those old fuckers still have a big fuckin bell in them like a fire alarm. I jump straight up in the air like one of those cartoon cats you see stuck to the ceiling, hanging by its claws. Fuck me, that livened me up. Gene's got a slim smile on his face like he's amused by my antics.

'Relax, son, it's only the flying tiddly-wink and his blazing moped. I get him to ring on his mobile when he gets downstairs. Before he buzzes up. I like to know who's coming round.'

It rings four times then stops. Gene laughs. I laugh as well. I realise Gene's taken the sting outta things, the last two days. My appetite's come rushing back with a vengeance. I have a long hit on the lager and, bollocks, why not, a big fuckin slug on the Irish.

'Now, is there anything else you can remember about anything? says Gene.

'Fuck off, please, Gene.'

That's a negative. I think I've told him every fuckin last detail I can remember and I'm sitting here thinking I really do worry too much sometimes. We eat some food and drink some more beers. Gene sits opposite and keeps my tumbler full. I've quickly grown a taste for the whiskey and very quickly the room starts to become a bit hazy. I feel warm and content, well off-duty.

'Do you think you need a bit of weaponry?'

'I fuckin hope not.'

'I can sort you out one if you wish.'

Gene gets up and goes into the bedroom. He comes back with a couple of guns. Cosy, lethal, black handguns.

'You really don't know what could happen. There's lots of crazy people about.'

'You know it ain't my scene, shooters, shooting people.'

'Okay, it's up to you.'

Gene sits back down by the low coffee table and puts one of the guns on the glass in among the tin-foil Chinky containers and plates, in among the leavings of rice, sweet-and-sour pork balls, crackers and noodles. He's got the other one in his massive hands and it looks tiny, like one of those pretend guns that are really lighters. I pick up the other.

'This isn't loaded is it?'

'Hang on, I'll check.'

He takes it, pulls out the magazine from the stock and flicks

198

out five brass-topped bullets onto the glass. They roll in semi-circles, backwards and forwards, for a couple of seconds and then finally come to a halt. Gene pushes the magazine back in, points the guns at the ceiling and pulls the trigger. It makes a click like a toy. He hands it back to me by the stock. I'm half pissed and I love the way it's so fuckin beautifully snug in the palm of my hand. I love the weight of something so fuckin powerful in my hand. Even empty I can feel the power that this little fucker can bring you. Someone made this little bastard with a lotta love. People say that guns are just dicks in disguise but if my dick was this heavy I'd walk with a limp.

Gene clears some space among all the shit and starts to dismantle his pistol. He's only half looking. It starts to fall apart in his hands and he lays out the parts neatly in rows, square with the table's side. He works in one long continuous action, his hands moving all the time. The metal doesn't resist, it co-operates, and very soon the parts are building up on the glass.

'You look like you could do that blindfolded.'

'I can and do.'

'Why?'

'I find it very relaxing. I find it's very good for meditation.'

'Meditation? That's chanting and that. I've seen those monks down in Thailand.'

'That's only one approach. Meditation is to concentrate the front of the mind with a mundane task, mantras or breathing, then the rest of the mind can find peace.'

'And you concentrate the mind with guns?'

'Yes, on occasions.' He laughs knowingly at his private little joke. 'It has been known, son.'

I can tell he thinks this is a fuckin classic, can't wait to tell his spars about it. He's got a double-cute smile on his boat. Don't be fooled. Gene the convivial host is also capable of deeds dark and deep, concentrating people's attention with a shooter in the mouth or under the base of the ear, so don't be fooled, don't be beguiled. Enjoy your food, your duck with plum sauce, the sweet-and-sour king prawns, your beer, your whiskey, your warmth, Gene's funny stories about the old fellow, the late seventies, souped-up mark-three Jags, fruity

Crazy Larry, the Cricklewood Cartel, no joke if you fucked with 'em, the three-piece suits for thirty-three quid, lotta money in those days, outta the Take Six boutique on Wardour Street, nutty twenty-four-inch flares but don't forget what this geezer's capable of. I look at my watch. It's quarter to twelve.

'I better be goin.'

'Relax, son. It's only early yet.'

Gene opens another can of lager and hands it over to me. It's there now, in front of me, so I think, fuck it. He tops up my tumbler for the umpteenth time. After that it starts getting hazy, very fucking hazy indeed.

'You forgot your fortune cookie, son. What's it say?' says Mister Geno, completely sober.

I open the paper, shut one eye and read it.

'Beware flattery.'

'That's always good advice, son,' says Gene with a wink.

Thursday?
Not a Good Day for It

People think the hangover they've got at any moment in time is the worst hangover in the history of the world but for once it's true. I'm waking up not knowing where the fuck I am but I soon realise I'm at home in my own bed. I can barely open my eyes cos every little bit of brilliant white light is painful and the blinds are wide open. My mouth's completely arid. I think I've had nails driven into my temples at each side and my whole body aches like I've been run over. I've got bruises on the top of my arms and my hands smell of fags. The clock says five to ten. I feel like shit warmed over, my skull's tight around my brain, I'm soaked in sweat.

If I tried to get upright I'd fall straight back down. The thought of getting up is too much. I'd love a glass of water but the idea of making the journey out to the kitchen makes me feel like chundering. My clothes are strewn across the floor. One loafer is missing, the trousers are inside out, my shirt's missing and the new jacket is in a pile. I need to go back to sleep for a couple of hours. This needs a rethink. I remember Freddie, Kinky, Germans, Yahoos, pills and feel even worse. I think about some poor fucker whose heart wasn't in it waking up next to Crazy Larry. It chills me to the bone. My mobile starts to ring. I can't see it but I'm fucked if I'm answering it anyway. I'd love to trust myself to get up and close the blinds but I reason that if I double-up one pillow under my head and put the other over my head I'll be okay.

As I go to pick up the pillow I jump back cos there on the sheet is a big black semi-automatic with a homemade silencer, just lying there on the bed. It's neither of the guns Gene had out to play with last night. They were this bastard's little brothers. The thought of last night makes my head hurt more. This is a monster of a weapon, like a hand-cannon. The silencer looks snidy, chunky, with old-school black electrical tape wrapped round and round it. It's like waking up with a black mamba in the bed with you, dangerous but very beautiful, lethal and powerful, but how did it get here? It's obviously one of Geno's little orphans but what's it doing in my kip? And Gene, he's probably jogging round some rose garden somewhere with a hundredweight bag of cement strapped to his back after getting me in this state. I can't remember getting home. Top of the morning to ya, Geno, thanks a bunch, thanks a fuckin million. The mobile stops ringing.

The phone by the bed starts to ring. Four shrill rings and it goes on the machine, but each feels like someone's sadistically tapping the nails in my temples. I pull the pillow over my ears. The message plays, then Jimmy Price's voice starts booming out.

'Are you there, son? Where the fuck are you?'

Without thinking I pick up the phone. 'Hello, Mister Price.'

'Oh, so you are there, son.'

'Yeah, I'm here all right. I was asleep.'

'What, at ten o'clock in the fuckin day? That's no fuckin good, is it?'

'I had a bittova night last night.'

'Listen, I couldn't give a fuck what you did.'

I wish I'd left the fuckin phone alone. It's very unusual for him to ring anyone at home. 'Listen, Jim, I ain't usually in bed at —'

'Don't fuckin call me Jimmy, yer little prick. What's the idea of tellin JD that those fuckin pills ain't worth shit, who the fuck are you to be tellin anyone what those things are worth, yer cunt. Then you go runnin up north to your fuckin scouser pals and tell 'em they can fuckin have 'em for sixpence each. And what the fuck you think you're doin gettin people at it, shittin your pants about some dead schwartza, spookin people, tellin 'em he's been fuckin topped by fuckin ghosties ... '

If I, or James Lionel Price, was under surveillance, being ear-wigged, by Crim Intel, the Regional Crime Squad, customs, the Drug Squad, the Fraud Squad or even the Metropolitan Police Latin-American Ballroom Dancing Team, he could not possibly make it any easier for them. They don't even have to sit around in draughty old make-believe laundry vans with cumbersome headphones on anymore either. I've got a mobile phone over there, in that jacket, and it can do anything short of give me a blow-job. Ask any young kid who works in telecommunications what Mister Plod can do with a phone these days and it'll make the hairs on the back of your neck stand up. If anyone in law and order, maintenance department, has any kinda interest in who I chat me business to on a daily basis they've only gotta do their own little version of call divert. They can sit in the comfort of their offices in an anonymous building somewhere, feet up, doing *The Times* crossword, eating a tuna Sicilian sandwich, drinking Java coffee and listen to me and Jimmy, loud and clear, on the speaker-phone. If anything juicy occurs they can listen back, at their leisure, to the digitally recorded, automatically enhanced, crisp as you like, tape recordings.

'And another thing, you dainty little pouf, "That's an expansive question,"' he lisps. 'You find a fuckin buyer for those fuckin pills or I'll find someone who will, you fuckin understand, you cunt, and don't fuckin leave it to some up-his-own-arse fraudster to be findin that fuckin bitch, you fuckin go and you fuckin find her, yer little prick. Get off yer fuckin arse and get to Brighton, and don't be getting too fuckin cosy with those fuckin irons down there either ... '

Mister Price, I have a question for you. Why don't you fuck off, Fuck Right Off, you Mister Price, your slag of a wife with her two-bob pretensions and her complete collection of Rod fuckin Stewart records, your double-moody, over the top, make-believe respectability with your pretend mock-Tudor house, why don't you just go fuck yourself. Of course I don't say that. I ain't got foolishness mixed up with bravery.

'I'll see what I can do,' I say.

'Don't be lying in bed all day, pullin yourself about.'

'I'm ready to walk out the door right now.'

'Don't fuckin lie to me, yer little prick,' he spits.

'I ain't doing –'

'Stay off the fuckin booze as well. I don't like havin laggin boats round me.'

He's gone, thank fuck. What was that tirade all about? It's been four days since he wanted me to find the princess, who's now 'that fuckin bitch', and three days since I got the word about the pills and now he's fuckin panicking cos he can't get his own way, like a big fuckin baby.

What I need's a horny little nurse like Tammy to coax me back to life. What I don't need is a day spent driving in circles in a hot, stuffy motor with unpredictable Morty and Clarkie, who never stops fuckin talking, trying to find a buyer for a lorryloada pills with a seriously dodgy recent history. Of all the mornings he picks to ring me up outta the blue, he has to choose this one. The one morning he's gonna catch me out he rings. Well, fuck you, Mister Price, King Dinosaur, I won't be sorry to see the back of you. Maybe I'll skip school today.

I realise that while I've been talking to him I've absent-mindedly picked up the shooter, so I've got the receiver in one hand and the gun in the other and I'm waving it round, taking a lazy aim at the light fittings, the cactus plants, the Gucci loafer on the floor and talking to him as well. When I put the phone down I'm left with only the metal. I wonder if it's loaded. I try to remember how Gene did it last night. After some pushing and pulling, fiddling with some catches, the magazine drops out onto the bed and, yes, it's loaded, very loaded. I push the bullets out onto the bed, one by one, and count them all the way up to sixteen. There's sixteen plump bullets in a pile on the bed-clothes and the clip's empty. This is all a bit of a mystery and it's getting deeper all the time.

Then, bang, like a knee in the guts, this evil sense of fore-boding. What if I've been out with this fucker last night and shot some poor bastard? I've heard tales of geezers being well pissed, or well out of it, doing some crazy but serious shit and remembering nish the next day. They've been captured later and they honestly don't know if they've done it or not. They go 'Not guilty' but get a guilty. They're sitting in the shovel for years not even knowing if they're really guilty or not, not knowing if they should be barricaded up on the roof of the nick protesting their innocence and mobilising the friends and family into a campaign to prove them non-culpable. It's the kinda thing that Crazy Larry woulda done. I'm panicking and sniffing the chamber of the tool. My heart's racing but it only smells of machine oil and metal. I'm relieved that it hasn't been fired. Thank fuck for that. I had some very nasty scenarios kicking about in my nut, some very heavy gravy. Panic over.

I start to push the bullets back into the gap and they fit so snugly, almost sexily, back into the chamber. Someone's been at these, filing the tops flat. I wipe my prints carefully off each one in turn, cos you never know where they could end up, do you. I don't wanna leave any bullets hanging about either, so I double-check by counting them back in, fifteen, sixteen, done. I flick the magazine back into the pistol. It all fits together so perfectly. It's so beautifully engineered, such a lovely weight in my hand, heavier than the ones last night, almost twice as heavy, a useful bitta kit, some might say. Right now I need a shower, shave and my arse in gear cos I really just wanna be out of here, maybe get an omelette, get a steam and a rub-down over Porchester Hall. I wanna day off after my striping from that old cunt.

In the shower I'm like a cat with hydrophobia but it slowly gets better. I give myself a pep talk in the mirror while I have a shave. I'm unsteady on my feet, still a bit pissed from last night as well as very hungover. I manage to down half a pint of water and a selection of vitamins and keep them down, so I make myself a cup of coffee. Maybe I need a hair of the dog. I pour a hit of brandy into the coffee. Maybe some of that flake coke behind the medicine cabinet would make the concoction complete. I get it out and sprinkle some into the brandy-coffee. All this misery is self-inflicted and that makes it worse. I put on a black suit, well cut but not at all flash, fine lightweight wool, to compensate for feeling like a paraffin lamp waking up among the dustbins. I put it with a beautiful gold polo-neck sweater in Merino lambswool by some guy in Barcelona. I tip over the other loafer in the front room, pair it up, put them back in the wardrobe. I've decided that they're definitely jinxed, definitely bad karma. I ain't thinking very straight today and at least I know it. I get out a pair of black Prada brogues and just as I'm lacing up the second shoe, the phone goes. If it's Price ringing back to go another few rounds I'm gonna tell him to go fuck himself, I've decided. I'm starting to feel much, much better. It's not so bad, this, being half pissed in the morning, the feel-good effects of coke are seriously over-estimated, though. I don't know how we get away with selling it.

'Hello?'

'Good day to you,' says a German accent in perfect English.

'Who's this?'

'My name is Klaus.'

'Should I know you?'

'Perhaps. I believe you may have some property belonging to me and my associates.'

'I think I know who you are, Klaus.'

'Mister Van Tuck gave me your number, eventually.'

Better English than me. A credit to their education system.

'Don't know how he could have had it in the first place,' I say. He was a collector of drug traffickers, a fuckin narcotics dealers' anorak.

'Well, he did. And he vouched for your organisation to my organisation.'

'What organisation? I don't have an organisation.'

'Led by your colleague name of the Duke, your personal and firm friend, I believe, no?'

'I never met this Duke in my life, Klaus.'

'They came to Amsterdam and quoted your name, and Mister Mortimer, Mister Clark and Van Tuck vouched for your credibility as honourable and noble men.'

'Listen, Klaus, why don't you come round? I'll have the maid prepare a bitta breakfast, we'll ground some coffee and we'll discuss this like grown-ups. How does that sound?'

'It sounds very hospitable, very adult.'

'Do you know where I live, Klaus?'

'No.'

'Well, fuck off then.'

Much Needed Rest and Recuperation

I'm just going out the door when my mobile rings. The display shows Clarkie's mobile number so I answer it.

'Listen. Go to the outside one, you know the one I mean?' he says. I can hear tannoys like he's in a mainline railway station.

'Yeah, gimme five minutes.'

'Okay,' and he's gone.

There's a bank of three phone-boxes about five minutes' walk from my flat. Clarkie will have all three numbers and he'll ring the first one in five minutes. If that's engaged, he'll ring the next one and so on until I pick up the phone. It's a beautiful spring morning, sunny, so I've got my shades on, but I'm already starting to piss sweat. I'm sure it smells of Irish whiskey. The phone's ringing as I arrive. I walk in the box and pick it up.

'Alright, Clarkie?' I say.

'How'd ya know it was me?'

He's on a payphone too.

'You're back from outta space then?' I say.

'Those pills. Fuckin 'ell. I'll tell ya when I see ya.'

'I'll look forward.'

'Listen, let's make this quick. Wassa industrial wardrobe?'

'Fuck knows. I woulda thought that it was a kinda locker affair that they use in factories and on building sites for overalls and that.'

'Like an ordinary wardrobe but made a steel?' asks Clarkie.

'Exactly, Clarkie. Why?'

'Old bill fished one outta the River Lee last night about sixish with two bodies inside. Get this, they had to use a crane on wheels to get it out. The thing was packed full of hundred-kilo bags of just-add-water cement to weigh it down.'

'That would sink a long fuckin way. How'd they find it?'

'A barge hit it cos it settled too upright in the water. Whoever dropped it in there, dropped it too straight.'

'How do ya know?'

'Some of it's on the news. Where you been? I been ringin ya.'

'Out and about. I'll tell ya when I see ya. Why did I have to come outside to hear that?'

'There's more. My old man got a bent gather. Two bods, right? No hands or heads, right. Geezer, huge fucker apparently. Bird, skinny as fuck, nothin of her. They reckon this geezer's mobbed up with you-know-who from outta town. You know who I mean?'

'Yeah.'

'They're both wanted for questioning about a shootin and weapons charges,' says Clarkie.

'We're not talkin JD, are we?' I say, but I already know the answer to that.

'No. The geezer's AKA the Duke, like John Wayne.'

'Do they know or are they guessing?' I ask.

'It's almost nailed on. All that lot have gone low-profile and maybe moved up town. See, Morty still wants to do a trade but if those fuckin Germans are on the rampage it might be better –'

'One of those fuckin Germans rung me up.'

'What!'

'Fuckin rung me up this mornin. Somehow Van Tuck had my number. This Duke's firm went to the Dam and used our names as credentials.'

'Fuckin 'ell, mate. What, me and Morty as well?'

'Yep.'

'Was they screamin and shoutin about their pills?'

'Nah. The geezer I spoke to was dead polite but I told him to fuck off.'

'You told him to fuck off? Are you all right?' says Clarkie like he can't believe it.

'Not really. I've had a funny coupla days.'

'You're usually the one wants to sit down and sort things out, chat, chat, chat, till it's sorted.'

'Clarkie, believe me, I'm regretting it now. I can see it wasn't such a smart fuckin move.'

'I hope we don't all live to regret it, brov.'

'Listen, Clarkie, me and Mort went to a meet with this Yahoo firm on Monday night in a gaff in Edmonton. Find Terry and go and see what's happenin up there.'

'The whole place'll be smash-alive with cozzers, heavy mob, Edmonton's where the two bods were found.'

'If ya see any old bill, sound the retreat but I'd like to know what's goin on, if anythin. I'll give ya the address. Look on a street atlas and have a look at it. You'll see there's a fuckin great patcha wasteground overlooking it. Get some binoculars and—'

'Binoculars!? Are you for fuckin real?' says Clarkie.

'Yeah. Big fuck-off ones from one of those shops on Oxford Street and go over there and see what you can see. Plot up and then drive round for a bit. Look for big flash, lemon motors. Look for clues. That's what old bill do.'

'And you're gonna be doin what?' he says with the zig as I give him the address.

'I'm havin a day off. I'm goin offside for the day. I've had him, Jimmy Price, on the phone givin me a ruckin, screamin. I know he's your old man's mate and all that but he's a —'

'My old man don't really like the geezer, reckons he's losin the plot, between ourselves.'

'Anyway, I'm havin a twenty-four-hour pass. You just made my mind up for me.'

'What the fuck did I say?'

'Nuffin personal, Clarkie, please don't take it the wrong way, but I'd just like one day, today, where people ain't tellin me all sorta unsavoury shit or wreckin gaffs or smashin people 'bout or tellin me 'bout two people chopped to fuck, without heads, in a fuckin industrial wardrobe in a fuckin river.'

'I think you maybe need it, pal. You sound stressed.'

I can hear the pips going.

'Don't tell me I'm stressed, Mister Clark, and don't be tellin anyone else either.'

'Fuckin relax, brov, deep breathin —'

He's gone. Clarkie's on a fuckin wind-up but I don't give a

fuck and while I'm here I'm gonna give Geno a double-quick
ring about his little baby back at the hide-out. I drop ten pence
in, ring the number and he answers, sounding fresh as a daisy.
'Hello, son. Good crack last night, wasn't it. I didn't know you
knew rebel songs.'

Neither did I.

'A fine voice you have when you allow yourself.'

'Listen, Gene, when do you want to collect this bitta property?'

'Start again, son, you've lost me.'

'I think I took home one of your aids to meditation last night.
You with me?'

'No, son. I'm getting more confused.'

'One of those things you use to concentrate the mind with,
yeah?'

'Son, this is as clear as Mother's shit soup. Was I there when
all this was taking place?'

'Yes.'

'Are you sure?' he asks.

'Fuckin 'ell, Gene,' I say, losing patience.

'Now, now, son. You may have a sore head this morning but
that ain't my fault.'

Like fuck it ain't.

'Gene, straight question, do you know what I'm talkin
about?'

'I swear by almighty God I'm starting to think I'm getting a
crank fuckin call here. I don't know what the fuck you're on
about,' says Gene with his edge.

Maybe he don't and I won the metal in a tombola. Maybe I
was out and about last night, on a mission, ended up in some
asylum and got to thinking buying a tool was a good idea.
Maybe at the time it was. Does happen.

'Listen, Gene, where did I go from yours last night?'

'Am I to believe you're seriously ringing me up to enquire
about your own whereabouts? Is everybody going mad?' I can
hear him tutting. I bet he's shaking his head.

'So you don't know?' I ask.

'Well, it would appear that there's two of us in the dark.

210

Listen, I've got to march on. Maybe you should just go away home and get your head down for a couple of hours. You listening, son?'

'Yeah.'

'I'll catch yer later, son.'

I definitely need a bitta rest and recuperation away from all this bollocks. I need a good charver, a bitta freestyle, a good bunk-up, doctor's orders, to get me thinking straight again. Who'd be pleased to see me, a little tatty round the edges, at eleven-thirty on a Thursday morning? I start to walk back down the hill to my flat. Fate favours the brave. I'm gonna give Tammy a ring and see if anything's going on, see if she's about and work from there. I push her number on the mobile.

'Hiya, Tammy, it's me from Saturday night.'

'Oh, hiya, what took you so long to call?'

'I've been busy, sweetheart. You sound sleepy, you just woke up?'

'Not long ago. I was out with Sid last night.'

'Your boyfriend, you mean?'

'He ain't me boyfriend. We just hang out. When am I goin to see you?'

'Whenever you like. What are you doin today?'

'Nuffin. I got a day off as it goes. I was just lying here wonderin what to do when you rang.'

'What, you're lyin there naked?'

'I've got a T-shirt on but that's all.'

I can feel a pullin in my strides.

'Listen,' she says, 'listen to this.'

I can hear a rustling sound.

'What's that?'

I can hear her teasing laugh.

'Listen again,' she says.

I can hear the same rustling, scratching sound.

'What the fuck is that?' I say.

'I was rubbing the phone against my fanny. Did ya like it?' she laughs.

Leave it out. That's how to get and hold a guy's attention.

I'm walking up the road with a tugging hard-on growing in my pants.

'So you're lying there, Tammy, with just a T-shirt on rubbin the phone on your fanny?'

'No.'

'No you ain't?'

'No. I've taken the T-shirt off now.'

I hear the rustling sound again and her laughing. 'Oh my, oh my, it's fresh this mornin. Look at my nipples.'

I wish I fuckin could. I bet they're erect as soldiers. I'm going fuckin mad here.

'I wish I had a horny young man here with me now, who'd really appreciate a nice bitta rumpy-pumpy.'

I can feel my knees buckling so I'm sitting on a wall. I can hear her groaning and moaning down the phone.

'Tammy, are you, like, touchin yourself.'

'What's a young girl to do?'

'Listen, Tammy, why don't you come over right now, get in a cab, don't bother gettin dressed, sling a coat on or something and come straight away.'

'I like that idea, but is it a long way? A girl could get cold,' she says.

'I'll tell ya what, I'll meet ya half way. I'll meet ya in the Churchill Hotel on Portman Square.'

'A hotel?'

'Yeah. It'll be a giggle. I could book in as Mister Smith. I got a nice bitta how's-your-father. Come over and meet me there.'

'Sounds good to me, lover-boy.'

'We could hole-up there for a day or so. It's easier, get a bitta room service.'

'I need a bitta bedroom service right now.'

She knows how to tease.

'Think about it, Tammy, we could be under the duvet, in the feather, in about an hour.'

'I'm definitely up for it. You know, a girl can tell a geezer who knows what buttons to press, knows what a woman likes, and you look like one of those geezers.'

212

'That's me, Tammy. No complaints, but I've never had a lesson in me life.'

'I'd like to, you know, relieve myself, go solo, just talkin to you now I'm gettin wet … ' She's groaning but laughing at the same time.

'Tammy, shall I come over to you?'

'No, lover-boy, but I'm gonna save myself till I see ya.'

'I'm gonna have to do the same cos I got a huge fuckin hard-on, Tammy.'

She's laughing. 'Save it for me, tie a big ribbon on it, you hear? You won't be disappointed, I promise.'

'I'm gonna do that.'

'Listen, Mister Smith.' Her mood's changed, her voice is a bit more serious. 'Yer know, I wouldn't want you to think I go jumpin into bed with any bloke that rings me up in the mornin. I kinda think you're nice. It could be good.'

She sounds tender and sincere.

'I think you're nice too, Tammy, very nice. I'll see you in the room at the Churchill Hotel in about an hour.'

'Give me an hour and 'alf cos I'll have to get a cab.'

'Any problems ring me on the mobile, okay? Missing you already,' I say.

'See you there, Mister Smith. Churchill Hotel, Portman Square. I'll be as quick as I can cos I'm feeling really naughty. Listen, here's something to be going on with.'

The rustling sound again. Then she's blowing kisses and laughing down the phone, then she's gone for the time being. I'm walking back home with a throbbing hard-on. She's really fuckin horny, Tammy, but really fuckin bright as well, you can tell after a minute. 'This could be good,' she said and I agree. Sometimes you get a woman who's horny but dozy or stuck-up but she's horny and wide awake at the same time. I could be out of this game earlier than expected if Cody gets me a result. I'd be looking to go on a nice long holiday and maybe Tammy would wanna tag along. Maybe I'm jumping the gun here but it could be a bit special.

I walk back to my gaff. I wonder if that's my shooter lying on the bed, my property, looking all criminal-lifestyle accessory on the bed linen. I slip it under the mattress. I put the coke and some poppers in my suit inside pocket, check I've got plenty of cash, go downstairs and get a cab. When I get to the hotel I get a double room on the third floor as Mister Smith and leave strict instructions that when someone arrives for me they're to buzz up straight away. I pay in advance for two nights and tip the porter a cockle, in spite of the fact that I don't have any luggage. As soon as he's gone I chop out another couple of lines of charlie cos I can feel myself flagging. The flake needs to be ground cos it's nearly crystal. I snort a line and immediately half my face goes numb. The room's perfect for this midday rendezvous. The bed's huge and so is the bathroom, with a massive bath and a shower cubicle. Me and Tammy can maybe have a little tub later. I'm itchy and sweating all the alcohol out of my system but feeling nicely charged. I need another shower to freshen up so I get undressed and jump in, leaving my clothes hung up in the wardrobe.

The pressure on the shower's strong and as the water's hitting me I'm remembering Tammy, how she looked so hot on Saturday night in her skimpy little outfit, how I wanted to have her stripped and willing in front of me, how, in a little while, she could be jumping in the shower with me. I'm wondering what she'll be wearing, how long after shutting the door it'll be before we're naked and rolling on that big old bed out there, if she'll really just throw a coat on, jump in a cab, come through the door and just let it slowly drop to the floor, flick off her shoes and away we go. My old bill's up and pointing at me again now. It's almost too tender or sensitive to touch. Maybe sexy Tam will have sexy underwear, black or red or deep, deep purple, and I'll have to go oh so gentle, patience, lover-boy, peel it off, slowly with care, with me teeth, to get to the prize.

Fuck the fuckin lot of them. This'll be our Cosa Nostra, me and you, Tammy, and fuck the world. Me and you in our own little world, our little room, for as long as we want, as long as it takes for me to calm down and relax, to get a bitta perspective back. I feel so horny I feel like I've had an ecstasy. This is what you dream about when you're young and wondering what your dick's for, waiting for a very horny, very game, very beautiful woman in a luxurious, three-hundred-quid-a-night hotel room, a loada coke if you want it and the spending power to whistle up anything – champagne, lobster – anything, in fact, that your imagination can think of. I was dreaming the dream on Saturday night and here we are on Thursday midday, getting acquainted. Sometimes the anticipation is better than the real thing but I somehow don't think this is gonna be one of those occasions. I don't think my old bill's capable of getting any bigger or any more upright. The blood's pumping, I'm pumping, I feel one hundred per cent alive. I can hear her voice in my ear, 'Save it for me', and that's what I'm gonna do. I'm gonna let her walk through the door and I'll be naked and proud, side-on so the midday light through the window silhouettes this magnificent hard-on perfectly. Tammy should be here any minute by my calculations.

I turn off the water, step out of the cubicle, reach for the towel. I've got water in my eyes. As I wipe it away I realise, for a split second before it gets hectic, I ain't in the bathroom alone. I jump backwards, shocked. I wanna shout but no sound'll come out. Two big geezers in identical blue poly-cotton boiler-suits, baseball caps and chunky black-rimmed glasses are there as well. One goes low, grabs my hands behind my back and pulls them together with a heavy plastic cable-tie, the other goes high, for my head. He grabs my jaw and sticks heavy tape over my mouth then snatches a black bin-liner outta his belt, wraps it swiftly round my head and tapes it around my neck. These twins, this very efficient double-act, have either rehearsed this very well or they've done it a few times before. My heart's going into overdrive, like I've had a big hit of amyl-nitrate. The two guys pick me up and place me on the floor of the bathroom, gently, like they were shifting a precious antique grandfather clock. Someone pinches my nose through the plastic and then tears a hole so I can breathe. He does the same with my ear. Maybe I shouldn't have told those German lads to fuck off.

'Listen, troop. Can you hear me? Nod your head twice if you can hear me.'

The geezer pronounces every syllable precisely in a slight Geordie accent. I nod twice.

'Do not resist and you will not be harmed.'

It's happened too quick to put up a fight but in a strange way I feel reassured by their professional attitude, his English accent, like I'm somehow safe. I'm alert enough to know that if this was the Germans or even the Yahoos, I'd be getting a serious kicking now. My head would be getting bounced off the bathroom walls, floors and maybe even the ceiling. I'm also wide awake enough to know that if these two operators were gonna top me, I'd be deceased, despatched, taken out, slotted, gonski. They could be taking me somewhere to kill me but somehow I doubt it. I can hear the phone in the room next door start to ring. That's gonna be Tammy downstairs. She's pulled out all the stops and got here early.

'Someone wants a word with you across town, troop. Be calm and no harm will come to you.'

They pick me up and put me down a couple of feet away on something softer but itchier than the cool bathroom floor. I can feel it against my body and I guess it's a carpet of some kind. The phone stops ringing. Suddenly I start getting rolled over and over.

'Watch yourself on that,' says 'Troop', laughing. 'That'll have someone's eye out.'

Troop's mate laughs too. I wonder what they're talking about. The phone in the room starts to ring again, like they've told Tammy on reception the room ain't answering and she's asked them to try again. I'm being stuffed into a long box. I can feel the sides and bottom. I hear a top being put on. The sounds of them going about their work are muted. I'm moved upright but I'm being manoeuvred backwards in small steps. Now I'm tipped backwards and being wheeled along. If I could talk I'd ask for a bitta Christian charity and beg my kidnappers to stop and explain to Tammy that I was being taken against my will, it wasn't just slackness on my behalf. I wouldn't believe it if someone used the old abduction excuse with me. 'Listen, Tammy, I was kidnapped!!' 'By fuckin aliens? Yeah, fuckin right, mate.'

Making New Friends All the Time

I once had a punter who used to take ounces at a time and get truly wasted. One afternoon he got so outta it he plugged up the gear and couldn't find it again. What did this genius do? Who did he ask for help in his emergency? He rang the old bill to come and help him look. He got eighteen months. Why's this occurred to me now? Maybe it's about having someone come and rescue me. I ain't eaten since six last night, so my body's weak and I can hear my own stomach rumbling and churning. My mouth's dry like I've been chewing sand. I've crash-landed off the bitta whistle I had earlier, hit the side of a mountain. I'm the ventriloquist's dummy. It's dark in the box but maybe if they take me outta the box, I won't like it, think it's nice and cosy in my dark box.

I've been in here an hour when suddenly I hear the top being taken off the box. I feel someone cutting the tape around my neck, removing the black plastic, the cool of the air on my face again. Through my squinting eyes there's Mister Troop with the tip of his finger placed on the middle of his slightly smiling lips, the boiler suit, cap and heavy-rimmed glasses gone. He's in a shirt and tie and black-leather jacket. 'Roll to your left, troop,' he says.

I do as he says. He cuts the plastic cable-tie.

'Get out of there and put those on, troop.' He points at a plastic bag from a sportswear shop, same one as Kinky used to shop at. We're in a portakabin. I can hear building work, drilling and generators. The floor is covered with a very fine layer of dust. I get out the wooden packing case and walk across, naked, to see what nice Mister Troop's brought me. Two geezers are standing in the doorway talking into their lapels so they're either deluded nutcases or bodyguards. I think they may have spent time in the military. And not the TA, either. The bag contains a black and gold Adidas tracksuit and Nike black-on-black old-school trainers in my size.

217

'Do you require anything for your immediate physical comfort, troop?' asks Troop.

It must be murder being this geezer's wife. Shall we have some sexual intercourse, Misses Troop? What do you think, dear?

'I could use a piss and some water.'

'Through there, and I'll get you some water.' He points at a door in the corner. I go in and use the chemical toilet. When I come out he's there to greet me with a two-litre bottle of water like he's pulled it outta a hat like a bunny rabbit.

'Can I ask a question?' I say, brave cos I'm alive.

'Listen, troop, curiosity killed the cat. Boredom killed the tarantula but curiosity killed the cat.'

This is obviously bodyguards' humour cos they all laugh. One guy's distracted by a message on his ear-piece. 'That's a roger roger, over and out,' he says into his lapel. 'The boss is ready down below,' he says to Troop.

He gives me a yellow hard-hat. Troop's on point. We walk out the room fast, along scaffolding boards, through corridors of old brickwork. We pass guys who look like civil engineers. Troop leads us, half trotting, till we come to a hoist-lift. Troop tells the geezer working it to go to the bottom. It creaks and squeaks. I'm wondering if it's safe to have these big guys and me on board but they ain't worried. At the bottom of the shaft the hoist inches to a stop and the door goes up and out we get and Troop again leads us but now we're moving across duckboards laid over broken clay. Suddenly he leads us out into a huge excavation, about the size of a football pitch, open to the sky but floodlit as well. We're about seven floors down. There's heavy plant, digging machines, bulldozers with orange lights, but it's strangely quiet, deserted like everyone's gone home. Troop leads me up some stairs on the side of two portakabins that are one on top of the other, into an office lined with plans and blueprints.

One man is stood facing guys in yellow hard-hats, steel-capped boots, cords and workshirts, engineering types. He has his arms folded across his chest but is holding a dimple on his chin, pensive like. He's got piercing blue eyes, a healthy-looking tan, silver-grey hair that's well groomed. The bespoke lightweight wool suit he's wearing must cost two-and-a-half gee from Savile Row. He's listening intently, digesting every word, nodding. He gets a French snout outta a packet and lights it, in spite of the 'Strictly No Smoking' signs. This guy's wearing chocolate-brown, hand-made, tasselled and fringed, suede pigskin loafers from Jermyn Street. He ignores us when we come in. Nobody interrupts.

I know this geezer. Or, more accurately, I know of him. Sometimes the last piece of the jigsaw will slot gently into place but on this occasion the whole jigsaw's fallen outta the sky and landed on my head. This gent's name is Edward Ryder. I never realised that he was from round our way but what I have worked out is that he's the mover and shaker, blood brother of Jimmy Price, the geezer I'm helping out by finding his daughter Charlie. She has a different surname so I didn't connect the two and I didn't recognise him without his dinner jacket and black bow tie. This geezer and his beautiful twenty-years-younger wife haunt the pages of those glossy magazines you buy at supermarket check-outs. Eddy and the wife will be in there, smudged-up at the charity dinner or the polo match, hobnobbing with the royal family and all those aristocrat Mafiosi, 'Mr and Mrs Edward Ryder, charity benefactor, businessman and multi-national entrepreneur' under the photo. Up-close and personal he could be the figurehead of his own runaway-success religious cult. He's gotta be fifty-five but looks good.

'Two weeks! They want another two weeks?' He shakes his head. 'Fucking hell, give some people an inch … Now, I need to have a little chat with this chap here,' he says, nodding in my direction. 'Come with me,' Eddy says, walking past me briskly and down the stairs. I follow him down and catch him up. Troop follows about ten feet behind. The clay has been turned over so it's rugged but dry.

'If it's about me finding your daughter, I just –'

He stops abruptly, gives me a glare with the beadies, raises a hand to silence me, then carries on walking until we come to the edge of a small gorge about thirty yards long that's been dug out along one side, a hole inside the main hole. I look over the edge and see that there's a small encampment of people, an archaeological dig, brushing away soil with dry paintbrushes and bagging it up. The whole site is criss-crossed with string in a grid system. Trenches have been dug and tarpaulins hung over certain areas. Students work in huddles, digging with tiny trowels and sieving the dirt. They go about it with enthusiasm. We're standing above the hole on a viewing area they've installed, made of scaffolding and duckboards. Eddy stops, looks down and shakes his head gently again.

'Here.' He beckons me over. 'Can you see that?'

He points at the side of the excavation. It's layered with different shades of clay, earth and mud, like a bottle of sand my aunt brought back from the Isle of Wight.

'Look at the layers of soil,' he says, 'the different colours and shades. You know what that is, don't you, it's history. See that man down there –' There's a geezer in a short-sleeve shirt, wellies and tweed deerstalker hat '– He could actually point out all the different periods of time, from the Romans, the Vikings, medieval times and right up to the time when they put up the building we knocked down.'

'Where are we?' I ask.

'Course, you don't know, do you. The City of London, about fifty yards from the Thames. The Romans built a harbour here. In those times this was an inlet right on the river.'

His voice is quiet and clipped like he's had elocution lessons somewhere along the line. Rover Rummages Round Rough Rambles. He sounds like a swell doing an impression of a chap from the lower order but, make no mistake, this guy, Eddy Ryder, could hold his own anywhere, from the boozer on the manor to the charity ball. The man in the deerstalker spots us and waves up. Eddy gives him a salute and a big smile.

'Wanker,' he says to himself. 'Total wanker.'

He has the delivery of a droll northern comic.

'See him, son. Complete authority on life in medieval times. Ask him anything about it and he can talk for hours; ask him the ingredients of an omelette and he's baffled. The Corporation of London asked me to give this mob some time. I said I would, of course, because if I don't they come back with a court

220

order. A site of historical value, they call it. Fifty-three grand a day, it's costing me and my partners, so I can't afford to get too Buddhist about it. I want them gone so I can throw up my office block, twenty-seven storeys. Beautiful, it's going to be.'

'When this lot get finished?' I say.

'If they ever do. They just told the Corporation that they need another two weeks.'

'You couldn't just say you need to move on?'

'And look like a vandal, a total philistine? I just have to be gracious, pretend like I'm really interested in what they dig up and come and show me, bits of old piss-pot and sheep bone. I had the Lord Mayor of London here the other day, standing exactly where you're standing now, chain of office and everything. We had our picture taken for the papers. I'm smiling, but in reality I want to aim him down the hole, stuck-up little cunt. And now they want another two weeks ... Do you know who I am, son?' asks Eddy Ryder, turning to me.

'You're Jimmy Price's mate Eddy Ryder.'

'He told you that?' He laughs gently.

'Yeah.' But something says that ain't the way he sees it.

'He also told you to find my daughter Charlotte? Why?'

'Mister Ryder, I've just realised I've been mugged by Mister Price.'

'But why? You haven't answered my question.'

I tell him what Jimmy Price told me on Saturday at Pepi's Barn. No point trying to be too cute.

'See Mister Troop over there.' He points with his eyebrows. 'He could find anyone in ten minutes.'

'So you don't want her found.'

'Not by you, son. I know where she is day and night if I want. You've been had over by Mister Price. I think we all have at some point, it's part of growing up. Maybe I owe you an apology.'

'For what?'

'I believe you were manhandled rather harshly earlier by Mister Troop, but I believe you're a cocaine dealer. Some dealers have been known to be a bit too free with submachine guns. Apparently you're a lover not a fighter.'

'Why does that geezer call everyone "troop"?'

'Old regiment thing, I believe,' whispers Eddy.

'What, SAS and that?'

He shakes his head but motions me closer with his finger. 'They think the SAS are a bit high-profile. His lot, I don't think they officially exist, Minister of Defence doesn't know about them even in wartime. He talks Russian, Gaelic and Arabic. Oh, by the way,' says Eddy like something's suddenly occurred to him, 'your two friends were picked up in Brighton at the same time as you. They were in a dealer's house up in Seven Dials asking lots of questions, pretending to be police officers. Two men who work for me impersonated police officers and arrested them. Ironic, really. Mister Troop wanted to plant heroin in their hotel room, enough for a charge of intent to supply ... '

Handy with a bitta brown, are ya, Mister Troop? You've only got to take one look at his eyes to know he's perfectly capable of entering a premises, giving an already-gouged-out semi-conscious smackhead a hot-shot. The Saff London kid was right all along, someone did sort out Kinky for taking the bung and still wanting the prize.

' ... but why make enemies, I said.'

'So why did Jimmy tell me to find your daughter, Mister Ryder?' I ask.

'Please call me Eddy. I thought you might be some urchin Jimmy had doing his dirty work but I can see you're a talented individual.'

I'm gonna have 'Beware Flattery' tattooed on my forehead. 'Thank you, Eddy. But why?'

'To hold as ransom. You're in trouble but not with me. I'm gonna mark your card for you. I've known Jimmy Price for thirty-five years. They don't give you that for murder. All that nonsense he told you is true to an extent, we did do a bit of junior time together but I always wanted away. Dewey, who you wouldn't remember, before your time, a real gentleman, he used to take me aside and tell me to get out, get far away. He used to say, "Jimmy's a crook but you could be a criminal."'

'What did he mean by that?'

'Dewey used to talk in riddles after a few drinks,' he laughs.

'I always took it to mean get out before Jimmy and that whole scene drags you down. I keep Jimmy where I can keep an eye on him. I learnt that off Dewey. He was a class act, shrewd, charming. You could walk into the pub that Dewey owned back in the early seventies and there would be senior police officers and villains all having a light ale.'

'And what was Jimmy doin the whole time?'

'Crawling up Dewey's arse. But Jimmy is not the same man Dewey was. He tries to emulate him, even down to buying Dewey's house when he died. Have you ever been there?'

'I only shift goods for Jimmy. We don't socialise.'

'You aren't a bad judge. The High Trees, out in Totteridge, beautiful house it was till Jimmy got his hands on it and started decorating like it was a whorehouse, like some two-bob gangster Gracelands. I've been there and he's just made a mess.'

'I don't wanna rush ya, but why am I in trouble?'

'I'm telling you. I believe you to be a sensible young man. I'm building an office block on this site when this circus clears out. The main investors are Russians.'

'Mafia?'

'Fucking hell, son. Where are your manners? You, like a lot of people, jump to the conclusion that just because these gentlemen are Russian they must be an organised crime organisation. A lot of this outfit were in the KGB, they're class, but a lot of people will tell you that the KGB and the Mafia are one and the same. As far as I'm concerned their money is as good as anyone's.'

Course it is, after it's been spun a few times by one Edward Ryder. I'll take that as an affirmative on the Mafioski connection. 'I'm sorry about that. Don't know what come over me.'

'These Russians are Muscovites, sophisticated, really, but Russia, the old Soviet Russia, is a huge place. A lot of their countrymen don't move with the same dignity. The Muscovites bring with them a lot of remoras.'

'Is that another republic?'

'No, no. A remora is an opportunist fish that swims with sharks. Here –' He points to the back of his neck '– the shark can't get at them or get rid of them. These remoras live in the slip-stream and benefit from the shark's protection but they are in reality scavengers, on the look-out for tit-bits of carcasses. The shark becomes used to them.'

Eddy refers to his partners as sharks.

'So who did the Muscovites bring?'

'Chechens. And they really are trouble. There's no love lost between the two camps either.'

'I think I've heard of them.'

'You may have done. Chechnya is a small but very dangerous province, an outpost, really. They wanted independence from Moscow so they fought a guerrilla war. The Russian Army, what was the mighty Red Army, went in, got a beating, so they put the place back into the Stone Age but they took a lot of casualties themselves.'

'So they're heavy?'

'Very heavy, like you wouldn't want to know how heavy. They'd break the ice on a frozen lake, throw some poor bastard in and stand around drinking vodka, smoking and laughing whilst he freezes to death. Ruthless, callous with it, but cunning, that's their mentality. The other outfits in Russia all steer clear of them because they know what they're like. Chechnya is like Russia's Sicily only ten times worse.'

'And they fired into you?'

'Well, they tried, but in this world there's no such thing as easy money. They entice and if one is too greedy, or not strong, they snare you. At first it's easy money but soon there's no walking away, not without ... ' Eddy draws his finger across his neck. 'The Muscovites explained to me that these people were without honour, could not be trusted, but if I wanted to do business with the Chechens I could, but they would cease to bring their business to me. I don't like an ultimatum but you can't have it all ways, can you?'

'So they went away?' I ask.

'Oh no. No way,' says Edward. 'They found someone else.'

'Who? Where?'

'Well, I throw a garden party every year, quite a date in the social calendar, though I say it myself. I always invite Jimmy because if I don't there's a fuss and also, to my shame, some of my friends are amused by his antics.'

'I can imagine Jimmy and his pretensions goin down well among the blue-bloods.'

'But I've come unstuck with my little attempt to provide cabaret for my chums. There's a lesson to be learnt here. Dewey always told me to learn from my mistakes.'

'Like how unstuck?'

'Jimmy made the acquaintance of the remora fish, three very charming gentlemen from Grozny, the capital of … '

'Chechnya?' I ask.

'Right.'

'Problems?' I ask, knowing the answer.

'Not many,' says Eddy, rolling his eyes.

Get the Atlas Out

'Jimmy couldn't even find Chechnya on the map. Gene the Hammerhead knew the score and told him to avoid them. I'll never know why Gene didn't just put one in Jimmy's nut the day after Dewey's funeral and start running things himself. Nobody would have said fuck all, not the Clarks or the Archers or anyone come to that. You know what happens to these backyard Don-types, don't you? They start to think they're what's called omnipotent, all powerful, God-like, and maybe in their own little world they are.'

I'm nodding in agreement but I'm also thinking that it would have kinda suited Eddy if the Chechens and Jimmy had got loved-up. It would take the dairy, the attention, away from him and the Moscow firm. It would have allowed him plenty of elbow room to shovel the bag-washed dollars, marks and pounds down his big old hole.

'Jimmy's telling me that I've gone soft, been around the good gentlefolk too long, but I'm telling him that these fuckers don't give a fuck if you are a big Charlie-new-potatoes gangster in London, these guys have taken on Hitler and Stalin. Where are those two loony-tunes now?'

'He wouldn't have it.'

'Arrogance. I know best. You can't tell Jimmy anything. They used it against him. He thinks he's having them over. They're playing it dumb and for someone who's so very fucking clever Jimmy can also be incredibly stupid. They grafted him like a Yank tourist gets grafted on Oxford Street with a three-card trick, because nobody messes with the good ol' US of A.'

'How?'

'It's as old as civilisation. They have goods over here.' He raises his right hand. 'And a buyer over here.' He raises the other. 'This one will not under any circumstances release the goods until he's paid in full, in full, mind. They have ninety per cent of the sum but now the buyer's getting cold on the deal, but he, distrustful soul that he is, will not under any circumstances front them any money so they're a bit stuck. They need a bridging loan and are willing to pay top dividend to the lender.'

'And Jimmy went for it?'

'These guys are very good.'

'What was the consignment?'

'Could be heroin, weapons, bomb-grade uranium, they're all abundant in that part of the world. I don't know, but it isn't important anyway.'

'So he pulled up his cash and mexxed up with these dudes?'

'I didn't know because they were telling him "Don't tell Mister Edward," so he doesn't. In some ways I'm glad he didn't and in other ways I wish he had because I could have put the kibosh on it.'

'How much we talking here, Mister Ryder?'

'Have a guess, son.'

'Million?'

'Up a bit.'

'Two?'

'Stick your neck out, have a decent fucking punt.'

'Five?'

'Double it.'

'Fuck. Ten fuckin million!'

'Then add three.'

'Thirteen million pound!'

'Yes,' says Eddy, dry as you like.

'Fuckin 'ell. Let me get this straight. Jimmy's been rumped for thirteen million quid by a loada East European grafters.'

'He didn't just hand over thirteen mill in readies after meeting these chaps the once. He didn't get a bit tiddly on the Pimms, cop for a drop of sunstroke and decide to pop down the bank and withdraw thirteen mill. These guys worked at this like a long-term project. They brought in a guy to say he was the seller, then guys to say they were the buyers, flying them in from all over the world. Then one day they tell Jimmy that they've had a break and thanks, but they don't need his investment after all and see you later, Mister Price. Jimmy's apparently gone fucking mad, "We've got a fuckin deal, you Russian cunts, and now you're trying to row me out," so he argues his way back in. But then one of the guys who's meant to be getting the money together their end is either arrested or killed or both. That's the tale they're telling Jimmy.'

'And he believed all this?'

'These Chechens are convincing. In your business you have to trust some people some of the time.'

'Not for thirteen million, I wouldn't.'

'In Jimmy's defence, this was all worked over an eighteen-month period and we, me and you, have the smug benefit of retrospective knowledge.'

'That's true.'

'It starts off, he's in for a mill and a half, five per cent dividend on the end profit, but they're playing it so he's increasing his holding all the time. They're pretending that there's disunity in their camp and Jimmy's getting palsy with each side and shit-stirring, all very human, all very James Price. They worked it so James thought he'd brought off a coup de grâce and was in charge. "What we do now, Mister Jimmy?"'

'Where the fuck did he get that sorta money?'

'That's about the lifetime's earnings for a man in Jimmy's position and he does have a few other strings to his bow, cash crops, which I'll come to later. Think about it, he's a canny boy with the shillings, is Jimmy. He's eased up over the years, gives the wallet an airing every now and again, but years ago he was very tight. If you sat him down and bought him a cup of tea in the café and he had even a suspicion that it could be cheaper somewhere else, Inverness perhaps, he wouldn't enjoy that cup of tea, even if you bought it for him.'

'But thirteen million. I'd be gutted.'

'I don't think he's being a Buddhist monk about it. This was done on a big scale. This was going to be Jimmy's World Cup Final. How much did you think he had tucked away?'

'I never gave it a lot of thought to be honest.'

'Surely you must have a bit of dough tucked away. Lucrative

business, the drugs game. I wouldn't mind a bit of that. I'll wait till it's almost nice and legal.'

'How did it come on top with Jimmy and the Chechens?'

'They just shipped out one day leaving Jimmy red-faced. Then he starts to lose the plot, thinks I've engineered the whole thing. His pride is hurt, can't believe that anyone would turn him over, thinks he's been betrayed, but you can only be betrayed by someone genuinely close to you and these people were only pretending, but he can't handle that, it's too real. He can twist things in his head, I know Jimmy, he starts to believe his own bullshit. After shuffling the pack he's decided that I introduced him to this gang of cut-throats to get them away from me. Some people can't accept that we all get had-over from time to time.'

'Ransom? You said ransom earlier on.'

'So I did. In his desperation he wanted me to negotiate with the gents from Moscow the return of his funds but they simply gave me a matron-size dollop of the old "We told you so, now he's only got himself to blame" and the old sideways look. See, Jimmy doesn't understand geography. He thinks all these Russian guys came over on the same coach trip. He doesn't understand that there's about the same distance from London to Moscow as there is from Moscow to Grozny. Jimmy can't be told that. He even accused me of orchestrating the whole swindle.'

'But you didn't, did you?' And up from out of nowhere, I wink.

'I like you, son. You have a good aura about you as my wife would say, but you also have a very reckless side that could get you in trouble on life's journey.'

'I'm very sorry 'bout that, Mister Ryder, it was disrespectful.'

'Fucking right it was,' he says, getting a snout outta his packet and lighting it.

I've got this riddled out now. 'Jimmy thought he'd use your own daughter as a hostage against you?' I say.

He nods.

'Bittova cunt's trick.'

He carries on nodding but says nothing.

'So I've been duped by Mister Price.'

'I think this is the least of your problems,' he says.

So he knows about the pills and the Germans.

'So Charlie's okay? I don't have to worry about her?'

He steps forward. 'Don't fucking worry about my fucking daughter, you understand, you little cunt.' He gives me the pointy finger in the chest, glaring eyes, genuinely angry, twitching, but then something else kicks in. He takes a deep breath and shuts his eyes for a split second like he's doing something he's been tutored into doing at times of emotional overload. I'm taken aback by this sudden flash of anger. 'I'm sorry about that,' he says. 'Thank you for your concern but my daughter is in excellent physical and mental health.'

That sounds like an official version. 'I'm glad to hear it,' I say with a forced smile.

'You should worry about yourself,' says Eddy.

'How did you know that Jimmy had told me to find your daughter?'

'You left some photographs of Charlotte on the table at Pepi's Barn.'

'For about five seconds.'

'That's as long as it takes. Angelo, the Maître d', spotted them and rang me, or rather rang Troop. I've dined with Charlotte there on many occasions and he recognised her from the glimpse you allowed him.'

'So you were keepin an eye on Jimmy?'

'I always keep an eye on Jimmy's lily-white arse. They detest Jimmy with a passion out at Pepi's. It was a bad day's work, the day I took him down there, because now he's got the place block-booked.'

'I got the impression that he's their favourite customer.'

He thinks that's funny.

'Well, it's not in their nature to tell people to fuck off, and maybe because I introduced him they give him a squeeze. They delight in getting him into trouble.'

'I can't see Gene goin along with kidnapping people, especially young girls, civilians.'

230

'I'm sure he wasn't delighted, but Gene's a tad too loyal for his own good. Loyalty can be a curse as well as a blessing. I think Jimmy wanted you out and about, blundering around, getting caught trying to find Charlotte.'

'To show he meant business?'

'Possibly. God only knows what goes on with some people. Now, you tell me something. What's these pills Jimmy was talking about on the phone this morning?'

So someone was listening in earlier. I shake my head and give him a blank look but he tuts.

'I think I've been very understanding to you, young man, someone who was conspiring to snatch my only daughter and hold her to ransom.'

I go to protest my ignorance but he puts his finger over his lips to quieten me before he goes on.

'Okay, you came here in a wooden box, got kidnapped yourself, but have I been unreasonable? No. I don't think I have. I could have Mister Troop over there inject you up with truth drugs and all sorts of chatty serums. You'd be telling us things you didn't know you knew. I've seen it before and it's ugly. Some people find it funny.' He nods over at you-know-who. 'I personally find it rather distasteful watching people become infantile.'

I have a sly glance over my shoulder at Mister Troop, who's pretending to be miles away, looking up, studying cloud formations, but I know he'd find it hilarious. He'd look upon it as reward for being a good boy all day.

'Okay, these pills … '

I tell him the story of the pills.

'So those were the Germans you were telling to go fuck themselves this morning?'

'I hope I didn't offend Mister Troop with my language on the phone this morning, Mister Ryder.'

'It's a bit bold of you to be telling a far-right politically motivated gangster to fuck off. How many of these tablets are we talking about here, son?'

'About two million, give or take a few thousand.'

'Fucking hell, that's a lot of pills.'

231

'I think the whole country could have a very good weekend with that lot. Apparently, and this is not my area of expertise, they're very fuckin good.'

'And do you have a buyer in mind?'

'Possibly. I think they're keepin us roastin so we take any price they give us.'

'Roasting?'

'Waiting, sitting on our hands, in suspense.'

'And how much would this parcel fetch on the open market?'

'That quantity, about one-fifty each. They're very good quality as well so they may go to two quid a pop. Why, you interested?'

It was meant as a joke but Eddy doesn't laugh.

'I think you're in too much trouble for me to be dealing with you. I could do something with those. I know people. You've got me thinking.'

'Trouble? I thought we'd straightened all that out, Mister Ryder. I was duped, played for a mug by Jimmy. Learn from your mistakes, you said, and that's what I'm gonna do. I'm gonna go and talk to my accountant and see how I can bob and weave to get outta town. I ain't gonna be havin anything more to do with Jimmy fuckin Price.'

'I think you're wrong. I think your fates are forever inter-linked. Getting away isn't always that easy.'

I bet Eddy fuckin Ryder's got the trippy-hippie, make-be-lieve eastern-mystic wife parked up at home. All this talk of auras, Buddhist monks and fate is a dead give-away. I reckon if he takes her from behind the feng shui's got to be right.

'You still haven't got it, have you, son. Me, these Germans or the Bushwhackers, are really the least of your problems right now.'

'You've lost me.'

'Maybe I better let Jimmy explain.'

'Fuck! You've got Jimmy coming here?!'

'Have I fuck. Be patient, son. You're in shit but … ' He shrugs, flicks his fag butt towards the deerstalker but narrowly misses. The archaeologist carries on brushing and scraping, oblivious. ' … Come upstairs, son. It's probably easier that way.'

Shit in Your Eyes

Eddy's motor is like one of those cars that, as a kid, we used to see the lagging-boat local mayor roll by in. Shiny, black, tall at the back and bulbous all over. In the back it's like someone's put a Chesterfield sofa in and built the coachwork around it. The black leather is as soft as silk. Separating us from the driver is a panel of polished walnut with small doors intricately built into it. The grain of the wood is uninterrupted across these, like the door fronts and main panel were cut from the same huge piece of wood. When Eddy's finished brushing small specks of dry clay off his suede loafers, he pushes a button on a control panel on his side of the seat and a glass window shuts, giving us complete privacy.

'You want a drink?' he asks.

'Some water would be nice.'

He pushes a panel in the walnut and the door jumps back. Inside there's a drinks cabinet. He looks inside and comes out with two bottles of soda water.

'This okay?'

'Any water, Mister Ryder. I'm dyin of fuckin thirst. I had a bit of a night last night.'

He hands me one, keeps one himself, shuts the drinks cabinet and opens another panel. Inside this one there's a music system that, because of its sleekness, all silver and matt-black, is completely at odds with the old-school motor. Maybe he wants some sounds on while we have our chat but he goes inside his immaculate suit and brings out a cassette tape. Maybe he's got a band. Eddy opens the tapedeck and puts in his tape, picks up the remote control and sits back. The tape is hissy even on this pukka system. I hear Jimmy Price's voice.

'Is that 'kin all, Albie, seven fuckin grand? Fuckin 'ell, hardly worth the fuckin bother.'

'Well, if you don't fuckin want it, pal, I'll fuckin keep it,' says a voice I don't know.

'I didn't say that, did I. I just said it's fuckin meagre, that's all, seven gee.'

'You'd fuckin moan if it was seventy grand, Jim. I fuckin know you, you old cunt, remember that.' He starts to laugh and I can hear Jimmy laughing too.

'I'm just sayin, ain't I, it ain't like years ago with your fuckin lot, you've all gone squeaky on me.'

'Tell me about it. I've gotta box so fuckin clever with those cunts from CIB3 sniffin around, listenin on the dog, firing people into yer all wired up, some dozy cunts ain't as discreet as you, Jimbo.'

Jimmy's talking to a bent cozzer, fair play Jimmy. CIB3 are the old bill's internal Gestapo, out to catch wrong'uns, CID gathers with big houses, multiple bank accounts and the holiday homes in Spain. Eddy stops the tape.

'Before you ask, the other gentleman is Albie Carter. He's a DS in the Regional Crime Squad, a plodder, bit of a dimwit, lacks a bit of flair.'

'And Jimmy's got him bent,' I say. I catch on fast.

Eddy raises his eyebrows, starts the tape again and looks out the car window across the river to the south bank.

'But is what you're doin that fuckin bad, Albie? You bring in some very good stuff, they always get their fuckin money's worth, don't they?' says Jimmy.

I'm getting confused.

'But I ain't meant to be gettin a whack out, am I?'

'You do okay, Albie.'

'And so do you, Jim. You'd be gone years ago if it weren't for me.'

'I know that, but don't start gettin all squeaky on yourself, leave that to the spotty herberts in your Squad.'

'I'm only saying, Jim –'

'Look, don't be a fuckin cry-baby on me now, Albie. You're up for retirement soon anyway, done your fuckin twenty.' Jimmy's half shouting now.

'Okay, okay, Jim, but you wanna tear the arse outta everything and there's only so much in those informer funds, they ain't made of money.'

That fuckin word 'informer' makes my blood run cold. Jimmy's at it. He's gone the other way, the cunt.

'So take more stuff straight into the banks, they'll always weigh-on to know when someone's fiddling in Aunt Maud's drawers.'

Eddy stops the tape.

'That means, apparently, the financial institutions will pay handsomely to be informed if outfits are committing organised fiscal fraud,' he says. 'You getting the hang of it now, son?'

He starts the tape again but my head's gone. Jimmy Price is the mystery informant that everyone who's any kinda player knows has been working for the last few years in London. Everyone knew it was someone big-time cos the kinda full SP the law were fronting people with could only have come from someone near the top of the Premier League. They've been getting a result too often, 'acting on information received'. If Jimmy's been at it, then me, Morty, Terry and Mister Clark are guilty by association cos Jimmy would be putting the bubble in and expecting a squeeze from the Other People in return. This is the cash crop Eddy was talking about. Jimmy brings information to this fuckin Albie and he feeds into the various squads, working through other gathers who are half bent and coming away with reward money, readies, outta the grasses' fund to pay a string of fictional informants. If Jimmy gets anything choice about people working long-haul frauds, like what Billy Bogus does, he gets his fuckin gofer, Albie, to take it straight to the finance house concerned. Their security teams, mostly ex-old bill, are always pragmatic, don't wanna undermine security with the public, take a powder, sort it out themselves or maybe sometimes they put together a snare operation where the guys walk in to collect but find they're nicked big-time instead. The old bill, not being stupid like some doughnuts think, always protect their source so they can do the same bitta work again. By the time I'm paying attention again Jimmy's talking about how a top white South London family, the Tylers, are bringing in shooters from Jamaica.

'He means people to shoot people, not firearms,' Eddy interrupts.

'I don't think anyone gives a fuck if spooks shoot spooks, Jim,' says Albie. They both laugh.

'I couldn't give a fuck about dead johnnie darkies,' says Jim.

'Jimmy, what about the O'Maras? They want anythin at all? Danny especially, any sniff at all?'

'Danny don't like me, tells people I'm sneaky.'

'Not a bad judge, is he.'

'Fuckin behave, Albert.'

'Calm down, Jim, it was just a joke. What about Gene?'

'They fuckin love Gene, those O'Maras, but I can't just send him over there on the earwig, can I?'

'Does he suspect anything, Jim?'

'Gene? 'Bout what?'

'Fuck's sake. About you being ... you know ... '

'Working it both ways? Listen, Gene can answer every fuckin question on those quiz shows on the telly, but he's a bit tick around people and that. He's my trusty gundog, is Gene. You know what I say, don't yer?'

'No, James, enlighten me.'

'Why have a dog and bark yourself, ay, Albie, why have a dog and call him "Fuck Off"?'

I can hear Jimmy laughing himself sick and slapping his thigh, probably slapping Albie as well. I bet his eyes were watering.

'Where did you get the tape, Eddy, one of Troop's extra-curricular activities?' I ask.

'Oh no. Albie Carter recorded it for me. Why have a dog and bark yourself?'

'Why'd he do that?'

'Money,' says Eddy in his speaking-to-a-child voice.

'I heard a little whisper that ... ' And Jimmy's off telling Albie the whereabouts of a guy who had to go on the trot over a very serious robbery, the kind that don't happen much these days. I'm so fuckin glad I'm getting out.

'Listen, Eddy, someone like Troop could've put this tape together, that's what them sorta outfits spend their day off doing, he could very fuckin easi –'

'Be your fuckin age, son. That's called denial. How old are

you? Twenty-nine and you don't want to believe that your sugar daddy's been a fucking supergrass for years, after hearing the man denounce himself on tape.'

'Yeah, but they splice different bits togeth –'

'Shoooosh, son.' He leans forward and playfully slaps me on the side of the knee. 'Don't you want to hear what he's got to say about you?'

'I got a nice one who's plucked and ready for the pot,' Jim's saying.

'Who's that then, Jim?'

'I ain't tellin you now, yer fuckin doughnut. I don't wanna reward on this one, I just want him out the way.'

'Why?' asks Albie.

'You're a nosy fucker, ain't you, Albie.'

'It's my job, Jim. I am a policeman, a detective to boot. Why do you want him out the way?'

'Got a few bob, ain't he, tucked away, but I'll fuckin find it, once I get my hands on the paperwork.'

'So who is this geezer, Jimmy? Would I know him?'

'Doubt it. Flash little prick but very low-profile. Thinks he's retiring, the silly cunt. He's gonna do a coupla errands for me then he's yours. I want him away for twelve.'

'If he's got over a kilo of Class A on board, brown rather than white, he's guaranteed double figures.'

'I'll guarantee he has on the day, even if I gotta put it there myself.'

I can feel my skin burning with heat but I can't breathe. I wanna cry, to be honest. I want my mum to come and take me home. I don't wanna play no more.

'It sounds personal, Jim. Ain't never been personal before.'

'Shut yer fuckin mouth.'

I can hear Jimmy spitting bits of cigar out.

'Okay, Jim, fuck's sake,' says Albie.

'There's something about this geezer that gets me at it. He's fuckin smug.'

'And you reckon you can get your hands on his goodies?'

'I fuckin know I can. It was me told him to go and see this dodgy accountant years ago and spread his readies about in moody names. The book-keep ain't gonna cause no fuss. He'll poop his pants when I go and talk to him. A snide name can be just about anyone,' says Jimmy Price.

'I'll put that down in the "forthcoming events" column, shall I?' says Albie and they both start to laugh.

Eddy stops the tape.

'The rest of it is just some pretty sordid sexual stuff, Albie pumping Jimmy again about the O'Maras, they seem desperate to lock them up, and Jimmy getting the hump with him about it,' says Eddy.

'I don't believe it,' I'm saying to myself with my head in my hands.

'Believe what you want to believe, son, that's what everybody else does in this life.'

'I mean I believe it but I don't believe it.'

'That's you on the tape he's talking about, the flash cunt who thinks he's going into retirement.'

I can only nod my head.

'I think Jimmy's got a different kind of retirement planned than you, different retirement home, too, Parkhurst, Isle of Wight.'

To be honest if I wasn't starving hungry and had a full stomach I'd be throwing up down the side of Eddy's motor or straight into the Thames.

'You seriously had no idea that Jimmy was at it?'

I shake my head.

'See, years ago Dewey would be obligated to put up names to stay in business. He indulged in a bit of habeas corpus, produce the body, as well. Truth be told, Dewey watched a lot of guys who were overdue but slippery go away for stretches on his say-so. If people didn't play ball, Dewey got the police doing his dirty work for him. When he marked your card with the law, you were gone.'

'So old Dewey was a grass as well?'

'Listen, son, while we're about it there's no fucking Santa Claus either. How the fuck do you think these guys stay in business? They buy a licence to work. Dewey accepted the inevitable and would use it to cull out all the toe-rags and blokes who would only be getting caught anyway. He fed them to the law. He used it to almost regulate the lawless, but Jimmy's psychological raison d'être is different. Jimmy saw it as an earner, a way of getting his retaliation in first. You heard it yourself on the tape, Jimmy's a spiteful, horrible, nasty man. My wife says he's a sociopath, incapable of feelings of attachment or seeing human beings as anything other than commodities to be used.'

I feel very, very naive all of a sudden. I don't feel angry, I feel ashamed. One time in school, I was seven, dreaming, contentedly picking my nose. The teacher pointed this out and the whole class turned to look. I was caught, bang to rights, finger up hooter, but too paralysed with shame and fear to move it. The whole class jeered and laughed and thanked God it wasn't them.

'I would have thought a smart boy like you would have worked this out on his own,' says Eddy.

'Can I have that tape?'

'I've already done you a copy.'

'When was this recorded?'

'Sunday night, live at the Café Royal.'

Rich tastes. Some poor fucker's paying their bill with his liberty. He hands me the tape.

'And before I forget, here's your hotel-room key. Mister Troop locked up for you.'

He hands me the key.

'Anyway, must fly. Got to get home, have the wash and brush-up. Going to the opera tonight. Do you like opera, son?'

'Dunno. The closest I ever got was Freddie Mercury.' I ain't really in the mood to chat about opera.

'*Damnation of Faust* tonight, about three-and-a-half hours too long. Man sells his soul to the devil but it ends in tears, these arrangements usually do. I might even see your German fascist friends there.'

'Why?'

'Oh no, of course not, what am I like, I'm only getting my Wagners mixed up with my Berliozs. Now, do you need some cab fare or can I drop you somewhere?'

'I think you've already dropped me on my head.'

239

The Simple Life

One time, a guy who was a friend of a friend sent us out two VOs, visiting orders, for us to come up and see him while he was doing a five stretch – for what, I can't remember. It's really bad manners or poor protocol not to go and see someone if they've gone to the trouble of sending you out the VO. I couldn't even try and slip outta it. My pal, I know for a fact, would've thought I was a right cunt if I even tried, cos the VO could have gone to someone who would've used it. We went up to see the guy, brought him up a joey of bits and pieces.

This guy who's inside, Colin, is in good form considering his circumstances, quite chipper, and he's telling us he's cracked it in here, mate. He's renting out a hard-core porn book by the night in exchange for Mars Bars and bits of puff. I was making about two grand a week clear at the time, had just come back from a week in Barbados and was having a scene, a singalong, with twin sisters, so I couldn't see what all the fuss was about. Soon, I'm thinking, that book's gonna fall apart through wear and tear, it's gonna get too sticky to rent out or someone's gonna decide not to give it back and you either got to say something or you look like a complete joe, a cunt, in front of everyone and then people really start taking libs and you can't decide to give these guys a wide or move to another part of town.

That's the idea of prison. It snaps your spirit quick or it grinds it down slowly until you start to think 'This is a bitta all right' cos you've got a Mars Bar and a bitta puff the size of your thumbnail. Very Buddhist, I'm sure Mrs Edward Ryder would agree, but the flip side of that is someone giving you a perceived snide look while you empty your piss-pot one morning is on a par with having your house repossessed or burnt to the ground on the out. It's all about fuckin with your perception. It curtails your horizons cos you may not see the horizon from the day you go in till the day you come out. You're lucky if you see the sky for an hour a day. This Colin says to me and my mate that he's looking forward to getting a move to a softer nick.

'When's that then, Col?'

''Bout two years.'

Great, ain't it.

Morty, for all his fuck 'em attitude, spends every waking moment dodging the very thought of being weighed off big-time. He likes to tell stories about being in the boob and how they had such a giggle but he ain't in any hurry to get back. Morty will tell yer about how he was glad to be banged up with a bitta puff and a good history book at eight o'clock on a Saturday night and Mort's a very intelligent man who's had his perception fucked with big-time. Some guys, when they're out, spend all their time reminiscing about being in and, no doubt, when they're in, all they go on about is being on the out. Mobbed-up guys getting put down for shifting powders watch straight-goers coming in after them for murder, kicking some-one to death in a pub brawl or strangling the wife, and getting their parole before them. How fucked up is that, geezers getting lifed-off doing less bird? I asked this guy who'd done a massive lump if he ever thought of escaping, making one. 'Everyone fuckin does,' he says, 'for the first five years.'

The Prison Service have thought about it too and you can end up sitting in a cosy cell in some purpose-built, brand-new nick, about a quarter of a mile from the outside fence and with about ten other electric fences in between. No open nicks for you either, son, kilos of Class A chemicals means years on Category A wings.

Getting a five, and with a drop of jam-roll getting out in three, is as much as I can get my head round but the thought of getting a twelve chills my blood on a hot summer's day. Twelve years ago I was seventeen and life was good, very good. If I think about all the good stuff that's happened since, all my hard work getting my money-pot together, and think it's all going down the drain, I shit myself. We're talking a decade of Tammy-and-the-like deprivation here but being stuck with the kinda sweet, sweet memories, rolling round and round the canister, that could drive a geezer permanently insane. One million in various enterprises, spread around, plugged up tight but Jimmy could, if he got the right bits of paper and the right little team round him, divert it in his direction. He's given it plenty of thought, I suspect, after getting his financial arse kicked round the yard by the Chechens. Life for murder or twelve to be going on with, yer shuffles yer pack and yer picks yer card.

I'm trying to get from east to west in a taxi down Oxford Street but one side the road's been dug up so the traffic's moving at a snail's pace. I'm distracted from my problems by two guys racing down the street. Sometimes the cab's overtaking them and sometimes the two guys are overtaking the cab. It's not a running race or anything like that. They're paraffins, tramps, and they're both dead psychotic and the idea of this game is to rummage in each and every single litter bin along the road. How long is Oxford Street? Two-and-a-half miles? And what you gonna find? The carelessly discarded tiara? The lobster dinner for two? No. What you're gonna find is a shit-load of half-eaten fast food that was dog shit in the first place plus a loada yesterday's papers along with all the debris of everyday living. Between each bin they break into a half-trot half-Olympic walk like they're desperately trying to disguise the fact that they're racing to their opponent, like it ain't happening.

The cab pulls away and I leave the two tramps behind. It occurs to me that some people, like those two back there, have got a simple life. Don't get me wrong, I'm not saying they've got an easy life, but nothing's complicated. No traitorous over-lords, no shape-shifting money launderers, no cut-you-to-pieces German posses, no bent cozzers or straight cozzers come to that, no bushwhacking here-we-go tourists to blow over the house of cards. You know who you can trust – nobody – and zero's a nice round number. Nobody's driving you mad, cos you got no plans, no ambitions, no responsibili-ties, no nothing, sweet fuck all, in fact, and the only thing to get excited about, to have a care about, to fight about, is the daily beat up and down Oxford Street, in and out the bins to see what new rubbish there is today.

242

Back in my room at the Churchill at five-fifteen, no messages or any signs of disturbance, I order the omelette I was gonna have at half-ten this morning. I pour a brandy from the mini-bar and drink it on my empty stomach in one big hit. It's like a karate chop on the back of the neck. I lay back on the bed, no TV, no light. I can hear the early evening rush-hour traffic down below. I need a good rethink.

Long time ago I was driving through lanes, not unlike the part of the world Pepi's Barn's in, Public Enemy's 'Rebel Without a Pause' pumping outta the stereo, with a pal of mine whose folks were top villains. We were going out to this Hawaiian disco affair in this country club. I had a couple of ounces, ballsed-up, to deliver and collect waiting readies on. The place was gonna be smashed alive with fit, scantily clad, gamey Richards. Life was good.

'Can I give you a bitta advice, brov?' says my pal, lighting a sensi spliff.

'Go ahead, brov,' I say.

I got the feeling that it's gonna be the kinda advice that's been handed down from his old lag grandfather to his father to him, he had that kinda pedigree. He gave it the pointy finger and pronounced every word like it was scripture.

'Be just as careful about what you allow other people to tell you as you would about what you tell other people. Yeah? Understand?'

'Yeah. I get yer.'

'And, obviously, I know this don't apply to you, it ain't your thing,' he laughs, 'but if you ever have to kill someone, yer don't tell a livin soul.'

Friday
You Gotta Go

You can buy latex surgical gloves in a high street chemist's, one pound seventy-five for ten. Wear two pairs, just in case. You don't want any powder hangin about on your hands. I don't know who you're talkin to in that fuckin mirror, you soppy vain cunt, he won't help yer, you're on yer own. Learn to get angry, son. Get outta this poncified bunhouse, the Churchill, get home, get your tool, be a man. Jimmy's gonna take your fuckin liberty. Leave the mobile there as well. Necessary evil, mobile phones, but it's voluntary electronic tagging. No mad ski-masks like some Seamus off the Falls Road. Get changed, nothing flash. Cut the sleeves offa oner those black jumpers with a carving knife. Make holes in 'em, to see through, stupid. Everyone thinks you're a bittova lightweight, don't wanna get your soft hands dirty, but it'll be our secret. Go home and get the shooter and the keys to the Rover. It's still parked up in Soho. Keep the room at the Churchill.

Oxford Street, chocka-block, first stop. Buy some big old chunky black-rimmed sunglasses that go dark in sunlight. Learn from a master, Mister Troop. Have a line, if you must. Put that brandy in the plastic water bottle, have a double when the time comes. Don't be getting steamboats and sloppy. Keep this quiet, don't know who's in the snore with the Other People. You do it on your own and only you will ever know. Buy big socks, woollen ones, divvy hiking boots, size-and-a-half too big, put a pair of socks over them, we don't wanna be leaving footie prints all over. In Selfridges, buy gloves, two pairs, driving ones. Don't get paranoid. Nobody's looking at you, pal. Buy a hat, little peaked affair, like old codgers wear, kids wear 'em back to front. Let them put it in a bag but walk outside and put it on. You're looking like someone else already. Go into another chemist further along, buy some binliners, will definitely come in handy, and your latex gloves, got a dirty job on? Yer not wrong. Do you think these birds on the check-out are paying you any attention? No barcode, you don't exist. Admiring yourself in the shop windows, are yer? Think anyone notices yer?

Get the motor. Drive out to Acton. Know what I'm looking for, nice light industrial estate, once heard some wank-stain estate agent saying the place was full of them. Stop and buy a street atlas, have a little drive about. This looks good. Loads of big industrial bins, dumpsters. There's lots of old oil drums catching rain water from the drainpipes. Nobody's gonna be looking in this part of town, seven miles away. There's a little park, full of black crows shrieking, manure over the rose beds, that's the spot. The charlie does the old appetite right in, get a nourishment drink, get a couple for the car. Find a hardware store, wire cutters, heavy tape, hacksaw, dark boilersuit, it'll come in more than handy. Find a garden centre, buy a soil shovel for bedding out plants from the glasshouse. Back to the park, stash it up in some bushes by the roses. Get my bearing by the skyline and trees. Be able to find that? Sure?

On the North Circular Road, round to Finchley. Off the dual carriageway and head north to Totteridge, bittova daylight reconnaissance. Totteridge Village welcomes careful drivers. Very nice part of town, a village on the outskirts of the city. The houses and cottages all higgledy-piggledy, tucked away off the road, down narrow lanes, cross open fields. Where's High Trees? Don't wanna be asking Postman Pat so he can have a day out up the Bailey. Could never find someone's house out here. You could very easily be a recluse out here. That's why people live out here, yer soppy cunt. That's why Dewey lived out here, now Jimmy fuckinsupergrassingcunt Price. Eddy gave yer the massive clue, didn't he. 'He wrecked that High Trees.' Maybe you're doing Eddy's dirty laundry so he can crack on, do his Russian bagwash. He weaved it in his act very nicely. If I wasn't cute with a capital kay, wouldn't have spotted it.

High Trees, fuck me, of course, look for some high trees, you fuckin doughnut. There, five in a row about five hundred yards away. Where's that map, along that lane and fuckin hell, this is it, High Trees right in front of me. No Jag out front. Have a little nose-up. Go around the back, park up, have a creep about. Back fence, old rusty barbed wire, could use replacing, Jimmy Boy, job for the weekend, cutters, clip, over. Brittle twigs underfoot. House hundred feet away. Burglar alarm, no surprise there. Dog bowls on the patio, big dog bowls, no surprise there either, two very big dog bowls, large red sink bowl for drinking water. French windows, steps down to manicured lawns, clipped flower beds, going into rambling, wild, wooded area. Plenty of cover but noisy shingle paths. Tall firs around the side of the lawn with the bottom branches lapping onto the grass. Kids could make camps under there. Heart's beating up a tempo, a didgy little rumba numba.

House looks empty. The dogs have started to bark. They're the key, son. He's either gotta walk 'em or turn the alarms off, send them out for a quick shit. You on it? You understand? Come back in the night. Go and check your tools.

Drive back towards town. Park up, pay and display off Hampstead High Street. Walk on Hampstead Heath. Find a secluded spot, latex gloves on, aim at tree. Trigger. Dooff. Shooter's working all right, tree splinters, leaves a hole as big as yer fist. This fucker's got a naughty kick to it, best use both hands, sweetheart, as the bishop said to the rent boy. Time to kill. Getting didgy now. More traffic on the roads. Kill more time. I want empty roads on the way out. More coke, nip of Andy Pandy, my mouth is always dry nowadays, frothy spit. Drive for an hour, then bang! time's right. I'm impatient all of a sudden. Back to Totteridge, everything quiet, misty cos it's high up. Tot-ter-RIDGE, it's high up, you dummy, course it fuckin is. Couple of people walking dogs. Jag out front. Park up off-road, in a narrow lane by a barred gate. Reverse in, might be in a hurry on the way back. Slip round the back of the Price residence. Pullover sleeve over head, boilersuit on, buttoned right up, latex gloves, two pairs, driving gloves over the top, small brandy bottle in one pocket, water bottle in other, divvy hiking boots on, socks over the top, clownish. Sit and wait this side of the fence. Wait an hour. Dew on deck. Quarter to ten.

Hear the dogs, big dogs? Rottweilers, barking out in the garden. Over fence, into the undergrowth. Itch all over, can feel my own heartbeat, hear my own heartbeat getting faster and faster, louder and louder. I need the dogs over here, in the dark, two-onto-one on the lawn, no chance, they'd rip me apart. Ain't no kamikaze mission. I'm going back alive.

Eyes adjust to the dark. I can see lights flooding up the side of the house. I wanna sit still and move at the same time. Can only breathe in the top of my lungs. I try and take a deep breath, sounds deafening. It stays stuck in my throat. I wanna cough. On tiptoe I see Jimmy watering the lawn and flower beds with a green hose. Two dogs, huge fuckers, big target. He's in a white towelling dressing gown. I come down, stumble, crack a large twig. Fuck! Dogs start barking, running in my direction, bandits at twelve o'clock. Final briefing: You may only get one shot at each. Make it count. You're doing this for the next twelve years of liberty. Don't fuck about. They've got the scent. They're charging into the trees. I make myself as small, still as poss. Both hands, remember, both fuckin hands. Rocky One comes galloping through the bushes, snarling, slobbering, fast. One time, I'm upright. Both hands. Finger on trigger. He sees me, he stops, split second, tries to change direction from his skid, aims to lunge. I aim. Nice doggie, big doggie, trigger, dooff, no side of head, doggie. Fuckin 'ell. Cartridge case goes up, into the undergrowth. Someone's tossed a two-pence coin. Rocky Two's tailed his mate in. Two seconds behind. Keep it together. The rest of your life, remember, the next half a second, don't fuck it up. Aim. Give him two, one for luck. Trigger, dooff, trigger, dooff. This is a fuckin tool. These fuckin dum-dums are the bomb. The first shot hits Rocky Two in the fuselage blowing a big hole. The second hits him in mid-air. The side of his head bursts open. Dead meat when he lands near my feet. Hear the bullet, and the skull disintegrates on impact. The silence has got me even more alert. I thought I was alert before. There's always another level. Got a film of sweat all over me, a puddle in the base of my back. This exact time last week I was counting the six-and-a-half gee I'd got from Jeremy the Swell. I can hear Jimmy calling out to the dogs, whistling.

I move out through the wood to my left, but edging in towards the house, closer to James. I can see Jimmy holding the hose absent-mindedly, preoccupied, worried about the hounds. I can hear anxiety in his voice, nice to hear. The mist from the spray is making a rainbow in the floodlight beam. Ain't so fuckin big without your fuckin dogs, are yer, cunt? You was gonna send me away for a twelve. In cold blood, you cunt. Nick my loot while I fuckin stewed in pissy nicks, the length and breadth of England cos you, yer arrogant cunt, got rumped by cunts from a country you can't pronounce. Keep it together, son. He could have had a whisper, have a little handgun tucked in the robe. Don't be even thinking about walking up to him, shooting him in the face, starting chase scenes, no slapstick! Keep the shit together, son. You're doing well. You've done the hard part, doing the dogs. Use a bittov stealth, lovely word that, stealth, who said that? Can't remember, couldn't be important. Keep edging over, one-man pincer movement style, closer all the time. The noise from that hose is well handy. Quick, crawl under the overhang of the tallest, widest fir tree. Now I can see you, Jimmy Boy, out in the light, but you can't see me, I'm all cosy in the dark, Jimbo. Shame your pal Albie ain't popped round for a drink and a chin-wag. We coulda done him as well. Can't start doing cozzers, son, it ain't on. Oh, ain't it now. If Jimmy had give him my name on Sunday, on that tape, he'd be going as well, no danger. Slow down. Fuckin 'ell, you're getting a taste for this, ain't yer. Jimmy's still shouting to the dogs. The soil under my tree's like fine dark powder, never seen water, brown like smack, 'Brown rather than white', judges don't like scag. Could you do a twelve? Do it standing on me head. How come he can't hear my heart, my breathing, is he fuckin Mutt 'n' Jeff, the old grass? Wonder how he got to hear so much if he's deaf. Let him go into the wood a bit. Go and have a fuckin look for your dogs, you selfish bastard. They died trying to defend you, fuckin ingrate. Biting the inside of my bottom lip. If I don't stop I'm gonna draw blood. Rolling my fingers, open and shut, clammy fist in the latex. Creep closer. Now closer still. I can see Jimmy's maroon-leather bedroom slippers, his milky white legs. He's studying the garden and the

248

woods, frowning. He's concerned, the dogs have just disappeared, into thin air. I move behind the trunk of the tree but the evergreen overhang gives me protection. I've got you ready-eyed, Mister Jim. You're in my sights. The hose is making a puddle on the lawn. He's standing like he's gonna fight off any invaders with it. He's edging into my tree but with his back to me, scanning into the darkness. Come to me, Daddyo. The hiss of the hose is like the hiss on the tape. Slow motion now. This is a gift, somebody up there likes me. Don't fuck it up. You wanna say anything to him? Fuckin 'ell. JUST SHOOT THE CUNT!! Let's get outta here, for fuck's sake. You sure you ain't got nuffin to say? Don't fuckin wind me up, just do it. Revenge or sentiment has no place in murder. I can feel my heartbeat at the bottom of my front bottom teeth. I'm Ninja. You're losing it big-time, you mean. Upright, and creep the three long paces across the dusty space beneath the branches. One, steady myself, Two, there's no air in my lungs, Three, but I'm totally alive. Jimmy's oblivious, surveying the wrong horizon, the wrong tree-line. His back's to me now, I could kick his arse. The tiny branches must be tickling his calfs. Do it, for fuck's sake. I'm so close I can smell the cigar smoke on his gown. He's just come out the bath, smell the sickly sweet aftershave, on a promise? I can hear him breathing deeply. Fuck's sake, he's there! Do it! This feels powerful. You're on, son. I raise my tool, stroke his earlobe, tender, like a lover. Tickles for a micro-second. He turns with a shriek.

'What the fu-!'

Trigger. Dooff. Trigger. Dooff. Top of Jimmy's head disappears. His body falls in an untidy pile. Give him another one! He's fuckin dead already. What, you paying for the fuckin bullets or something? Give him one more. Trigger. Dooff. No neck. Jimmy's head's got all expansive all of a sudden. Very good. Shame he ain't around to hear that one, would've liked that, all expansive. Jimmy's brain, looking like frog-spawn across the lawn, in the low branches of the fir. I'm covered in splashes of his blood, didn't plan on that. I should've shot him from a distance. Ya wouldn't listen to fuckin reason. Had to be fuckin clever. Had to let him know he was going. Who's in the fuckin house I wonder? Wife and fat-slag daughters? Shall we do them as well? Have you gone fuckin mad? fuckin 'ell. First you shit yourself about doing it at all, now you wanna start slaughtering non-combatants, in cold blood. This ain't a fuckin arcade game, son. Breathing through me nostrils, rushing, trembling with adrenaline, it ain't fuckin pretty. Hose's dancing like a epileptic green snake over the lawn. Let's go. Make it quick. Through the garden, fly over the fence, nothing left to chance, nothing left behind 'cept shell casings, nuffin we can do 'bout that. Jog back to motor. Nobody about, open back door, deep breathing, a car goes by up the lane, duck, didn't see me, binliners on back seat already opened out, ready to receive. I'm scared. I wasn't back there. I've just fuckin killed a human being. Big deal. I'm trembling so I can't get the boots untied. Composure. Think about the consequences if you get caught. You do sixteen years, that's five thousand, eight hundred and forty days, heavy bird, and that's if you behave and get remission. Focuses the mind, don't it. Boots off, in the binliner, damp boilersuit off, same, mask with blood and brain on, off, careful! Watch the fuckin fabric on those back seats. Any forensic could get yer well nicked. Don't panic, now. Driving gloves off, latex gloves same, in the sack. Shooter in the door panel, case we get a pull. Sacks, double-bagged then triple-bagged, in the boot. The murder squad'll be all over this patch of ground at daybreak, it'll have a tent over it, so check you ain't left nothing behind. Drag any footprints you left around with the *Standard*, like the Indian tracker in the cowboy films. DC, double-check. Okay? Okay. Let's go, chunky clear-glass spectacles on, old tosser's hat on, case I get caught in someone's full beam, let the motor free-wheel down the slight hill, listen for other cars, nothing, hit the ignition. 'Beware! This is a neighbourhood watch area.' See ya later, Totteridge. Head towards the route in red marker pen on the street atlas, all the narrow lanes, quiet roads. No ready-eye, CCTV, to control traffic flow. Need to put some distance in. Pick up the North Circular at Finchley again. Don't wanna go down the main road. 'A job is not finished till the clearing up is done,' said the sign in the hardware shop. 'No conspicuous fires either,' said Gene. Bob and weave for an hour. Glasses and silly hat off. Round to Acton. Park up motor. Put on black nylon Prada jacket, latex gloves. Bring new best friend over park fence, final wipe down with rag, find spade first time, dig hole, three foot deep by one foot wide, hard fuckin work, sweating, huffing and puffing, crows shrieking, won't fit, dismantle gun, does now, bury, start to back-fill, pat down, cover with earth, check footprints, none, latex gloves off, in bin, keep Britain tidy.

In car. Back over to industrial estate and bitta luck. Dustcart doing a night round with a big hoist on the back to empty industrial-sized bins. Touch. These dustmen ain't got time to be pulling bags apart. Drive ahead of it, round the corner. Quick. Bags outta boot, into the dumpster. Quick, drive around block and park up. They don't even fuckin notice you with your big silly glasses. These guys are on a bonus, on Lou Reed as well, driven to get the round done and get away. Sit, snort a big fuckin line, watch as the bright red industrial bin is raised, tilted, its cargo of rubbish comes tumbling out into the grinding mangle of the dustcart never to be seen again. Bye bye boiler-suit, boots, specks of Jimmy's blood and brain on the sleeve of a nearly-new Gucci sweater. They'll be buried for ever in a land-fill site somewhere out on the Thames estuary. Wipe down and drop the cutters and unused hacksaw in water-filled oil drum without getting outta the car. Home for a few hours. Park up Rover on a yellow line. I'm gonna be gone before eight in the morning. Strip naked. All the clothes I went to Totteridge and Acton in, off, ripped in two with kitchen knife, in another black sack, left by the street door. In the shower and scrub and scrub. Scrub till ya red, son, under nails and in yer ears, cos you never know. Never know what? I don't fuckin know, do I, son, for fuck's sake. Get dressed in tracksuit, trot this bag down to the bins outside for safe-keeping till the morning. Sling the fuckin coke and all, it's starting to weird you out. One last big line, okay? I'm not sure I like you on cocaine, you can turn on a sixpence, as your old man says. What was that word Eddy Ryder used? Omnipotent, God-like. Calls on the answerphone? Three. Social. Nothing to do with business. Good. Sit and watch the programmes you taped last night, attention to detail, drink coffee, come down a bit, keep ya shit together, son, almost there. Don't wanna be asking anyone for alibis cos if they crumble the spell's broken, away you go, you're gonski. Hurry up, clock, for fuck's sake, hurry. I wanna get going, wanna get done. Getting ready to leave, phone rings. Clarkie's voice on the answerphone. Clock says seven-fifteen.

'You there, brov? you awake?'

I pick up, pretending to be half sleeping.

'Fuckin 'ell, what time's it? Shit. Fuckin 'ell, it's seven o'clock.'

'Listen,' he says.

'What?' I say.

'The Legend got the worst.'

'What!?' I say.

'Yeah. Last night,' he says.

'The worst or the very worst?' I ask.

Nicked or killed, like I don't know already.

'The very, very worst. Could be the overseas or outta-town crew.'

'Really? Shit,' I say, glad the blame's travelling in the other direction.

'The Mister says you're to go offside for a while till him and Chief Scout can work out what's what, okay?'

Morty says I'm to disappear for a bit while he and Gene, Geronimo to me and Clarkie, try and work out what's going on.

'I'll catch ya later,' I say.

Dialling tone. He's gonski. Hope anyone listening in was convinced. Offside suits me fine. He don't sound exactly grief-stricken, does Clarkie. Wonder if he's a sociopath? Anyway, things to do. Gotta get Mister Clark's rental motor back, drop the keys in the handy little box provided. One can rent it in one place and drop it off in another, if one desires. They simply total it off on the credit card, very civilised. No point worrying Clarkie about where the car's been, what it's been up to, worrying the poor boy half to death. Out the door, pick up the black sack from the bins, back up to King's Cross. Glasses and hat on. African geezers doing the car-cleaning look like they couldn't give a fuck what yer been up to. I used to have a navy

252

boilersuit just like that. Why you telling me for? After I've gone through the serious buffing machine they drive out with high-pressure hoses every last bit of Totteridge dirt and dust from every nook and cranny, even underneath. They wipe down every surface, inside and out, and leave enough finger prints to confuse the issue. It pays to go deluxe every time.

I go for a little stroll with the bin bag, drop it in another large bin outside a council block. I come back and tip the guys three quid and drive over to the drop-off point. Park up, put the last pair of latex gloves on. Wrap some heavy-duty tape around my hand, play patter-cake, patter-cake, baker's man, dabbing my hand over the front seats to make sure, DC there's no incrimi-nating, guilt-ridden little fibres knocking about. I wipe down the steering wheel, plastic surfaces and door handles. Shut the door with a paper hanky, Howard Hughes style. It looks like it just come off the production line. If the murder squad did get a plate number from some busy cunt out in Totteridge the motor wouldn't come back to me. Clarkie would certainly be alibied-up cos he's never at home. They'd need forensic to get a guilty. I drop the keys off in the drop-off box and walk. I can start to relax.

Back at the Churchill I pay for another night. Now listen, this is very important, you hear? If you get nicked, stick to your story, son, everything's gonna be all right, okay? You're get-ting weird, son. I don't know why you think you gotta be sat talking to mirrors all the time. You've done well. Why don't yer have a drink, a vally and go to sleep. Nobody knows you're here. Stop it, it's spooky. You're starting to scare me, laughing like a fuckin lunatic, drinkin toasts to geezers you shot dead last night.

'Raise your glasses. Alas, poor Jimmy, we knew him too well.'

Saturday, PM
Savoy for Drinkipoos?

Years ago you could wake up in a gaff like this, the Churchill,
fuck the chambermaid, stick it on the bill. These days you gotta
suffer with a Continental breakfast or make your own arrangements. I feel like shit. I've been taking care of business but I
ain't been taking care of me. I crashed out about ten this
morning. It was hazy. My watch says it's three-fifteen now. I
could kip for another ten hours but then I'd be living on Los
Angeles time, wide a fuckin wake at three in the morning.
That's guaranteed to weird yer out and look a bit suspect. The
plan of action now is to see if anything's happening with the
pills. If nobody wants to punt, and punt quick, I'm gonna sort
out my affairs and scarpa on an extended holiday. North Viet-
nam could be the place to lay low, take a breather, or Curaçao,
off the coast of Venezuela, short hop from Amsterdam via
Caracas.

The law are gonna be all over Jimmy's affairs like a nasty
rash, any known associates can expect a pull. When they realise
it's been Jimmy who's been feeding them juicy titbits on all the
top London firms, north and south of the pipe, for the last
couple of decades, they'll increase the list of suspects to about
two hundred. It muddies up the cesspool very nicely. Who's got
a motive? Who ain't fuckin got one is a better question. I hope
Albie Carter, Jekyll cozzer, knows better than to tell his col-
leagues that he did the tape and sold it to Edward Ryder. My
hunch is Albie's got enough self-preservation instincts to keep
that bitta severely incriminating data to himself.

I give the room a wipe down before I leave, it's becoming
second nature to me, pay my room-service bill and head for
home to see what's occurring. The mobile I use for work says
I've got fourteen missed calls. I get a pen and make a list.
Billy's rung up irate, I don't fuckin blame him, after getting

254

released without charge from the nick in Brighton, wants to talk, sounds like he wants a row. Later he rings up, says don't be avoiding me. Finally he rings, concern in his voice that I might be dead somewhere. Gene's rung the once to say 'Ring me as soon as possible'. That's a long message for Gene. Clarkie's left four messages, one saying that there's method in my madness, him and Terry have got a bittova result with the binoculars. That could be interesting. Morty wants me to give him a shout as soon as. These are all from yesterday, Friday, before Jimmy died. Everyone's keeping a low one today. Last but no means least, Mister Edward Ryder's rung. His message is more than interesting.

'Hello, son. I enjoyed our chat the other day. That two million you were looking for finance on, I think I may be able to help. Listen, it's Saturday, midday, give me a ring on this number.' He leaves a number, I write it down. 'Oh, and have a little punt on Jolly Smuggler in the two-thirty at Kempton Park. It's priced at forty-to-one but don't let that deter you. Ring me when you get this message.'

Nothing about his old pal Jimbo and he'd fuckin know, all right. I've missed the race and getting a bet on. I turn on the telly to get the result but I kinda know already that Eddy's horse pissed it. Forty-to-one usually means they're just showing a young gee-gee what a racecourse looks at. Here it is, Jolly Smuggler, won by seven lengths, but they're holding a steward's inquiry. I ring the mobile number Eddy's left.

'Hello. This is Ryder,' he says in his best swell's voice.

'Good afternoon, Mister Ryder. I'm returning your call.'

'Well done, son. Can you meet me in the Thames Foyer Bar at the Savoy in about an hour?'

'I guess so. Sooner if you wish,' I say.

'Good. That's what I like to hear. Half an hour, then. Smart dress essential, but I don't need to tell you that.'

'Half an hour. See you then.'

He's a smug bastard, is Eddy, but he may be the answer to my prayers. I need a quick pit-stop, a change of clothes and a splash about in a sink full of cold water to liven me up. I walk downstairs, get a cab and nonchalantly tell the driver, 'The Savoy, please.'

The bar is quiet as I arrive but Eddy is plotted up at a table by the window, facing the door so he can watch all the comings and goings. Old habits die hard, I guess. During the week at this time, six-thirty, this bar would be heaving but on the weekend it's slow. We shake hands, I sit down, the waiter comes over. I order a vodka and tonic. Eddy says, 'Make it a large one,' with a wink to the waiter.

'How are you son?' he asks.

'I am in the best of health, Mister Ryder. Thank you for asking.'

'You okay, son?'

'Yes. I am very well today. How are you today, Mister Ryder?'

'I'm okay,' he says.

'How was Thursday's performance of *The Damnation of Faust*?'

'Too loud. I heard the overture then got my head down till the interval.'

'I hope your family are in good health.'

'Fucking hell. What's this, a fucking English-conversation class? What's with you, son? What's the fucking problem?'

'Well, Mister Ryder, you have been known to record conversations for posterity.'

'Oh, so that's it. Trying to be a clever bastard, are we? How do I know you ain't wired up?'

'I ain't,' I say.

'Right, so we are going to have to trust one another, aren't we? This is one conversation I definitely would not want recorded. Those space pills, I want to buy them, how much?'

'The lot?'

'Of course.'

'The price is two and a half million sterling but we will take the equivalent in dollars or gilders. Cash, used, large denominations.'

'Sounds about right,' he says.

I wish I'd asked for more cos he don't bat a fuckin eyelid, two and a half mill's fuck-all to him.

'Are these going to Moscow? Get the Ivans and Ivanas livened up?'

'No,' he says, shaking his head, 'Tokyo.'

'Japan?'

'That's where Tokyo was last time I looked.'

'You're gonna sell them to the Japanese?'

'I'm going to give these to the Japanese,' he says, lighting a fag.

'Give? What, free in packs of Rice Crispies?'

'No. You're being slightly foolish, now, slightly English as well, if I may say so. How much would one of those tablets fetch in the United Kingdom?'

I do that thing builders do, intake of breath, and drop the rap I gave JD on Monday night. 'Well, that all depends on the quality, availability, seasonal fluctuations, police activity ... blah ... blah ... and then if you factor in the –'

'Fucking hell. You don't half go on, do you. Just answer the question approximately. How much, to the person who pops it in their mouth, does it cost?'

'About a ching, a fiver.'

'Right, about five pounds. In Tokyo they cost about forty pounds each.'

'Very nice, chicken and rice. So you're gonna give them away instead of charging forty pound a pop. And I thought you was a businessman, Mister Ryder.'

'It's none of your business what I do with them after they become my property. But, between ourselves, I intend to make a gift of them to some businessmen I wish to do business with.'

'Oh, I get it. Yakuza. Japanese Mafia.'

'Have I spoken to you before about your manners? I have, haven't I? Do you think everyone I do business with is some variety of international gangster?'

Yes. 'No, of course not. No way. I'm sorry. I was just being reckless, don't know where it comes from, I'm sorry.'

Just because they've got BANDIT tattooed across their forehead and half their fingers missing don't make them Yakuza.

'You're forgiven. So when can I have them?' he says.

'As soon as we can make the arrangements, Mister Ryder. Everyone's gone off-duty, it's the weekend.'

I need a couple of days to work out how we're gonna do it our end.

'You don't work the weekend?' asks moody toff Eddy, pulling a face like I was a plumber.

'Well, neither do you. I'm surprised to find you in town at all,' I say.

'True. No wonder the country's going to the dogs.'

'I still can't see why you don't sell them to the Japanese gents,' I ask, intrigued.

'Kudos. It's a good-will gesture.'

'Seems they're getting all the good will.'

'See what I mean about you having an English attitude.'

'This lot stand to make about eighty million pounds or a fuckin lot of yen outta your fuckin good-will present.'

'Well, so be it. Transpires these ecstasy are the new aphrodisiac, the new white-rhino horn in smart Japanese society.'

'Well, they had to find an alternative, what with wiping out all the white rhinos.'

'Manners. I can get them landed and away at Tokyo airport, no problem.'

Well, lucky you.

'I'll get it sorted,' I say, 'but as you can understand with the Jimmy situation things are a bit up in the air.'

I'm looking for his reaction.

'Yes, poor James. The police are talking about a highly professional contract killer. It solves your little problem quite nicely, though, doesn't it?'

'Well, it does. If you think, Jimmy might have died and I would never have known he was out to nobble me up and steal my assets. Without your help he might have died a hero in my eyes.'

'It's part of growing up, son. Poor Jimmy.'

'You know, in spite of that business with your daughter, he thought the sun shone outta your arse.'

'He was a good man, James Price. "Misunderstood", I

think's the word best describes James,' he says like the vicar at a wrong'un's funeral.

'He just lost the plot a bit towards the end,' I say.

'True, son. That's what true desperation can do to a man.'

'He started to have fantasies about people. You, for instance, he was very jealous of you.'

'Me?'

'Oh yes. My dad used to say envy's worse than cancer, can eat ya alive. Maybe I shouldn't speak ill of the dead.'

'What did he say?'

'He ain't even in his grave yet and I'm slandering him. You're right, Mister R, I gotta learn to watch my manners.'

'I thought you said you never had much to do with him?'

'I'm talking about last Saturday. Fuckin 'ell. This exact time last week. I just felt like someone walked over me grave.'

'And the fuckin slag was sayin what?' he says, the elocution lessons flying out the window.

'No, I can't repeat it.'

Eddy grabs my wrist and squeezes it. The barman catches it, looks alarmed but turns away quick.

'Listen, stop fuckin 'bout and fess up, okay?' he spits.

'Fess-up? I don't understand?'

'Tell me, you fuckin cunt,' he says with a clipped 't', like a market trader.

'Okay,' I say in a hushed whisper. He leans closer. 'He said, God rest his soul, that he was going to kill your first wife, Charlie's mum, as a favour, but you was scared that he'd blunder about, fuck it up, you'd both get nicked for putting the plot together, it's conspiracy.'

'He said that?'

'Yeah. This time last week. He said that you had the murder done instead, to stop him fuckin it up. Now ain't that a fuckin sick thing to say 'bout anybody, even in his deranged state.'

Mister Ryder's gone very pale, very sudden. He coughs and signals to the barman for two more.

'He told you this? On your own?'

'He fuckin said it to me, Gene and Mister Mortimer. Gene wouldn't have it, said "No fuckin way, Jim." Jimmy got the

259

hump cos it was one of the few times Gene ever stood up to him.'

'Gene didn't believe it?'

'No way,' I say.

'And this Mister … '

'Mortimer. Couldn't give a fuck.'

'And Mister Mortimer's the large black fellow, bit of a tearaway?'

'Funny you should say that, but Morty's the quiet one in the family. His brother's are fuckin ravin lunatics, real head-the-balls. He's quite reserved by comparison. It's funny that, ain't it? Everything is relative, don't you think, Eddy?'

'How many brothers does your friend have?'

'Four. Oh fuck, by the way, I forgot to mention, I saw your horse won.'

'Yes it did,' he says with a quizzical face on, thinking is it worth the blood-bath to get rid of me, Mort and Gene, probably not. 'After a steward's inquiry, said it was a suspected betting coup, and to a degree it was.'

'Really? Well, well. Let me ask you something, Mister Ryder. I hope you don't think I'm being about myself but why does a geezer, with all your shillings, have to get involved in betting coups?'

'Sport.'

'But I thought that hobbling horse races would be the opposite of sport.'

'The sport is in beating the system. I have to make my own entertainment.'

'Oh, I know that one all right, making my own entertainment. That's interesting what you say about sport, though, beating the system, havin 'em over.'

But he's a bit preoccupied, is Eddy, thinking about London, early seventies, disappearing acts, things he's always thought he'd got clean away with. He's nibbling his bottom lip.

'Fuckin 'ell, Eddy, you can see the whole fuckin river from here.'

Teach him to fuckin kidnap me.

Afters

Walking back along the Strand, two large vodka and tonics later, I'm experiencing the calm after the storm, thinking that for a minute I can allow myself to think I could be trotting towards Easy Street. The pills could be on the way to Tokyo and yours truly could be travelling in the opposite direction. I could use a sauna and a Thai massage, some little Thai bird walking about on my back, nothing saucy, just a sweat and a rub down, get all these fuckin toxins out. Him back there didn't seen to think it was anything more than a coincidence that he dropped the tape on me Thursday afternoon and last night Jimmy got the top of his canister blown off. Eddy just wanted to get his bitta business done, couldn't give a monkey's about Jimbo. I'll talk to Morty and Gene about it in the morning.

It's Saturday night, I've had a bittova week, I feel like going back home to bed. I wonder if Tammy will be up for that? I could make it up to her for letting her down the other day. I push her number on my mobile. It rings three times then someone answers it. 'Hello? It's okay, I've got it, Tam,' they shout. It's gormless Sidney. She must be in the bath or something. Now there's a thought. I stay silent. 'Hello? Who's that? Talk, will yer,' he says aggressively. 'Who the fuck's that? Talk, you cunt.'

He must be able to hear the traffic noise my end.

'Listen, you cunt, don't fuckin ring this number again, you hear?'

He's gone. Luckily I've got this phone rigged so it withholds my number. Sid's obviously on some jealous-suitor tip but Tammy said they only hang out, he ain't the boyfriend. Maybe he thinks different.

The phone rings. I check the incoming number. It's Morty's mobile. He rarely carries it. I answer.

'Where the fuck you been?' he says, all up-tight.

'Hello, Mister Mortimer,' I say.

'Where you now?'

'On the Strand. Why?'

'Gene wants to see you. Have you done anything to upset him?'

'No,' I answer. Nothing that he knows about.

'Well, he wants to see you, now.'

'Yeah?' I'm curious.

'See you in Loveland,' he says.

'Is that a Barry White number, Mort?'

'You always gotta be the funny cunt, ain't ya. Twenty minutes, okay?'

He's gone. Obviously had a tough day with Gene running around trying to get a clue about dear departed Jimmy. One fuckin minute ago I was walking on air, thinking I might have a buyer for the Jack 'n' Jills and maybe I could even get Tammy back to the hideout to consummate this liaison once and for all. A minute later, crash, verbal from Sidney, crash, verbal from Morty, and my world-view's totally spun. I stop a cab and get in.

'Where to?' says the driver.

I tell him to go to the corner of the street that Loveland is on, but as an afterthought I ask him to go on a detour by my car, parked round the corner from my place. It makes me late but something in Morty's voice tells me that it could be a good idea. The taxi stops. I get out, open my car door, open the glove compartment and start emptying out, onto the front seat, all the pre-recorded cassettes and mix-tapes. Near the bottom of the untidy pile is the one I want, the one DJ Eddy Ryder, top mixer, gave me on Thursday. I get back in the cab and head for Loveland.

A pal once told me that him and his bird once went on holiday and he left eighty grand in bricks of cash lining the sides of a drawer, third one down, in an old dresser, in a hardly used upstairs boxroom. For some reason he could never explain, just as he was going out the door to get in the cab to the airport, he went back upstairs and took the lightbulb outta the socket in the boxroom. He put it in the rubbish bin in the kitchen. When he came back, from Ibiza or Thailand or wherever he's been, the whole fuckin house had been ransacked by local teenage toe-rag burglars, and all the valuables were gone. His gaff had been systematically racked over, room by room, all except the small, seemingly neglected, boxroom that hadn't been touched, cos it didn't have a lightbulb. I asked the guy, Why on that occasion did you decide to remove the lightbulb, you go on holiday four times a year, why that time?

'Fuck knows,' he said.

When I get to Loveland the whole place is in uproar. Morty's shouting and screaming at Nobby and the two kids who work there. He's telling the two shop workers that they're bone fuckin idle, doing dead people outta bodies, he's never seen people putting so much effort into being lazy, they can have a clump if they want one. You want some? They stand there terrified, scared to move from the spot, saying nothing. Nobby actually looks on the point of tears. Morty's rucking him about the unwanted porn cluttering up the place. You should be in the ladies' hairdressing game, putting in curlers, Nobby. Get those two useless cunts out there to start sorting out what you want and what you don't want, get it boxed up, I don't give a fuck if it's Saturday night or Christmas Eve, I'm sick of you moaning like a girl every time I come in for my readies. Okay, Nobby?

Morty walks past me out the door and gestures with his head for me to follow him. We walk up to Morty's car in silence. He's putting out a didgy, volatile vibe like the last time I saw him, flitting down the canal steps after the Freddie Hurst thing. We head off north, making towards the Edgware Road. He's all huffing and puffing, swearing under his breath and shaking his head all the time. If yer try and talk to Mort when he's like this he'll either eat yer alive or ignore yer. Finally he speaks to me properly.

'The geezer we used to get our merchandise off, through Jim, don't wanna know us for the next few months. Says we're too fuckin warm.'

'We might have the pills sold, the lot at two and half mill.'

He doesn't seem impressed. He shrugs like it's none of his business. 'Gene's been on the fuckin warpath all day, getting reckless, driving people mad.'

263

'Who does he think did Jim?' I ask.

'Nobody's got a sniff. I've been out with Gene since eight this mornin, all over London, no cunt knows anything, but Gene's been lookin to get that felt.' He grabs his collar and tugs. 'He went off to see some geezer he could only see alone. He told me to sit tight at Loveland. Now he wants to see you. I don't know why, before you ask. I told him you're no good in combat but he wants to see you all the same.'

'Where?'

'You'll see when we get there.'

Gene's in a sitting room above a boozer in Kilburn nursing a very large whiskey. His suit jacket's off, he's listening to Elvis crying in the chapel. I hope Gene hasn't got all morbid and sentimental cos someone shot his mate. The room is furnished with affluent Irish publican taste, beige-leather sofa, religious ornaments, massive telly and along one wall a gigantic chest freezer. They must do a roaring trade in burgers downstairs.

'If you want anything, lads, I'm –' the landlord says.

Gene's up in a bound. 'No, that's grand, we're okay now. I'll see you in a bit.' Gene's shooing him out his own door. He shuts it very neatly, then turns, grabs me by the throat. He hurls me across the room against the wall. I put my arm up to try and stop myself but I bend my wrist back sickeningly. I hear a nasty crack and immediately it's agony. Gene swiftly follows me over and kicks me hard in the stomach, knocking all the wind outta me. I feel like throwing up.

'Fuckin 'ell,' says Mort, shocked. 'Fuckin leave it out, Gene.'

'Shut the fuck up, Morty,' says Gene with a cold anger. 'I'll explain in a minute.'

Gene picks me up by the back of my collar, bangs my head against the wall and drags me effortlessly over the chest freezer. The landlord's had a cheap padlock screwed on it to stop pilferage. Gene grabs the lock, wrenches it hard and it comes off with a snap. He pulls the door open and slams my face inside. I feel the bitter, freezing cold straight away. I'm inches away from frosty trade boxes of eight-ounce hamburgers and crinkle-cut chips. Gene pushes me in further. The heavy frost on the box burns my face. A sinister smoky mist rolls slowly up and out over the side of the freezer. Gene pulls my head up, grabs my jaw with one massive hand and bangs my head against the wall so I'm on tiptoes. He pushes the barrel of a gun hard into my forehead, it's cutting, like it's gonna draw blood.

'Now, you're gonna tell me what I want to know or I'm gonna put you in there, understand?'

There's plenty of room. I can smell the snout and whiskey on his breath.

'I don't fuckin understand, Gene. Why?'

'Alive or dead, you can go in there, you understand?' says Gene, who's gone the colour of chilli sauce, breathing hard through his nostrils.

'What do you wanna know, Gene?'

'I might put you in there anyway, you murdering cunt.'

'I ain't never killed anyone, Gene, I fuckin swear. On my mother's fuckin life,' I lie.

'Yer fuckin liar,' screams Gene, banging my head against the wall then hitting my nose with the gun butt.

'Gene,' says Morty. Gene's head spins. 'He ain't a killer. I'll swear to that. He ain't got the bottle. Relax, Gene.'

'He killed Jimmy,' says Gene, putting my face back down into the freezing cold, jamming it against a box of chicken Kievs, scraping the frost off with my cheek, wedged so I can't talk but I can see blood from my nose, claret on the frost.

'No way, Gene, no fuckin way,' says Morty. 'Let him up, you're gonna break his fuckin neck.'

'Maybe I will as well, break his fuckin neck. Take your fuckin hands off me, Mortimer,' shouts Gene.

Is this some mad fuckin paranoid deluded hunch from Gene or does he know something? The biting cold is burning into the side of my face. It makes me forget about my wrist.

'Gene,' says Morty, pleading for my life, 'let him out. Talk to him properly.'

In one movement, Gene drags me outta the freezer, throwing my head back. He hurtles me across the room, over a coffee table, and I land on one of the sofas. Gene marches towards me.

265

He's gonna pull me apart. I'm gonna die, but Morty, God bless him, jumps in between Gene and me.

'Calm down, Gene. Please,' he says. I've never heard Morty use the word before.

'Don't tell me to calm down. That little toe-rag killed Jimmy.'

'What makes you say that, Gene?' says Morty, desperately trying to pacify him.

'Okay, you pair of cunts, you stay there, I'll fuckin tell ya, don't fuckin move.'

You ain't gonna stand for that, are ya, Mort, I'm thinking. He called you a cunt. If they get into a bitta ruff and tumble, I could slip past them, out the door or maybe get out the window and jump.

Gene snatches up the dining chair that his jacket's hung over. He goes to the inside pocket and comes out with a bitta fax paper, unfolds it and hands it to Morty. 'Here, read that. Better still, Mister Mortimer, fuckin read it aloud.'

Morty scans it. 'Fuckin 'ell. Where'd you get this, Gene?'

'Never fuckin mind. Just read the fuckin thing.' He's breathing heavy, glaring at me.

To senior ranks only: murder squad investigation, victim: James Lionel Price. Under no circumstances to be revealed to press or below rank of inspector. Preliminary ballistics report, repeat preliminary. Further information to follow within forty-eight hours. No rounds recovered, disintegration on impact. Recovered cartridge, casing-eject pattern consistent with murder weapon used in unsolved 1994 homicide of Lawrence Francis Gower, AKA 'Crazy' Larry Flynn, case number –

'You get it now, do you, Morty?' asks Gene.

'Yeah. Whoever killed Larry killed Jimmy?'

'No. The gun was the same but I gave that gun to him –' pointing at me '– on Wednesday night and he went off and killed Jimmy with it or gave it to someone to kill him.'

'But where did you get it? Oh fuck, hang about,' says Morty. Me and Morty fall in at the same time.

266

'I killed Larry,' says Gene.

'What! Why?' says Morty, shocked and surprised. They were best mates.

'He was getting out of hand, strangling rent boys, couldn't help himself. He always made me promise if he went over the edge, I was to do the decent thing and pop him. Now, out the fuckin way.'

'Larry liked boys?' says Morty, disbelieving.

'Now stand aside, Morty. This isn't your quarrel.'

'You said you knew nuffin about Larry's murder, swore blind,' I say, up from out of nowhere.

'Don't fuckin contradict me, you murdering cunt,' screams Gene. Morty turns on his heel, gives me the pointy finger and glaring eyes. 'Why'd you kill Jimmy? Talk. Don't try and be funny.'

'Cos he was a police informer, Mort.'

'I don't believe it,' says Morty, shaking his head.

'What, you don't believe I killed him or he was a grass?'

'You'll have to do better than that, you lying little cunt,' says Gene.

'Give me a chance. I've got the proof,' I say, desperado.

'What, you going on the word of some gobshite in some old boozer, listening to all the envious gossip, are yer?'

'I'm going on the word of Jimmy Price. Listen, I've got a tape. Get ridda Elvis and put the tape on. Just listen to it.'

Now I'm feeling brave.

'If you ain't convinced, the pair of ya, I'll jump in the freezer and shut the door.'

'Gene, we gotta hear this,' says Mort. 'And Gene, put that fuckin gun away. Someone'll get hurt.'

I rummage in my pocket and bring out the tape. Morty turns off the Elvis tape just as another little baby boy is born in the ghetto. I can hear a stumbling, tumbling version of 'Material Girl' coming up through the floorboards. Then he puts on Eddy's tape. The same hiss, then Jimmy and Albie's voices fill the room. I've heard this a few times now so the novelty's worn off. The side of my face is burnt, tender to the touch, my nose is dripping blood onto my suit and my wrist is starting to swell and throb.

Sometimes I wish I was one of the shit-kickers downstairs in the bar, living the simple life. Boozed up, maybe get lucky, blag a sloppy knee-trembler bunk-up once a fortnight, have the crack or the row in a Turkish kebab house on the way home but be content with my lot. I spot Morty flinching and tutting when he realises the coup, works out Jimmy's little sideline. He starts to comprehend the implications and possible consequences, especially if other firms get to know that we've worked under Jimmy's informant's licence. Heavy people have got brothers, cousins, pals, wives, husbands, sons and daughters who've gone away for long lumps on the back of Jim's bubble while we jogged on scot-free, getting fat. Are they gonna believe we weren't in on the swindle? I never had direct contact with Jimmy so I never told him anything but I can see Gene and Morty rolling with body-shots cos information they'd relayed to him in idle chit-chat, over a sherbet, was now being served up to old bill via Albie Carter.

'Wassa "spook"?' asks Mort.

'That's old-school cozzer-talk for an IC3, a black geezer,' I reply.

'Cunt,' says Mort, shaking his head.

Morty's no Nelson Mandela but he don't like being called snide derogatory names cos he's black.

I know what's coming next and I'm watching Gene's face but pretending I ain't.

'He's a bit tick around people and that … gundog . . why have a dog and call him "Fuck Off" … ' Jimmy's laughter fills the room. Gene looks hurt. It's in the eyes. Two minutes ago he was prepared to slaughter me and lob me in a freezer, do the bird-lime, sixteen-year tariff for murder, remember, if captured. Now he's listening to the geezer he was devoted to for twenty years selling information Gene's told him in confidence to the odd firm and not only that, belittling him, talking about him like he was a fuckin dog. Gene pours himself a double double, pours it down in one hit. He refills his glass as the band downstairs go into 'I Will Always Love You'.

The guy on the trot for the serious armed one is a close personal friend of Morty, I know that for a fact, although I've never met the gent. By this time they've both got their heads down, shaking them gently, looking at the swirly carpet. When the bit about 'a flash little prick' comes, Morty looks up at me.

'That's you, ain't it?'

I nod.

'You don't fuck about, do ya, pal?' says Mort, looking at me in a new light.

'I thought you said he was no good in combat, Morty,' says Gene very dryly without looking up.

I say nothing. I let it sink right in, soak right up, let them absorb it. I get up and walk over to the music centre and push the stop button with my good hand.

'Jimmy was always calling other people grasses, everyone was a wrong'un, according to him,' says Gene quietly into the carpet.

'For all our sakes, I think it's a sensible idea if we keep this to ourselves, in this room. Gene? Morty? Agreed?'

They both nod.

'And we don't know who did the biz on Jimmy, do we? Agreed?

Neither of them has stopped nodding.

Dare, True, Kiss, Promise and Plot

'I fuckin asked you about that shooter on Thursday morning and you categorically denied it was yours.'

Everyone's calmed down a bit.

'Listen, you was round my house, you was well pissed, more pissed than I've ever seen ya. You was performing, acting the goat, you was gonna fucking shoot 'em all, the Here-we-gos, the Germans, the Northern Lads, the fuckin old bill if they came near yer. You'd declared total war, blitzkrieg. There wasn't a gun big enough for yer. You came right out of yourself. I tried to put ya to bed but you said you wanted to wake up at home, in your own bed, but you wouldn't give the gun back, grew attached to it, you did. I ran you home and you fell asleep straight away, like a baby.'

'But when I rang up the next day you said –'

'I know what I fuckin said, lad, but sometimes you're so fuckin serious 'bout things, so earnest, so fuckin up yourself –'

'Okay okay, I get the fuckin picture, Gene.'

'I thought it was funny, a wind-up, you waking up in the feather with a big ol' piece like that, with a silencer. I didn't know you was gonna do Jimmy with it.'

He and Morty smirk at each other like little kids.

'Is that your idea of a joke, planting guns?'

He leans forward and gives me the pointy finger. He's serious now. 'Listen to me and listen good, lad. I Did Not Fucking Plant It. You was gonna shoot me with it if I tried to get it off yer. Where's the gun now?'

'Why, do you want it?'

'Jesus fuckin Christ.' He throws up his hands. 'Ya fuckin jokin, ain't ya? Tell me you are. I don't want it within a fuckin million miles of me. That bitta kit'll get someone twenty years. You got rid of it somewhere safe?'

'I buried it in a park, in a flower bed.'

'How deep?'

'Three foot.'

'That'll have to do. It'd be too risky going back now.'

I've got a packet of frozen fish fingers wrapped in a tea-towel on my wrist, my nose is full of bloody snot and the side of my face is burning still. 'I'm a bit better, thank you very much for asking,' I say to myself cos these two here don't give a fuck. Morty and Gene are getting chilled out, drinking the Irish.

'So Eddy wants the pills now?' says Gene. 'That's a turn-up, if you're a fan of irony.'

'I probably would be if I knew what it was. Why's it a turn-up though, Gene?'

'Because it's Eddy's fault, this whole fuckin mess. Him getting Jimmy, may the Lord have mercy on his soul, involved with those Chechen fuckers.'

'Who are they? Red Indians?' asks Morty.

'I'll explain later, Mort. Have another drink,' says Gene.

'Eddy reckons he told Jimmy not to get involved with them, said you told Jimmy to give it a wide as well.'

'So Eddy's taking notice of me now, is he? It's highly fuckin debatable that, but my theory, for what it's worth, is that Eddy swerved these swindle merchants into Jim to get them offa his back.'

'And it worked very well.'

'It worked for Eddy but not Jimmy. He went down for the thirteen mill.'

'Jimmy got rumped thirteen million quid!' says Morty. 'Fuckin 'ell.'

'At the time it seemed plausible, very fuckin plausible. They were flying in ex-government officials from Timbuktu and beyond. They would argue about shares, percentages, minute, tiny details all night long, throwing wobblers, crying cos they thought they were getting turned over. Remember this, cos this is important. Jimmy only bought, with thirteen million pounds, a forty-two-per-cent share. They were looking to divvy up about one hundred million pounds. It was worked big.'

'So he was looking at walking away with a forty-two-mill whack. That's temptation. What was the cargo?'

'Heroin that had been seized and parked up by a Pakistani political party when they were in government but who are now in opposition.'

'Going where? To who?'

'Montreal, Canada, and then overland into the United States.'

'But Gene, whose property was it?'

'One of the Italian, New York families who farm it out to pro-democracy, anti-Castro Cubans, who've got a network in place in the southern USA, Miami to Dallas. They in turn punt it into the black communities there.'

'But surely the Eyeties got the finances in place to do this kinda thing every daya the week.'

'They've got very heavy currency laws out there now, anti-racketeering statutes, RICO, so they find it hard to get cash-dollars moving around. The Pakistanis wanted cash so they could send half to Antwerp and Prague to buy weaponry and the other half delivered to Zurich to split among the top boys.'

'Couldn't the Eyeties pay in weapons? Easy to get in the States, firearms. It's the one thing they ain't short of.'

'See what yer did?'

'What'd I do?'

'Yer started asking serious questions about something you already know to be a total fiction, an elaborate fabrication, a bollix. It's already got in yer nut, ain't it? A little whiff of intrigue and big money and you're being led by the nuts.'

'True.'

'You're sitting in a room above an ol' roughhouse boozer in County Kilburn and you was seeing all those places, Miami, the US-Canadian border, Pakistan, Belgium. Admit it, you was already sending postcards.'

'You're not wrong. If you're gonna tell a lie, tell a big one.'

'Exactly, son. Trying to sell Jimmy a non-existent holiday home in Portugal wouldn't have worked, give him the opportunity to be a big-time international player, stroke his ego, he's a fuckin sucker, got wiped out.'

'Was he potless?'

'More or less. That's why he put the thing together in Amsterdam, the bushwhack, with the Banditos. That's why he was after your shillings, knows you ain't a spunker,' says Gene.

'Jimmy put that skank together? Put the Yahoos up to that?'

Morty looks at me, shaking his head. He doesn't know either.

'I thought you'd worked that out already,' says Gene, 'a smart geezer like you. I'd have given you that much credit.'

It's easy spotted in retrospect.

'How?'

'Manna from heaven, Jimmy called it. That gobshite Duke, that priceless prick, came to see him, skint because his drug-addled girlfriend had shot up his house and the police were after him. He wanted help, thought Jimmy might know some likely candidates to turn over. Jimmy thought that it's a bit risky over here, that it might cause problems, so he suggested Holland instead. He gave him some plane-fare, arranged passports and Darren, the Duke, as he liked to be called, took the bait, gobbled it down.'

'What, Jimmy just wound him up and pointed him in the right direction?' I ask.

Gene winks and nods. 'Listen, son,' he says, 'I've seen Jimmy put teams together to rob banks, get a gullible four waifs together, appoint a leader, tell them that he's got it all worked out, he's plotted up and cased the joint, put together a master-plan. The bank's got two doors right? You run in the first one, do the cha-cha with the sawn-off, get the money and run out the other door, okay? You got it? Back in the jam-jar and away and don't forget to bring me back my share. If you're captured, name, rank and serial number only. I know for a fact that he'd only ever driven past the bank in his motor. That was Jimmy all over.'

'And they would? Bring him back the readies?'

'They would run round to give him half. Wouldn't stop to take the balaclava off sometimes.'

'Why?'

'Kudos, reflected glory. Strength of personality, Jimmy had it, can't be denied.'

'I bet he had double-bubble sometimes, copped for the reward money as well.'

'That's a point. I hadn't thought of that till now,' says Gene. Jimmy's died a double-death, physically and reputation-wise. 'You know,' he says, 'there's no such word as "gullible" in the dictionary, it's a made-up word.'

'Really?' I say.

'Course it's in the fuckin dictionary, you stupid cunt, but I got you thinking, doubting your own intuition for a split second, didn't I? And listen, son.' He gives it pointy finger. 'All fuckin words are made-up words.'

'So Jimmy worked the old go-and-rob-a-bank-for-us-son number on Duke, only on a bigger scale.'

'Exactly, but Duke was made of sterner stuff, bittova Don himself, was the Duke. He didn't see why he should split the take with Jimmy after he did all the graft, the shovel work, over in Holland.'

'Fuckin ingrate. But the German firm found him and liquidated him.'

'Who told yer that?'

'Clarkie told me the other day.'

'Why does he think it was the Germans?'

'We was assuming.'

'Good. If everyone's happy to assume that the Germans did the business on those two, great. Let's hope the out-of-town posse thinks the same.'

'You did him, didn't yer, Gene?' says my reckless good self.

The band downstairs are playing 'Everybody Hurts' painfully. Gene stops and lights a fag. He looks at me, then at Mort, like he can't believe what he's heard, but he did give it a bittova drum-roll.

'You've grown balls before my very eyes, son. Seeing as we're all being so very honest and seeing that the hear-say evidence of a pair of reprobates such as yourselves would be thrown straight outta court, I'll tell ya.'

'Not if you don't want to, Gene. I was outta order askin, even.'

Remember, be cautious what you let people tell you.

274

'Oh no, you've asked now –' says Gene a little bit sulky, rolling the Dunhill, '– so I'll tell ya. They turned up at the Paddington car-front, Tuesday, out of the blue, day after you'd told JD those pills weren't worth shit, him and the wife, Slasher, demanding money there and then. She started making threats about the law, he told her to shut the fuck up, started hitting her, knocked her spark out. Metal Mickey showed his first bit of initiative ever and shot the Duke in the head while he was stood over her screaming at her to get up. What you two laughing at? It ain't fuckin funny, two dead people, two bodies.'

'It's the way you tell it, Geno,' says Mort, crashed out on the sofa, getting cosy with the Irish. 'I'm starting to feel right left out here, I ain't never killed nobody in years, I'm starting to feel a bittova wuss.'

'So she had to go as well?' I ask.

'Well, you have to be pragmatic 'bout these things, don't ya. I don't like doing birds so Mickey … you know.'

When Gene the Gentleman was dividing up the pork balls the other night he used his fingers, ''scuse fingers', he said. The same fingers hacked off their heads and hands. Fuck knows where they are now. I don't wanna know.

'I think,' I say, 'we should get those pills, out them to Eddy Ryder, carve the two and a half mill, then shut up shop for good, go our separate ways.'

'Shank them outta their share?' says Mort.

'Call it what you like. I'm saying do unto them as they would do unto us.'

'We could pull together some awesome firepower. Young Mister Clark reckons he might know where they're holed up with the loot,' says Mister Mortimer, sitting up, rubbing his hands, getting excited.

'I don't want no blood-baths, no comebacks, no messy implications. There's more than one way to skin a cat.'

'I not with yer,' says Geno.

'Slowly, slowly catchy monkey.'

'One thing been buggin me,' says Morty. 'Did this Eddy Ryder or one of his outfit have my little cousin Trevor killed?'

'I made a point of askin him that and he categorically denied any involvement, was sorry to hear about it in fact, hoped the two gee hadn't contributed to the poor young man's death.'

'That's all right then, cos ... you know.'

You'd have to do something, so I've saved you a loada grief, maybe getting one in the temple from Mister Troop. It's getting too easy to lie these days. I wanna be outta London early next week. It's grown stale and dangerous for the time being. I wanna be as far away from these two as humanly possible. Nothing personal, but I need blue ocean, seafood and fit birds, not growlers, shooters and grim-boat Londoners.

The music from downstairs stops abruptly halfway through 'The Greatest Love Of All'. It's replaced by screaming and shouting, glass smashing and the rumbling of a crowd stampeding. Gene and Morty don't seem to notice. I walk to the window and from my first-floor vantage point I can see a huge brawl, western style, has begun on the forecourt across the pavement, with the landlord and some bouncers, black bow-ties, one black-leather glove, on one side, and twenty roughneck head-banging tea-caddies on the other. They have a mêlée for a few seconds, then a stand-off, then they charge again and attack each other with glasses, clubs, tools and bits of furniture. It must be empty downstairs now cos everyone's outside.

A TRU patrol unit arrives in record time, sirens wailing, blue lights flashing. The old bill come hurtling out the back and side doors, truncheons out, ready to rumble. It then becomes a complete free-for-all with everybody hitting one another. The police are trying to arrest people but girlfriends jump on their backs and scratch their faces, hysterical, getting a smack in the mouth from other old bill for their trouble. Another wagonload of old bill arrive. There's a young Seamus who's stumbled up the road, pissed and oblivious, swaying, having a piss against the side of the first law wagon. A cozzer, walking past, cracks him cross the head with a truncheon without missing a beat. The geezer falls so his head's holding him up, wedged against the van. He carries on pissing down his trouser leg. The old bill appear, as ever, to be loving it. Ambulances start to arrive like they've been pre-booked in advance, like some sensible souls book a mini-cab for eleven-fifteen. This time next week I wanna be in Mexico or Sri Lanka.

I'm starting to feel like one of those Herberts who join the army to see the world. They get promised the healthy life, skiing, rock-climbing and sailing but they end up in a barracks in Moenchengladbach or Essen, wanking too much and eating mountains of fried food. I didn't sign up to be an official observer to mini-riots in Kilburn on a Saturday night.

I need to be outta town. The official mourning period of James Lionel Price may now be officially over, exactly twenty-four hours after his death, but the police investigation will just be warming up. At Jimmy's funeral, which hopefully will be a long way away cos they won't release the body until they've got someone charged or convicted, Gene and Mort will send large ostentatious wreaths with simply their first initial on the condolence cards, cos Crim. Intel. and RCS have been known to go nosing round in graveyards, but in reality they'll both go on the missing list cos Crim. Intel. and the murder squad will be smudging up the proceedings with a telephoto lens. Eddy'll no doubt send a large one too, 'RIP, my misunderstood pal'.

'You know what yer man here's after becoming, don't yer, Mister Mortimer?' says Gene. I turn round and he's smirking like a fuckin schoolboy.

'What's that, Mister McGuire?' asks Morty.

'A right feckin gangsterman. He has it in him to be a Don,' replies Gene.

'So what's the next move, genius?' Morty says to me.

'Yeah, what's the story, killer?' asks Geno O'Hammerhead, trying to keep a straight face.

They're both giggling, looking at me with their hands out and palms up, waiting for me to say something. They obviously find themselves hilarious, the old double-act. My wrist is killing me, it's swelled up huge. The fish fingers have melted and are now dripping, fishy and salty, onto the carpet. I'll have to keep a beady eye on these two jokers. I click my fingers on my good hand. I've just remembered something needs doing.

'Right, Morty, before I forget, explain to Shanks that the cargo's gone, tell him not to fuck about next time, but get one of his shooters down here. I wanna instigate the final solution on Klaus, the Germans' top kiddie. I don't want him fuckin things up at this stage in the game.'

'We'll have to find him first,' says Morty.

'He rang me up the other day.'

'Fuckin rang ya?!' says Mort. 'You didn't say.'

'I ain't seen ya. Van Tuck had the number. I'm prayin he rings again.'

'I'll get on it in the morning. We've got all sorts of codes and shit worked out.'

'Tell Mister fuckin Shanks I don't want him sendin down some scally muppet, either, who's gonna waste our time or spunk our readies on trainers and smack, go rabbitin all over the gaff.'

'No, no. Shanks and Big Trevor have got some serious but very sensible people on the firm.'

'Someone who can deliver a headshot,' I say.

'Right,' says Mort.

'From a distance. First time. In the canister. JFK style.'

I clock Gene's right eyebrow going ever-so-slightly upwards.

'You know who's the key to this, don't ya, you bright sparks? Billy Bogus. Think about that. I'll see ya tomorrow. I wonder if one of those ambulances'll give me a lift down the casualty department.'

Sunday
Accident and Emergency

If you ever decide to have an accident or an emergency, try not to have it on a Saturday night. I thought I'd box clever and get a cab as far away from Kilburn as possible cos I could see their local hospital being overwhelmed with casualties from this Saturday night medieval battle, but it transpires it's the same wherever you go. I went in the University College Hospital by Euston Station at about eleven-thirty and emerged the next morning at eight. My broken wrist – it *was* broken, thanks a bunch Gene, lucky my nose wasn't cos you'd be in trouble – rated very far down the list of A and E priorities. The whole place was smashed alive with walking wounded, mostly alcohol-related it has to be said, and ambulances were arriving all the time with more severe stretcher cases who were rushed straight in to see the doctors without waiting. Some people seemed to think this was unfair, queue-jumping cos you're dying.

The people who feel themselves to be the most powerless in society make the most fuss in the casualty department cos they know nobody's gonna give 'em a clump. There's geezers in there with glass wounds in the face, guys with great big bandages round their heads from being hit with blunt and heavy objects or simply falling over lagging and landing on the bonce. There's an orderly with a mop and a bucket on wheels cleaning up after them.

Homeless people appear to book in for the night and get their heads down cos they know they ain't gonna be disturbed for about five or six hours, it's nice and warm, ponce snout, a few cups of tea or coffee in the morning, take advantage of the camaraderie of bewilderment. I'm sitting in there tripping out, but it ain't too psychedelic, from lack of sleep, seeing imaginary cats and rats dashing and darting about just outta my field of vision. I'm almost too tired to sleep, too alert mentally, too charged with adrenaline and vodka. I've drank more, taken more drugs in the last two days than I have in the last two years and I'm not used to it. You need to be in training to be doing that shit.

I get back indoors about nine, starving hungry, cos I don't eat properly anymore, only shite. I've got another hangover after Jimmy's Kilburn wake, with a plastercast from the top of my fingers up to my elbow, a plaster on the side of my nose and some ointment for cold-burns smeared up the right side of my face that's glowing red. The nurse asked me how I got such a big cold-burn. I said it was a prank, a childish one at that, don't ask. I couldn't tell her this big mad Donegal lunatic was going to forcibly imprison me in a chest-freezer till I froze to death cos I shot dead, yeah two in the canister, works every time, love, some geezer he thought was his best mate for years but he found out. Now could I?

I could sleep for a week, go to a health farm for a month. I would be within my human rights, but if I'm to get outta town this week I've gotta march on regardless. I ring Cody and arrange to meet him later. I also try to ring Clark but he ain't at home and his mobile's switched off so I leave messages at both places for him to ring me after twelve, midday, important. I get in bed and go to sleep. I think I'm asleep about thirty seconds when the phone by the bed rings. After four rings I can hear Klaus on the answerphone in his perfect English.

'After conferring with our leadership in Holland I have to inform you that unless we receive an undertaking from you that either our goods are returned to us intact or suitable compensation is paid to us, we will be in a state of war. We will have no alternative but to enter into hostilities between our two organisations.'

That's just childish, irritating, playing at war, using big words. You've got all the power of a box of dead matches, Klaus. It might be okay thinking you're a soldier cos you and your pals tortured a jolly-jack-tar boat-trader to death in some kinda fruity sado-masochistic turn-out gone horribly wrong, but it's also my prayers answered.

'Klaus, you just caught me. I was on my way out to church,' I say in my very best English.

'Did you hear my message to you, Sir?'

'I did, but before I say another thing I really need to apologise to you, you and your organisation, about my behaviour last Thursday morning. I have been under a great deal of stress lately and I think it was unfortunate that you just happened to ring at the wrong moment. Again, I'm very sorry.'

'I accept your apology, Sir. It's very gracious of you to accept your responsibility.'

'Klaus, I really am just on my way out. Could you leave me a mobile number? I promise you I will ring you later. I don't wanna know where you're staying or anything. Give me a mobile not a land-line.'

Will he go for it? He starts to give me the number but I have to go and get a pen and paper. I get one.

'Today we change hotels anyway, for ideological reasons. It was pointed out to us, by our leadership, Otto, that the hotel was named after the Jew-loving, notorious war criminal –'

'Whatever, Klaus. I've got a pen. Give me the number again.'

He does and I write it down. And Gene reckons I'm up my own arse. Changing hotels cos you don't like the name?

'Thanks, Klaus. Now, I'll ring you later. I need this thing cleared up as soon as possible. I'm thinking along the lines of pointing you in the direction of the people who stole, and are still holding, your merchandise.'

'That would be very excellent,' says Klaus.

'Then you can take it from there. Till later, then. Again, my apologies.'

'No need, my friend. We all experience stress from time to time.'

How very understanding.

'Later, Klaus.'

I put the phone down and ring Mort's number. He answers it with a groan, real tired.

'That thing we discussed last night, the very last thing? Yeah? You fuckin awake, Mort?'

'Yeah, I'm with ya,' he mumbles.

'Soon as. On the hurry-up. Okay?'

'Okay.'

I put the phone down and go back to sleep. There is a God in heaven after all.

Calling the Shots

'What happened to your face and arm?' says Clarkie.

'Don't fuckin ask,' I reply.

'Okay,' he shrugs. 'Listen to this, brov, this'll crack ya right up, yeah. One of the O'Mara brothers, Johnny, the quiet one, has gone to see that Freddie Hurst geezer's old Doris and told her that Freddie was bang outta order talkin to this geezer who did him like he did. She's sayin like, "Tell me about it, Mister O'Mara. I know what Fred's like." He's told her that the mister who did the business wants to settle outta court and he's talkin about fifteen grand. How's that sound, Mrs H.?'

'About right.'

'No. That's what Johnny says to Mrs Hurst, "How's that sound?"'

'Seriously, is Freddie still in a coma?' I say.

'Best place for him really, brov, cos Mrs H. wants the fifteen large to take the kids to Disneyland and Freddie's not included in the deal. See, Johnny O'Mara thought he'd really have to convince her so he really pulled out all the stops and did the big hard sell. "You could go to Disneyland, Florida, when Freddie gets better." But she's got right on it, it's gone right in the canister, she's ready to pack, get a double-script of Valium and leave straight away, fuck Freddie in the intensive care.'

'I bet he's a right fuckin tyrant to her.'

'Johnny's said, "Listen, I don't know anything about who did this to Freddie," to cover himself, yeah? "But I might be able to get you a few thousand to be gettin on with."'

'But if he dies, all bets are off,' I say.

'But if he lives, he goes in the witness box and says he's never seen Morty in his life, who's that bloke over there? In fact it wouldn't even get anywhere near crown cos if the victim don't wanna know,' he shrugs, 'what can old bill do? Fuck all. If he dies, that's different, they don't need him. Funny, ain't it?'

'Hilarious.'

'So I've gone round there with Johnny O.M. My old man's got the sweet all round. I've met John outside and he's warned me that the gaff's a shithole, stinks, brov, and we've gone upstairs and this Freddie's misses has asked us if we want a cup of tea, brought us through to the front room, the whole family's sat round watching the lottery draw, eating chocolate and crisps, they're all quite lumpy, and you know what?'

'What?' I'm actually genuinely inquisitive for once about one of Clarkie's stories. I usually wanna tell him to switch off when I'm tired.

'What's the date? D-A-T-E,' asks Clarkie but he already knows.

'April the tenth,' I say, looking at my watch.

'Well, they still had their decorations up, from Christmas, maybe they've been up for years. Mrs H. was treating me like I was the geezer from the lottery company come to give her a prize. I felt like a right fuckin celebrity, Jim Davidson or someone. I thought I was gonna get smudged-up for the local paper. Johnny's flirtin with her, for the crack, gettin her goin, "Oi, Mrs H., you're still a handsome young woman, you could play the field," and she's gettin all worked up cos she probably ain't had a portion in stretches. She's all over the gaff, wobbly on pills for her nerves. It's tragic, really, what with him on the life-support machine up the hospital, shouldn't laugh really.'

'You give 'em how much?'

'Five grand. I reckon she's only ever seen five kay cash in the movies.'

'Morty can afford it, won't break Mort, five large.'

'I meant to ask you. What happened to the Rover we went up north in?' he says.

'The one you got so out of it you couldn't drive back? That Rover, you mean?'

Clarkie's embarrassed.

'I took it back,' I say.

'Cos I'll end up payin for that.'

'See Mister Mortimer for an expenses claim-form.'

'I ain't gonna get paid, am I?'

'Take it outta the money we get on this lot. Okay, now listen, this is important. Don't be tellin your old fella what we're up to here, cos certain things we're gonna do are just plain sly, a bit naughty, bit slippery, bit crafty, very tricky. Are you receiving me loud and clear?'

'Like what?'

'Like wait and see, Mister Clark, but your whack's gonna top up to about two hundred and fifty grand. How's that sound?'

'We're gonna shank 'em, ain't we? We are, I can tell by that little grin on your face.'

This geezer's going right to the fuckin top. Rings exactly on the dot of twelve, sun's straight up in the sky, says on the phone he'll be round at five o'clock meaning one o'clock case anyone's listening, there on the doorstep at exactly one o'clock, ready to go to work, ready to go and pick up Cody Garret, AKA Billy Bogus, at one-thirty in Camden to go and have a bitta Sunday lunch up in Highgate. You can look at Clarkie and see breeding counts. They've been villains in his family for generations, second nature to check whether we're being tailed, learnt in the cradle, first words outta their mouths, 'No Comment'. Old Man Clark Senior apprenticed the youngest son Clarkie with the firm of Jimmy Price and Company to get a solid foundation in his trade. If only he knew.

'Johnny was havin a little sniff, askin what the fuck's going on with us lot, you know, first Morty uppin Freddie then Jimmy gettin served. It ain't our usual style. He reckons they used to call us "The Quiet Team" but not any more.'

It could go further the other way yet. When we arrive at the gaff where Cody's staying, I ask Clarkie to stay in the motor while I go upstairs cos I've got six grand for him to be getting on with, maybe he'll wanna plug it up inside rather than dragging it around with him. Six grand can be bulky. Cody lets me in and brings me upstairs.

'I was gonna kill you dead on Thursday night, serious, I was gonna have one put in your nut.'

'I'm sorry about that, what can I say, mate?'

'I've calmed down, luckily. What happened to you?'

'Don't ask. Here, it's some of what I owe ya.'

285

I give him the six. He throws it nonchalantly onto the sofa.

'The geezers who nicked us were playin the old impersonating-a-police-officer swindle, but they had accreditation from someone real in Scotland Yard, the Brighton old bill checked them out.'

'How do you know they weren't real gathers?'

'I could tell, takes one to know one, and they half admitted it at the end. If they were for real they would've nicked us. You ever heard old bill refusing a collar after they've got a body in the cells, not botherin to check if there's any outstandin warrants?'

'No.'

'They were very good, looked the part, looked like they got all their clobber outta mail-order catalogues. You never told me it was Eddy the Swell's kid we was lookin for.'

'I didn't know meself.'

He gives me a dubious look and the pointy finger. 'Fuckin hope you ain't lying to me, pal.'

'It's actually turned in our favour cos Eddy wants to buy the shipment of pills.'

'Did he have Jimmy shot, do you think?'

'Possibly, but I think it's quite a long list of candidates. I'm doin this bitta business then I'm takin a leaf outta your book and gettin outta town for a while.'

'I think you owe me big-time for the inconvenience,' says Cody.

'If you say so. I can do it like that or I can put you into somethin that'll set you up for a long fuckin time. You'd have a big enough chunk to start makin legit investments, money goes to money.'

'How much we talkin?'

'Between three hundred and fifty thou and four hundred thou. We'll have some ex's and we might need to bring in some specialists. That's your department.'

'It ain't no hare-brained kamikaze mission, is it? Cos if it is I don't wanna know,' Cody says.

No point worrying him, telling him about the Duke and Duchess Slasher.

'Let's go and have some lunch and talk about it.'

'It's on you, right?' says Cody.

'You didn't bring me back no Brighton rock, very thoughtless that, Cody.'

'Don't take the piss. You ain't forgiven yet.'

In the restaurant I explain to Cody the coup. Clarkie and Terry went to Edmonton on Thursday with two sets of binoculars, plotted up, and tried to see if anything was going on at the lock-up, but it was all quiet on that front. Cos they had fuck-all better to do and Clarkie's desperate to succeed, he left Terry keeping dog while he drove round and round in circles looking for big lemon motors with big muscle-bound bouncer-types inside. This is, according to Clarkie and his driving-school lessons from ex-old bill, exactly what the gathers from one of those top squads would do if they wanted to find a little team working in a certain area. After an hour, very tenacious boy, Clarkie, and a few false alarms tailing yard-dogs and almost getting plunged at traffic lights by over-paranoid twitchy local dealers, he's come across a Merc G-Wagon jeep, white and gold, looking completely out of place in a side-turning offa Tottenham High Street a couple of miles from the Edmonton lock-up. He's got outta the motor and had a little recce, a stroll past, and in the back there's four boxes that look like the boxes refrigerators arrive in. Clarkie knows about numberplates as well, it's a hobby, can tell yer where in the country the motor's registered, like traffic plod, but on this occasion he didn't need to cos the dealer's name was on the plate as well. It fitted the profile. Across the street was a Merc sports rag-top, definitely not a North Tottenham motor, same thing, same dealer from outta town. Good front business, car dealership.

A traffic warden comes past and tells Clarkie that if he don't move his motor, meaning the jeep, in five minutes he's gonna ticket it. Clarkie tells him he's just going to get his hair cut, 'ain't havin it washed, mate, just cut, don't need washin, washed it this morning', and please give him a squeeze but the keen young African warden ain't havin it. Mister Clark goes round the corner to make further enquiries and comes across a café, full, with steamed-up windows. He opens the door slightly, whistles with his thumb and first finger, shouts 'Merc jeep gettin a ticket, anyone?' and who comes running out past Mister Clark but gormless, lovesick Sidney, according to Clarkie's very accurate description, with a 'Cheers, mate,' over his shoulder. Another guy comes out of the café but he's strolling, no sweat, no panic, and gets into the Merc sports while Sidney gets in the jeep, starts it up and pulls out into the High Street.

Clarkie jogs back to his motor and follows the jeep. It goes round the block and pulls up outside the café again as four guys are emerging from it. They've stayed to finish their nosebag while Sidney plays the martyr. One goes off and gets in the Merc and the other three get in the jeep with Siders. Six-handed, now, and it don't take six big lumps like these to move four fridges. Now Clarkie knows he's got a result if he keeps his cool. A white and gold Merc G wagon is nice and easy to follow, you can see it from about six or seven cars back. The jeep starts heading south, into town, while the Merc disappears in the other direction. Clarkie's surprised cos he was absolutely certain they would head back outta town as well, hitting the motorway as soon as possible, but instead they head further in towards the centre of town. They hit a big main road so Clarkie don't stick out cos everyone's moving into town. If you see someone at three or four sets of traffic lights in a row it ain't really suspicious. They come to Finsbury Park and turn off the main drag and into smaller tighter roads and Clarkie uses all his driving skill and expertise to keep outta range, poking the front of the motor round the corner just as the jeep turns the next one.

Eventually they drive into a small entrance beside a railway bridge. Above the entrance there's signs advertising bodywork, spraying, general car repairs, MOTs, wheel-balancing and engine-tuning. Between the arch doors and the garden fences backing on there's lots of cars in various states of repair. Terry rings up to say that a Merc sports has pulled up outside the lock-up in Edmonton, two geezers have gone inside and come out again with a big weighty sports hold-all, 'reckon it's tools or dumb-bells, brov', stuck the bag in the boot, that's visibly dipped, looked all over the gaff and fucked off. They didn't see him cos he's plotted up three football pitches away but he can see them through his brand-new binoculars.

Meanwhile, back in Finsbury Park, Sid and his three pals are out the Merc jeep and unloading the boxes into a railway arch. Clarkie gets Terry to come down from Edmonton, sit in the motor and keep the arches ready-eyed while he goes to get some grub and make some calls. I'm across town in the City of London, either in a box or in a deep excavation having my card marked by the geezer Cody calls 'Eddy the Swell', so I'm unavailable for comment. Between them they keep the place under observation day and night. The first night, Thursday, a kid on a pizza delivery bike brings a lorryload of grub. Last night, Saturday, he brings two pizzas, two Diet Cokes and cheesecake. Clarkie's got him sweet, so the early vigilante has waned. This lot's eating habits give them away every time. If they hadn't have stopped for the mid-afternoon fry-up they would have been clean away from Edmonton and we'd be pissing in the wind trying to find them.

After lunch we drive over to Finsbury Park to have a recce. Terry, who it seems I ain't seen for ages, is sitting in another hired motor about twenty-five yards from the entrance reading the paper and listening to the football on the radio. We jump in.

'Listen, Terry, the joint chiefs of staff have decided that we ain't payin for those pills. They robbed 'em so we're gonna rob 'em off them. How's that sound?'

'I'm up for it. You know we could go over there right now and take those cunts apart. There's three of them in there.'

'That'll lead to a shitload of complications, Tel. Their heavy mob'll come after us. We've gotta be a lot cuter. Cody, do you think it can be done?'

'Two things worry me: are they tooled up in there? If they are, will they use 'em? That bitta road in front of those arches is only a glorified alley. Where's their out, their escape?'

'That's three things, Cody. Can it be done?' I ask.

'Sure it can be done,' he says, 'but I ain't fuckin goin in first.'

We leave Terry keeping an eye on things in Finsbury Park, under protest, and drop Cody back in Camden. He reckons he needs to get himself a shopping list, get out and about, buy and hire, all the bits and pieces he needs for the work. He also needs to find some guys he's worked with in the past and put them in the swindle, on wages, very good ones.

'Morty says he's over by the swans havin a cup of coffee. He says you'll know where he means.'

'Knightsbridge, by the Serpentine, let's go.'

There's a cafeteria on the edge of the Serpentine in Hyde Park, a spit from Harrods and all the creamy shops on Sloane Street. Me and Morty like to have a serious shop-up in the locale and then go and get a proper cup of coffee in the café that's been built from moulded concrete so the veranda hangs over the boating lake. The swans that Mort was talking about were the governors who ruled the roost in that little part of the world. A swan up-close is a large, frightening, volatile bird, especially if they've got a few kids in tow. Next down the pecking order come the geese, then the ducks, then the mundane grey pigeons and last the tricky little sparrows. Some days it was peaceful to sit, drink coffee and fizzy water, gaze out across the water and do nish while the rest of the world grafted, observing the urban wildlife.

By the time we get to the café by the water it's three-thirty and Morty has been plotted up, shades on, for over an hour, but he seems chilled enough, sat outside with a couple of Gucci bags, watching people come and go. The punters are mainly tourists in this part of town, rich ones, well dressed and assured.

'This guy, this German, he's gotta go?' asks Morty.

'I think so.'

'Why?'

'He could fuck things up. Remember what Shanks said.'

'What did Shanks say? I switch off a bit with Shanks to be honest.'

'About these guys wanting one of us dead.'

'Yeah, yeah. I remember now,' says Mort, more interested in the rich tourists.

'So you ain't made the call yet,' I ask.

'If you say he's gonna go, he's gonna go. You seem to know what you're doin lately.' Morty fishes his mobile outta one coat pocket and a piece of paper outta the other, rings the number. 'Good afternoon. How are ya, young man?'

I know from experience that this call will go on for about twenty minutes. What needs to be said could be said in about twenty seconds but anyone listening, either now or at a court trial, wouldn't, hopefully, get the gist. If the Other People played the tape in court, saying that this twenty-minute pow-wow about football was actually two parties negotiating the terms and conditions, whistling up a contract killer, the jury would think old bill's whacked out, been getting too high on all the seizures. Morty could talk in gobble-dee-gook and codes the rest of his life. I get lost before kick-off.

One time I was having this scene with this bird and I rung her one afternoon to ask her if it's all right to pop over.

'It's okay but I've got the painters in,' she says.

'Well, that's okay, they go home at what? Four or five? They gotta take their boots off sometime,' I say.

'No. Arsenal are at home,' she says.

'What the fuck have Arsenal got to do with anything?'

'You can come over, but I'm flying the red flag.'

'Are you all right love?' I ask, concerned.

'Yeah, but I'm on my period.'

'Oh right. Why didn't you say?'

So I leave it to Morty.

'We need someone who can hit a ball from outside the penalty area, Shanks ... need to pay top wage to get anyone half decent ... can't entertain messers, they can get ya relegated ... need to stop the rot, sharpish.'

Mort's been on the phone fifteen minutes, concentrating on every word. Suddenly he snaps the phone shut, gets up and starts walking out the café. He gives a nod and a wink to Clarkie to get the Gucci bags and follow. We fall in behind. We let Morty walk on ahead for a bit. A swan has lost its bearings and is walking, slowly and awkwardly, not so agile outta water, are ya son, across the path in front of us as we come level with Morty.

'Tomorrow, Shanks says tomorrow. Work out what time the first train outta Liverpool arrives in Euston and your man'll be on it,' he says.

'Right,' I shrug.

'Shanks didn't wanna go and see the geezer cos there's football on the telly, lazy cunt. Says you'll recognise the geezer, you've met him.'

'I can't think who that'll be.'

'Maybe wait till tomorrow and you'll know. Slowly, slowly catchy monkey.'

Clarkie curls a snout between his thumb and trigger finger and then lets fly, flicking it hard. Miraculously it hits the swan on the side of the head. The swan twitches and hisses like he can't believe it more than anything, ain't used to this disrespect, this hostility. Clarkie's got his arms out, looking for a bitta praise, like he's scored a goal or something. 'See that, chaps, a direct fuckin hit.'

'I bet you can't do it again,' says Morty. 'Fifty quid says you can't do it again.'

Monday
Bing Bong

Bing bong: Announcing the arrival of a mercenary, paid assassin on the scheduled InterCity service departing Liverpool Lime Street at five forty-five, arriving at London Euston at eight-thirty.

Bing bong: Announcing that this one's a freebie, on the house, cos Big Trevor was a rotter to you on Tuesday night, dropping you at a petrol station in the middle of nowhere, and this neo-fascist crowd were responsible for nausing up their puff deal.

Bing bong: Announcing that the shooter will have a ski-bag with his tools in, looking like he's off to catch the last of the snows on the pistes. He usually needs more time and information but it can be done and apparently I've met this geezer before.

Off the train at eight-thirty, with all the early-bird-gets-the-worm businessmen, comes Trevor's mute chauffeur, dressed like he's on his way to Austria or Switzerland, with a big, long bag, five-foot long, bobble hat and black puffa jacket.

'You better lose the hat, brov, you look like fuckin Noddy,' I say as I shake his hand.

He nods, removes the hat and we walk down to the hired motor I've got in the underground car-park. The ski-bag won't fit in the boot, will only go in across the back seat. I drive outta Euston Station and head north towards Primrose Hill.

'Far?' asks Chatterbox Scouser.

'No, not at all. I'm gonna show you the place I thought was good now. You can have a wander about, pick yer spot. We can disappear for a few hours, I'll get the target up there for about one o'clock and you can be back on the rattler back to Liverpool at about half-past. How's that sound?'

He nods and gets a personal stereo outta the pocket of the

293

puffa jacket, very fuckin sociable, but I suppose it's preferable to stand-up comedy, the usual scousers routine, at nine in the morning. He puts the earphones in and pushes the play button. He's looking out at the London streets like someone's waving a lolly-stick with shit on it under his nose. Probably listening to one of those thumbs-up, you-gotta-laugh-ain't-ya, scally bands who think they're the Beatles.

'Bon jour, savva?' he says.

'What's that, brov?' I say, startled.

'Madams, miss-yours, mays on fong.'

I turn and he's listening intently.

'Char mar pell Jean-Paul, ja swee Angliese.'

He's fuckin only learning French on the old speak-and-repeat tapes.

'Char mar pell Jean-Paul, char swee Angliese,' he says again with the beck, scouse accent, tearing the arse outta all the Cs. I tap him on the arm and point at his ears.

'French,' I say, nodding.

He nods, distracted, humouring me. I tap him on the arm again.

'Learnin French,' I say, making my mouth big so he can lip-read. 'Very good, tray be ann.'

He nods and looks out the window but I tap his arm again.

'Europeans,' I say, pointing at him and me, backwards and forwards.

He rolls his eyes.

'It must be great,' I say, 'to be able to say fuck all in two languages, you mute cunt.'

He nods.

I park up round the back, away from the main road, where it's nice and quiet. Primrose Hill is a park, about the size of about twenty-five football pitches, that rises up into one peak with a splendid, panoramic view across London, rain or shine. Someone standing at the viewing platform, or sitting on one of the benches conveniently placed on the pinnacle, would be at best silhouetted against the sky and at worst wide open, free from any protection. They'd make an ideal target for someone with a telescopic sight and hunting rifle. The shot could come from any vantage point surrounding the peak. Me and the shooter go for a little walk around. He's nodding seriously the whole time. He asks which direction the target will be coming from but I don't know for sure. From the main road, I think. He nods.

'You got a picture of the target?'

'No I haven't, but I'll know this guy. I've got binoculars in the motor. I'll give you a signal, we'll be three hundred yards away. Listen, this guy is responsible for Trevor los –'

He's shaking his head, turning away, waving his hands like Al Jolson, he don't wanna know what the target's done or hasn't done.

'Does it make a difference shootin up-hill?'

He shakes his head, rolls his eyes, like it was a rank amateur's question. He produces a telescopic sight from outta the puffa and starts eyeing-up, walking at the same time, staying close to the brick and wooden perimeter fence, looking over his shoulder to check the windows that look out onto the park.

'Here,' he says at last, pointing at the floor. He turns, starts walking briskly back to the motor so he's waiting when I get there. We get in and I go to start up.

'Maybe leave the motor here. Will we get this space again? This is good for the out but you desperately don't wanna be gettin any tickets. When we move from here to the spot I said, okay, the rifle goes in two, so you'll have half and I'll have half. It only takes a second to put it together, get gloved up then sling 'em. Okay? Good. Now you gotta get your man here. That's the hard bit. I would like to be on the five-past two back or failing that the five-past three. After we do the business, walk back here. Remember that, walk, don't fuckin run, whatever you do. For about five minutes after, nobody's gonna have a scooby-doo what's goin on, it'll be pure confusion, so stay relaxed and don't bring any attention on yourself or me. You drop me at Baker Street station and I'll take care of myself from there, okay?'

I understand now. This geezer only talks business. He puts his earphones back in and presses play. I get out the motor and ring Klaus's number.

'Hello, this is Klaus.'

'Good morning, Klaus, it's me. I must say I'm extremely sorry that I didn't ring you yesterday as I promised but I was detained. I've been busy and I've got some maps, photographs, names, other bits of information on the party you're after. How does that sound?'

'Very good indeed. I'll come to you now?' he asks.

'I was gonna say I'll meet you later at Primrose Hill, any cab driver'll know it, at the top.'

'Is it a hill?'

'It's a park. It's ideal cos we'll be up there all alone, there's nowhere for anyone to hide. We'll be able to see each other comin. Go to the top and I'll see you there.'

'At what time?'

'Twelve-thirty?'

Plenty of time for him to catch his train.

'That is good,' says Klaus.

'I'll have an envelope in my hand. I wanna restore our reputation. Who knows, Klaus, there may be some business to be done in the future.'

At exactly twenty-five past twelve the shooter gives me a nod and we get out the motor. This geezer's as fuckin cold as ice, no nerves at all. He opens up his bag, reaches and emerges with my half of the rifle. I put it under my raincoat. He tucks the other half under his puffa. We stroll into the park, along the fence, about three hundred yards from the top of the hill, till we reach the bushes and small trees that he's selected to be the best vantage point. I hand him the half of the rifle I was carrying, unbutton my coat and get the binoculars outta the case hanging round my neck. He slots the rifle together and again I'm impressed with the way the metal clips together as the result of loving craftsmanship. There's not a soul on our side of the park but in the distance I can see people walking their dogs. A group of four people are descending from the top of the hill and with my binoculars I can see a very large blond-haired guy in a similar trench-coat to mine hiking purposely up the hill with big strides. Sturmbannführer Klaus is right on time, punctuality being a Germanic virtue.

The shooter is standing with his hands behind his back, Prince Charles style, holding the assembled weapon behind him, outta sight. Through the glasses I can see Klaus arrive at the top and put his hand across his eyebrows to shade the sun while he looks down onto London. How do I know that's Klaus? Who else is it gonna be?

'Listen, that's our boy on the hill there,' I tell the shooter.

'You sure?'

'I'll tell yer what, for your satisfaction I'll ring him.' I get my phone out. 'Be ready, cos as soon as he answers he's gonski, okay?'

'Whatever you say. You're the client.'

He looks about, left and right, to double-check there's nobody about, then raises up a very serious-looking hunting rifle, complete with silencer.

I push the button to dial the last number, Klaus's, looking through the binoculars at the same time. It starts to ring. Klaus reaches into the pocket of his raincoat and comes out with his phone.

'Do it,' I say.

Dooff. Klaus drops like someone's cut the puppet's strings, into a cross-legged position with his head down.

'Hello.' Someone answers the phone. 'This is Klaus. Shysen! Mein Gott!'

Fuck! Panicking, I look up and down, back to the dead body. It's a fuckin disposable four-ninety-nine camera on the ground beside him. I'm confused, gone burning red instantly. Halfway up the hill, fifty yards from the top, I spot a short, dark, dumpy guy, stood still, paralysed like a statue, with a fuckin mobile phone welded to his ear. Not very master-race. He looks like a kid in a grown-up's suit. Suddenly the figure turns and starts to run back down the hill. I can hear quick, heavy footsteps and breathing at my end cos the connection's still live. Klaus drops his phone. I can hear it crackling and sliding across the gravel path. He stops, grappling to pick it up.

'Shoot that geezer runnin. Quick! That's the fuckin geezer,' I'm screaming at the shooter.

'Listen, pal,' he says, calm as fuck, already dismantling his rifle, 'life ain't a fuckin fun-fair. Trevor's only paying for one. Comprendi?'

'Please.'

'No. I don't do massacres. And I thought you Cockneys were cool.'

Take It Like a Man

'Come in here and sit down right there. Now, maybe you just think I'm some tick, shit-shovelling Paddy, some shit-kicker fresh from off the bog, just got off the fuckin steam-ferry at Holyhead, but let me tell you something, you gormless little cunt, I've spent the last three hours sorting out the abortion of a bollix that you caused this morning. I've had to send sensible blokes out, on top fuckin money, that you're fuckin payin, every fuckin penny, by the way, to try and find this Klaus character and his fuckin crowd and they'll do the fuckin job properly, no mess. That man you had shot today was an American national, a systems analyst from Portland, Oregon, first time in London, had a wife and four kids. He was a fuckin decent, hard-working man and because you wanna start fuckin playing the gangster, calling on button-men, been watchin too many fuckin pictures, a man is now dead. If you wanna play the gangster, go play somewhere else, because if you do it round me I'll fuckin cripple yer. Shooting people in public parks is not fuckin on, with kids and all sorts wandering about. Maybe I should've had more fuckin sense, you shoulda had more fuckin sense, what the fuck was you thinkin of? Who do you think you are? I'll tell yer who yer ain't. You ain't Michael-fuckin-Corleone. You think that's funny, do you? So why you got that insipid grin on your face? Don't fuckin smile at me, son. Nervous, yer say? I'll give yer fuckin something to be fuckin nervous about, yer little prick. Do you know what happens when an American gets shot in the fuckin head with a sniper's rifle overseas? They send over the CIA, FBI, DEA. It becomes a diplomatic incident and that's before you start to worry about what Scotland Yard are gonna do. We're talking Anti-Terrorist Squad, MI6, Crim. Intel., SO11, Home Office, Foreign Office, that's even before they put together a shit-hot murder squad. It's one thing shooting a nut-case Nazi who's probably known to Interpol, is up to all sorts of drugs skulduggery and has, no doubt, made enemies all over the fuckin place. If you'd shot the proper bloke today the old bill would probably wanna give you a medal. They'd be looking for other neo-Nazis because those fuckers are always falling out but, no, you gotta have Mister American shot fuckin dead. Have you seen CNN? They doing *This Is Your Life* on the guy. They're ready to go to war with half a dozen countries, got the armed forces ready to go and bomber planes in the sky. Say what you like about Yanks but if one of their own guys gets fucked over, they don't fuckin stop till someone's crying. Every little sneaky little grass in London's gonna have his arse set on fire by old bill. You wanna pray that the guys I sent out there this evening find these Germans and take care of them properly, dissolve the bodies, because if they find this Klaus before we do and he puts your name up, you're fucked, you're doing life plus twenty, hard time, behind the door. They'll wanna put you on trial in America as well, on fuckin TV, so you better get down on your fuckin knees and pray, yer fuckin cunt. Does it bother you me talking to you like this? You got a fuckin problem with it? Maybe you think I'm just a fuckin gundog too, a shit-for-brains Mick. Maybe you think you can go dig up yer metal and you're gonna come round, sneak up on me, and put one in my fuckin nut like ya did Jimmy fuckin Price. Well, you better not miss, yer cunt, cos I'll take that fuckin gun and stick it up your arse sideways. Do you think I'm a cunt? Do ya? Think I'm a cunt? No? Yes? No. Well I'm fuckin glad you said that cos you sometimes look at people like you do, like yer think we're here for your own fuckin personal amusement. You're on probation with me, okay? I said, okay? You fuck this thing up tomorrow and I promise you I won't kill ya, you'll wish I had, I swear on my mother's grave I'll cripple yer, I'll break your arms, then your legs, then your fuckin spine. I'll put yer in a fuckin wheelchair. I swear they'll have to feed yous with a spoon. You start a war with these fuckin geezers with the pills and I'll bury yer alive. I swear I'll dig a hole and bury yer. Tonight I've got a guy from Stockwell bringing up some Smith and Wesson revolvers, same as what the law use, and some vests, stab-jackets. You send Clarkie over early in the morning to get them, he's still got a fuckin brain. You reckon your pal's gettin the caps and the radios? Tell him he better not fuck up either. And Morty, I'm holdin five uncut kilos that are paid for. Take it over to Sonny King tonight and he's gonna sort ya out sixty grand in cash while ya wait. I know it's too cheap but we need the cash for expenses. By the time he's slapped it around he'll have eight fuckin kilos outta that. Now you, listen to me, I'll be round tomorrow, in Finsbury Park, with Mickey and a couple of other lads, just in case it does go crooked, but if you've got anything to say to me, tell Mister Mortimer here, and he can tell me, cos I don't wanna talk to yer, in fact I don't even wanna look at yer. Now get outta my fuckin sight. Morty, get this fuck away from me before I change my mind. Did you hear me? I said fuck off, now! Get outta here. Get!'

Tuesday
This Is a Raid

Gene gets into the back of my rented motor. I'm half expecting a clip round the ear. I don't really wanna look at him. I can feel his presence, smell today's snout and last night's whiskey. I'm at one end of the short street and Morty's at the other, keeping an eye out for old bill. We've got phones, short-wave radios and a couple of scanners tuned to the local police frequency. We've driven past and seen the Merc G wagon and Merc sports soft-top parked up in front of the archway.

'Right, son,' he says, all top-of-the-morning, giving me a playful slap on the thigh. 'What happened to your hand, son?'

'Don't ask, Gene,' I say without turning to look at him.

I think I work with a loada fuckin schizophrenics. I've taken to carrying my false passport and money at all times.

'Gimme your phone a second, son. Oh look, you've got quite a collection, quite the command post, ain't ya?'

I hand him over one of the mobiles I've got in the back seat with me. He gets a piece of paper outta his pocket. 'I'm useless with these. Get this number, will you?'

It's JD's number. I feed it in, press the send and hand the phone to Gene.

'Good morning, Sir,' he says to JD. 'The boys have been busy on your behalf. We'll have a meet later today. I think it's fair what they've come up with ... Not over the air. I'll ring you later.'

It was decided that Gene shouldn't lure the sentry party away, too obvious, but should tickle-up the theory that we have buyers on their behalf. It would be relatively simple to go blasting into the arch, take the cargo, but that would have massive implications, maybe start a war. They've got to think they've got a squeeze. If there's an almighty steward's inquiry it's been a complete failure.

The boys have been busy on their behalf getting everything we need. Terry and Clarkie have been up here day and night, watching the comings and goings. Cody's been up here taking photos with a long lens when he ain't been running all over London recruiting, putting people to work acquiring, sometimes making or printing the necessary props. Cody's had some excellent reproduction police baseball caps made, with the chequered sides that the heavy-mob use on raids. The badges on the front are photocopies of the crest of the South East Regional Crime Squad, embossed then laminated. If you studied it under a lamp it wouldn't pass serious inspection but in the confusion we hope to produce it will, hopefully, work, especially when teamed up with Gene's pal's Smith and Wesson revolvers, stab-jackets that look much like the Met's, yellow hi-visibility vests with POLICE surgically cut from stencilled blue and white plastic and then very carefully stuck on along with thin strips of reflective plastic running lengthways. Cody has obviously been watching *The Colditz Story* on telly, the bit where the English public-school boys make a very convincing Field Marshal's uniform outta Red Cross parcels. He's hired radios, hand-helds, lapel and ear-piece microphones.

On Sunday night he sent a geezer over the wall into the car-pound of a police station in deepest South London. The creeper was in the yard for three hours, in the early hours, opening the boots and doors of all the vehicles, seeing what he could find. He was disappointed with the haul, a bin-liner of odds and sods, POLICELINE tape, a truncheon, police-issue gloves, clipboards, but to Cody it was worth the five hundred he paid him. The two-quid-per-hundred-metres police tape was the real prize, well worth a monkey on its own.

Terry has made his way through back gardens into a decrepit garden shed about twenty feet from the doors so he can hear laughing and joking from inside. From his forward observation post he could ring back whispered intelligence but we couldn't ring him for an update. Cody told him to hold the phone as far up and in their direction as was possible. Sometimes he rings another phone, we let it ring and decipher the signal. Three rings means movement in the G wagon, two rings in the Merc sports.

Terry rang earlier to say that there was six, repeat six, geezers inside. Three had spent the night and three had arrived early. When Cody's firm went in they would have mobiles with them, tucked in a pocket in the front of the stab-jackets with a line open going back to me so if things got outta hand we'd know and then it becomes a straightforward skank. If we heard anything over the scanners, we could tell them over the radios. There's a danger that they could cause so much commotion that some get-a-life neighbourhood-watch nuisance calls the real old bill, they come down here in cavalry-charge mode and the swindle's blown. I keep a listening ear on that scanner. Gene goes to get out the motor.

'I'm gonna go in with the first wave but I'll be staying in the van, unless … ' He winks and pats his chest where an awesome weapon's secreted. He shuts the door, walks away, takes two steps, returns like he's forgotten something, opens the back door again and leans in. 'Oh yes, that business. It's sorted, lads found 'em in a mucky sauna in Swiss Cottage. Lifted 'em outside.'

'And I gotta pay? That's okay,' I shrug.

'I'll treat yer. We'll take it outta our winnings.'

He shuts the door and tiptoes off up the street. One of the phones rings so I pick it up. It's Terry holding the phone up. I can hear laughing and joshing, about who's going to brekkie first, complaints, play-fights, insults and pretend threats. They're in good spirits after Geno's call. Morale's just taken a massive surge upward. One of the other mobiles rings three times then stops.

'Movement in the big Merc. Get ready,' I say over the radio.

Terry's whispering over the sound of an engine. 'Three are going. JD, Sidney and Gary are staying.'

This is an early away-goal for us cos the three getting in the Merc, Big Frankie, Paul the Bouncer and Sammy Fisher, are the hard-core, trigger-happy loons. They've pulled rank, are trotting off for their feed. JD's the only serious heavyweight contender in there. Gary will show a clean pair of heels if shown a chink of light but Sidney ain't gonna shoot fuckin nobody. But he may be reluctant to make one, do a runner, might need a shove. Half lying, half sitting, one eye shut, using one side of the binoculars, I see the Merc G wagon emerge from the entrance and turn off in Morty's direction. One of my mobiles rings. It's Mort.

'Three on board. Frankie, Sammy and Paulie, a result.'

'Billy's gonna give it five minutes then hit it.'

Now I'm back to sweaty palms, shortness of breath, hearing my own heartbeat, looking at my watch every five seconds, wondering if Billy's decided to turn it in, decided not to bother, maybe having a Darjeeling and almond croissant himself, when round the corner at Morty's end comes a white box van, the Trojan horse, as Cody would have it. Driving is one of Gene's head-the-balls. He puts full-lock on the steering wheel, into the entrance. A mechanic from one of the garages, outside having a smoke, tries to stop him driving up the tight, pot-holed track but he totally ignores him, almost runs him over instead. The gears grind and burn, the gearbox cries for help, the van shakes backwards and forwards, catching the kerb, scraping the brick wall on one side of the entrance. All the geezers in the back push the call button on their mobiles at the same time. They all ring together. I hit the green receive buttons. I can hear the screaming engine through all six phones laid out neatly in a straight line on the back seat.

I hear the roller-shutter of the back door go up and geezers dropping to the tarmac, war cries going up, like Red Indians, howling and savage, a door going in, shouts of 'Armed police!', curses, a fight. If anyone was going to be shot, it would be now. Combatants are grappling, one phone's dropped to the floor. Cody's told his team to get the three outside as soon as possible so they can leg it. Ordinarily old bill would be trying desperately hard to incapacitate their prisoners, dominate them, but our crowd are trying to aid and abet their escape, without it being obvious. I can hear a bit of metal hitting the brickwork, JD's voice cursing. A scattering of mechanics and paint-sprayers come running onto the street to get away from the mêlée. I can hear Terry's voice shouting my name on one of my phones.

'Terry?'

'Yeah, brov. Listen, that Gary went straight through the slips, over the fence like a gazelle.'

'What about the other two?'

'They're getting near the street. We may have a result, brov, it's a stand-off.'

I can hear shouting, JD's voice above the rest, about burying it in yer head, ya cozzer cunts.

'Go on, me son, run. They ain't gonna shoot ya,' Terry's shouting over the phone. 'Let me get a better view. Yessss, they're on their way, you fuckin beauties, JD's out-flanked them, they'll be with you in five, four, three, two, one, zero. You got 'em?'

On zero, JD and Sidney come hurtling out the entrance into the street, running faster than two big guys should. JD drops a steel bar onto the road. A car has to break hard, with a skid, to avoid hitting JD but he's oblivious to it. He swerves past it, curses and runs full pelt in my direction, while Sidney, who looks absolutely terrified, takes a tumble, gets quickly up and dashes off the other way, completely panicked. I duck down. I hear JD go darting past. I count one-two-three and put my head up again slowly but he's already rounded the corner. That's the hard part. Now comes the clever part.

The Clever Part

Outside the arch the 'old bill' are having a screaming match, the major stewards with one another, accusing each other of bottling it again. There's a lot of the old hold-me-back I'll-swing-for-the-fuckin-cunt business. Some conversations are meant to be overheard. All the mechanics and sprayers are outside ear-wigging and watching old bill fighting amongst themselves.

'Get on to the local nick, get a description over the air. Neither of them fitted the description of the chap we're after anyway.'

What we're praying for now is one of two things, that one of these mechanics in the neighbouring arches is a pal of the Yahoos and will slip away, ring Big Frankie or one of the others and mark their card that the slaughter, the hideaway, is crawling with filth, worst kind, CID, heavy mob, it's on top, I'll-see-ya-when-I-see-ya. The other is that JD, Gary or Sidney will find a phone-box and tip the others the wink. The crime-scene tape will be going up now. Cody's little team will be all over the Merc sports with latex gloves, smudging it up. They'll have their radios turned up so the scanner will be getting re-broadcast, Alpha, Bravo, Charlie, Delta, old-bill radio traffic going out on the airwaves again, lending a nice air of authenticity. Sitting on my back seat I can hear conversations. Tiptoes rings me on yet another phone.

'It's bolted up here, mate. It was scary for a minute, thought they were going to put their hands up, but the big fella freaked right out.'

'Any shooters in there?' I ask.

'A bored-out Mach-10, serious tool. It's in an evidence bag.'

'Did he go for it?'

'Luckily they were caught off-guard. It got slapstick in there, bittova chase round the boxes. We've got a mobile as well. What shall I do if it rings?'

'Turn it off. Are those grease-monkeys being nosy?'

'Yeah. Really nosy. Moodying they ain't.'

'Good.'

I can see a few wandering out onto the street, taking an early day. Half this lot'll be signing so they don't really need the old bill asking loads of questions, taking names. That's what Cody's posse are doing right now, clipboards out, asking questions of all the geezers in the surrounding arches, meeting resistance. They need to stay in place just in case the other three do turn up, and that takes bottle.

'Do you know the occupants of this arch, the end one?'

'Do you know who owns this Mercedes sports? Is it here for repair, for spraying, perhaps, Sir?'

'Have you seen the occupants come and go?'

'Did you know the three who absconded earlier? When we catch them I hope they don't say they know you, Sir, because that would be most unfortunate, wouldn't it?'

'Am I Drugs Squad? That's very interesting. Who said anything about drugs? I certainly didn't. I'm actually from the South East Regional Crime Squad on detachment, looking to serve an extradition warrant.'

'Do you know a character by the name of Darren Anthony, AKA Duke, AKA the Duke, been naughty over in Holland, he has, been naughty over here as well but they've got first go at him. Bollocks, ain't it, that's the EC for ya.'

'Take my card, ring me if they come back, Sir. You'd only throw it in the bin, well, well, well. That's not very polite, didn't your mother teach you any manners?'

'You don't need a lawyer, you ain't under arrest, been watching too much telly. I'm conducting an inquiry and you're helping me.'

'You can have a kick up the arse, you want one, you 'orrible cunt? I've nicked criminal household names so don't be givin it the big'un, yer greasy little arse-wipe. Okay? Go on, fuck off, get back to yer carburettors, yer greasy cunt. You wanna have it? Don't worry about me being old bill, son. I'll come back later if yer want, we'll have the straightener right here.'

'Hope all these wrecks got the proper papers. I'm gonna send some locals to check 'em out, then you'll need a lawyer.'

Cody Garret is floating about, masquerading as a high-ranking Dutch detective, wire glasses and big bag of paperwork, telling the English detectives, in a perfect Dutch accent, that they have only an arrest warrant, not a search warrant, this could prejudice any trial in Holland if correct procedures are not fully carried out.

'This is England, mate, you're a guest here, remember.'

Cody and Tiptoes start having an argument about European Extradition Treaties, giving each other the pointy finger. It's all being taken in by the observing crowd.

'But the geezer you want isn't here. His vehicle is but he isn't. He's gone.'

'What is a "geezer"?' asks Cody.

'Fuckin hell,' sighs Tiptoes.

Tiptoes is earning the twenty grand he's gonna get for the work, ten now and ten in two days' time. He's now riddled out who's the top honcho in the next-door arch. Off he goes, clipboard in hand, to ask a few questions. He's been waiting for the right moment.

'I don't know nuffin,' the top man says before Tiptoes opens his mouth.

'I haven't asked you anything yet.'

'Well, I don't know anything.'

'I don't believe it's possible for someone to know nothing, it's impossible,' says Tiptoes provocatively.

'I don't need some smart cunt givin me grief.'

'Listen, pal, don't call me a cunt. I'll tell you what I told your oil-rag boyfriend. I can come back here later and me and you'll have it, man to man.'

The exact timing is essential. Cody was stressing it over and over last night, again this morning. It goes to plan. One of the pretend old bill walks quickly into the garage and grabs Tiptoes and tells him to come next door, straight away, quick-sharp.

'Can't you see I'm talkin to Al Capone,' says Tiptoes.

'Fuck him,' says the other cozzer furtively, all itchy, flicking his head. 'Come and have a look at this.'

'I'll be back,' he says, all Arnie and pointy finger.

But when he emerges from the garage he's alight, electric, charged. He trots straight over to Cody, Dutch Super-Sleuth, begins to tell him there's nothing left to find here, maybe they should be going. Cody is perplexed, baffled, asking if he's finished questioning witnesses. Tiptoes is almost dragging him along.

'But what about this motorcar. It is evidence, is it not?' asks the Dutch detective.

'I'll have it impounded, Sir. I'll have forensic go over it here before I have it moved.'

'I'll wait and have it done properly.'

'Please, Sir, I'll get someone to drive you back to headquarters, you can advise Amsterdam on developments.'

Tiptoes must have spotted the garage owner ear-wigging, making notes for the Yahoos when they debrief him later.

'Ain't you got any fuckin work to be gettin on with?' he shouts at him.

'But I thought you wanted to talk to me,' he replies.

'Fuck off.'

'That's no way to talk to a citizen, Sergeant, no way at all,' says Cody the appalled Dutchman. 'Now, I know you put in a lot of very good detective work, finding the car, you're disappointed, but there is no reason to be rude.'

'I'm sorry, Sir. I am disappointed but I'll tidy up here.'

Tiptoes sneaks off and rings me up.

'This mechanic is definitely mexxed up with the other lot. He's plotted up on a car bonnet, drinkin tea, looking over here. No sign of the other three?'

Fuck. Speak of the devil. I catch a glimpse outta the corner of my eye. The Merc's turning into the street.

'Tiptoes. They're on their way back. Let the others know,' I shout down the phone.

'It'll fuck it up this end. I'll be there in a second.'

The Merc goes past. I pick up my binoculars. Tiptoes must have run the distance between the arch and the street. Just as the slowing Merc's about to turn up the slip, Tiptoes comes wandering down and into the road, POLICE chequered hat, clipboard, POLICE yellow vest, stab-jacket, but preoccupied like he's dreaming. The Merc breaks hard and wakes Tiptoes outta his dream. He raises his hands apologetically, shaking his head. The backs of their heads seem close enough to reach out and slap. They're all rubber-necking up the turning. Tiptoes goes to the window of the Merc, briefly talks to them, like he's saying sorry, then walks towards me a few paces. Then he stops, swivels on the ball of his foot, starts talking into his radio but trying to disguise it. They get on it quick-sharp. He's pretending to do a vehicle-check on the plate number. They speed up, ignoring the entrance, trying to remain inconspicuous, like an elephant in a football kit. They turn the corner Morty's end. Morty comes on the phone.

'Listen, brov, you gotta be payin fuckin attention down that end. That came as a big surprise.'

'Sorry. I was talkin to Tiptoes. What they doing?' I ask.

'About seventy,' he replies.

Life Ain't Fair

Cody doesn't wanna leave, he's having too much fun. Tiptoes is getting genuinely pissed off. Eventually he manages to get him off the plot accompanied by another 'officer'. At last he gets into a hired motor round the corner that has sixty grand in the boot to pay the others. About ten minutes after 'the Dutch cunt' has gone, after two hours of keeping the 'clog dancer away from those fuckin boxes', the 'old bill' load them up into the van and off they go. They drive the van over to the car-park of a DIY superstore on the North Circular Road, where we are waiting to meet them. In the back, Gene has been sedately reading the newspapers all morning. Someone suggested that Metal Mickey had a colouring book to stop him misbehaving. The 'old bill' take Morty's car.

Ten minutes later a recovery truck reverses up the narrow alley backwards, hooks up the Merc sports and tows it away. Someone has written 'Do Not Touch. Awaiting Fingerprint and Forensic Examination' on it with yellow crayon. The beautiful run-around is taken to a crushing plant that specialises in insurance jobs and turned into a cubic yard of metal. Inside the arch they leave dust that looks frighteningly like fingerprinting powder on the shiny surfaces, a scattering of heavy cable-ties, used for holding prisoners' hands together, and a scattering of POLICELINE tape.

Who wants approximately two million Class A pills dropped on their toes, hanging round the house? Nobody. That's why they were holed-up in a lock-up in Edmonton and then a dank railway arch in Finsbury Park. Morty and Clarkie take them over to Loveland. I've got a feeling that these are gonna have to be delivered out to Heathrow. It's conveniently on the way. Gene tells me to drive along the North Circular. After five minutes he tells me to pull over into a lay-by.

'Get me this number on your phone.'

He hands me a matchbook with Big Frankie's number on it.

'Frankie. It's Gene. I've been ringing JD all morning but getting no joy. Is he with you? ... Let him explain what? ... Get him on the fuckin phone. Where is he, down the gym or what? ... I've got people here ready to rock 'n' roll ... I thought you lot wanted to get going ... Explain what? Listen, take this number and get him to fuckin ring me straight away.' Gene gives him the number and he hands me back the phone.

Last night I had a conversation with Cody and Morty. Mort was treating us to an instalment of his ol' jailhouse wisdom. An old lag used to tell him that for a story to be truly convincing it must contain inconsistencies.

'So what was he doin in the boob?' I asked.

'Fourteen years, but his point was a good one.'

That's why Cody's team went looking for a dead man. Something like that's gonna jam your radar. You try and riddle out the big picture. Maybe someone's had us over but you keep jumping back to why old bill come crashing in looking for someone who's dead as Elvis.

We sit in silence watching the traffic going by. Gene and Mickey smoke a couple of fags each then the phone rings on my lap. I press the green button and hand it to Geno.

'Hello, JD. What's the story ... What you fuckin mean, gone? ... Sold? ... What the fuck you lot fuckin playing at? ... Where are you now? I'll find that, will I? ... I'm fuckin coming straight over. Don't fuckin move.'

He hands me the phone.

'Walthamstow, head for the 'stow dogtrack.'

We find the drinking club where the Banditos are holed up. It's a scruffy doorway between a newsagent's and a chemist's. Gene leads me and Mickey out of the sunshine and down into the semi-dark of the tatty club. Frankie's sitting up at the bar with Sammy Fisher and Paul the Bouncer. One look says spirits are at an all-time low. The seductive lighting can't disguise the fact it's a khazi.

'You all right, Gene?' says Frank.

'I dunno, I'll tell ya in a minute, Frank,' says Gene without missing a beat. He's spotted JD sitting with Gary down the far end of the narrow basement.

'All right, Gene?' says JD.

'Everyone's so concerned about my welfare,' says Gene.

'What's he doin here?' says JD, nodding at me.

'Him? He's here cos I want him here. Does that answer your fuckin question? And because he's spent the last week getting a very good deal done on some goods you reckon ain't around anymore. Mickey, take Gary here up the bar and get him a shandy.'

Mickey and Gary go and join the others. There's only three others in the gaff, a trio of career lagging boats.

'Now,' says Gene, sitting down opposite JD. 'What's this you was saying on the phone?'

'The pills, they're gone,' says JD.

'Gone fuckin where, Jay?'

'The old bill. We got a spin.'

'Now listen,' says Gene, looking straight into JD's eyes. 'Jimmy's gone, I'd like to get hold of the cunt that killed him, everyone's a suspect till I say different, he had a share in those fuckers, maybe not the half he wanted, but that comes down to me, you understand? I fuckin hope you ain't been clumsy with my inheritance.'

'We got raided and the stuff got captured.'

'So how come you lot ain't all in fuckin custody?'

'We managed to fight our way out.'

'That's very convenient, mate. You just walked out?'

'Me, Gary over there, and a geezer called Sidney were guarding them when it's come on top.'

'Where was this?'

'A garage in Finsbury Park, this mornin, about ten. The law flopped on us but we got out.'

'I ain't convinced. It ain't in the papers? On the telly? Old bill would scream about it, they'd go garrotty.'

'They came to nick Duke, Regional Crime Squad, but Duke's dead. They wanted to hand him over to this Dutch old bill who was gonna extradite him back to Holland for murder, over that business, the geezer gettin shot, the Belgian geezer. Does he know about that?' says JD, nodding in my direction.

'I had to tell him after Jimmy got ... you know ... ' says Gene. 'How did they find you?'

'The car,' says JD.

'What fuckin car?'

'Duke's misses had a Merc sports and we was using it.'

'Fuck's sake,' says Gene, 'have you got no sense at all?'

'We didn't think the law wanted the Duke in Holland.'

'Don't fuckin believe it, not a word of it,' says Gene, shaking his head. 'The law musta fuckin known yer man's already dead. Do you think I'm some thick-as-pig-shit Paddy? They've got computers that'll tell them anything they need to know, tell 'em ya shoe size. And how the fuck do you know all this if you didn't hang around? Go on, answer me that, you cunt.' Gene's shouting now.

'It could happen, Gene,' I say with raised eyebrows. 'Old bill ain't all that organised. Sometimes right hand don't know what the left one's do –'

'You,' interrupts Gene, giving me the pointy finger to the nose, 'shut the fuck up. Who are you? His fuckin lawyer?'

The group at the other end of the bar are looking concerned. Gene's got a Browning handgun in a holster under his shirt. JD's got on it.

'Well? Do I get a fuckin answer or what?' says Gene in full flow.

'We managed to get away, the three of us, the others were away getting ready to move the goods. We thought they were on their way after you called. The law interviewed all the people in the other arches. The guy who sorted us out the arch was there, heard them talking, they interviewed everyone. He's coming here in a minute. He's rung me, told me the griff. I ain't moodying, Gene.'

'And the police just told him all their fuckin business, did they? Maybe he was asking the fuckin questions? That's why he knows so much?' says Gene, getting twitchy.

'Here's Minty now.'

JD calls him straight down to our end of the bar, gets him a drink and sits him down. If this geezer was on a fortnight's holiday in Malaga you'd still know he was a mechanic cos they

315

never get rid of the grease on their hands, under their nails. He's forty-five, dressed lampish, and is totally blown away but is trying to appear unaffected. He offers us a mint from a crumpled, greasy bag of Mint Imperials. He's embarrassed when we refuse.

'Tell these geezers what happened today, Minty,' says JD.

Minty starts to go though a detailed account of the morning's events. Geno questions him relentlessly, buys him a large Scotch and feeds him Rothman's.

'So this old bill's talkin to me and this other old bill comes runnin out and says for him to come and have a look at somethin next door. His mate, the other old bill, was trying to keep it dark, and when this old bill comes out again he's like lost it, gone all fuckin didgy. He's tryin to get rid of the Dutch old bill but the Dutch geezer won't fuckin go. They had him nobbled, wouldn't let him near the inside of the arch, like they were workin in a team to get rid of him, makin little sly signals, thought I didn't clock 'em but I fuckin did.'

'And who were these lot? From the local nick? They ever been in your yard before?' Gene asks Minty, calmer now.

'No,' says JD. 'I said before they were South East Regional Crime Squad. One of them says they're on detachment.'

Me and Gene look at one another, shaking our heads, looking resigned, sighing deeply.

'You didn't say it was Regional Crime Squad,' says Gene.

'I did earlier but you was … like, upset. What's the matter?' says JD.

'They've got a little bitta previous. Did ya get his name, the cozzer who was talkin to you?' I ask.

'He offered me a card, to ring, to grass, like,' says Minty.

'Did ya take it?' I say.

'Have ya got it?' says Gene at the same time.

'No. I wouldn't let him give it to me,' he says like he's done something wrong. 'He was a sergeant, six foot, big cunt, fancied himself, you know, handy in a tear-up.'

'Well, that could be any one of a million cozzers,' I say. 'Did he say his name was Cox?'

'Coulda done.'

316

'Think about it, Minty,' says JD.

'It rings a bell, could well be. Why?'

'There's a right flash detective sergeant on the South East Regional Crime Squad. Luckily I've never met him, a lot of people reckon he's bang at it. They seize ten kilos but only three end up on the charge sheet. Nobody's gonna say they had more, get another five, are they? That's why it ain't in the papers, Gene. They look up Duke, old file comes up, them computers are only as good as the people programming them. Cox goes in there with this Dutch cozzer, right, they've traced the Merc, thinkin they've got Duke, got a body, but it's a fuckin wild-goose chase but he tumbles into ... How did you have them? In boxes, sacks, bin-bags or what?'

'Boxes, four boxes,' says JD, egging me on now.

'They stumble across these boxes, open 'em up and Bob's your uncle, they're lookin at a nice fat pension.'

'They didn't have a search warrant,' says Minty, leaning forward, anxious to please Gene.

'They musta had a search warrant. You can't go busting into premises without one,' says Gene, shaking his head.

'The Dutch bloke, the old bill, was tellin the English ones that they've only got the power of arrest, could nause any trial if they didn't do it right. That's Dutch law, is that. After they come across whatever was in the boxes, they kept trying to get rid of him for two hours, but when he went they give it ten minutes and then fucked off sharpish. They left one cozzer there to go with the break-down truck that come for the Merc sports.'

'You leave anything inside, Jay?' I ask, already knowing.

'Some bedding stuff, my phone and a Mach-10.'

'A Big Mac! Fuckin 'ell,' says me and Gene in unison.

'A reactivated one,' says JD, a bit sheepish.

'Does that make any difference then?' I say sarcastically.

'Don't fuckin start. I ain't in the mood,' he says. Minty looks like he don't wanna play anymore.

'So they got your phone and a Big Mac semi-automatic,' I say. 'Loaded?'

He nods.

'That'll get ya about eight years,' I say. 'Was the weapon ever used on a bitta work?'

'I dunno.'

'Fuckin 'ell. You don't know where it's been? Could have notches on it, a right history. You don't know what ballistics could turn up. Is the phone registered to your address?'

'Sister's,' he says, shaking his head, looking gutted.

'Did this Cox geezer get a good look at ya?'

'Good enough.'

'Can I give you a piece of advice, Jay?'

'Go on.'

'Go on holiday for a little while and start praying like fuck that those Regional Crime Squad geezers have gone through with your pills, you know, nicked 'em, cos they won't wanna proceed with the gun and phone thing if they have. They won't wanna risk you being up at Snaresbrook Crown Court or the Bailey sayin you only had the hardware to protect you from a bogeyman robbin the missin Jack 'n' Jills. What would the chief constable say? Where's the fuckin pills? Maybe they've got a hunch they're crooked now. They'd reason you've got no need to tell porkies, you're going for an eight already. Cox would keep the phone and Big Mac knockin around, just in case, could come in handy.'

JD and Minty are shaking their heads, lookin sick.

'I tell you what, Jay,' I say, bucking up, 'Sergeant Cox'll wanna punt them. You could always go and buy them back.'

'Are you fuckin mad?' he says, his nut spun. 'Tell him they're our pills and we want first refusal?'

'It was only a thought,' I shrug. 'But if ya think about it you've had a right result.'

'I'm not with ya, pal,' says JD curiously.

'You got bent old bill floppin on ya this mornin. If they were straight-goers, which the majority of old bill are, you'd be fucked, lookin at eight stretch.'

'Put like that, you've gotta point,' he says.

'You know,' says Gene suddenly, 'you've convinced me, JD. You know why?'

'Why, Gene?'

318

'Cos between the lot of you, your whole fuckin crowd,' he nods towards the foursome at the bar, 'you ain't got the imagination, the wit and gumption to make up a ludicrous story like that.'

JD smiles and looks relieved like it's a compliment.

'Thanks, Gene. I'm sorry about the gear. What can I say?'

'That's okay, son, worry about yerself. Like yer man here says, start praying those pills end up back in circulation. Look after Mister Minty here for us, a few bob,' he says with a wink.

'Shame,' I say as we get up, 'I was looking forward to a nice earner outta those pills, six figures at least.'

Gene turns to me. 'That's the most selfish thing I think I've ever heard in my whole life. Yer man, JD here, is looking at eight years and you can only think of yourself. Jesus wept.'

'All I'm sayin is I'm disappointed, that's all. I've been up and down to Manchester three times this week.'

'How many times have I got to tell yer, son, Sometimes Life's Not Fair.'

Wednesday
At Your Own Risk

Today's the day I get paid. Two and a half million in used banknotes, various currencies, fits snugly into one of those massive red and white gingham laundry bags you can buy on street markets or in anything-one-pound-crash-out shops, but it'll take two people to carry. To count two mill, to check, it should only take about two hours if everyone pulls their finger out. The carve-up has been decided. After a hundred grand's taken off the top, expenses, to pay the outstanding due to Tiptoes and the other guys and to sort out the crew who did the Klaus business, Gene will receive six hundred thousand, twenty-five per cent, because he, in some respects, already owned a share in the pills and without his say-so we couldn't have skanked the Banditos. Me and Mort will get four hundred and thirty-two grand each, eighteen per cent, and Cody, Clarkie and Terry will each receive the three remaining thirteen-per-cent shares, three hundred and twelve grand. Not bad work if you can get it.

I need time to catch myself up. Things are happening too fuckin fast right now. I've booked a ticket out to Paris on the late Eurostar so I can plot-up for tonight and riddle out where to put my whack. I think overland to Zurich on a first-class sleeper might be a better idea than jumping around on aeroplanes, booking in my suitcase with my readies in it, leaving it at the mercy of all those robbing bastard baggage handlers.

I wake up this morning and the rain, the first in weeks, is battering my window. Rain like you only see in movies is moving in sheets over the rooftops of the houses overlooking my bedroom. The drops are hitting the glass like someone's fired them from a gun, and the wind, changing direction every split second, gets behind it and drives it so it appears to be coming in horizontally. The morning papers are still full of the shooting of the geezer on Primrose Hill, first three pages, editorial, 'Is This London or Beirut?', where they've linked it with the shooting of a known organised-crime figure in sedate, sleepy Totteridge, North London, and the more sinister discovery of two mutilated bodies in a navigation canal in Edmonton. 'Gun-law, blah, blah, blah, Home Secretary resign, blah, blah, blah, more police powers' and so on and on. Not a dickey-bird about a seizure of ecstasy with a street value of twenty million pounds. The old bill always exaggerate figures, indulge in wishful thinking. They think of a number between one and ten, then double it a few times. I know some guys who will be anxiously, but with growing relief, scanning the linen drapers this morning for any mention of 'Scotland Yard are very happy to announce the seizure of ... '

I rang Eddy yesterday evening and he told me to ring again at midday today to arrange the exchange, said he might have something else I might be interested in but I told him I'm going off-duty for a little while, thanks but no thanks. The money we get from Eddy will no doubt be naughty readies, diverted from another dubious source, but if yer start getting too greedy with geezers like him you can end up not being able to get out the other end. I've learnt my lesson well with Jimmy. My thirtieth birthday is rumbling into sight and I fancy being on the beach in Barbados or hanging hard in the South of France, moodying that I'm a film producer at a film festival, not running around London in the pissing rain, accumulating even more readies that I ain't got the time to spunk.

By the time I leave my house, the weather's changed again. Now it's bright sunshine, blinding white light hitting the pavements and puddles. All the debris of twigs, leaves, paper and small pebbles has been driven into the gutters by the downpour but now the air is fuckin alive with ions, positive or negative or both, the birds are back singing in the trees and I know that today's the last day in this fuckin life before I sever the ties and ride into the sunset. Shades on, brolly in broken wrist, large empty Samsonite in good hand, nod to the neighbour as I pass on the stair, post the spare set of keys over to the letting agency in case I'm outta town for a while, and get a cab over to Loveland to see the boys and ring Eddy the Swell.

When I get outta the cab, Gene's got the white box van parked up in the alley, with the roller back up and the two back doors of Loveland wide open. Metal Mickey is standing, huffing and puffing, with a huge box so I can't see his face and Gene is teasing and poking him with a broom handle.

'Leave it out, Gene, I'm gonna drop 'em,' says Mickey.

'Don't stand there gawping, watching a man struggle, either shut your eyes or help him,' says Geno.

'I can't be schlepping boxes, I've got a fuckin broken wrist, Gene.'

'How did you do that?' he says.

'That joke's a bit worn out now, Gene. It was only half funny the first time and now you've got every cunt sayin it.'

'Well, you never did a day's work when you had two good hands, yer good-for-fekkin-nothin bastard,' he says in a culshie accent, brandishing his broom.

I can hear Mickey laughing from behind the box so I snatch Gene's stick and give him a smart whack on the knee-cap.

'Ouch! Leave it out, Gene, what was that for? That fuckin hurt, that did,' says Mickey, doing a little dance.

I give the broom back to Gene, who takes it before thinking. Mickey grapples the box into the back of the van. He looks to take a breather but Gene points with his thumb inside and Mickey troops off to get the next one.

'Where's Morty and Mister Clark?'

'They're inside counting counting machines. And Billy, or Cody, or whatever his fuckin name is, will be along in half an hour with the motor you gave him yesterday.'

'They the goods?' I point at the two battered, taped-up, corrugated cardboard boxes on the wagon already.

'Yeah,' says Gene.

'Don't look two and a half mill's worth.'

'There's another two inside as well. Morty and young Clark bought them inside overnight, got their heads down here, stop them getting pinched. There's a lot of it about, you know, robbery, streets ain't safe these days.'

'Not like when you was a boy.'

'Don't be fuckin cheeky, son,' he says, waving the broom.

Inside, Morty, Terry and Clarkie are drinking coffee and eating toasted sandwiches, but they don't look all that well groomed. Indoor camping obviously doesn't agree with them. In one corner are electric scales, the very accurate kind, that weigh things down to the last gram. These are usually used for weighing books or parcels. If you wanna know if you've got two million pills, you don't count them all, it'd take too long. What you do instead is put ten thousand through a pill-counter, weigh the ten thou, weigh the rest, deducting the weight of the boxes they're in, weigh one empty box, get your calculator out, paper and pencil, do your sums, and hopefully things'll tally up and you'll have the correct amount of pills.

There's also six money-counting machines, a pill-counter from a medical supplier's on Wigmore Street and calculators, so me, Mort, Gene, Clarkie, Terry and Cody can crack on and get the money counted and get back here, carve up the two point five mill and go our separate ways for a while. I ring Eddy's number before they start giving me grief about spending the night at home, in a nice warm bed, while they were the martyrs, suffering for the cause in a grubby sex shop.

'Afternoon, Mister Ryder. Ready to rock the casbah, I hope.'

'Good day, young sir. Most certainly. Had a little trouble getting your wages how you wanted them but it's okay now. Three o'clock out at Heathrow. Follow the signs for Terminal Four but go past it. Turn into the Southern Perimeter Road, follow it round to Redbridge Road and turn into it. Look for the Cargo Terminal, but before you get there you'll see "International Shipping and Freight Corporation". I should be there from about three onwards but forgive me if I'm a little late,' he says.

'I'll see you there, Mister Ryder,' I say, just as Cody and Nobby come through the office door at the same time.

We saddle up, Gene, Terry and Metal Mickey in the truck, and me, Morty, Cody, with Clarkie driving, in the rented motor. Mort's rubbing his hands in anticipation. The sun's got warm now for April, and it's evaporating the rain off the ground so steam rises eerily. There's shoots of pink cherry blossom on the pathetic-looking trees in the square but life is coming alive again, life tastes good again. We pull outta the alley and turn into the street just as Nobby comes running out of the front door of Loveland.

'See that old cunt? Run him over, Mister Clark,' says Morty as Nobby waves, trying to get his attention. 'He's drivin me fuckin mad.'

How Does It Feel?

When we arrive at the International Shipping and Freight Corporation at five to three, everything is quiet, deserted, nobody to be seen. In the sky above there's the deafening noise of planes taking off and landing continually, like they're coming in just over the top of your head. The freight sheds are open but Mickey pulls the truck up outside and we wait. Clarkie and me go inside and have a recce but there's nobody around at all. It appears to be a vacant warehouse the size of a penalty area. Traps have been placed for the rats and mice, there's even a few dead and mummified ones. Along one wall there's three bright-red dumpster bins, like from you-know-where, with bits of old chocolate-coloured carpet on the top. The glass-fronted offices in the corner are empty as well, except for some locked wardrobe-sized metal cabinets like the ones that Duke and Slasher got buried at sea in. The carpet is newly laid. Clarkie goes and has a piss in the khazi that's been built from breeze-block in the opposite corner from the offices. He's asking me if I'm sure I've got the right address but I tell him that there can't be two firms called the same in the airport, maybe they're just moving in. He did say he may be a bit late.

After about half an hour, when we're starting to think that maybe we should sack it, return to base and rearrange for another day and after five or six calls to Eddy's unobtainable mobile, Eddy's car, a black brand-new top-of-the-range Range Rover, comes sweeping round the corner, up Redbridge Road and drives straight through the roller-shutters and into the warehouse. We're on.

'We thought you weren't comin, Mister Ryder,' I say through the window of his car as Mickey and Clarkie drive the motors in. Mister Troop pushes a button that automatically closes the shutters. In his car with him are two other quite heavy-looking guys.

'You must forgive me. I underestimated the journey-time across town. Are all the pills in the van, young man?'

'Sure. Please help yourself, open up a box, anyone ya like. I accept you'll wanna examine them, do some tests.'

'Oh, it would mean nothing to me, just another commodity to me, my friend.'

'Shall we get going on the paperwork then? I've got places to go, people to see.'

'It's a bit gloomy in here, isn't it, Mister Troop.'

Mister Troop walks slowly over and hits the lights. The neon flickers. I look up for a split second and squint. I hear sudden movement, people shuffling about. Outta the big red bins come geezers in black combats, boots and heavy-duty machine pistols, from the offices come the same, from the pre-fab office roof two guys jump, roll and come up with rifles aimed at Mickey and Gene's heads. No fuckin shouting, they move like Chinese gymnasts. I turn and see Morty with his hands outta our car window already cos there's a geezer in a ski-mask, completely motionless, pointing a lethal-looking heavy-calibre machine pistol at his head. A guy sneaks up and puts Cody on the ground with one quick, silent kick in the back of the legs then stands above him with a rifle pointed at his face. Terry's sitting in the back of the motor, I know he's got a tool in there, is flustered, trying to get the door open. A guy in a ski-mask walks calmly up from behind, stops, leans forward, tap, tap, tap on the glass with his weapon, and gets his attention, or rather the tool does. Terry slowly raises his hands. Morty, I can see, is telling Terry to take it easy, don't do anything stupid, don't do anything at all.

When I turn around to face Eddy again I realise that one of the guys from the back of his motor is out now, with two arms laid out across the roof of the car, clutching a pistol aimed right at my forehead. His face is completely emotionless and I know that if someone said 'Terminate the prisoner' I'd be dead before the words came outta their mouth, before I realised what was going on. I'm starting to regret telling Eddy that Jimmy said he killed his wife. The lights were the simple signal. These geezers, army special-forces types, were plotted-up, camouflaged

326

in a fuckin empty warehouse, in bins, locked office cabinets and water-tanks. Four of our team are tooled-up. They never even got to think about using them, which is probably just as well cos once one person gets shot dead they'd just follow the exercise through, do the lot of us. Eddy wouldn't be able to fuckin stop them either cos once the switch is thrown, it's goodnight Vienna to anyone who's not on their side. This other lot have been in training, wishing and hoping for a fire-fight like this all their fuckin lives. Life's not fair, who said that? The other guy from outta Eddy's motor walks silently over to our hired truck and starts the engine. Mister Troop has pushed the button to raise the shutter again. They cover each and do everyone's hands with heavy-duty cable-ties, like the ones we used as props yesterday to such good effect. I see it now, why he put me off until three o'clock. They needed more rehearsal, time to get it off pat. I can see Mister Troop putting them through their paces till they had it drilled to perfection. Everything's done to a signal. It's all about co-ordination, everybody being a designated target.

This exact time yesterday JD was shaking my hand, telling me he don't like me but he really respects me, punching me playfully on the top of my good arm and giving it 'Cheers, brother'. I feel angry now. I wanna spit. If this cunt with a pistol to my head was gonna shoot me he woulda done it by now so I move over to Eddy's side window with my hands up.

'Stay still! Do not move again!' shouts the geezer with the gun.

'I wanna word with your boss, pal. You've got what you fuckin come for.'

'Stand still!' he shouts again.

'Look, they're going outta the door right now. See ya later, next stop Tokyo.'

The truck moves slowly towards the door. Troop jumps up on the running board, opens the door, climbs in, shuts the door again and the truck speeds away. One of his comrades comes shuffling up, throws me against the car, pats me down, searches me for a shooter. Eddy motions with a finger, Roman Emperor style, to let me to come to the window.

'Son, did you really think I was going to give you two and one half million pounds for those goods?'

'Why not? You can fuckin afford it, can't ya? It's called commerce, pal.'

'Listen, son, it's not me who needs the lesson in the ways of the world. By the time you get outta here, those goods will be airborne.'

'So we are getting out alive. Is it Princess Charlotte's birthday so King Eddy's granted an amnesty?'

'Don't be cheeky. But seeing as you ask, young Charlotte's found God in Brighton, actually.'

'I'd wondered where he'd been hidin. Where they goin, still Tokyo?'

'Of course, via Romania. They're waiting for them. The relief flight's taxiing right now. They'll go straight into the cargo terminal, straight through customs. They'll be covered in red crosses by now. They're travelling out as medical supplies as far as Bucharest then they miraculously turn into much-needed exports for the journey on to Japan.'

'That's fuckin out of order.'

'Amoral is the word you're looking for. And you can fuckin talk. I've been thinking. Thursday I tell you James is planning on trading you to the forces of law and order and the very next day someone as good as decapitates him with a gun that would kill an elephant and, I hasten to add, shoots his fuckin pet dogs as well. Now that's some kind of coincidence is it not? Now I knew Jimmy for forty years, from kids. I see these pills as compensation for putting up with him all that time, not to mention, if I'm honest, the sporting angle, of course. Do you think I'd get this kind of satisfaction chasing a fox around? Well, do you?'

'What makes you think we wouldn't come at ya later?'

'You're all too clever, can see the way the odds are stacked. Look at Gene and the big black guy, Mister Mortimer, they're too long in the tooth to be rampaging around looking for revenge. Drug-dealing's meant to be easy money, not grief. I don't think they'll risk life sentences, but as insurance maybe I'll leave dossiers with my lawyers, to be opened if anything

328

happens to me, destroyed if not. It's in your interests if this thing finishes here today. Be your age, son. It's the way of the world. They might not be the Maltese Falcon but those pills, or tablets, or whatever they are, do have a chequered past, so why shouldn't I be the one to make a killing, someone's going to. I'll give my chaps a nice little Christmas bonus out of them. I wasn't lying when I said they were a gift to the Japanese, I promise you. You've got a childish, sulky look on your face. Be a man about it, put it down to experience. One day you'll look back on this and laugh. In 1965 Dewey caught me with about a thousand lepers, purple hearts, half a crown each or five for ten bob. Drugs were bad news back then. He called it confiscating them, I called it theft, end of the day it makes no difference. It spurred me on to better and higher things. I wanted to get where he couldn't touch me. Listen, you're a smart guy, can tell just by looking, and one day you'll be sat here, in years to come, in the back of the motor, telling some young Turk the facts of life.'

'And?'

'You're born, you take shit, get out in the world, take shit, you climb higher, take less shit. The higher you climb, the less shit you take, till one day you get up in the rarefied atmosphere and you've forgotten what shit even looks like. Welcome to the layer cake, son.'

With that he pushes the electric window and without a word the car moves off, swings round in a circle and goes out the door, leaving seven of us with guns pointed at our heads feeling very stupid indeed. It's all about power and when someone's got a gun pointed at you, they've got the power of life or death over you. It's humiliating and deep. Suddenly another two cars swing into the warehouse and again on a silent signal the guys with guns walk, don't run, covering us the whole time, to the motors. They get in and they're gone.

My old man used to have this speech off pat, his own composition but rehearsed like some people learn an epic poem, about if you think you're a tough guy there's always a bigger, tougher chap somewhere. His theme was bullies and bullying and it used to irritate me before I was old enough to even understand it but right now I can't get it out of my head. It's going around and around and around. There's a big part of me that feels sick to my stomach. I've just lost four hundred and thirty-two grand, in cold fuckin blood, but there's another part of me that feels that what went down here in the last two minutes was the work of an amoral class act, a fuckin master-class, no two ways. There's also a feeling that if you're gonna hang around in this game, that's where you gotta aim to be: sitting in the back of the box-fresh Range Rover, with highly trained ex-professional soldiers obediently doing your dirty work, delivering the highly suspect philosophical lecture to baffle the enemy and cover yer tracks, make them think you're doing them a favour, contributing to their emotional development, and then away, at speed, back home to fuck the wife, or the nanny if the misses ain't home.

The End of the Road

It got a bit slapstick, bit ugly, out at the airport. This afternoon's argy-bargy, push and shove, was for real. Recriminations and pointy fingers aplenty were flying about. Some people pay good money to be tied up and dominated but others, it fucks their heads up totally, gets 'em wild. It wasn't a group-therapy situation and I got the fuckin very worst of it cos it was my deal. That's why I was getting a fat chunk if it went right, serious grief if it didn't. Terry seemed to think I was just a bit too fuckin pally with the swell-mob geezer, having a little chat about this and that, maybe even in on the fuckin swindle, brov, while they were having shooters pointed at their heads. Good job the Actionman Posse fucked off with the heavy weaponry, is my thinking on the matter. And fuckin Cody still wants fuckin paying for the drop of work yesterday. Fair enough, brov, but your fuckin timing's a bit out, you fuckin pick yer fuckin moments. Someone's gonna put one in his fuckin nut if he don't fuckin watch himself.

Eddy's got Morty and Gene sussed dead-right. Although they ain't saying it, it's the end of the road for them on this one. Sometimes yer gonna say something or otherwise people are gonna shit on yer but here and now, they've already been shit on, so it's time to wipe yer mouth and move on.

'Nine letters, to be judged by results, beginning with P?' says Gene to himself.

'Wassat, Gene? You all right?' says Clarkie.

'Pragmatic,' says Gene all enigmatically.

'Yeah, all right, mate, whatever you fuckin say, big man,' says Clarkie, giving me a who's-your-mate nod.

Might take a little while to get over it but if Mister Eddy Ryder ain't in their face all day long, hanging out in the old neighbourhood, they will forget. It might take a good few Guinnesses with the double-shot of brandy or in Morty's case a few lick and shines – that's smoking rocks of crack-cocaine

331

while a hooker sucks your cock – but the sting will go away eventually. I wish Terry and Clarkie had heard Eddy the Swell's little lecture cos something like this, getting rumped, will definitely propel them both into orbit. I'm cutting out but I can see Mister Clark especially as the geezer sat in the back of the Range Rover in years to come.

Clarkie had to drive over to Terminal Four and get a taxi to come back for some of us. Gene took Terry, Cody and Mickey over to some boozer in Ealing to get them paralytic, calm them down, cos it was looking to get outta hand, Cody and Terry wouldn't shut the fuck up. Me, Morty and Clarkie headed back to Loveland to work out how to pay Cody's little troop. It looked like I was gonna have to tell Mister Lonsdale, my crafty accountant, to find me some funds quick-smart, sell! sell! sell! The blossom on the skinny trees that looked so full of promise a few hours ago, like an omen of new life and hope, now looks like it's just taking the fuckin piss, wasting its fuckin time even trying.

As we pull into the alley beside Loveland, Nobby's outside the back doors smoking a slim panatella. He walks anxiously round to Morty's side of the car and is looking in the window, waiting for Morty to get out.

'That's just what I don't fuckin need, this cunt drivin me fuckin mad.'

As he gets out, Nobby's on him like a police dog.

'Morty, I've been trying to ring you all day.'

'I know, Nobby. I saw your number come up on my mobile so I didn't answer it, okay? Does that solve yer little fuckin mystery, Pops?'

Nobby looks hurt. 'It's just you took the wrong boxes this morning. I tried to tell ya as you was leaving but you all just waved and drove off.'

Morty and Clarkie are grinning. I am too. We're back in business.

'I fuckin love you, Nobby,' says Morty. 'What was in the box we took?'

'Well, it was all that shit you told me to send back to those

332

geezers in Amsterdam. The boys parcelled it all up yesterday after you give 'em the ruckin the other night.'

I can see it now. Eddy, all kimonoed-up, bowing from the waist, down the number-one paper-tea-house in Tokyo with wall to wall geisha girls and the Don of Dons from the Yakuza. Eddy's telling him he's got a little gift for him, you can make a right few bob with these, but listen, my friend, if things ain't all that clever in the bedroom, you wanna get some of this kit, take the bullet train up to that little cottage you got tucked away on the slopes of Mount Fuji and see what develops. I doubt if those Japanese gangster types like being told they need a blow-up doll or a life-like vibrating vagina to spark up the old love life. It's all about face and all that funny old Samurai code-of-the-warrior shit. They'll probably slice his bollocks off, cere-monially, of course. Quite funny, really.

'So, Nobby, listen to me now. Where Are The Other Boxes?' says Morty.

Nobby looks at his watch.

'About now they'll be landing at Amsterdam Airport. It wasn't anything important, was it? Bit of a fuck-up, I'm afraid. See, the two boys from the shop was like … scared, you know, they wanted the job done, so they come in early and took them down the cargo terminal themselves. Have you ever been there? Heathrow? They told the Dutch geezers to collect them the other end. You're always telling them to show initiative.'

'Nobby, you're a complete cunt. Didn't you fuckin stop them after you knew they were the wrong ones?' says Morty.

'I'm sorry, Morty. I went next door for two minutes to put a bet on. When I came back they're gone. They ain't answering their phone either.'

'Here's what we do,' says Morty, pointy finger to me and Clarkie. 'We get Gene, Terry and shit-for-brains Mickey who loaded up the boxes in the first place. We get on a plane out to Amsterdam, right now, tonight, and we go and crash the gaff and get that fuckin parcel.'

'You'd have to be a bit polite with these geezers, Morty, they're right bleeding heavy,' says Nobby.

'And we're not heavy?' says Morty, rolling his eyes.

'This lot are fuckin Nazis, you know, neon-fascists. That's why they do all the po –'

'Their Führer ain't a geezer called Otto, is he?' I say.

'You must be telepathic, son. Do you know him?'

'We've never met.'

He beckons me to come closer, looks right and left. I can see Donna bouncing around inside. Clarkie's mobile rings.

'People reckon they're into drugs and all sorts,' Nobby says.

'Okay, Dad,' says Clarkie, 'he's here now. I'll tell him.'

Clarkie puts the phone away.

'Morty, Freddie Hurst just died. This is gonna cause complications.'

I'm outta here.

Curaçao
Twenty Miles Off the Coast
of Venezuela
1 April 2000
Life Goes On

When I woke up six weeks later, after floating through the dark, running up tunnels with bright lights at the end then deciding to run back down the other way, tripping out, seeing myself from above and dreaming guys in green overalls were messing with my brain, I was told I was incredibly lucky to survive. Lucky to be shot.

I better explain that. What happened was I was due to leave London on the Saturday, after laying low for a couple of days, leaving instructions with my accountant Mister Lonsdale and the guys who worked my properties and other businesses for me, but on the Friday I decided to follow my gut instincts and give Tammy a ring. I thought that maybe after I'd got based-up somewhere funky she could come over for a visit and maybe we could take it from there.

I arranged to meet her in a pizza gaff in Camden Town and the second she walked in the door and skipped down the three steps into the main floor of the restaurant I was hit with a strange but brilliant sensation that come from my heart rather than my dick. I could see us old together, a lifetime away, surrounded by grandchildren and living out in Australia, well-to-do and content, winking at our private jokes, children asking how we met, a few business investments ticking over nicely, shrimps on the barbie. It was to remain to this day a mirage.

The reality was that jealous Sidney had tailed her across town and into the restaurant with a handgun. He walked over before I had time to think, put three bullets into me, two into my head and one into my chest. Thankfully they were quite small calibre, point two-two. Piece of advice, Sidney, always use dumdums. Anyone would think that if you shot a guy twice in the fuckin canister it would be game over but that ain't necessarily true. I felt like something had picked me up by the hair and thrown me across the room like I was nothing, a bitta rag. They travelled between my scalp and my skull, they weaved about for a while and then stopped. I ain't saying that they didn't hurt like fuckery but they didn't fuckin kill me either. As I was trying to crawl under a table, like a paralytic drunk, he walked across the room, aimed, and put one in my chest from about an arm's length away. He fired more times but the gun was empty, click, click, click, like Geno's toys. I remember the sound late at night if I can't sleep. Then he turned round to Tammy, who's screaming hysterically, covered in my blood, and said that she's coming home with him, he forgives her. A team of have-a-go on-leave squaddies wrestled Sidney to the floor and gave him a kicking. A psychiatric nurse who knew the basics put his hands over the wounds long enough for a paramedic on a motorcycle to arrive.

My surgeon, Mister Masters, said it was a fuckin miracle that I'm alive, calculated the odds somewhere up in the millions. He showed me my X-rays, he showed all his mates my X-rays, put them on the internet for all the other surgeons to see. It's pretty impressive the way the bullet missed the heart and lungs, whistled around the head like that. He started giving me the 'You are a very lucky man' speech. Maybe I wanna start believing him.

I finally woke up outta my coma to be greeted by a team of the top old bill who wanted to ask me a loada questions. I was plumbed into one of those machines that gives you a shot of pure morphine when the nurse pushes the button. You hear a bleep, you get your hit. I'd been coming-to slowly over the previous couple of days, watching and feeling, semi-conscious, then just awake but smacked outta my head, looking forward to the next bleep, a fuckin junkie's dream, on tap, one hundred per cent pure, top-quality morphine. I could never see what smack-heads saw in smack, all that goofing and gouging was never for me, but I suppose if you've got nothing planned, nothing going on in your life, it's a good enough cop-out as cop-outs go, just drifting along in your coma. I could hear through the fog, Mister Masters marching them out, telling them only come back when I'm well enough to be talked to. They argued of course but he was very fuckin insistent, saying his only duty was to me, his patient.

When I did wake up one day to find just one cozzer on his own, sitting next to my bed reading the *Guardian*, I was a bit surprised cos usually old bill are pack animals and they are, according to their working practices, meant to work in pairs, but this one was, you could tell, a cut above your usual gather. He's got graduate written all over him. He's young, about the same age as me, middle-class, wearing a navy Barbour. He don't really look like old bill. I bet he didn't spend a lotta time on foot patrol. This geezer is a product of the Met's elite fast-track promotion policy, outta university with the degree, a couple of years on the beat, just so the foot soldiers don't get the hump, and then nudged upstairs, into one of the creamy sexy outfits who go up against professional criminals. Always remember, only very stupid people think the police are stupid.

He puts his paper down and gets straight to the point. Don't you say anything, just listen. We've thought about maybe trying to get you to turn informer but you don't really fit the profile. We could blackmail you, we could use coercion, but after the recent attempt to murder you I wouldn't fancy your chances of bringing in anything worthwhile anyway. Very amateur dramatic, he was. He had a certain clipped delivery, dry and passionate at the same time.

'We are engaged in a war,' he says like we're in an old black-and-white movie. 'The same way you are,' he goes on. 'All is fair in love and war, but for you the war is over, you're going into retirement, believe me, we're serious about this. If you don't accept this and resume your pernicious trade we'll fit you up, as your fraternity would term it. We'll provide the correct evidence, coach a scattering of witnesses from our pool, have the chaps in our squad queuing down the Bailey to give evidence. You'll do twenty years. Think I'm kidding? Call my bluff. My governor will get you a life sentence if you want it. Do you want it or do you get outta here when you're able, tidy up your legit affairs and go away and remain inactive? And remember, we'll be watching. Now, I'm going to ask you a straight question, okay? Am I talking to a man in retirement? Just nod your head if you agree.'

My head hurts like fuck but I can see I'm the one getting a bargain so I move it slowly up and down enough for him to get his answer.

'Good,' he says, 'and this conversation never happened. That's part of the deal.'

He gets up, folds his paper and leaves.

So did I. I left London. But one time I got in touch with Tammy from a hotel in Lisbon. She says: girls like dangerous guys but you're seriously fuckin life-threatening. How many girls do you know end up covered in blood, chief prosecution witness in an attempted murder trial on their first date? I think I'm gonna give it a miss, mate. All the best, I wish you well.

Sidney got ten years, even with me on the missing list, cos the old bill had two dozen witnesses. Make all the difference, witnesses. He pleaded guilty.

I ended up here cos I ran outta places to go. Bought a little bar. Sometimes people from London come over to see me. Morty brings the news and gossip from home. The law don't leave him alone because of the Freddie Hurst thing, know he did it, just can't prove it. Target criminal, but he lives well outta the three tom-shops he owns in prime locales. Mister Clark Junior took over much of the business that we had going on and it transpires that the geezer who did the business with Jimmy Price would've dealt with young Clarkie if only he'd known. The Clark family work tight around the youngest member of the family and that apparently is the only way to work back in London now cos prices have tumbled but everyone still wants to earn top dollar. People have to go armed to drop off an ounce. Costs about a grand these days, but people think it's worth their while to turn ya over. Guys have their bitta personal taken offa them at gun-point.

Just to make things interesting, MI6, who ain't got no reds under the beds to chase anymore, no cold warfare in Moscow or Berlin, are after all the top firms, families and outfits. Drug

338

trafficking ain't the lucrative giggle it once was. Morty reckons it was one of these ex-spies who come and give me my ultimatum in hospital. Old Man Clark had his suspicions about Jimmy's little sideline, or so he says now the whispers've got back to him. Everyone, villains and cozzers alike, are in the dark about who did the hows-your-father on him. The South East Regional Crime Squad was disbanded due to widespread rumours of corruption. Every time the USA has a bitta grief with any Middle Eastern country they wheel out a head and shoulders picture of the systems analyst from Portland, Oregon, and I have to duck cos it's still getting blamed on Muslim fundamentalists.

Terry, who was working tight with Clarkie, got shot dead after an altercation at a T-junction. After some verbal between him and another driver, he got out to sort it but two game black dudes – Yardies? wassa fuckin Yardie? – opened up, emptied their pieces into him, twenty-six rounds. Thankfully he was gonski before he hit the floor, gone to join all the other dead heroes. Nobody, not the law or the Clarks, could find these geezers, so nobody could work out if it was business or personal. Old-school London villains, black and white, yellow and Turk, are bubbling up the new chaps from Jamaica, then complaining that the law ain't doing nothing about it. It's a different game nowadays, it's all about financial resources. Gene spends a lot of time in Ireland, catching up with his daughters. He's squirrelled away a great deal of readies over the years, so he lives well.

A guy told me once that you never stop learning. This is true, but I never stop forgetting either. I always wanted to get in and get out before I was thirty, have my wedge neatly tucked away, out of harm's way, but I've got a metal plate in my head, fun and games at airports, and people have to tell me their names four or five times before I remember. Sometimes I'd start to miss the bollock-tingling excitement of making ten grand for an afternoon's work, so I bought myself a huge red parrot, called him Jimmy. He talks too fuckin much as well. I taught Jimmy the Parrot a few of Jimmy the Don's choice sayings – 'You're lookin at a twelve, son,' and 'Why have a dog and call

him Fuck Off?' – just to keep the mind from wandering backwards.

My name?

If I told you that you'd be as clever as me.